HMS *Hazard*

HMS *Hazard*

David Donachie

McBooks Press

Guilford, Connecticut

McBooks Press

An imprint of Globe Pequot, the trade division of
The Rowman & Littlefield Publishing Group, Inc.
4501 Forbes Blvd., Ste. 200
Lanham, MD 20706
www.rowman.com

Distributed by NATIONAL BOOK NETWORK

British Library Cataloguing in Publication Information available

Library of Congress Cataloging-in-Publication Data
Names: Donachie, David, 1944– author.
Title: HMS *Hazard* / David Donachie.
Description: Guilford, Connecticut: McBooks Press, [2021] | Series: A John Pierce novel; #16 |
    Summary: "Can John Pearce resist the lure of a valuable capture and risk his ship in a dangerous
    battle to gain it, or will his duty come first?"—Provided by publisher.
Identifiers: LCCN 2021020671 (print) | LCCN 2021020672 (ebook) | ISBN 9781493060658
    (hardcover; alk. paper) | ISBN 9781493063383 (epub)
Subjects: GSAFD: Sea stories. | Adventure fiction. | LCGFT: Sea fiction. | Action and adventure
    fiction.
Classification: LCC PR6053.O483 H63 2021 (print) | LCC PR6053.O483 (ebook) | DDC
    823/.914—dc23
LC record available at https://lccn.loc.gov/2021020671
LC ebook record available at https://lccn.loc.gov/2021020672

♾™ The paper used in this publication meets the minimum requirements of American National
Standard for Information Sciences—Permanence of Paper for Printed Library Materials, ANSI/
NISO Z39.48-1992.

To my grandson Alex Donachie, a boy with a mind of his own

Chapter One

If anyone had suggested to a young John Pearce he would come to appreciate routine, he would have laughed at the notion. With nothing even approaching domesticity in his early life, such a thing had never been possible, while not very much had occurred since to alter matters. He'd spent his early years wandering the highways and byways of Britain in the company of a politically radical father, known to the world, or at least within the British state, as the Edinburgh Ranter.

A polemical orator, Pearce senior was intent, through fiery speeches and rancid pamphlets, on changing the living conditions of the politically disenfranchised, poor folk on whom an indifferent society bore down with endless hard knocks or total indifference. It was impossible, outside riot, for their voices to be heard, but Adam Pearce sought to convince them a change in their blighted lives was theirs to take, certain it would never be given.

Too many times, in a peripatetic existence, which had taken them all over the country, where they would lay their heads and take food was continually varied, no preparation for a future in which the business of the day was endlessly repetitive. Yet here was the very same John Pearce, in the early summer of 1796, in command of the 14-gun brig HMS *Hazard*, steeped in the constantly recurring and content to be so.

No ship of war could be run any other way, especially with a raw crew consisting mainly of so-called quota men. Every municipality in the country had been legally obliged to provide bodies in order to man a wartime fleet sorely short on numbers. It was hardly a surprise to find the citizens who ran these electorates despatched from their locality those least upright or naturally competent. Supposed to be leavened throughout the fleet, mixing the new with the experienced, malice had landed Pearce with too many of the former and too few of the latter.

New to the life and resentful, they had to be moulded into a crew able to sail the ship, while being willing to also fight and subdue Britannia's enemies. It was the job of John Pearce and his officers, petty, warranted, and commissioned, to teach them their duty where it was appropriate, or force them to it when it was essential. A process begun in the calm waters of the Thames estuary only served to show the alarming depth of the task. The number of flaws this exposed was endless, while not enough time was afforded for remedy.

Obliged by the mission of which they were employed to weigh anchor, Pearce had finally put to sea, assured by the ship's master of good weather. In doing so, Mr Williams had sailed HMS *Hazard* into a full North Sea gale that, by luck, Pearce and his crew had managed to come through unscathed. The experience had gone some way to blooding them, engendering a communal feeling of gratification in having survived what had been a true tempest. Only those with more knowledge of the sea knew how close they'd come to disaster.

His novices had, in the loosest possible sense, then participated in the taking of a merchant ship of indeterminate nationality. Here was a vessel that flew no flag and lacked a name on its stern, this having been dropped overboard on *Hazard*'s approach. It turned out to be an English vessel engaged in smuggling, sailed by a pair of vicious criminals called the Tolland brothers.

A coincidence almost too uncanny to accept, they were no strangers to John Pearce or his close companions, being men who laid, at his door, the theft of a ship and cargo, of which he was innocent. Given nothing could convince them they were mistaken, and the real culprit had disappeared, in revenge, they had tried to kill him on more than one occasion.

Both Tollands, along with those serving under them, had been decanted as pressed seamen into HMS *Bedford*. The 74-gun ship of the line, part of Admiral Duncan's North Sea Fleet, was on blockade duty off the Texel, set to contain the Dutch, now allied to France. Given the conditions of the navy, when only peace would see them freed, it was as good as a prison, one which relieved Pearce of the burden of their presence.

What then to do with their unnamed ship, full of a valuable contraband cargo, without anything to identify the owner. It was assumed any documents it carried had been dropped over the side as soon as they identified who was approaching. So, with a degree of subterfuge, if not downright chicanery, Pearce had taken the nameless vessel in to Ramsgate, declaring it to be an enemy merchant ship and thus a prize.

The hull would be assessed by an Admiralty Court prior to a sale and the cargo auctioned, with the value of both going to the ship's company. This held out a promise of hard coin for everyone aboard HMS *Hazard*, helping, amongst his so-called "volunteers," to mitigate the feelings of a malignant fate.

If the money was not yet in their purse, it would be waiting for them when arrangements could be made to pay it out. This stood as a rare example of the promise of riches, always touted as there to be gained by joining the King's Navy, being met. Too often it was nothing but a recruiter's lie.

Beating down the English Channel into the prevailing westerly wind produced signs of improvement in some. Yet too many failed to rise above the downright clumsy, showing little natural aptitude for anything requiring dexterity. Given so few could be rated as competent, everyday tasks, outside the most simple, tended to require double the number usually employed: those to carry it out, overseen by the men who could instruct or correct matters when things went awry.

Pearce had hardly been off the deck the whole time since they'd weighed, his presence and aura of command necessary to ensure instructions given were fully carried out. That said, he had absolute trust in his two lieutenants. Hallowell and Worricker were both competent seamen, which left him well aware he would have been at a loss to run the ship without their equally tireless endeavours.

Other responsibilities went by the wayside. The commanding officer's logs were left as rough notes, given there was too little time for accurate record keeping. As a captain lacking a schoolmaster, he was supposed to undertake the education of *Hazard*'s midshipmen. Gifted four raw youths, all of Scottish parentage, equally new to their occupation, meant there was much they required to be taught. All four would be required, in time, to assume positions of authority, which would include command of a section of the crew. Added to this was the responsibility that went with their role as inferior officers when it came to the standing of a watch.

If he could have spared the time to do so, Pearce would have enjoyed teaching these youngsters things at which he reckoned he enjoyed some competence: manners, deportment, plus the use of firearms and swordsmanship. Similarly, he would have been at home with sails, knots, and rigging. At one time as new to the profession as his tyro seafarers, time at sea had made him truly familiar.

He was less sure of his ground when it came to subjects in which it was unwise to delay the instruction of a putative naval officer. This was especially true when it came to mathematics, use of the sextant, and the kind of nighttime star mapping necessary to provide competence in the article of celestial navigation. This task was undertaken by his rather uninspiring master, he who had so badly misjudged the weather when they'd first cleared the Thames. Williams felt himself under a cloud and had offered, as a form of recompense, to devote two hours a day to this serious scholastic burden.

Bouts of seasickness were an obvious and serious impediment to efficiency, the "chops" of the English Channel being notorious in this regard. Even in reasonably good weather, the short, vicious waves, added to their uncertain impact, so unlike deep-sea rollers, had a deleterious effect, even on those long accustomed to the sea. Blue-water tars of many years' experience could be reduced to misery. For the kind of landsmen who made up *Hazard*'s crew, the debilitating novelty was even worse.

Being an affliction that seemed never-ending, this rendered the wretchedness doubly hard to bear. Yet no allowance could be made for anyone suffering the malady; the ship and the duties required to sail her had to be carried out and completed regardless of the state of the crew. This led to some harsh but necessary treatment, not something John Pearce, at any stage in his life, would ever have foreseen himself imposing. But apply it he did, caring not if it endeared him to his crew or led them to curse him as a tyrant.

It was with palpable relief they made their pre-arranged landfall at Falmouth. In the calm waters of the Carrick Roads, once at anchor, the required flag saluted and a berth designated, the afflicted could begin to recover. The ship, the deck especially, could also be put to rights, and John Pearce could write a long letter to his lover, Emily Barclay, the mother of their infant son. Another was penned to his friend Heinrich Lutyens, a final missive to his prize agent, Alexander Davidson, repeating the details of the capture of the Ramsgate "prize."

While this was happening, HMS *Hazard* was cleaned from stem to stern with diluted vinegar, especially below decks, where the effects of the last seven days were most obvious, while hammocks were washed and aired. Only when Mr Hallowell, the premier, was satisfied, was it passed as fit for a full inspection.

The fellow Pearce knew as Samuel Oliphant, his partner in the mission on which the ship was engaged, had gone ashore as soon as they made their berth. His task was to collect any last instructions sent down to Cornwall by Henry Dundas, the Minister of War in the Pitt government. It was on his need for information they were both employed, the task to assess the security of what had become a possibly less-than-solid Spanish alliance.

As captain, John Pearce was likewise obliged to go ashore, his duty demanding he visit the port admiral and pay his respects, though in no way was he obliged to state his business. Sailing under Admiralty orders, he had no requirement to be open about the mission that, on its own, would have rendered any meeting awkward. Senior officers, when probing for information, were unaccustomed to being stonewalled by a mere lieutenant, even if he was rated as a master and commander.

The nature of the officer dodging these enquiries made it doubly so, the name of John Pearce not being one to elicit much joy in any naval breast. Having got his step from midshipman to lieutenant on the express orders of King George, without a proper examination, he'd run a coach and horses through what the service saw as the proper way to promotion. The royal gift had been awarded for conspicuous bravery, but this did not, in any way, mitigate service hostility.

Added to this burden was his very name, it being coupled with that of his father, Adam, seen as a dangerous revolutionary by a profession riven with reactionary opinions. They thought Pearce senior akin to the kind of Jacobin who'd overthrown then cut off the head of the King of France, a man who would, if given the chance, do the same to their own sovereign.

Such abhorrence fell similarly upon the son, so the admiral had been frosty in the extreme, manifestly so in the way Pearce was not offered refreshment of any kind. No wine or coffee was provided, this being a pointed and deliberate insult. Such lack of even common decency was rendered doubly galling when, back on board, he found Oliphant, while ashore, had treated himself to a capital dinner and was happy to crow on the fact.

'And, no doubt, a pint of good wine, when I was not even offered bilge water.'

'Don't blame me if your name stinks.'

'Am I allowed to say your breath could be so described?'

This barbed comment said much about their relationship. It was one of a mutual dependence, which neither took to well, this being rendered more so by the treatment Pearce had just experienced, coupled with the amusement the story had provoked.

'While you were filling your face, I was having to bite my tongue in the face of the most aggravating condescension. I was tempted to give the old booby a slap.'

'You clapped in irons would have served us well' was the sarcastic response.

'Was there anything from Dundas?'

'A great deal.' Oliphant pulled a packet of letters from his coat pocket and threw them over. 'He sent a courier down with the latest intelligence he has garnered, as well as a pair of homing pigeons.'

'What have you done with them?'

'They're housed in your pantry, so make sure your man doesn't make a mistake and cook them.'

Looking at the thickness of the bundle that had landed on his desk, Pearce asked for a summary, given they already had plenty of information, brought down from London while Pearce was trying to get *Hazard* ready for sea. Most of it related to the terms of the Treaty of Basle, which had ended the two-year-long War of the Pyrenees, fought on both the east and west coasts of Iberia.

The Dons had made early and substantial gains, but it didn't last. Once properly deployed, the forces of revolutionary France had pushed them back over their own borders, so the Spaniards had been obliged to sue for peace, which produced a strange outcome. It had been assumed the terms came with a price, but the territory taken by a victorious French army was given up, the previous border restored, with no financial reparations demanded.

The question of what had been traded for such a generous settlement was now solved in the letters from Dundas. The Dons had ceded the eastern two-thirds of the Caribbean island they called Hispaniola, to give Paris possession of the whole, which would now be named Saint Domingue.

'Possession?' Oliphant scoffed. 'There's nothing to give up, the whole island is probably now under the control of ex-slaves.'

'Who, if you recall, have pledged allegiance to France.'

The French no longer really controlled their third of the island; the slave revolt five years past, led by a Toussaint l'Overture, had sent packing any planters and their families who'd not be slaughtered. Yet he had quickly made known his loyalty to France, while the revolutionaries in Paris, to accommodate his demands, abolished slavery, a move much applauded by Pearce *père et fils* along with a goodly section of international opinion.

Control of the island by France was an outcome to seriously affect the balance of power in the region and not in favour of Britannia. It might not be as sound as Paris would wish, but anything that advanced French interests in those waters was taken as a threat to the British Sugar Islands.

'Dundas thinks the French have done well, possibly too well for merely withdrawing their armies, so he fears there may be other concessions. Yet there's also an assertion by the Spanish ambassador, who is desperate for another subsidy from London, that both peace and treaty are merely a delaying tactic to buy time. He has assured Dundas the

Dons will take up arms once more, when they've rebuilt both their army and border defences and have the funds to pay them.'

'He could be lying.'

'Really' came with the requisite amount of irony. 'It matters not. Whatever he's telling our government will be on instructions from Madrid.'

'Where we, too, surely have an ambassador.'

'He'll be getting the same story.'

'Which leaves much up in the air.'

'He is at us again to proceed with all speed, so when you read the correspondence, take note of the dates. This tells you how much lingering in the Thames and your shenanigans with that merchantman have cost us in terms of time. The courier and his pigeons have been waiting for ten days.'

There was an underlying sense of injustice there. Oliphant was, in reality, no more than a passenger aboard *Hazard* and, as such, any gains that accrued from the aforesaid capture would normally do nothing to fill his purse. As a sop, Pearce had rated him as a midshipman, which, if it granted him something, ranked as tiny compared to those with whom he shared the wardroom. It was in the nature of sailors to talk of spending their windfalls long before they had them in hand, and he dined with the ship's officers, so the difference in anticipated reward had to be a running if unmentioned sore.

'Which tells anyone who cares to enquire,' Pearce insisted, 'Dundas is no sailor. It's not unknown for ships to take a month to get from the Thames to the Lizard.'

'Oh, I know, time and tide and all that rot.' Ignoring the glare this got, Oliphant continued. 'The most important communication is to tell us our initial destination has changed. Dundas wants to know what's happening on the western side of the Pyrenees as well as the east, so that's where we must first seek out information. We're to send him a message by pigeon on anything we discover.'

Oliphant carried on, explaining Dundas was desperate to know, being in receipt of mixed messages, what, if anything, could come next. Would Spain remain as a sound and committed member of the present league against France, if not on her own borders, in the waters of the Mediterranean, which depended on a scoundrel called Manuel Godoy.

The country might be a monarchy, but it was common gossip, both King and Queen were in thrall to their powerful chief minister. Godoy had risen rapidly from being a mere member of the Royal Guard to achieve power at age twenty-five, this in a country where royal officials tended to the septuagenarian.

Reputedly a handsome cove, and suave, malicious rumour had him as lover to the Queen, seen as probably true, if not paramour simultaneously to both her and the King. This was an accusation too common with royalty everywhere to have much credence, but what could not be gainsaid was his grip on policy. To this was added the most telling factor: He was known to be no great devotee of the present coalition, one which was as much a wonder to most within the British Isles.

If there was an enemy in the lexicon of historical British foes, it was Catholic Spain, not least in the national myth of the Armada. In what was seen as a fit of monarchical solidarity, the Dons had elected to fight the regicides of Paris. Their fleet had been deployed alongside the Royal Navy at Toulon, taking an equal part in both the capture of the main French naval base as well as suffering the subsequent loss.

There had been a degree of bad blood following the need to evacuate Toulon because the intention had been to leave nothing of value behind. Naval stores were to be utterly destroyed, a task that fell to the British. The French capital ships taken at anchor, when the main naval base was captured, were to be likewise set on fire. Yet in too many cases, this had failed to occur, the Spaniards, to whom this assignment fell, too slow to carry out the allotted task.

The suspicion arose and could not be quieted; had it been deliberate? A purposeful dereliction, to avoid favouring their British allies too much, for the time may come when they would revert to being mortal enemies. It was a suspicion that could neither be proved nor dismissed, with the Spanish capital ships then withdrawing to Port Mahon in Minorca, seemingly now in no mood to put to sea once more and re-join the fight.

Pearce, who'd stopped there on the way back from the Tuscan port of Leghorn, had been able to pass to Dundas his impression this could be on orders from Madrid. Further disturbing information, to back up his contention, had been provided at his next port of call by the governor of Gibraltar, Sir David Rose. He had raised the spectre of serious difficulty for his vital station in the near future.

Might Godoy be edging towards outright hostility? If there was one secret protocol on the Treaty of Basel, there could be more, making it essential to find out his and his country's intentions. Gibraltar, connected to the Spanish mainland, having been placed under siege more than once, could never cease to be a worry. Yet the impact this might have on the Royal Navy vessels masking Toulon, under the command of Sir John Jervis, could be calamitous.

If Spain swung decisively against Britain to the point of war, Jervis would be faced, far from home and support, while massively outnumbered, by a combined French and Spanish fleet. This might lead to a battle he would struggle to win and one his nation could not afford to lose.

Pearce found himself harbouring feelings of increasing resentment as Oliphant related the ministerial concerns. It was all very well for the likes of Henry Dundas to badger, but this took no account of his difficulties, even before you accounted for the possibility of delay brought about by foul weather.

He'd been ordered to take over a well-manned ship, only to see it stripped of its experienced crew and competent officers by a malicious Admiralty, with no idea if such an action had been a ploy to humbug Dundas or to personally spite him. It took a while to calm down, to come round to the view it made no odds.

Besides, he was damned if he was going to show any kind of bitter reaction in front of Oliphant, lounging on cushions atop the casement lockers with a smug expression on his face. He would be waiting for, as well as relishing the thought of, a vocal explosion of resentment. Pearce was damned if he would give him the satisfaction of letting his feelings show.

This would have held but for the arrival of Midshipman Maclehose. The eldest of his midshipmen knocked and entered, to tell his captain a verbal message had come from the port admiral, carried by a civilian clerk in a hired wherry. This was a demand to know when he planned to weigh, since his berth was required.

'The messenger also said,' the lanky youngster added, a nervous note in his soft Scottish burr. 'Since we're not on the Channel Fleet or Falmouth establishment, his superior saw no need to make up on our needs in food, wood, and water from his stores.'

'Which tells you, young man,' Oliphant said with a sneer, 'something I suspect you already know. For advancement in the King's Navy, you've nailed your colours to the wrong mast.'

Clearly preparing to expand on this with more of his so-called wit, Pearce cut him off, throwing the retied bundle of letters into his lap. 'I don't recall that my cabin is, for you, a place of repose.'

'Oh dear,' came the reply, delivered with studied serenity, as he stood and made to leave. 'Wounded pride.'

It was the sandy-haired midshipman who blushed, not his captain. He'd known Oliphant long enough to expect no other kind of response. For Pearce, the wound to his pride, which he felt acutely, was something he again wished to keep hidden. It was a near-blasphemous discourtesy, one made deeply personal by being sent by the hand of a civilian messenger.

The admiral was within his rights to deny him the items listed, yet it was anything but normal behaviour. The man had no idea what HMS *Hazard* carried in the way of stores. For all he knew the crew could be on short commons, so it was nothing less than a studied, deliberate, and likely soon-to-be-public insult. The anchorage was busy, but hardly overcrowded, which also made it nonsense to talk of needing the berth.

'Are they waiting for a reply?'

'They are, sir' came out guardedly.

'Then kindly tell the fellow, we are in no need of assistance and also stress this. I will take the liberty of letting the admiral's attitude and actions be known to the powers that be in Whitehall. Not least, this will include the King's First Minister, upon whose business we are presently engaged. Make sure he understands the last part and have him repeat it.'

'Aye aye, sir.'

'And, Mr Maclehose, please tell the premier to make preparation to weigh as soon as the tide permits.'

He was on deck when the time came, observing the various activities being carried out, this done with less-than-sparkling efficiency. There would be others watching, not least that damned admiral, as well as, no doubt, a gaggle of his officers. Each would be competing to make the most degrading comment, and there was much to disparage. *Hazard* was slow over the anchor, while the catting and fishing of the article took time, added to no end of shouted frustration.

Benjamin Hallowell finally gave the orders that sent aloft the topmen to let fall the sails, and this looked reasonably smart. In all of his tyro crew, the men carrying out this duty were the ones, young and less set in their ways, who'd shown a modicum of application. Their less-adept mates were on deck, their actions requiring no more than pulling on ropes. In this they were guided by Pearce's good friends Michael O'Hagan, Charlie Taverner, and Rufus Dommet.

The trio proudly termed themselves Pelicans, as did Pearce, boon companions with whom he'd been pressed into the navy from a tavern thus named. Truly seaman now, they were overseeing the sheeting home and this, too, while not crack-frigate impressive, went quite well. HMS *Hazard*'s sails took the wind and, with creaking timbers, she got under way.

'One day,' he said, very softly, in his mind the vision of a gaggle of sneering officers. 'You will be struck dumb by what this ship will become. I'll make you eat your jeering.'

'Sir?' asked a curious Midshipman Livingstone, a lad so young and small in stature, he was known as the Mite.

'Nothing, lad,' Pearce replied, patting his shoulder.

'The salute, sir?' called Hallowell as they came abreast of Admiralty House, home to the flag officer who wanted them gone.

This was merely a request for when, not if, given it was common practice to salute the flag of the resident senior officer on both arrival and departure. It was with a feeling of savage delight Pearce responded to his premier, indeed to the whole crew on deck, even if he knew, in future, it would be held as yet another mark against his name.

'I think,' he called out in a carrying voice, so to include the whole crew. 'This is one occasion when no such courtesy is required.'

CHAPTER TWO

Edward Druce was a man of fixed habits, so much so, any deviation was a thing to be remarked upon. Thus, a decision to forgo his breakfast within the confines of his own home, to decide to partake of it elsewhere, was bound to be the cause of speculation, not least by a wife accustomed to catering for his morning presence.

He could hardly tell her his brother-in-law was the cause, yet it was the truth. Not a man he'd ever been inordinately fond of, the constant appearance of Denby Carruthers at the breakfast table bore down on Druce like a sword aimed at his very soul. This was made doubly unbearable by the way his sister treated her brother like some visiting deity. In her eyes he could do no wrong.

This enforced lodger had been obliged to quit his own substantial house in the city, in order to avoid the constant attention of the morbidly curious, folk who wished to visit the home of his late wife, the victim of a most heinous and bloody crime. Crowds gathering outside was bad enough, but there were those bold enough in their ghoulish curiosity to haul on the bell pull and request an interview, even to petition for entry to the late woman's private quarters.

Pamphleteers, wielding their pens in lurid words and images, made sure the story of the murder of Catherine Carruthers was kept both alive and profitable. This had been extended because Cornelius Gherson, the man accused of her sexual molestation, then carnal mutilation, in a trial by jury, had been found innocent. This left open the obvious speculation: If he wasn't guilty, then who was?

The usual rules of a nine-day wonder had thus failed to apply, first prolonged from the actual crime, then the sensational trial and its result. It thus had made what was supposed to be temporary relocation by

Denby into one that had lasted for close to a month. Edward Druce knew more than was good for him about the nature of his brother-in-law, as well as the circumstances of the crime. This presented a problem of tangled loyalties added, in his more vivid imaginings, to a potential threat to his own person.

To arrive at the offices of Ommaney and Druce in the Strand did not bring any sense of relief. There he was faced with the fallout from a previous association with none other than the named villain. It was one the firm of prize agents, of which he was a partner, had been required to pay out a substantial sum of money to the widow of Captain Ralph Barclay, Cornelius Gherson's late employer and their one-time client. Barclay had been very successful in the taking of valuable enemy prize vessels, the proceeds of which were substantial and overseen by the company.

Questionable trades on the Barclay account, facilitated by Gherson, had left the firm exposed to a hefty bill. Despite each transaction being jointly agreed, it had been Druce's duty to oversee the day-to-day arrangements. Added to this was the subsequent and voluminous correspondence, the truth of what was taking place hidden from their client, if not his clerk. This allowed his partner, Francis Ommaney, senior in both experience and the level of his investment, to act as if Druce was somehow the sole malefactor.

Thus the atmosphere within their suite of rooms was far from contented, quite the opposite, given the strain on the company finances. Hints were being dropped by Ommaney of a dissolution of the firm, a move that would leave Druce exposed to potential bankruptcy and incarceration in a debtor's gaol. The only man who could save him, should it come to such a pass, was the very same person who'd bankrolled him initially and to whom he still owed money. None other than his damned brother-in-law.

Business had to go on, given the firm looked after the financial interests of a great number of naval officers. This, given the nature of their clients, added to the circumstances attending on the taking of prizes, generated a great deal of correspondence. Too much of this was with lawyers employed to argue for and against claims in the Admiralty Prize Court. Then there were disputes over value, since agreements on the level of remuneration a serving officer should receive for a successful capture were never simple.

This was endlessly complicated when more than one vessel was involved in an action, the only thing to make it palatable being the fees Ommaney and Druce could levy for their efforts. The Battle of the Glorious First of June, two years past, was a case in point, the subject of numerous competing claims, hardly surprising given the defeat of the French fleet yielded a reward for vessels captured, as well as gun money for everything from cannons to muskets.

In addition came the value of weapons like pikes and even knives, crews taken prisoner. Added too, were what stores they carried in their holds, down to the very last nail, barrel of tar, and bolt of canvas. In a fleet action, several vessels engaged simultaneously, with each individual commanding officer entering claims. All were utterly convinced their ship had done more sterling service than their contemporaries, indeed going as far as to utterly dismiss certain assertions.

This doubled in disputes between the lower-ranking admirals, the only one secure in his reward being "Black Dick" Howe. He commanded, and still did, the Channel Fleet. He was, in essence, though he showed little inclination to do so, the one person who could arbitrate in these disagreements.

'Writing to him is getting us nowhere, Druce, and I seriously doubt we're the only folk doing so. Someone will have to coach down to Bath and beard the old fool to get the answers we require.'

Francis Ommaney, a man of substantial belly and high colour, in a face of bulging cheeks and full lips, pronounced this with the air of a rhetorical point: He was not suggesting for one second he make such a tedious journey and to such an awkward personage.

'He's not an easy man to get to see, Francis.'

Druce suffered a certain pang then, one of which he was only too familiar. In just the way they named each other stood the very nature of their relationship. Ommaney rarely used his given name and then only when, and this was annoyingly obvious, he was seeking some favour or petty advantage.

'How the devil the old sod can command the Channel Fleet from Bath escapes me.'

This was taken as a deliberate change of subject, a ruse by Ommaney to indicate the decision about the need for the journey and who should make it had been made. A few weeks past and Druce might have challenged it; now he was not sure he dare, which took no cognisance of another worry.

What could happen if he were absent for any length of time. Things might take place of which he would be unaware. In a partnership that relied on trust, he was far from sure he now enjoyed or had any.

'I suggest another letter be tried, firm in its composition.'

'Firm?'

'He's too complacent, too successful, Francis, with his own profits from the Glorious First secured and basking in the gratitude of the nation. Let us hint at a move from his inferior officers to claw back some of what he's received in prize money and have it paid to them.'

'He will see it as vexatious, Druce.'

'As long as it displeases him enough to stir him from his sulphurous baths.'

'And if it fails?' came with a cold stare.

'We will know in a few days. To such a threat to his own purse he's bound to respond. If we can see no progress, I will undertake to challenge him face-to-face.'

Ommaney moved with surprising speed and grace for a man of his bulk, so quickly his affirmative agreement to this course of action was delivered over his shoulder, leaving his partner to reflect he was as light on his feet as he was flexible in his principles. Also, if the attitude of Admiral Lord Howe was of concern, it was, at present, a secondary one.

From a desk drawer he took out two sketches given to him by the well-known and successful thief-taker Walter Hodgson, these laid on his desk and, not for the first time, subjected to concerned examination. There was a strong element of self-pity in the thoughts and memories such perusal produced, the recollection of acts and favours that had seemed blameless at the time. They had, in reality, drawn him into a conspiracy and may have made him, in his darkest reflections, an accessory to murder.

He'd certainly been inveigled into an attempt at the same crime, three years previously, in providing to his brother-in-law a couple of press-gang hard bargains. These bullies were to be employed to chastise, with a sound beating, the young and handsome buck of a clerk who had, while residing within the walls of his own house, cuckolded Denby Carruthers.

Edward Druce had no knowledge of the Gherson name then and was now wishing it had remained that way. Denby, furious at what he saw as the seduction of his wife, Catherine, had gone much further than he'd hinted at when the request was made. It was impossible, given what he'd subsequently discovered, to imagine Denby's intentions had been anything other than permanent removal.

He now knew the proposed victim to be the very same Cornelius Gherson. It was he who'd lain with Denby's much younger wife. The cuckold was thrown off London Bridge with the certainty, in a fast-flowing Thames, the sod would drown. Here was a crime reckoned to be without much in the way of consequence. Any such person so disposed of would end up as just another cadaver pulled from the water.

Half a dozen such finds a day were not uncommon, the bodies sold to the dissecting ghouls at St Bart's Hospital learning to be surgeons. Failing such an outcome, the victim would wash up on a sandbank downriver, a bloated, unidentifiable corpse. Gherson had indeed been tossed over the parapet but had also, miraculously, survived.

The pair of faces he was looking at now, sketched representations, were far from pretty, both villainous looking with one seriously facially scarred. The pair looked to be evil personified. If Hodgson was right, they might be the murderers and abusers of Catherine Carruthers, seeking in their actions to pin the blame on Gherson, which would see him hang. The troubling question was stark. To whose benefit did it accrue? Had they acted on their own volition or on behalf of another? If the latter, there was only one possible candidate.

The prospect of returning home went from being unwelcome to abhorrent, which had him call for his clerk to send a message to his wife, to say his workload this day was so heavy he would not be home for supper. The next request was brought on by hope rather than certainty, looking for aid to a man he felt had betrayed him already. Providing services to the widow of Captain Barclay while simultaneously working for Ommaney and Druce should have made this impossible.

'You know where to find the fellow Hodgson. Ask him to call upon me at his earliest convenience.' There was a pause, caused by the sight of those two penned and unprepossessing faces, a consideration of where it all might lead. 'It may be necessary to hint at an enhanced reward for his services.'

'I fail to see the need for an establishment of your own, when you're perfectly free to stay here as my guest for as long as you please.'

There was no polite way for Emily Barclay to say, staying in someone else's home was never quite the same as one's own, regardless of circumstances. Heinrich Lutyens was a dear friend, the closest she had, and he'd been kindness itself. In spite of the complications of her relationship with John Pearce, Emily knew she had to make a life for herself and their son. This was hard to accomplish as a guest, however welcome.

Being married to Ralph Barclay had radically changed her life, not all of it in a way anticipated. She'd come to so despise him, the thought of living under the same roof was anathema. Having separated from him, then embarked on an affair and become a mother, allied to the absences this had entailed, had turned her into a very different person. Even residence in her own family home felt altered enough to induce disquiet.

She was no longer a child, to live within the constraints imposed by her parents, however well-meaning they might be. The three years since leaving as a girl bride turned her into a woman in every respect. Time spent in Italy especially, added to her liaison with John Pearce, meant she'd seen a different world. This drove home the limitations of what was a very provincial setting.

Necessity had brought her to London but, in a short time, Emily had seen it as a better place to reside. As the widow of a successful naval captain, she was a woman of more than independent means, doubly so since her claim against Ommaney and Druce had been settled. Just into her twenties, she would, when her period of mourning came to an end, be able to launch herself into society.

She could cast aside the widow's weeds convention obliged her to wear. Black garments, which drove home a feeling of deep hypocrisy every time she caught sight of herself in a mirror. Emily Barclay could hardly be said to regret her late husband's passing, but society expected her to show the opposite and to this she must conform.

Added to this was another more pressing consideration. She had every intention of marrying John Pearce, but before this could happen, he must pay court to her as a respectable widow. He would be required to do so for some time, so decency was not offended. Such attention would be so much easier to undertake in a bustling metropolis than in her sleepy Somerset home. In Frome, everyone knew each other's business and was ever ready to perceive scandal, even where none existed.

'You'd find us a burden eventually, Heinrich,' she said in an emollient tone. 'Adam does not trouble you now, but it won't be long before he's crawling around your feet and, may God provide patience, when he's walking and beginning to talk.'

Much as Lutyens sought to hide his consternation at the prospect, he lacked either the guile or the features in a somewhat fish-like face to carry it off, which made his verbal response sound very insincere.

'Perhaps I could come to welcome it.'

'You will be very welcome to indulge Adam when you come to visit, which will not be hard, since I intend to look for a property close by.'

The ringing of the doorbell was enough to distract them both, to conclude a conversation that, continued, might cease to be pleasant. Lutyens not being much of a social creature, he did not appear to have many friends and so was wont to overvalue those he did possess. There was also the fact he, at one time, even if nothing had ever been said, had harboured hopes of a relationship with Emily himself.

She'd worked alongside him in Toulon, nursing the wounded in the hospital he'd set up to treat battle casualties, the port under siege by the forces of the Revolution. Being in close proximity over several weeks, as well as a growing bond of friendship, had no doubt fuelled his hopes. It was a blessing, seeing them dashed had not affected either his regard for her or the man on whom she had come to bestow her affections.

The door opened to reveal the footman with a letter on a silver salver, this passed to his employer. Lutyens examined it before passing it to Emily, given it was addressed to her. As soon as she looked at the writing, it caused her to bite her lip.

'Gherson. I know his hand.'

'Don't open it,' Lutyens insisted, 'it will only distress you.'

'Wondering what the schemer is up to while not knowing would distress me more.' Emily broke the plain wax seal and unfolded the single sheet, reading it swiftly before passing it over.

'A request for money doesn't surprise me, Heinrich.' This engendered a humourless chuckle as the missive was read. 'But no threat, which has ever been the case before.'

'Can he still be a threat?'

'It may not say so, but it is there between the lines. It is true I have done well out of bearding my husband's prize agents . . .'

'No more than your due' was a hasty interjection.

If this was correct, it failed to measure the scale of what Ommaney and Druce had been obliged to pay. Not only all the monies they still held on her husband's account, but a large additional sum, one calculated to make up for the expropriations gained by their nefarious dealings on Captain Barclay's account. Added to this was the substantial compound interest due on the difference.

It was a hard truth to acknowledge, but none of those monies would have come her way without Gherson. He, as Ralph Barclay's clerk, had been the sole channel of communication between the prize agents and their client, able himself to benefit financially from concealing the true nature of the fraudulent trades. A portion of the Barclay account had been used to launch highly risky investments, subsequently boosted by their own funds, to secretly raise the stock price to a ridiculous level.

At which point Ommaney and Druce would sell out at a profit, leaving Ralph Barclay and other investors to bear the losses on the scheme's collapse. Given the major portion of the Barclay fund was working as it should, such malpractice was easy to explain away as the normal workings of the market.

'I doubt,' Lutyens suggested, 'he'll be any more upright as a purser than he's been in any other walk of life. The man is wedded to criminality. If John were here, he'd point out to meet such a request opens you up to being endlessly importuned.'

If this had to be acknowledged, Emily wondered if either man understood her position, regardless of the fact, especially in the case of John Pearce, it had been explained to him dozens of times. She was the mother of a child conceived out of wedlock, a married woman who'd had an adulterous affair. The nature of this had already been subjected to a degree of speculation by suspicious minds, her only salvation being irrefutable evidence of her infidelity was lacking. Gherson could provide that.

It made no odds Ralph Barclay had turned out to be far from the man she'd thought she was marrying, nor how much parental pressure had acted in her decision to accept his proposal. None of this would matter if the truth of Adam's illegitimacy became common knowledge, a stain that could destroy her and be left with him to carry throughout his life.

His father might say he didn't care and she had to believe him: Society would, and therefore so did she. Thus, anything that was required to protect the truth had to be met. Gherson knew how little she'd seen of her husband after Toulon, as well as how estranged they'd become. He knew a legitimate conception for her child was impossible, just as he could point the finger at the real father.

This was why he'd communicated with her from prison, seeking her help to prove his innocence. She'd paid for Gherson's defence, employing the brilliant advocacy of William Garrow, the only lawyer who had a hope of getting him off the charge of murder. Thanks to information gleaned by Walter Hodgson, Emily had no doubt Gherson was indeed blameless, probably, given his background, for the first time in his miserable life.

The arrangement on acquittal had been for him to proceed to Portsmouth, armed with a letter from her as Captain Barclay's widow.

This attested to his sterling character, so he could get another place as a captain's clerk. But in this, he claimed to have been unsuccessful. True or false, there was no way to tell from a distance, while the thought of her coaching to Portsmouth to beard him in person was impossible on several counts.

Not least, she found his presence and his carnal insinuations, and always had since the first meeting, to be repulsive. There was, however, a possible solution, an emissary she could send who knew, and this had been proved already, how to be both discreet and firm with such a slippery character.

'I think, Heinrich, I will require the aid of Mr Hodgson once more.'

CHAPTER THREE

For John Pearce the wind had not only eased, it had swung round to the northwest so, by mid-morning, two days out from Falmouth, the ship was off Ushant, the British sailor's corruption for the French Iles d'Ouessant. These formed a deadly outcrop of islands and reefs off the tip of Brittany, marking the point at which a vessel could be said to have finally left the English Channel.

They lay in an area of huge tidal flows, vicious cross currents and varying winds. Despite this, Pearce had *Hazard* steer closer than was strictly required, making sure the crew were treated to the sight, albeit at a fair distance, of what a lethal menace they presented. Troubled white water marked the iron-bound shoreline, while spume-filled spouts sprang from rocky outcrops, some barely visible on the surface, sobering in its effect.

It was also necessary, employing a pun on the name of the ship, to loudly point out there were other unseen dangers, just covered by water, lying ahead, this to drive home a simple fact. The seas through which they would sail contained equally perilous hazards, underlining a message he'd been repeating ever since these quota men first came aboard.

Strict obedience to any given instruction and absolute attention to their duties was essential. Not to do so, on a shore like the one before them, could see a ship founder, in seas where rescue was impossible and death by drowning a certainty.

'Mr Worricker, a course to take us well clear now, if you please.'

Out in the open sea, on a steady and regular Atlantic swell, life became more comfortable for the majority, if not all. This was something to which those few still suffering the *mal de mer* would, over time, become inured. It also allowed Pearce a future in which he could look forward to enjoying some proper rest, the downside being the need to catch up with the numerous other responsibilities that fell to the captain of a warship.

He was afforded time to take the full measure of his standing officers, as well as, after time at sea, to inspect the areas for which they were responsible. He also sought their views of who in the crew were showing well, as against those who could never aspire to any other duty than mindlessly hauling on a rope. This saw some suggested for temporary positions as mates or yeomen in the various disciplines overseen by the master, bosun, gunner, and carpenter.

Likewise, he was afforded a chance to quiz his Pelicans, albeit formally, in the presence of Mr Hallowell. Michael O'Hagan was holding down the position of master-at-arms, just one of the many areas in which the ship was lacking a properly experienced petty officer. Charlie Taverner and Rufus Dommet had been rated as watch captains, so were, in working with the quota men, closer to the crew than any commissioned officer could ever be. They were thus able to give advice on who might, with encouragement and help, improve their level of skill.

Those named were then called into the cabin, the aforementioned having departed, to be individually addressed and heartened by their commanding officer. He made a point of emphasising, feeling slightly fraudulent in doing so, what was possible in the future. If they studied their various crafts, in a service always in need of expertise, it could lead to positions of responsibility.

In time this might be aboard larger vessels up to ships of the line, granting them the pay and status that went with such increased responsibility. The truth was, such elevation depended on recommendations from highly regarded captains; any from him might be the opposite of helpful.

About to retire at the day's end, he felt reasonably content. If things were far from perfect and real efficiency a long way off, the ship was making decent progress, on a set course and sailing easy on a regular swell. The overnight watches would be taken under experienced hands, so he could look forward to something he'd sorely missed these last ten days. An untroubled night for, once in his cot, sleep should some easily.

Quite apart from his own weariness, the regular creaking of the timbers, as well as the sigh of the wind as it whistled through the rigging, would always provide a sure aid to sending him under. Yet, as ever, there was an interlude when his mind turned to other matters, those he'd left behind, as well as the contents of the letter he'd sent to Emily. Not that they occupied his thinking for long: Why brood on matters about which you could, at present, do nothing?

So, eyes closed, he imagined on a happier prospect, in which he envisaged a life of settled happiness, free from any of the concerns of naval life, a warm place to be and one into which he could happily drift off. This rendered the knock on the door of his sleeping cabin most unwelcome.

'Mr Hallowell's compliments, sir, but he believes it necessary to request your presence on deck.'

There was no choice but to reply in the affirmative. 'Thank you, Mr Livingstone. Please inform him I will be there presently.'

His premier was not the type to ask without purpose. Born in what had been the American colonies and related to a captain of the same name, the very experienced Hallowell had been sent to him as a favour by the commanding admiral at Portsmouth.

Sir Peter Parker was a rare creature, who cared nothing for the crabbed opinions of his fellow flag officers or the officials and senior naval personnel who ran the Admiralty. Secure in both his rank and the depth of his purse, thanks to a three-year spell of command in the West Indies, he could ignore their prejudices, to become the only senior officer from whom Pearce had been in receipt of kindness.

Admiral Sir John Jervis was the polar opposite, a man known for his trenchant opinions and strict discipline. He had sent Pearce back from the Mediterranean to get rid of a man he saw as unfit for either the duty or the rank he occupied. Given this, Sir Peter had posited the possibility, along with the despatches carried, would have come another less official communication to their lordships of the Admiralty. This would suggest John Pearce, in the Jervis opinion, was not fit for future employment.

It was sad to reflect, without Dundas and his intelligence requirements, it was a view that would resonate with almost the entire service. This meant the best he could hope for was life on the beach as a half-pay lieutenant. Given the problems in his relationship with Emily Barclay, this was not a prospect to savour. Wrapping himself in his boat cloak, knowing these depressing thoughts had to be dismissed, he made his way up and out into the stygian darkness, the sound of cooing pigeons coming from the pantry as he passed by.

It was a night in which thick cloud obscured both the moon and the stars, leaving only a tiny modicum of seawater phosphoresce as illumination. As he came close to the faint light of the binnacle, his attention was drawn to a rippling orange glow, reflected off the clouds far out to sea, followed in a few seconds by the faintest of booms, surely caused by cannon fire.

'Third salvo, sir,' Hallowell said, confirming it was not the only other possibility, an explosion, before apologising for disturbing him.

'You marked the time of the first sighting?' was an automatic enquiry.

'Aye aye, sir. I felt the need to know what you would make of it.'

In the reflection from the binnacle, the face might be indistinct, but not the tone of voice. With its distinct twang, it betrayed Hallowell's curiosity about what might follow. The natural response would be to close with the evidence, but *Hazard* was sailing on a specific mission upon which many a delay had already been imposed. This Hallowell knew, even if he was unaware of the exact purpose, which made questionable how his captain would respond.

There were many factors on which to ponder and one was their proximity to the coast of France. They were passing through waters made dangerous by more than rocky seaboards and hidden reefs. Not far to the south of their present position lay the Goulet, the entrance to Brest, the main Atlantic base of the enemy fleet. Pearce had ensured the master set them on a course to avoid it by a wide margin.

Another set of flashes lit up the western cloud base, he counting on his fingers the time between the sight and the sound, trying to calculate the distance, as he would for thunder and lightning. He concluded, when he got above ten, it had to be many miles distant, which did nothing to provide enlightenment.

Yet one notion had to be considered: It might be a British warship engaged in action, perhaps one of the patrolling frigates of the Channel Fleet. It was never going to be a line of battleships: They were at anchor in Plymouth, ready to weigh and offer battle only if the enemy capital ships put to sea. This seemed an increasingly unlikely event since the drubbing they'd received at the Battle of the Glorious First of June.

'Your opinion, Mr Hallowell?' was a courtesy; the decision about how to react would be his alone.

'If our duty permits, sir, I would be inclined to investigate. Our own comrades aside, there are likely to be a number of French privateers in the area. It could be a merchant vessel of ours in difficulties.'

'Not in convoy?'

Cargo vessels sailing alone, in the third year of the war, were supposed to be a thing of the past and rightly so. Safety lay in numbers, meaning convoys which ran, very often to hundreds of merchant vessels, travelling in company, under protection from the Royal Navy. Gathered from many different ports, but mostly from London, they would congregate in the spacious anchorage off Deal, there to join with their naval escort.

Given such a duty was akin to herding cats, it was not a one to which a King's officer happily subscribed, but their presence was essential. The escort had to be strong enough to contest anything but a main enemy battle fleet, such commercial armadas being the lifeblood of the nation's trade. These convoys were thus the source of the funds needed to both fight a war and support and subside continental allies.

They formed an assembly of vessels heading for multiple destinations, the first being Lisbon for the Port Wine trade. Part of the armada would continue on in to the Mediterranean, while the remainder sailed down to the Azores, to detach from there the vessels heading for the Caribbean. This left, to carry on south, those heading for the Cape, India, and the Far Eastern Spice Islands.

'There are always those who will take a chance if they have a speedy vessel. Of course, I can think of many other possibilities.'

There was a tone of eagerness in the premier's voice, and Pearce was not immune to the emotion. Yonder lay the prospect of action, and what kind of naval officer would either man be if they did not crave to be part of it. He looked at the slate to assess the speed they were making, in truth no great shakes, which allowed for an appreciation of the time it would take to close with whatever was taking place.

'I'm disinclined to increase sail, Mr Hallowell, for reasons I hardly need explain.'

'Of course, sir.'

He knew, as well as his captain, the risks of sending aloft men of limited experienced on a pitch-dark night.

'If it's a fight,' Pearce suggested, 'it would be too much to expect we can come upon it in time to affect the outcome. But it could leave men needing succour, so it would not serve to just pass on by. Alter course to close, but I see no need to clear for action.'

Hallowell's ghostly voice denoted quiet agreement, while the orders he issued, which brought the duty watch on deck to trim the yards, were enthusiastically bellowed. Midshipman Livingstone, sharing the quarterdeck, was ordered to go and tell the various bodies who, on hearing the noise, might think their presence was required, to stay in their cots. The youngster came across as confused, which had Pearce proffer soft reassurance.

'Adventure, Mr Livingstone. This is what you joined the navy for, is it not?'

'Aye, aye sir' was an uncertain whisper, which got the Mite a gentle push to send him on his errand.

Pearce stayed on deck, waiting for more evidence of gunfire, the lack of which had him entertain the thought he'd made the wrong call. But it was done now and, in terms of extending the time to reach their proposed destination, it could only be minimal. To reverse his decision might not sit well with the crew, who would now have heard what was afoot. Having tasted action once, albeit in a limited fashion, in which there had been no real risk but the promise of reward, they would be eager for a repeat.

'Am I allowed to enquire what we're about?'

Pearce turned to face the very recognisable voice. Oliphant moved closer to appear, like everyone else, spectral in the glim, he, too, wrapped in a cloak.

'Young Livingston told me I had no reason to stir, so I couldn't help but wonder why anyone would be required to.'

'He should have passed you by, but I cannot fault him for failing to do so.'

'As it was, I was awake. It is not easy to sleep with the ship never silent. How you slumber through constant bells every half hour I cannot fathom.'

'Can I suggest you engage in more activity during the day, as well as fresh air, instead of reading and napping in your berth?'

'I prefer to take my ease when the chance permits, Pearce. And, as you know well, I lack duties and do not choose to partake of any. I doubt the safety of the ship would be improved if I decided otherwise.'

'Which I would be obliged to most heartily concede.' Pearce moved closer to add in a very soft tone. 'Do I have to remind you, in public, you must address me as captain?'

'No doubt to stroke your self-esteem.'

The tone of the exchange, though icily polite, could not disguise the constant undercurrents in their relationship. Ever since he had first encountered Oliphant, there had been an air of uncertainty around the man, one he almost willfully encouraged, which extended even to his name. He'd been introduced by Henry Dundas as Oliphant, but Pearce had heard him confidently called by another name, something the man had declined to explain, even when challenged.

This had occurred in Paris, on a mission to encourage those seeking to overthrow the Revolution. It had proved to be not only a fiasco, but actually a deception and a trap. Forced to contrive an escape back to England, circumstances had obliged them to split up, which allowed Oliphant to get home first. Henry Dundas, the man who'd sent them on this wild goose chase, had thus been fed a very tall tale, suggesting an unqualified success instead of complete failure. This aura of fabricated achievement led to their present assignment.

'You have, I'm informed by the same young man, altered course.'

'By a few points only, to investigate something of interest.'

'You feel you have the luxury of wasting even more time?'

The response was sharp. 'I feel I have the deck and the right to choose.'

Aware of others on the quarterdeck, Oliphant indicated, with a jerk of the head, the need to talk without being overheard, one to which Pearce felt obliged to respond.

'I will be in my cabin, Mr Hallowell. Call me if anything requires attention.'

They entered to the smell of coffee, which had Pearce smile at what had been a commonplace with Michael O'Hagan. The giant bruiser of an Irishman had to be the least likely looking servant any captain had ever employed, albeit he'd been assiduous in carrying out his duties. On taking up the responsibilities of the master-at-arms, Michael had taken care to ensure his replacement, a fellow called Derwent, knew the ropes, as well as the captain's habits.

If chalk and cheese had a physical manifestation, it would have perfectly described the difference between the two. Derwent was a slight, soft-spoken, corn stalk–thin fellow from Dorset, and this extended to a subservient manner. Michael's brute strength and bulk were only half of the very sharp contrast: He had habit of treating his captain as an equal in private and quite often guying him too.

'I took the liberty, your honour,' Derwent said, tray and pot balanced on one hand, the other used to steady himself against the door jamb. 'On account of Mr O'Hagan saying it were the way you liked things if you was hauled out overnight.'

'For which I'm grateful. Put it on the desk and fetch a cup for Mr Oliphant.'

This obliged them to wait several seconds, in silence, until the request was fulfilled, which pointed up another difference, the requirement for discretion. Pearce would not have cared a jot if Michael overheard what was about to be discussed. He trusted him absolutely, indeed, many times in the past, his opinion on important matters had proved not only valuable but lifesaving.

Oliphant didn't sit, even when invited, until the cup had been delivered and Derwent had once more departed for his pantry. Even then he waited a few seconds, before opening the door to ensure the servant was not eavesdropping.

'You never cease to demonstrate distrust' came from John Pearce, with a sardonic chuckle. 'I've no doubt this extends even to me.'

It was not taken as amusing; indeed, the response was deeply serious. 'How many times have I said to you, the habit is why I'm still in one piece? Trust has killed more fools than stupidity or happenstance.'

'We are on a ship at sea, man. Even if you have a host of secret enemies aboard, none can harm you. That is, unless any of the crew have found a way of communicating by sorcery. You are safe.'

'If not entirely content, and I have not been so since we left Falmouth.'

'Really?'

'You spent two weeks, much of it dithering in the Thames, which was bad enough. Now more than another week has gone by and we're sailing as if on some form of pleasure cruise. Surely we should be going as fast as the wind will carry us? And by what right do you choose to deviate from the direct course you have set, without consulting me?'

'Consulting you!'

This was shouted loud enough to pass through the bulkhead, Pearce only able to contain his temper for so long. Yet he was annoyed at himself and worked hard to calm his irritation. The raised voice must have been heard on the deck and would set tongues wagging.

Besides, it seemed to have no effect on Oliphant, who said calmly, 'Do not seek to deflect me. I'm justified in asking.'

'You're not' was imparted in a normal tone, not without difficulty. 'But there are sound reasons.'

'Which are?'

'Those that fall to me as the captain to decide. So accept it, only as a courtesy, if I choose to explain.'

Pearce poured the coffee, then indicated Oliphant should sit down, in a manner that left him no choice. Still suppressing his annoyance, he outlined his motives, this to a fellow not in the least willing to accept an explanation. Not even the fact, at sea, if it was felt another vessel was in danger, there was an obligation on all to seek to assist.

As he was talking, another matter was nagging him. Given how little Oliphant knew about ships and sailing, Pearce was left with a query of his own. Where did that remark about a 'pleasure cruise' come from?

'Do I sense you've been asking a few questions of the crew you so mistrust?'

The response was defensive. 'And why would I not?'

'The fact it may be bad for discipline should be a consideration.'

'Which I term as rot. I say again we are well behind where Dundas expects us to be, which leaves no time for sailing slow. You were present when he insisted time was pressing, and this was driven home in his letters. So you cannot plead ignorance, in which case my previous question stands.'

'I daresay you anticipated a better set of hands, as did I, proper seamen. But we must do the best with what we have.'

'I know the reasons why it was the case. I'm less sure as to why this is so now.'

'They are the same as pertained previously.'

Oliphant made to speak, but a sharp gesture stopped him.

'If you want to criticise anyone, take it out on the sods at the Admiralty. I didn't consider myself that high in their judgments as to be the cause of such malice and, if I am partly so, it's a sideshow. I suspect in taking out the experienced crew they set out to humbug Dundas, by making it plain his ministerial authority, by which he oversees the army, did not extend to the navy. So when he demanded they provide a ship, they gave him one, but then ensured he was gifted with men utterly lacking in skill and with no time to change matters. Yes, I can crack on, setting everything we have aloft and seeking maximum speed, which would be a good way to bring on the exact opposite.'

'Stuff' was Oliphant's uncertain reply.

'To do as you ask would see the crew never off the deck and me and my officers with them, a situation we have only just ceased to require. They would be shifting, setting, and altering sails every hour of the day and, if you had your way, at night as well for days on end. How many men would make a mistake, would be injured by being fatigued and pushed into tasks they are as yet uncertain how to perform, sometimes like tonight, in the pitch dark? How would it play with hands still new to their duties, to be worked to the bone, and how long do you think it would be until we suffered some damage to the ship or the rigging?'

Oliphant sought to look defiant; to Pearce it came across as petulant.

'As of now, they are, in the main, slowly learning their duties. So I should go back to our master. Ask him if he would be happy to drive the crew hard to gain a few knots of speed, risking, in the process, the contentment of these men as well as the safety of the ship?'

'How do you know it was Williams?'

'Because you're not the only one aboard with a deductive ability. My officers would never talk to you about such matters and my midshipmen are too ignorant. You're not the type to condescend to conversations with a common seaman, even if you could find one who knew anything, which the majority don't. It doesn't leave much to guess at.'

'I have good reason to speak with him.' Seeing Pearce's irritated curiosity, Oliphant added, 'Mr Williams obliges by keeping me informed of our position.'

'What difference does it make to you knowing?'

If Oliphant was stuck for a reply, it did nothing to dent his air of justified frustration.

'You should share my concerns instead of deriding them. I doubt failure will endear you to Dundas and I don't have to spell out what that could mean. You have this command by his gift, one that can just as easily be removed. That's something, I feel, given the lack of esteem in which you're held, the entire naval service would cheer. In the face of their low opinion, what hope can you have of another command, or even a place?'

The sound of the bell being rung on the quarterdeck, to signal seven bells, informed Pearce the watch would change in half an hour. It also told him he would have to be on deck in less than four hours himself. Dawn came early at this time of year.

'A risk I will have to take and one by which you will just have to abide. Please do not pretend it's me for whom you are concerned. It's your own future employment which is causing you to worry. Lose the trust of Dundas and he'll throw you on the scrap heap.'

'I will not deny I have reasons for wishing to keep his good opinion.'

'Nor should you, but they do not extend to our progress. Now I suggest you go back to the wardroom and get some sleep, something I fully intend to do the minute you depart.'

It didn't come easily, and no amount of seeking distraction in other thoughts could keep Pearce away from recalling the conversation. It was only after half an hour he realised, when the bell rang once more, how long his fruitless ruminations had kept him awake. Not that the determination to remedy the matter helped much.

Chapter Four

He was fully dressed and on the quarterdeck at the appointed hour, as was Samuel Oliphant, as ever, far from happy at being roused out pre-dawn by the hullabaloo of the ship coming to life. With no repose possible, he'd chosen to come on deck, granted permission to be there as long as he stayed out of the way of John Pearce. He also had to avoid impeding Hallowell and Worricker, the four midshipmen, Mr Moberly, the lieutenant of marines, along with a half dozen of his eight men, now lined up, muskets at rest.

The ship had been cleared for action, bulkheads down to provide a clean sweep fore and aft, with the cabin and wardroom furniture struck below. The gunner, Mr Low, in his regulation felt slippers, was sat behind a wetted screen, the passage to the gunroom covered in damp sand, while the fellow newly designated as yeoman of the powder room was standing by in the filling chamber or light room.

The carpenter, Towse, had a small band of helpers standing by to effect repairs should they engage in battle, while the surgeon, Mr Cullen, and the pair chosen to assist him were below, ready to receive casualties. All was as it should be for Pearce, bar one concern: The excessive amount of time it had taken to man, load, and run out the guns, a precaution mandatory at first light in wartime to guard against surprise.

He had, in the Thames, instituted as much practice as he could within the limited time left over from other vital tasks, even buying extra gunpowder in Faversham to facilitate extra firing drills, hoping the excitement of actual firing would bring on encouragement. If it had brought a better standard it was nowhere near enough to even hint at what was required.

Worse was the evidence of fumbling, not too much of a problem in what was a routine daily duty, with time to make adjustments, which would not do if they found themselves in sight of an armed enemy. Even then, there was usually time to prepare, matters at sea rarely being subject to immediate gravity.

But it was what would follow which lay at the seat of his concerns. The first discharge could be controlled, even carefully aimed if properly supervised. It was the rate at which his crew could reload and get off a second or any subsequent salvo that mattered. They needed to achieve the rate of fire necessary to subdue a foe, as well as strike home on their target in a rolling broadside. It was upon such ability to outgun the enemy the Royal Navy depended, the source of their battle superiority. Lacking it could put HMS *Hazard* at a severe disadvantage.

There was nothing he could do about it now. It had to be put aside so he could concentrate on the present duty, keeping alert to any threat that may appear with the dawn. The first tinge of grey had begun to show to the east, though the western seascape was still in darkness, which made surprising the cry from the masthead.

'On deck there, two lights off the starboard bow.'

Pearce used his telescope to sweep in said direction but with little initial success. It was some time before he spotted them, two distant pinpoints, which soon disappeared again, boats rising on the Atlantic swell, before falling to become invisible in the troughs. The call from the masthead had sent Worricker racing for the mainmast cap, soon pointing more precisely from his higher elevation.

'Lanterns! Got them in plain sight, sir.' As the light increased, he added, 'A cutter and a jolly boat fully loaded.'

'Mr Hallowell, a course to close.'

With the guns manned, this took time. Pearce was not going to take a chance, calling men away from his ordnance so close to Brest. It was possibly some subterfuge by a French warship, one that still might not be fully visible. His concern was eased as the light increased to show the sea barren of an enemy. By the time they closed with the two bobbing craft, they were plain to see from the deck and packed with men, it was full daylight and *Hazard* was back to normal.

Initially they were greeted with waving and barely distinct shouting as the boats came round to aim for *Hazard*. Then the occupants went quiet, though there seemed, judging by the many gestures, a great deal of communication between the two boats. This was not in doubt when they'd eventually closed the distance between them, whatever was being exchanged far too faint to be heard, eventually because of the noise aboard ship.

The crew had to be cajoled into ignoring this apparition and concentrate on their duty of wetting, sanding, and swabbing the deck, others being sent below to put the lower decks back to rights. Finally, they were close enough to show a silent set of tired faces.

As they came alongside, the command was issued to say breakfast should be held back until they could identify and deal with the now-silent occupants. Standing by the open gangway, Pearce counted some thirty souls, easily picking out the man who, merely by his dress and the size of his feather-trimmed hat, had to be in command. With a hand to his mouth, Pearce called out his name and that of his vessel.

'Captain Brendan Gilligan,' came floating back, 'of the *Arklow Lass*, taken by some swine of a Frenchman not many hours past. May God bless you and be thanked for bein' where you are.'

'Irish, John Boy,' commented Michael O'Hagan, who was close enough not to worry about being overheard. 'And Christian most like, thankin' the Lord for their deliverance.'

'Best get it done quickly,' Pearce joked, 'for they'll struggle for divinity once aboard.'

'As I do' was the response.

O'Hagan accompanied the remark with a swift sign of the cross across his breast, underlining one point on which these two good friends would ever part company. Michael was deeply religious, while Pearce was a vocal sceptic, forever calling out, while careful not to deride it, the Irishman's superstition.

'Permission to come aboard, Captain Pearce?' came from the cutter.

'Granted. Michael, get a message to the cook. Tell him we will have a few more mouths to breakfast. They can't be carrying much in such crowded boats either. The purser will be obliged to provide hammocks and maybe a bit more, possibly without payment.'

'Sure that'll cheer the sour bugger.'

It took time, on the swell, to get the boats alongside without damage to themselves or *Hazard*'s scantlings, but those manning the oars were competent in themselves and well ordered by the men on the tillers. When they did finally make their way up the side, they managed the man ropes and battens, always a trial in open waters, with an ease born of long practice. More obvious was the weariness brought on by what must have been a hard haul on the oars, over several hours, in darkness.

Gilligan was last on deck, a sturdy leather satchel over his shoulder, to lift his hat and repeat his profuse thanks. The temptation Pearce had, to ask for an immediate explanation, was put aside while he was introduced to the first mate, Mr Macklin. He seemed a rough-looking individual, with a smallpox-scarred face, added to a less-than-cheerful demeanour, which stood in sharp contrast to the smiling geniality of his superior. Both were introduced to the trio of lieutenants, as well as the master, before Macklin was led off to the reinstated wardroom.

The crew, none of whom had spoken a word, were taken below, carrying in dunny bags what few possessions they'd managed to salvage. HMS *Hazard* got under way again on its original course, the execution of this watched briefly by Gilligan, who was then taken to have breakfast in the main cabin.

A nosy Oliphant forced his own attendance, no doubt curious to know what had caused the merchant captain to be in the predicament in which he found himself, and he was not alone. Pearce, equally intrigued, considered excluding him, but reasoned it would be too public an embarrassment to do so.

Once seated and provided with the wine he requested, it being the only drink he could partake of even at this time of day, the merchant captain was encouraged to relate his tale. It was quickly established he'd owned the vessel lost, as well as the cargo she carried, having sailed from Izmir on the coast of Turkey, bound for the Pool of London with a cargo of spices and carpets.

'Now possessed by a dog of a French privateer, sir. Came upon me in the night and opened fire before I even knew he was in the offing.'

Pearce masked his wonder and the obvious question: How had the so-called "dog" found him, in the dark, on a cloudy night? The conclusion, reluctantly and hesitantly confirmed, admitted Gilligan had been sailing along with his quarterdeck lanterns alight, which indicated a degree of foolishness in waters known to be far from safe. This obvious error was not a point to emphasise without being rude, but there was another.

'You were surely not sailing alone?'

Gilligan pulled a face before replying, implying discomfort, seemingly assuaged by hiding his face behind a hearty and lengthy gulp of wine. Goblet back on the table and with the enquirer awaiting a reply, he responded with a gloomy air.

'No choice, Captain Pearce. We'd lost our upper mainmast around forty north, in what was close to a hurricane. A real corker, it was, for sure, which I reckon came all the way over from the Caribbean, losing none of its power on the way. It had me saying Hail Mary's by the dozen, I can tell you. We fell behind the convoy and, with only a jury rig, had no way to catch up. Fired off blue lights to the alert escorts in the hope of a tow but, if they saw them, they chose not to respond.'

'Such weather would surely have scattered them as well as all the other vessels.'

Gilligan's expression seemed to indicate this as a thought not previously considered. This being illogical, Pearce reckoned to have misread the expression, so he moved to refill his guest's empty glass. It was taken as very welcome by the immediate way it was drained, an act which went some way to explain the Irishman's countenance.

The face was full, bluish on the cheekbones and not just from the effect of wind, sea, and what seemed an affection for alcohol, given it overlaid what appeared to be a natural high colour. There was about him an air of prosperity, for he was not short on belly in a squat frame. If his brass-buttoned red coat was a touch sun bleached, as well as stained with salt from his being in a boat, it was of a fine quality, still showing enough of its colour to outdo the ruddy cheeks.

A wig covered what had been ginger stubble, not previously worn as he came aboard, now atop his head, despite it being in dire need of powder. Considering his loss, the voice was far from melancholic, which was also the case with his appetite: The boiled fowl he was chewing on, added to the drink with which he washed it down, seemed not to be diminished by misfortune.

Pearce could not avoid a comparison in the speech, if not the height and build, between him and Michael O'Hagan. He noted the accent, although strongly Irish, to be different, softer in tone if not in level. Gilligan was a boomer, hearty in making his points and not afraid enough of the deity, to which he often referred, to eschew the odd blaspheme. This occurred as he sketched out the voyage from the Levant to where his ship had been taken.

'I suppose I can say, at least the bastard was a Christian. He put us in our boats, along with water and biscuit and didn't just slit our throats, Jesus be thanked.'

'Can I say, Captain Gilligan, you seem remarkably sanguine, given you have lost not only your ship but what must have been a valuable cargo.'

'Only because it's insured, sir, at the Lloyd's Coffee House and to the full value of the manifest. With you to witness the position where you picked us up and in what circumstances, I anticipate no difficulty in submitting a claim. I assume I can trust you to provide written testimony.'

Pearce agreed with a degree of reservation. 'I can certainly attest to the location.'

The hull had a price already determined, but the value of the cargo was another matter entirely. This, with insurers always looking to evade their terms, was bound to be a subject of a dispute as to the accuracy of the manifest. He assumed this to be in Gilligan's satchel, easy to inflate if the ship's master was inclined and able to do so.

Pearce had no intention of becoming involved and so burdened, given the degree of correspondence disagreements could engender. Gilligan's eyes narrowed slightly, as if to imply this were not fulsome enough, but it was fleeting and his expression changed to one of query.

'You have not, sir, enquired as to the course set by the swine who took my ship?'

The brow was now furrowed and the reason was not hard to fathom. The "French dog" could not be very far off, which raised the possibility of recapture, surely the first course to adopt for a King's officer, which obliged Pearce to add a reason for inaction.

'I think you'll agree, whatever course he took within sight of you and your boats, will likely not be the one he subsequently chose to pursue. I cannot, in all conscience, go chasing around the ocean in search of the fellow. Indeed, in altering course to find you, I have already exceeded my orders.'

'Your destination being?'

'As yet undecided,' Oliphant blurted out, before Pearce could reply.

This got him an irritated look, one, judging by his slightly arch expression, not missed by their guest, surely the cause of what followed.

'Can I enquire as to the purpose of your orders?'

Pearce got his response in fast. 'Let's say it is not for open discussion.'

'I just wondered if I could persuade you to a detour.' Given neither man responded, if you excluded astonishment, he continued. 'I would, of course, make it well worth your while.'

'Detour?' Pearce asked eventually, breaking what was too long a pause. It was clear, having proposed the notion, it was a stimulating one to his guest, for he continued with palpable enthusiasm.

'Sure, how many days sailing are we away from the southwest coast of Ireland?' Getting no response, Gilligan added with brio, 'Three, maybe, if you were to crack on and the wind favours.'

'I don't think you understand the ways of the navy, sir.'

This remark produced a chuckle and a sly look. 'I understand every man's need for a coin or two, Captain Pearce, and I know neither a uniform coat nor civilian attire does not much diminish such longings. I have, in the satchel I brought aboard, the means to meet a fair fee.'

Pearce didn't know whether to be affronted or amused. He could hardly deny his naval peers were inclined to avarice, or that he himself was immune to the sin. Had he not just falsely named a vessel as a prize when it was anything but, happy as anyone aboard to accept whatever share of reward it produced?

'I'm afraid I must decline to oblige you.'

'What Mr Pearce is trying to say, sir, is we have certain tasks to fulfil.'

That got Oliphant a sly look from Gilligan, added to another impatient glare from Pearce. Why could the man not just shut up!

'Sure, the navy issues directives, which I have always understood to be flexible enough for variation.'

Oliphant responded, ignoring a look from Pearce to be quiet. 'I fear the captain would be obliged to tell you that is not possible in this case. Also, we are somewhat pressed for time to fulfil our instructions.'

This got raised eyebrows, added to a look of disbelief. 'Looking at what you had set aloft, when I first sighted your sails, I don't see you being in a hellfire hurry to get anywhere.'

'Something,' Oliphant replied airily, with a sideways glance at a now-fuming Pearce, 'on which I'm apparently not competent to judge.'

Gilligan's gaze swung back to him and, if the answer was available, it was not one John Pearce was willing to divulge. So he covered for his lack of an experienced crew with an excuse, one which sounded feeble, even to him.

'I have no desire to emulate you, sir, and lose a mast.'

The merchant captain demonstrated his disbelief with scant attempt at dissimulation, a crooked smile exposing yellowing teeth; he saw it as weak too.

'You have not asked what I'm prepared to pay.'

'The amount would have no influence upon my intentions, which are to proceed with all despatch.' The rest Pearce added hurriedly, as he realised the inconsistency of the statement, made obvious by the arch look it engendered. There was, also, the need to stop Oliphant butting in. 'It is, of course, commensurate with the well-being of the ship.'

'And here's me, having promised my lads I'd get them home in good time to harvest the potato crop.'

Oliphant was quick into a gap left by Pearce's inability to think of any kind of sensible reply. 'You will have to take passage from where we can put you ashore. As to how long that will be, well, we may have other matters to see to beforehand.'

They had decided, just after weighing from Falmouth, a first call would be off the estuary of the River Bidassoa, to seek intelligence on the attitudes of the one-time combatants, the river forming the Atlantic border between Spain and France. Depending on what they discovered, it was uncertain where they would go to next, the eventual port of call, if they bypassed Lisbon, being Gibraltar as originally intended.

From the Rock, Gilligan and his crew could take passage on any number of homebound vessels, including fast-sailing postal packets. If this didn't serve, they could heave to beforehand off the mouth of the Tagus. There was no need to actually access the port of Lisbon: Gilligan and his crew could be dropped off into their boats to make their own way upriver.

As of this moment this was a secondary concern to the man becoming more and more irritated at the way Oliphant was commenting on matters that were none of his concern. He was also employing a tone which implied he stood equal to the ship's captain, and it had not been missed by Gilligan.

To Pearce, Oliphant was a junior partner and would remain so until they touched land. Even there it was debatable if his particular skills would produce the kind of result Henry Dundas required. Such had been the original nature of their association on the prior mission to Paris, he to the fore and Oliphant there as support.

If circumstances and flight had enforced more equivalence, Pearce saw no reason on this new venture to allow it to resurface. It was in such a fit of pique he asked a question designed to knock the sod off his perch.

'I wonder, Captain Gilligan, did you, on your travels, pick up any information pertaining to the actions of our Spanish ally?'

It was pleasing to see Oliphant stiffen and sit bolt upright, the fear obvious something of their mission was about to be disclosed. It was in a spirit of pure and pleasant mischief Pearce added, 'It was a matter Mr Oliphant and I have been discussing, agreeing it to be unnatural, when you consider how many times the Dons have been our deadly enemy. We wondered at their fortitude in pursuing the war on our side now they've made peace with France.'

'Have they indeed?'

Nodding, Pearce explained the basis of the treaty the Spaniards had signed.

'Holy Jesus, peace. It's strange indeed' came the response. Gilligan then looked from one to the other, in a way that underlined he'd more than sensed the tension. 'Unnatural is the word I'd use, sir, to be even talking to those murderous revolutionaries, devils who should be sent to the pits of damnation for their sins.'

'A cause for curiosity, of course,' Oliphant cut in, employing a dismissive tone. 'Worthy of idle speculation but nothing more.'

'To which I am in no position to add, sir.'

'You did not call at Minorca perhaps?' Pearce asked. 'And catch sight of the readiness of their fleet?'

An attempt to keep the discomfort alive, it was successful: He could almost hear Oliphant's grinding teeth. So he added, in a pedantic, schoolmasterly way, information of which Gilligan might expect a civilian to be unaware.

'Port Mahon is a timely stop on the way to Gibraltar, Mr Oliphant, a place to take on basic requirements if we are, as of now, not in conflict. This is especially the case after a long voyage from the Levant. If anything was amiss in how the Dons intend to act, there could be signs there for a merchant captain to observe, as well as gossip to pick up.'

This got an excessive head shake, which nearly dislodged Gilligan's wig. 'We made no attempt to close Port Mahon, indeed, it was a place I chose to bypass, being secure in wood and water.'

'Then I am obliged to assume you victualled elsewhere?' Pearce commented, in a rhetorical way. 'An Italian port perhaps.'

'At Palermo, sir' came the strident response. 'My primary aim, on weighing from there, was to catch up with a homebound merchant fleet gathering at Gibraltar, whose proposed date of sailing I had from the outward voyage. And, Christ in Heaven, it was nip and tuck when we did succeed, with barely hours to make up our stores before the signal came for the entire convoy to weigh.'

'A pity,' said Pearce.

About to ask for more details of what happened next, the loss of the mast and contact with the convoy, he never got the chance.

'If you will forgive me,' Gilligan announced, abruptly. 'I thank you for your hospitality, but I think it best I see to the welfare of my crew.'

Tempted to say they had been breakfasted and so would be content, or to point out his first mate was available to oversee anything requiring attention, good manners gave no option but to accede. He then explained he had sent instructions to the purser to provide hammocks, while his master-at-arms would sort out the slinging arrangements. What was added next was underscored by a bit of malice, designed to further put Oliphant in his place.

'You will, of course, berth here. I'll have part of my cabin set aside for your use.'

'Holy Christ, that's generous, sir.'

By the look of genuine surprise, he meant it. A courtesy being granted to him, which would have been automatically extended to a fellow naval captain, was obviously seen as flattering. It hit its mark, too, being one he'd not and could have extended to Oliphant from the very outset. He was just as surprised, but not in the same way.

'I'll say' came out crabbed.

'Let us hope it will be only for a few days,' Pearce added gaily, pleased with the effect of his ploy.

'I shall beseech the Good Lord it is so.'

Which led to a scraping of chairs and the Irishman's departure, allowing Pearce to challenge his so-called compatriot.

Chapter Five

'Why in the name of the devil can you not stay out of matters that are none of your concern? You had no right to make any comment on things which fall to me to decide.'

'Oh dear.' Oliphant sighed, seeking to cover his obvious and continuing irritation at what he must have taken as a deliberate snub.

The option to share the cabin had never been offered and with it the comfort such a gift brought, better food and a less-crowded living space. Not least it would allow access to the privacy of the captain's privy, obviating the need to use the windswept heads, which a man like Oliphant must find demeaning.

'Have I pricked your precious authority again?'

'You act and sound as if we're equal partners. We are most certainly not on board and perhaps not even if we find ourselves ashore.'

'What do you make of our sudden guest?'

The disinterested look that had appeared on Oliphant's face, as he asked this, was a mask to hide his true feelings regarding his accommodation. But the words made clear he had no intention of entering into a discussion on their relative standing. It was as good a way as any of telling Pearce he did not, and would not, accept the interpretation just enunciated. When he got no reply, he asked again.

'I'm merely curious if you see anything to wonder at?'

Well aware there was quite a lot, Pearce still answered, 'For instance?'

'A fellow made uncomfortable by being so closely questioned.'

'Are you implying I was rude?'

'Heaven forfend' was delivered with unmistakable irony.

'Are you intending to put an oar in there as well?'

Oliphant looked set to react positively, when the voice at the door stopped him.

'Permission to clear away, Capt'n?'

The bent-over figure of Michael O'Hagan filled the doorway in such a way a mouse would have struggled to get by. But it was the look on his face that amused Pearce. It was bland, innocent, and utterly false, given he must have overheard the last exchange. Tempted to ask what he was doing in the cabin was tempered by the presence of his fellow diner, but it did present another chance to assert his authority.

'Mr Oliphant is just about to return to the wardroom, so yes.'

In the face of such a comment, the man was left with no choice and so was up and off in a second, which allowed Michael to explain his presence. He admitted to overseeing Derwent to ensure all was done properly, Gilligan being Pearce's first invited guest, even including the ship's company. It rang a bit hollow, the suspicion being Michael was more curious about his fellow countryman.

'And where is Derwent now?'

'Sent him to get hot water from the cook' was the reply as he began to clear up. 'Asked me, cause he's a'feart to hisself, if you can find another berth for them pigeons. Says the never-ending noise they make is not to his taste.'

'And where does he suggest they go?' came in a less-than-accepting tone, which was as good as saying, they're not going to be kept here.

'Seems the Mite's been poppin' in an' feeding them since Falmouth. Tells Derwent he had turtle doves at home.'

'Which he still misses, I would think.'

'Time will make him what he needs to be, for he's a good lad. I can ask him to take them into the gunner's quarters if you say it will serve. Reckon he'll look after them proper.'

'If you think it a good notion, Michael.'

The next remark was delivered in a much-less-friendly tone. 'Sure, he's a prickly one, your Mr Oliphant.'

'Not much loved by you, I fancy' avoided the need to answer.

'Not by any of us, John Boy, as you well know. Our Charlie is sure, as the day is long, he recalls him from somewhere. He said so since first clapping eyes on the bugger. It's not a notion to cheer him and nor should it you. Given where Charlie hails from and his past life of crime, it does not point to honest endeavour.'

'And Rufus?' Pearce enquired, having no intention of hinting at agreement.

'Following the lead as ever. Happen you should talk to them and ask for yourself?'

'I'll leave that to you.'

The suggestion was impossible, even if Charlie Taverner and Rufus Dommet were people he considered companions of a particular stamp. Circumstances aboard the ship into which they'd been pressed had caused them to combine into a solid grouping for reasons of communal protection. Subsequent events and palpable threats to their continued well-being had seen this bond grow and they'd rarely been apart since. On many occasions, Pearce had needed to rely on them for his own safety and his fellow Pelicans had never let him down.

How long ago that fateful night seemed, as distant as that pair being able to address him in the mocking way they had on first acquaintance. Only Michael had ever had a chance to talk to him privately, outside a few occasions when he'd met all three ashore, away from prying eyes. and even this was now constrained.

Being so shorthanded, Michael was no longer with him in the cabin. The other two, being rated as watch captains, might be a position well above the common herd, but it was still one which precluded friendly public chats with their commanding officer.

'How are they faring?' he asked, as Michael re-entered the cabin.

'Charlie reckons he's bein' worked to the bone by your lubbers. That's afore he starts on what they have aloft.' Michael tapped his forehead to indicate to what he was alluding. 'Claims he knows planks of wood with more wit, but carping is his way. Rufus, as ever, takes what comes.'

'Any notion of the crew guessing what we're about?'

The remark got a knowing looking. His quota men would not yet be adept at fishing out things they were not supposed to know. For experienced tars, it was a game never to be abandoned, which usually made information on course, duties, and destination near impossible to keep secret. This accepted, anything that could be called a fact had to be sorted from the endemic, daily-changing rumours. Sailors spent as much time making things up as ferreting out the truth.

'Sure, guessing would fit for all, me included' came with a look that struck home. Used to knowing more than most, Michael was making it plain he was unhappy about the present situation. 'They know we're bound for Gib, but no more.'

Pearce had no intention of providing anything extra, given Oliphant's obsession with secrecy, but the information demanded a response.

'No doubt from the master?'

'Unlike some, I reckon he sees no cause to hide it.'

And nor would the crew, which meant Gilligan would find out, which made irrational the way Oliphant had dissembled. He could have just said Gibraltar and left it there. It seemed to be integral to his nature, a man who would fabricate even when the truth could do no harm, a trait it had taken Pearce time to discover and one he reckoned it was unsafe to forget.

'Tell Derwent to get a bulkhead set up, to make a sleeping cabin for your fellow Irishman.' Again his expression demanded Pearce say more. 'I offered to berth him here.'

'He's not navy, John Boy.'

There was an oddity to think on. Michael was the least hierarchical soul in creation, evidenced by the relationship he had with the man he could so address in private. Yet he appeared put out by the notion of what he saw as proper being set aside. A courtesy to a King's officer was not seen by him as one to extend to a civilian.

'The wardroom is far from spacious and neither are we well found anywhere else. It will flatter him, and he strikes me as a fellow who might like a bit of soft soap.'

'Not alone there' was Michael's parting shot, as he carried the last of the used dishes out of the cabin.

The lower deck required to be rearranged to accommodate the extra hammocks, cutting space for all, and this for men who would not be called upon to work the ship. It didn't sit well with those forced to make room and required to suffer the much-truncated gap between swaying bodies, as well as more crowded mess tables. Michael, being a sounding board for the crew, carrying out duties which took him all over the ship, brought this to the attention of his captain, as well as another matter, one he found strange.

'I tried to talk to some of the men who came aboard and not one of them speaks a word of English.'

'Can you not address them in your Irish tongue?' That got a look to which Pearce responded, 'I assume they're fellow countrymen of Gilligan.'

'Sure, I tried, but they don't understand that, either, bar one word in ten. Jesus knows what kind of Erse they talk, for I can't get any sense out of it. I was down to making signs until that creature Macklin came by.'

'So what did you learn?' was an idle enquiry, from a man busy making late entry calculations on stores consumed, his quill poised over one of the ship's ledgers, just opened.

'Nothing. Soon as he appeared they turned clam. And neither did he give ow't away, leastways to me. Made a sharp gesture and the men moved away. Gave me a hard look and off he went too.'

'Not a cheerful soul, I reckon.'

'Not like Gilligan then.'

'No' came with an arch look. 'How upset are the crew?'

'Never having served on a fully manned ship, they're not to know what's normal, an' your being kindly makes them mouthy.'

'Am I kindly, Michael?'

'A day aboard the ship I served on, without you, would show you are and still their tongues. Even if you've been driving them hard, it's not with cursing and the cat.'

Quill still poised, Pearce thought for several seconds before speaking again.

'It occurs to me there may be an obvious solution.'

'Which is?'

'What if Gilligan's crew were also working the ship?'

'Sure.' O'Hagan snorted. 'I give you joy of finding the means to ask.'

The quill was housed and Pearce stood. 'The person to ask is their captain.'

He found Gilligan below decks, in earnest conversation with Macklin, though it looked, more by gestures observed than anything Pearce could overhear, to be some kind of divergence of opinion.

'I have a request to make, Captain Gilligan.'

The first mate moved away at a glance from his captain, Pearce noting the taciturn look aimed at both. Gilligan's attitude was similar until Macklin was out of sight, when it turned to the opposite. The Irishman's green eyes, in that well-rounded, cheery face, when he gave Pearce his full attention, positively twinkled.

'Would I be allowed a guess as to what it might be?' Slightly thrown, Pearce nodded. 'I couldn't fail to note, when you backed sails in order to pick us up, your crew are a bit low on knowin' their duty. In getting under way again, it was even more obvious. Not hard to guess why, when near all are new to the life.'

'You've been questioning them?'

This was delivered with a frown. It seemed a discourteous thing to do without asking his permission. Gilligan responded, not the least put out by the obvious disapproval.

'By Christ, why should I restrain? I'm not navy, am I?'

Which was a good way of saying the constraints binding upon naval officers, it keeping a proper distance between themselves and the men, did not apply to him.

'And what did this enquiring produce?'

'Jesus, nothing you don't already know. They're ignorant of the sea, as well as their duties, and worried about what the future holds.'

'I believe you were about to advance a guess.'

'My lads know their trade where yours do not.'

'And if they were asked to lend a hand?'

'They'll do what I tell them' was imparted firmly. 'In fact, I was about to suggest such a course.'

'And Mr Macklin agrees?'

A shrug indicated his opinion was of no account, which had Pearce wonder if he was against the idea and had been saying so when interrupted.

'They are enough in number to make up a watch, which will more than ease the burden on your lads, both below decks and above.'

'My master-at-arms, who's Irish, tried to talk with them, only to find they lack English. Nor could he make headway in Gaelic.'

'They're far West Country and island folk, Mr Pearce, and have their own way of speech. Some have never set foot on the mainland at all, seeing they have no love for the bodies who abide there. Especially anyone in authority, who would be looking for tax money. But they're honest, hardy types, not given to the complaint and never a one looking to do anything other than make some coin, then get back home to their families.'

'So you will ask?'

'No need, as I say.'

'You feel you can just volunteer them?'

'They've got to earn their vittels,' Gilligan insisted. 'Sure, if they don't work the same as the crew, they can't ask to be likewise fed.'

Sensing the doubt in Pearce's expression, which hinted he was not one to deny any man sustenance, Gilligan was quick to claim it as a joke. 'And when it's put them to right, as the fastest way to get back to their own hearths, they'll be as eager as you are to crack on.'

Off he went to corral his crew, it being plain, for all his confidence, added to the indistinct buzz of difference and the time taken, it required a degree of persuasion. Pearce, who listened for a short while before going back to his cabin, reckoned it had to be about the thought of toil without pay and it would include the first mate. Yet Gilligan was successful, for they came on deck at four bells and remained throughout the duration of the watch.

More importantly, a number, at Macklin's request and in an incomprehensible tongue, made their way aloft when his men were called upon to do so. Their very obvious competence allowed Pearce to risk an increase in sail, all orders processed through Gilligan's knowledgeable first mate.

Studding sails were fetched from the hold, articles he'd reckoned, apart from airing, were weeks away from employment, these being sent aloft and bent on with an efficiency his crew could not match, and the effect was immediate.

For the first time he could experiment and seek the best point of sailing. HMS *Hazard*, well-handled, had the lines of a flier and she began to show her paces now. When the cloud cover parted and the sun came out, it was as if the gods of the sea had decided to bless their progress. Blue sky brought an increase in what had now swung round to a favourable northeasterly wind.

This had Pearce calling for even more canvas so, by the time Gilligan's men stood down, getting an appreciative nod as they filed below, the picture was very different. Instead of rising and falling easily on the ocean swell, the prow was now slamming into the waves, the dipping bowsprit sending cascades of water over the foredeck. Hitherto gently canted, the main deck was now seriously sloped, being regularly sluiced with foaming seawater, a combination that sent some of his quota men, in failing to use the man ropes, tumbling into the scuppers, engendering many a bruise and one broken wrist.

Gilligan had stood throughout on the quarterdeck, commenting with perspicacity on the sail plan, which underlined he was a proper seaman, able to handle more than a lumbering merchant vessel. He was enjoying the speed as much as any man aboard, which had Pearce allude to the position they were approaching, added to a concern from which he was now reckoned to be free.

Hazard was coming on to the same latitude as Brest, with a wind that favoured the enemy if he wished to put to sea, posing a threat which could have been serious. The addition of the men of *Arklow Lass* to the crew meant danger was eased: Should anything be sighted, which looked like a French warship, he had, on that very same wind, every hope he could outrun them.

'Not inclined to fight?' Gilligan asked, with some surprise, when this was mentioned. 'Even if it looked to favour you cannon to cannon?'

Shaking his head, Pearce realised he was on the same hook as existed previously, the mission upon which they were set. It was one that precluded even a minor risk to the ship, which there would surely be with the way the crew handled the guns. The Irishman, clearly doubting, asked in an idle manner about friendly warships, which would be patrolling such waters, to which the answer was equally firm. Pearce would acknowledge but not close to confer.

'Even if ordered to do so?' was an obvious rejoinder. Any such vessel would likely be a frigate and under the command of a superior officer, who would expect to be obeyed. 'Sounds like hot water to me.'

Tempted to point aloft to the Admiralty flag, Pearce demurred. To allude to it could only bring on more questions.

'Trust me, Mr Gilligan, any such instruction will be ignored.'

Over dinner, just the two of them, Gilligan avoided any further enquiries about the loss of his ship, stating it as too depressing to dwell upon. Instead, he became angrily vocal about the difficulties war imposed on the carrying trade. High insurance rates, allied to the rapacious wartime prices being charged by those selling the cargoes, eating into what an honest merchant captain could earn.

When this was exhausted, it looked as if the conversation might swing back to his loss, which was deflected as he alluded to the trouble he would have encountered had it not occurred in hanging on to his crew when they came into soundings.

'I had intended, if I failed to find the convoy, to go for Bristol, it being less dangerous when it comes to pressing. It would have led to a loss of profit due to the need to barge the cargo to London, of course, but hanging on to a crew for a merchant captain, one you know and can trust, is just as important as it is for the navy.'

Unknowingly, Gilligan had touched a Pearce nerve; he'd experienced the very thing, having been pressed into the service for a second time in those very waters. It had been early enough in the war to see any number of merchantmen sailing alone on their homebound journey, probably unaware the conflict with France had broken out. This allowed any short-handed naval captain, and too many were at the outset of a new war, to strip from them what men they required.

Convoys were safe from interference, but this didn't entirely mitigate the risk. Having made a landfall at Deal, most of the captains would discharge and pay off most of their crew. Only those necessary to get the ship up to the Pool of London would be kept on, as few as possible, so any diminution in numbers would risk the safety of the ship, something the Impress Service was required to respect.

Yet the Thames estuary remained a dangerous stretch of water when it came to press-gangs, not all of them official. Freelance bands were based in the numerous creeks downriver of Sheppey, men eager to earn a cash bounty for every man forcibly entered and handed over and damn the safety of the vessel.

This they indulged in, while at no danger to themselves from the Admiralty. Bodies would disappear on to warships from which they would not be discharged till the peace, while their relatives would ask in vain for their whereabouts. Illegal it might be, but it was subjected to, like much that took place in the service, the blind eye.

'Nowhere is safe, not even the Bristol Channel. But sure, the Thames is where the devils are most active.'

Voices raised in dispute stopped their conversation, and Derwent entered to say Mr Oliphant was asking permission to call.

'Tell the sentry he has my permission.'

Chapter Six

Allowed past, Oliphant made no attempt to mask his fury, nor could he cope with the heel of the ship, which had kept him off the deck for most of the day. Now he was obliged to put a hand out to the bulkhead just to maintain a vaguely upright position, which rendered somewhat feeble his palpable anger.

'I need to have a word with you.'

'Indeed,' Pearce responded, well aware of why the sod was upset; never before had he been obliged to request entry in such a manner. 'I daresay we will be done in very short order. Do you wish to come back or sit down and join us in a glass of wine?'

The jaw was already tight, but Oliphant managed to make this even more evident. Gilligan, well aware of an atmosphere, which would require a knife to cut, pushed his chair back, saying he must look to his responsibilities.

'I wasn't aware you had many, Mr Gilligan,' Pearce responded, in a languid tone, taking advantage of the possibilities this barb afforded. 'Aboard this vessel, they fall to me and to me alone.'

'What ship's captain is ever free from them, sir? But you gentlemen clearly have matters to discuss and they will be none of my concern.'

'Are you deliberately setting out to insult me, Pearce?' Oliphant hissed as the door closed. 'That damned marine sentry of yours was insolent.'

'He was acting on my instructions.'

'I guessed as much' was the reply as a lurch of the stern had him hanging onto a candle sconce.

'As to insults,' Pearce snapped, 'this does not seem to apply to you. Every time you fail to properly acknowledge my rank, you embarrass me and, I suspect, if they overhear, my officers, while no amount of reminders seem to dent your behaviour.'

'You might be their captain, you're not mine.'

'For the love of God, sit down!' Oliphant had to launch himself towards a chair, to be told, once he was seated, 'Do you really think I care personally about such things?'

'It's mentioned often enough.'

'On deck or in earshot of the crew. You have no idea of how gossamer thin can be the acceptance of discipline and the ease with which it can be undermined. Call me what you like in private, but in public I am to be addressed as Captain Pearce.'

'Which does not make me a person of no consequence,' Oliphant barked.

Pearce found it hard to comprehend why he was feeling a twinge of guilt. If anyone deserved to be taken down a peg or two it was Samuel Oliphant, whose attitude of condescension was far from unusual. Yet for all the pleasure to be had in guying him, there was also the knowledge of it being petty and, in a way, self-demeaning. This accepted, withdrawal was not easy, so Pearce kept his tone quite firm.

'If you behave as you should you will be treated so. Now take that look of annoyance off your face and let us make arrangements to have the discussion we should have had days past. All that has been decided is where to land. What I need to know is your view on the best way to carry out our instructions once we do so.'

The reply came with a sneer. 'Don't tell me you're seeking advice?'

'This was in some measure put forward as a peace offering. If you decline to take it as so, please vacate my cabin.'

The mutual glare held for some time, until Oliphant asked, in a voice which had lost its aggrieved edge, 'How long before we make the required landfall?'

'Ask me tomorrow when we have read the wind.'

'Tomorrow then?'

'After breakfast. I will ask Gilligan to allow us some peace to confer.'

'I'd make sure he's not listening at the door.'

'You think he'd sink so low?'

'If he wants to know what we're about, yes.'

Tempted to say Oliphant should not judge everyone by his own low standards, Pearce held the comment in check; having just made a sort of concord, it would be foolish to breech it for the sake of one barbed comment, even if it was accurate.

Having eaten up the miles during the day, it was down to topsails and a drop in speed on the approach of night, this again efficiently carried out with the assistance of the *Arklow* men. With the pitch and roll of the ship eased, Pearce invited Gilligan to a supper of toasted cheese, asking Oliphant as well, to indicate a restoration of normal relations. With him being on his best behaviour, pleasant it was, conversation being uncontentious, about the state of the world and the prospects of the war, in much of which Oliphant did not participate.

The changed nature of things below decks was obvious as the sound of singing, not all Irish in origin, came filtering into the cabin, until the time came for a clearly exhausted guest to retire: He had, after all, been given little sleep the previous night.

'If it would not trouble you, Mr Pearce' came with a meaningful look at the near-empty port decanter. 'After partaking so well of the bottle, I generally take a turn around the deck before I lay down my head.'

'Of course. I have the ship's logs to complete and, being the end of the month, I have others to check, which will take some time.'

A look at Oliphant was enough to tell him to likewise depart. Being busy and required to concentrate, Pearce barely noticed how long Gilligan was gone. He did register the singing had stopped and the ship, bar the usual creaks and groans, was now quiet. His quill moved as he penned the various notes made in the course of the day into the more formal log. Course, speed, position, stores consumed, those of his crew suffering minor injuries, all had to be listed and agree with the various others.

Those of his standing officers he now examined, cross-checking the entries of the master, boatswain, gunner, and carpenter, which would, at a future date, be examined by the clerks of the Navy Board, those of the surgeon going to the Sick and Hurt Board. Eagled-eyed sods staffed these bureaucracies, clerks who saw their task to find and raise discrepancies, some of which could be charged, if at all possible, to a captain's account. When Gilligan came back, Pearce's timepiece, laid on his desk, indicated how long he'd been absent, which was remarked upon.

'I had my devotions to see to, sir, which I thought best to do on deck, in which my men chose to join with me, not least to thank the Good Lord for our deliverance. I fear it might embarrass you to hear our Papist entreaties, you being a King's officer.'

'One who has a jaundiced view of the Thirty-Nine Articles, Captain Gilligan, to which I'm obliged to pretend to subscribe.'

'You're not one for prohibition then?'

'It is an affront to good sense to bar Catholics from serving as officers in His Majesty's forces, for the sake of what I see as Protestant intolerance added to ignorant bigotry.'

'Heaven allow,' Gilligan boomed, 'you'll not find an Irishman south of the Ulster Plantation who'd disagree with you, sir. It cheers me to hear what you say.'

The temptation to mention David Hume arose, he being his father's old mentor and friend, as well as a worthy whose opinions and pronunciations the younger Pearce held as valuable. It was put aside, probably it being a name, if he knew of it, which would not sit well with a man so intent on nightly prayers.

Hume the philosopher, as opposed to Hume the historian, was cynical on the whole notion of a divinity, even more particularly of one claimed to be ever-present and all-seeing. It was a view to which John Pearce was partial and the fact must have shown on his face. Gilligan had sensed he wanted to say something more and was waiting, so it seemed better just to shut it off.

'Good night to you, and let's hope for good sailing weather in the morning.'

The Irishman nodded and passed through the temporary bulkhead, which shut off a space big enough for a cot and not much more. Door closed, his host dipped his quill once more and carried on until his ledgers were closed for the night. This set him to another task, the continuation of the letter he was writing to Emily Barclay.

In comparison to the filling and checking of books, it was a much more complex and contemplative process. Given the fractured nature of their relationship, he was required to exercise great care with his words. Lovers for coming up two years now, it could not be said to be a romance running smooth. He had to avoid much they disagreed about, mostly his desire they should live under the same roof with their son, Adam, and damn the opinion of others.

This was set against her sense of propriety. As a widow, she must wait a prescribed period before any new relationship was seen as socially acceptable. Nor would she countenance an open admission he was Adam's father, sticking rigidly to the fiction the boy was the legitimate offspring of the late Captain Ralph Barclay.

That was a name to stop the quill as his bile rose, he being the man who'd first illegally pressed John Pearce into the navy. If he'd prospered since the night it happened, the man named had no part of it; his successes had all been his own. Before a cannonball removed his head, Barclay probably thought Pearce's affair with his wife was undertaken just to spite him.

There was some satisfaction, as he lay aside the quill and sanded his missive, before folding and sealing it with wax, in thinking the miserable bastard had nothing to do with that either.

Dawn found him on deck as duty demanded, fully ready to do battle, guns run out, flintlocks fitted, officers with swords to hand and the weapons used to repel boarders in place; pikes, tomahawks, the short-curved swords called hangers sat in an empty barrel. Once more the marines had their muskets ready for use and bayonets to hand. The only folk missing were the men of *Arklow Lass*, not being required to vacate their hammocks to be brought to such a duty.

Gilligan, roused from his cot as both it and the bulkhead that shut it off disappeared below, was last seen stretched out on the casement cushions. Given, as daylight appeared, there was nothing to cause alarm, the crew were stood down to go about their daily duties. Pearce could hand over the deck to the present watch, covered by Martin Worricker and Midshipman Maclehose.

Tall and skinny, Maclehose was a lad whom the crew had come to call "Jock the Sock." Of the four Caledonian mids, he was the one who showed the most promise, being a quick learner and seemingly able to oversee, without much difficulty, the work of men twice his age. Mr Williams had reported he was also rapid on his numbers, able to absorb instructions of navigation to the point where he could already be relied on to accurately record local noon using his sextant.

Pearce entered his cabin to find Gilligan standing by his just-replaced desk and the pile of ledgers Pearce had been working on. He smiled and then stepped back without haste, settling himself, once more, atop the casement lockers to observe his pleasure no merchant captain was obliged to record so much information. To this Pearce replied, in an acid tone, the navy ran on paper as much as water. They chatted amicably while breakfast was laid on the table, it being hardly surprising this centred on the weather conditions, for those of the previous day were no more.

Overnight they'd altered significantly, not surprising given, in darkness, they'd opened the Bay of Biscay, a stretch of water notorious for its sudden changes of weather, as well as generally challenging conditions. From sailing along easy at midnight, dawn had brought a lowering grey sky and a much heavier swell, which indicated foul weather in the offing.

'And the glass is falling,' Gilligan noted, with a glance at the barometer.

Pearce removed his weapons, hanging up his sword and putting away his pistols, the mahogany box which held them stuck in a desk drawer, then locked. Gilligan got up to take another look at the glass, tapping it to disturb the mercury, with a look of concern that failed to match his words.

'It's not dropping fast, Jesus be thanked.'

Time proved him wrong. By the forenoon watch, they faced a stiff southwesterly and a seriously troubled sea, which obliged Pearce to haul aboard all the boats and double-bank Gilligan's pair over his own. As the day wore on, the glass fell farther, which brought with it the odd nasty squall, sudden tempests which overbore the gusts of what was now taken as normal.

It was a danger against which it was required, whoever had the deck, to be alert, small cyclones that could seriously affect the trim of the ship. Rare, they came suddenly, only a visible rippling of spume, blown off the wave tops in the offing, a sign of their speedy approach. The lookout in the tops had strict orders to keep his eyes peeled for the first sign, anticipation allowing time to adjust.

The wind, steady or not, was now producing high waves and deep, irregular troughs, which indicated a more serious storm out in the vastness of the ocean, with many a studied glance to the west for any sign it might be coming their way. This rendered impossible the rate of sailing achieved the previous day, constant changes to the sail plan and the altering of course being required to make progress.

Such tacking and wearing also meant endless calls to bring the duty watch on deck, with great care being exercised on each manoeuvre to avoid being caught in stays. It also barred the arranged conference with Oliphant on possible future plans, not that it would have been fruitful: The steep rise and sudden fall of the bows, as well as the heel of the ship each time they changed course, kept him in his cot.

There was much to make him and the inexperienced kind nervous, the worst being the heavy thud of a more potent wave occasionally slamming hard into the hull. This seemed to stop, for a very brief moment, any forward progress. It reverberated alarmingly through the ship's timbers from stem to stern, producing fearful looks in the raw crew members. Clearly, they took no comfort from the shrugs of indifference displayed by those more accustomed.

It also made convivial eating impossible, so dinner was a snatched affair, after which Gilligan came to stand alongside Pearce on the quarterdeck as he took over the watch, careful not to comment on any instructions given. Every time they altered course, he was witness to the activities of *Hazard*'s unaided quota men, emitting an occasional grunt as to the obvious rawness of their efforts.

This was delivered not as criticism, rather, given the accompanying look, with professional understanding. He also moved forward from time to time, taking note of the information being added on the binnacle slate, the timing of the changes as well as course and speed, then made a point of chatting to the master. Williams seemed flattered by the attention and, judging by the gestures displayed, there was much discussion of the sail plan as well as the quirks of this particular vessel, given every ship possessed them, once more underlining his grasp of their shared profession.

Eventually he went below, making his way, he informed all who could hear, to ensure the continued well-being of his crew. This raised him even more in Pearce's opinion, such concern not being common with those who commanded merchant vessels. Men who tended to have risen from lowly beginnings to their present elevated positions, they were generally careful of their standing. Often aspiring to the status of gentlemen, this could stretch the nature of such an appellation in the less naturally polite of their tribe. There were many who could not shed the evidence of their humble background, which made them the butt of many a naval joke.

Gilligan was back on deck at eight o'clock, when, in the fading light, his crew took the first watch, chatting cordially to Mr Hallowell, who now had the deck, while observing his own men at work until darkness brought an end to toil. He went below when they did, though not to the great cabin, instead seen to take turns at each mess table, to talk quietly to his crew in what appeared to be a paternal way.

Late evening found him again sharing a quick bit of toast and a glass of wine with John Pearce, prior to both men turning in at two bells. It matters not that a ship is never silent: The timbers groan and the wind, if it has even mild force, whistles noisily through the rigging. This takes no account of a bell every half hour plus the sound of a change of watch every four.

In the sea through which they were currently sailing, with the constant calls to tack or wear ship, and the thud of those occasional heavier waves, HMS *Hazard* was far from restful for anyone, a ship's captain least of all. It was necessary to develop the skill to sleep as if with one eye open. John Pearce, and the entire crew and vessel for whom he stood ultimately responsible, were always at the mercy of an endlessly unpredictable element in itself and one doubly dangerous in wartime.

So when the door of his sleeping cabin creaked slightly as it was opened, the light from the exterior tallow wad playing on his eyelids, Pearce woke up. He was not fully enough to be alarmed and certainly not quick enough to react to the low voice, added to the feel of cold steel on his throat.

'You being such a generous soul, Mr Pearce,' Gilligan hissed, 'you won't mind if I take from you your fine vessel.'

As HMS *Hazard* rose, pitched, and fell, and it was seriously doing so, it had no effect on a cot slung from the overhead deck beams. Thus a rigid Pearce was in no position to react, given he feared any movement by him could see his gullet sliced open. Gilligan's frame was nothing more than a dark outline, silhouetted against the light from the main cabin, with no sight of his face. But a hand on one of the cot ropes, necessary to keep his feet, was visible.

'I'll be asking for the key to your desk, pistols being required for what is to come.'

'Go to hell.'

This seemed a feeble response, yet the only one coming to mind which might buy a bit of time. The pressure of metal on his neck increased a fraction but there was no sensation of cut flesh, and it occurred the Irishman was not looking to kill. That was soon seen as a supposition too far, so Pearce whispered, 'You'll never succeed, Gilligan.'

This got a low chuckle. 'Against your mob of useless lubbers? Sure they'll run a mile at the sight of a weapon. That is if they don't seek my good opinion and offer to join me in sailing the high seas.'

'They'll be equally lost under your hand as mine.'

'Don't seek to stall me, Pearce. The key, or I'll cut your throat, then rip the desk drawer open. A pity since it's a fine piece of furniture and soon to be mine own.'

He was about to say where his coat was hung—being dark blue, Gilligan couldn't see it in the limited light—when a sudden squall hit *Hazard* hard enough to put her on her beam end. It was sheer good fortune, in trying to keep his feet as the whole ship went over to larboard, Gilligan eased the pressure of the blade instead of letting it press down. This still left his victim vulnerable, with only a second to react as the ship began to groan and right itself.

Sheer instinct had Pearce get a hand on Gilligan's groin to squeeze the man's testicles as hard as he could, desperation making it effective enough to get a loud gasp. More vital was the loss of secure footing, which had caused the weight of the Irishman's body to fall across him, the weapon now off his throat, though it had to still be in his assailant's hand.

One fist came out from under a blanket to take a wild and un-aimed swing at the faint shape of a head, lucky to connect with a cheek, just enough to slow any reaction. It was quickly followed by another, though neither could be said to be forceful enough to stun. What saved him was the ship continuing to right itself, to naturally overcompensate with an excessive roll to starboard, just as Gilligan was seeking to find his feet and had let go of any support.

With nothing to hold on to, he fell backwards as the deck dipped behind him, to become an utterly unsteady indistinct blob back-stepping into the main cabin. Pearce swung his own feet to the floor, only to find the same canting deck propelling him forward. If Gilligan could have got the blade up and ready, he would have gutted him: Luckily, he was a fraction too slow, which allowed the staggering Pearce to swipe it aside with one hand and belt the Irishman with the other, this time a proper knuckle-hurting punch.

Not that he could arrest his forward movement, which threw him into actual contact. So close were their faces, he could feel the heavy breath on his cheek. Both careened into the temporary bulkhead that formed the wall of Gilligan's hutch, a Pearce knee coming up to take the Irishman in the groin. He would have doubled over had not Pearce still been pressing against him, but again the ship intervened as the deck canted once more gently to larboard. Pearce was now forced back, the Irishman grabbing at the open door jamb to steady himself.

There was a split second of hiatus as the pair glared at each other, Gilligan's yellowing teeth bared before, knife point out, he lunged. With difficulty Pearce swung away to avoid being the target, the weapon, now seen to be a bayonet, slicing through his flapping nightgown to a sound of tearing cloth. Desperately, he hooked an arm over Gilligan's and hauled him close, to nullify his chance of taking a swipe with the point.

Finding himself right by the man's head, Pearce got an ear between his teeth and bit hard, before wrenching his head furiously to one side, tasting blood as he did so while forcing a screech of pain. Next he swung a leg under those of his now off-balance opponent, taking away both his shod feet. Gilligan seemed to hang in the air for a moment, before he fell bodily and hard on to the deck, both arms out but uselessly, contact, by the sound of exhaled breath, winding him.

Pearce was without footwear, thus unable to deliver any kind of meaningful kick. Instead he put one bare foot on Gilligan's chest and used him like a stepping-stone to get to his hung-up sword. It was out of the scabbard before the Irishman could get to his knees. Tempted as he was to run him through, it was the hilt which was used to crown the sod. This was applied not once but several times, until he was flat on his back again and the point could be put just below his eye line.

Panting heavily, Pearce gasped, 'Drop the bayonet, or I'll run this through your neck and into your heart.'

Chapter Seven

Chest heaving, on a still rising and falling deck, there was a moment when John Pearce felt ever so slightly absurd: His nightgown, ripped almost in half by the bayonet, was hanging below his waist, so for a man lying flat out on the ground, the view from there would be unedifying. This was proved as the Irishman's eyes, when he rolled onto his side, flicked towards his exposed genitals, no doubt with a view to attempting a reverse of his present disadvantage by a swift blow. The point of the sword was waved slightly to discourage him.

Not that there was mortification: HMS *Hazard*'s captain was not one to be shy in the area of being seen lacking in clothes. In an opinion to which many who knew him well subscribed, he was one of those mad creatures given to immersing themselves in water for pleasure. When opportunity and weather permitted, he'd dive in to the deep unfathomable sea, as if there were no creatures unknown and unseen waiting to eat him or drag him under.

His shout for the marine sentry, even repeated, got no response, bar a look from Gilligan, one he quickly sought to disguise. This seemed to imply such support had been taken care of prior to coming for his superior. To such a probability the bayonet, now feet away from both, seemed to testify, which left Pearce at something of a stand. If he moved to seek help, the man might get on his feet and they'd be back to battling each other, which led on to other thoughts.

It seemed impossible Gilligan had acted alone, this while the image surfaced of what had been reported to him. The Irishman talking quietly, in the last part of the day, at each of the mess tables in turn, to the men of his crew. Was it really a paternal form of care, as had been assumed, or to finalise the execution of a plan? It was not the sole thought, as every moment spent in the man's company, as well as every word exchanged, was reprised to be seen in a different light. This made things, seen as innocent at the time, deeply suspicious.

Was it really possible his crew knew not a word of either English or the Irish Gaelic tongue? The only evidence he had for Gilligan being the captain of a merchant vessel was his own word. And what of the circumstances of its loss? Oliphant had referred to an interrogation, much to the annoyance of the man asking the question, who had no notion of engaging in any such thing. But had he properly assessed the answers or the manner in which they were provided, or had he been too keen to cut Oliphant out of the conversation to notice? Was Gilligan making up a false tale, not recounting a true event?

Then he recalled the long conversations with the master, also the careful noting of information on the binnacle slate on how *Hazard* sailed, made up of course, wind strength, and speed. Surely it could not any more be above suspicion, more a cunning preparation for the coming larceny.

Right now it was the man's crew who posed the greatest danger. For all Pearce knew, beyond the outer cabin door, could be waiting those very same creatures Gilligan had brought aboard, impatient for his word to act and in numbers no sword could contend with. This was true especially of the lightweight one he was holding, thin bladed and designed more for ceremony than combat.

Staying in this position would solve nothing, while the notion of waiting for the ship to come alive as a new day dawned seemed equally unpalatable. He required an immediate solution, and a glance at the door to Gilligan's temporary berth produced a possibility. Pearce moved the sword tip just enough to drive home the command he issued, employing as well a threatening snarl.

'Up and on to your knees, Gilligan, and no farther. Do exactly as I tell you, for as God is your judge, I will run you through.'

As the man complied, blood dripped from an ear half torn off, more showing on the back of his head from the blows the sword hilt had delivered. Once on hands and knees, Pearce took a chance on balance as the deck heaved, using a bare foot on his backside to encourage him forward.

'Crawl into your hutch, all the way through the door.'

Gilligan moved slowly, the man ordering him well aware of the way the Irishman's mind was working: Positions reversed, his would be doing likewise. On a dip to larboard he saw the right hand raised more than was necessary, so he lifted his sword high and then came down in one movement, again using the solid metal of the hilt. This was delivered to the kidneys, which brought forth a gasp of pain and had said hand swiftly back on the deck.

Once he was half through the door, another problem presented itself. With Gilligan so disported, the inward-swinging door in such a confined space wouldn't shut. Another gentle jab with the sword point was required, not to draw blood but pressure enough, through the thick red coat, to make it plain the risk of not complying.

'On your feet.'

'I can be a forgiving creature, Mr Pearce,' Gilligan growled, while failing to obey. 'An' even if you have sorely used me, if you belay this nonsense, I will do you no more harm than was done to me.'

'Stand up.'

'I'll gift you the boats you need and provender, too, enough to get you safe to England's shore.'

Pearce had his free hand on the door jamb to steady himself from the swaying of the deck. 'Be quiet and move.'

'But if you carry on in the manner you've adopted, it might be from your very own yardarm you'll be swinging.'

Pearce needed to filter this. First, Gilligan's tone was one of breathless urgency, but the implication was not beyond imagining: He was trying to tell him it was too late. This conjured up some unpleasant visions of him and his officers, along with his Pelicans, the only men he could certainly rely on, trying to take back control of a vessel already in the wrong hands. If it was so, he had no option but to engage in such a fight. Yet there was another more hopeful possibility, the one he had to act upon; Gilligan was bluffing.

'With your true colours now flying,' Pearce hissed, 'I think the rope is at the heart of your concerns, not mine. Now do as I say and stand up.'

He tried, no doubt because he felt he had no choice, to do to Pearce what had been done to him and take away his assailant's feet. A hand, nearly invisible in the gloom of the hutch, swiftly reached out and sought to grab an ankle. He was close to succeeding, only foiled by deft footwork as Pearce pulled his leg back, his hold on the door jamb keeping him from falling away. It did, however, put his sword in a temporary position of being no threat.

The Irishman did try to get up then, not at speed, his tub of a body was not built for dexterity, so a bare foot was stuck onto his back as he was halfway up. Lacking balance, this propelled him in to and over his own slung cot. Pearce grabbed the latch ring and pulled shut the door, then slid his sword, up to hilt, through the ring, so the blade ran down both the door and the bulkhead in which it set.

This proved enough to secure it when hauled from within, only able to open and shut a fraction. This occurred several times, enough to test the blade as well as allowing out furious cursing and blaspheming. Pearce moved quickly in case the thin blade didn't hold, dashing into his own sleeping quarters to fetch his hanging coat and the key kept in the pocket, this taken out and inserted in to his desk drawer.

The means to load the pistols were in the same mahogany box as the weapons. To the sound of endless muffled cursing, he carefully loaded both. Having fetched his clothing, he laid them on the desk and got dressed, in his mind running over a series of questions, to which he had no answers. He had to assume the store of small arms was safe. He lacked an armourer, just one of those positions he'd been unable to fill thanks to Admiralty malice. Michael O'Hagan was doubling up on this duty, though the gods knew he was no man for the kind of metal repair the position called for.

Pearce allowed himself a grim smile as he reflected on the name. It would take all of Gilligan's crew to overcome Michael and many of them would be bloody specimens if they tried. But it couldn't have happened, given the sod had come at him using a bayonet. This he would not have done if he'd possessed a more telling weapon, and certainly he would not have acted alone. Had he not wanted access to the very pistols which now lay on the desk?

Nor would the marine sentry's musket have provided him with a usable gun. Unless action or mutiny were threatening, such weapons were never loaded and with good reason. Carrying a primed and ready musket on a vessel at sea was a very unsafe notion even on a calm sea, and they were far from that now.

Not only was there a trust issue—marines, even if it was very rarely the case, could be as dangerous as any mutinous tar—but anyone staggering on an unstable deck, with a ready-to-fire musket in their possession, could allow for the accidental discharge of ball, one which could go anywhere. Thus, the bayonet was the basic weapon of security.

Moberly would have his pistols and so would Hallowell. But Worricker, on deck with the Mite, would be without, so he had to be discounted. Not least because Macklin had taken to acting as watch captain for his own men and, given they were on duty, the *Arklow* crew would be present as well.

The other midshipmen had only their dirks and were hardly old enough for the kind of close-quarters contest Pearce could envisage. He totally discounted his quota men, now asleep; they might have been suborned, as Gilligan had indicated, but even if it was not the case, such men could well stand aside to see which way matters lay.

His standing officers and he had not been together long enough to guarantee the kind of loyalty that makes support automatic, which left Michael, Charlie, and Rufus. They would stand with him he knew, for they'd done so in the past and he made his mind up, there and then, if he could get to where they were sleeping, they should be roused out first.

One pistol stuck in his breeches, the other cocked and in his hand, Pearce pulled the sword to release the door, which showed a glaring and still-bleeding Gilligan. His eyes were immediately drawn to the waving barrel. Behind this lay the determined look on the face of the fully dressed naval captain, which did not allow for bravado. With such a man, however, it did give room for bluster. Gilligan smiled, teeth just visible in the glim of light.

'Sure, if I'm set to hang anyway, you might as well pull the trigger.'

Pearce had intended to put Gilligan ahead of him as protection, a sort of human shield, but these words caused a rethink. The man would surely try to reverse matters, even if it was only by making a noise to alert his men. He would see no other choice, so was the idea of ball in his back enough to stop him?

With no idea what he would face beyond the cabin door, it was best he never got the chance to find out. The sword blade had held in the time he'd been confined, let it continue to do so. The door was pulled slowly shut and the weapon reinserted, with Pearce saying as he did so, 'Show your face and I'll put ball in what passes for your brain.'

Next he lifted up the bayonet, this too, a bit uncomfortable given its length, also housed in his breeches, then made his way out of the main cabin, past the empty pantry, to the outer and should-be-guarded entrance. The comatose body of the marine lay against the door and, when examined, Pearce could see he had been crowned with a belaying pin.

This lay beside his hat, rolling back and forth between it and the corridor bulkhead, the useless musket underneath his body. How Gilligan had managed it he couldn't fathom; the sentry was placed outside the door, yet somehow he'd managed to get him to the other side before doing his worst. Speculation at this point was useless, but a mental note was made to send Cullen to the man as soon as it was safe to do so, which could only be when everything else was sorted.

Body moved, pistol at the ready, the door was pulled open to reveal an empty afterdeck, the only thing visible another cause for wonder: one buckled marine shoe. Above his head the ship was once more changing tack, so the men of *Arklow Lass* were not at their mess tables, only then to wonder if such a named vessel actually existed. His own crew were asleep in their hammocks.

Pearce crept along a silent deck trying to imagine every possible scenario he and those who would back him might face, seeking out Michael first. In this ship, there being no junior lieutenants, he was berthed with the gunner, so it was to those quarters he went, drawn by the sound of heavy snoring.

O'Hagan was not a man to be brought awake while staying close, so Pearce shook him hard and stepped back sharpish, in case a fist came flying at him, one he first experienced swinging at his head long ago in the

Pelican Tavern. Having seen it since, and in use, he knew it was a good notion to be outside the arc.

'Michael,' he hissed as the eyes opened. 'Up and be sharp about it.'

His friend didn't blink or ask why; he swung out of his hammock to stand bent over under the deck beams, a questioning look on his face, both fists ready for employment. The explanation, of necessity, had to be swift and filleted, but it was enough. They were soon unlocking the chain which, running through the trigger guards, held secure the small arms and muskets. A few pistols were taken out to lay in Michael's hammock before the chain and padlock were replaced, conversation continuing in whispers.

'We need to get Charlie and Rufus armed, then rouse out Hallowell. What about help from the warrants?'

'They're not fighters to my mind, John Boy, and are still ill content at being under your command. Of the mids, which you're yet to ask of, sure, I'd give only "The Sock" credence.'

'Gilligan's men might be waiting for him and Mr Hallowell to appear and take over.'

'Which will not happen,' O'Hagan hissed. 'We can catch them off guard when I call for the watch change.'

'You rouse out Charlie and Rufus, I'll do Moberly and Hallowell. And Michael, if anyone looks to challenge you, shoot them.'

A barely visible ham of a fist came up and he knew Michael was grinning. 'Jesus, there's rarely cause for such, John Boy.'

Pearce quietly roused out his premier and then went for Moberly, close by in a screened-off wardroom cabin. Not the liveliest of minds in the opinion of his captain, it took a while to get him up and appraised of what was required. Pearce declined to accept his suggestion he get his small squad of men dressed and ready for whatever might come, especially the fellow on duty outside the spirit store. Such activity and the movement it would engender might not go unnoticed, in a situation where surprise was essential.

At the same time Michael was wading carefully through swaying hammocks to rouse out Charlie and Rufus Dommet. Taverner, as usual, was the one who required persuasion, not ever having been a man for automatic obedience to anyone. The pistol pushed into his hand did more to underline necessity than all the urgent whispers. This had others, who'd been woken by even such limited noise, asking what in "Christ's name" was going on.

'Stay slung until you're roused out, mates, or face me come the light of day.'

No one declined to obey.

Once everyone was alerted, with the sketchiest of explanations, there was only one place to gather without accidentally drawing attention, and that was the captain's quarters. The first task was to get the comatose marine into the pantry, where, a lantern lit, he could be properly examined. Making him as comfortable as was possible, they then proceeded to the main cabin.

The first object to take attention was the sword confining a now-silent Gilligan. His proximity, and the man in command was particular about this, precluded any normal conversation about what was to come. Signalling Michael should bring Charlie and Rufus quietly up to date, Pearce took Hallowell and Moberly into his sleeping cabin for a quiet briefing on where they should take station, as well as what to do when matters came to a head.

His orders had to be paused when the ship changed tack again, all listening for any sound which might portend trouble, with every creak, usually seen as normal, the subject of exchanged and concerned looks. As *Hazard* settled on her new course, Pearce outlined what he wanted done. There being two companionways down from the deck, he and his Pelicans would take the main one, which led from the quarterdeck, in order to catch Macklin as he came off duty.

'Mr Hallowell, you are slated to take over from Mr Worricker. I require you to do so early with your pistol concealed and to hand it to him without it being observed. You must also find a way to alert him to join with Mr Moberly when he vacates the deck and so, even if it will scare him rigid, must young Livingston. I charge you to keep the Mite safe.'

Aware of what he was asking for and how difficult it would be, Pearce was pleased his premier just nodded and asked no questions, so he turned to the marine.

'Given the noise of the change of watch, this will be the time to alert your men. Take station at the rear of the forward companionway with bayonets fixed. As soon as Gilligan's men come down, they are to be confined. Please do not hesitate to use force to make it so, even to the point of spilling blood.'

There was a moment when all three did what was natural: contemplate all the things which could go wrong, added to an unstated and sobering fact. The captain had as good as said there could be no placing reliance on any of their own crew.

'I think,' Pearce added, 'from first coming aboard and since, we've already had too much against the grain to contend with. HMS *Hazard* is our ship and it will remain so.'

Once back in his cabin, Pearce consulted both his pocket watch and the local, time-set chronometer. 'Time to get into position. Michael, rouse out our crew.'

O'Hagan went first, followed by the others, as Hallowell asked about Oliphant.

'Damn me,' Pearce hissed, genuinely taken aback. 'I'd forgotten all about him.'

Chapter Eight

The change of watch was ever a rackety business, not least for the amount of grumbling, which came from men woken from their slumbers. Now, given the extra numbers, they were required to strike down their hammocks, soon to be replaced. Nearly everyone aboard was moving about for a very brief time, while on the lower deck it was possible, with no slung canvas to block vision, to see from one end to the other.

Benjamin Hallowell quickly and quietly alerted Martin Worricker to the fact something was amiss, without being allowed the chance to go into detail. A man to follow orders, the premier was yet a fellow of enterprise, who could see the plan as laid out by John Pearce might have a flaw. Gilligan's first mate, on the quarterdeck, if not right by the wheel, would see his men off the deck before going below himself. Thus the plan to catch all at once might fail.

Instead of slipping the second lieutenant his pistol, he pulled it free and pressed it into Macklin's back, while quietly informing him, if he so much as sniffed in too loud a fashion, he was in danger of the trigger being employed. With no further explanation, he pushed him towards the after companionway to march him down, leaving Worricker issuing an order to the newly roused-out quota men, telling them they were forbidden to go below until further notice.

Behind the forward companionway, Moberly waited till most of the Gilligan gaggle were down and making ready to sling their hammocks. He was shrewd enough to allow for those slow to make it, the lookout brought down from aloft and the fellow in the bows casting the log. Both had to be physically relieved before leaving their posts. At the fitting moment the marine lieutenant, pistols ready, appeared, his men to his rear, weapons cocked and bayonets lowered. Clad in shirts and little else, without any sign of a red coat, they moved forward to push the mass of confused sailors back into a tight huddle.

'Mr Macklin,' Pearce said, as the mate appeared, Hallowell at his back. 'I desire you to tell the men you lead they are in danger of being shot if they do not comply with every instruction given.'

Macklin looked around at the stony-faced Pelicans, the minimal light seeming to exaggerate the smallpox-scarred nature of his own face, but what was of more interest to Pearce was his lack of reaction. A man who should have been startled was not. He was calm, driven home, as he cast an eye to the rear.

'If you want to address them, you may do so yourself.'

'How so,' O'Hagan demanded, 'when the captain has no idea of their tongue?'

Macklin slowly shook his head. 'That one held and I never reckoned it to be so, but a tar is ever up for a jest. They know enough English to get your meaning.'

'And the Erse?'

'Not the mother tongue, I'll grant, which is confined to the island, but they would harken to it also.'

'I need you,' Pearce cut in, 'to obey me and for them to obey you. So tell them to remain where they are and behave.'

'I'm bound to ask the whereabouts of a certain party?'

'Gilligan?'

'If you choose to call him so.'

'Not his real name then?' Macklin responded with another almost imperceptible headshake. 'Which makes me wonder about the *Arklow Lass?*'

'First I heard of the name, as well as the one you just used, was when Keoghan shouted to you from our boat. Conjured it up on the spot, but then he was always one with a quick wit when it came to making up a story.'

'And the idea to take over the ship?'

Macklin turned slightly to take in the silent huddle. 'Worked out, if such words apply, in the double glass of time it took us to get alongside, with each man sworn to silence.'

'And you saw sense in this idea?'

Macklin chose to shrug. 'I reckoned it close to folly.'

'Yet you went along with it?'

'Did I?'

'Let's say you chose not to oppose it.'

'When you have few choices, Mr Pearce, you go with what you have no way of stopping.'

'And taking *Hazard* would have served?' That got a noncommittal look. 'My cabin, Macklin. But beforehand, tell your men if they seek to cause trouble, the weapons they see before them will be employed. I've given orders to kill if need be.'

What the first mate then said was incomprehensible, but it was effective; to a man they sat down on the deck and kept their hands visible.

'How come you know the tongue?' Michael asked.

'I'm wedded to an island girl.'

'Charlie,' Pearce ordered. 'Rouse out Mr Cullen and fetch him along to see to the marine in the pantry, the man is out cold. Mr Hallowell, I wish you to stay with Mr Moberly and ensure there's no trouble.'

Pearce waved his pistol and Macklin moved, Dommet using his to give him a gentle and encouraging push in the back. At the door, Rufus was left outside to ensure ample warning if anything went awry, Michael staying with Pearce as he led the way into his cabin. Once seated at his desk, one pistol very obviously to hand and pointing at the opposite chair, he invited the man to sit. O'Hagan took up a position by the door, arms akimbo but his weapon also obvious, using the pressure of his back and well-spread feet to compensate for the roll of the ship.

'From you, Mr Macklin, I require the truth of what happened to you before you came upon us added to the reasons it came about.'

'Then I hope you'll not be disappointed if I decline to provide it.'

This came as a surprise, it being so blank a refusal. It had Pearce seeking the reason, another question Macklin refused to answer.

'From which,' he concluded, after a lengthy period of consideration, 'I sense the truth does not show you in a straightforward light.'

This also got no response, if you excluded a bland stare. Pearce, after another significant pause, responded with a wry smile. 'I doubt everyone you have so recently helped to lead will be as reticent as yourself. Even if being open presents to them some danger of retribution for acts which rest outside the law.'

The reward to this was a stiffening of the jaw and a wary look in Macklin's eyes.

'It is a well-noted policy, when seeking evidence of wrongdoing, to offer a man leniency in order he may suffer less than others. Be assured, I will employ such a route to anyone willing to be open with me, which applies as much to you as to anyone, possibly even more so.'

A muffled cry came from behind the temporary bulkhead door. 'Keep your mouth shut, Deacon.'

Pearce slowly shook his head. 'I now suspect your true names are enough to see you face justice for acts unknown. This is a possibility you will most certainly be exposed to when I hand you over to authority?'

He was good, whoever he truly was, for there was no discernible reaction this time. 'Gunfire at night, leading to the loss of a ship, whatever the name of the damn thing, not a merchantman I can be fairly sure, but the other vessel . . .?'

The question was left hanging, with again no response, not even a blink.

'No British warship I can be certain, for they would never have cast you away in boats. Not a French ship of war either, given they have galleys on which to chain those they capture and do not look to exchange. A Spaniard, assuming we're still allies, would hand you over to our own navy, likewise a Portuguese. So, who took your vessel?'

'Happen if you'd chased the sod, you might have found out.'

Meant to deflect the line of enquiry, it was an error. While not revealing the truth, it opened up in Pearce's mind a number of possibilities, each one examined only to be dismissed, because well-armed vessels in these waters and not from a national navy were few.

East Indiamen yes, but they carried enough cannon to fight anything less than a man-o'-war and were strong enough to inflict serious damage on anything less well armed. Quite apart from such factors, they would never allow themselves, being so valuable, to fall out of the protection afforded by a convoy. These were, very often, assembled around their needs.

Barbary was a remote possibility outside the Mediterranean, yet they did sometimes prowl these waters. But they took crews captured, if they didn't just slaughter them, to sell as slaves. This didn't leave very much except the packets carrying post, which regularly traversed the Bay of Biscay. Fast and trim vessels, they were designed to outrun threats, not fight them, and were adept at doing so. This left only one other alternative, arrived at after more silent contemplation.

'Michael, I wish you to go on deck and ask a question of the men sitting under guard. I want the name of the Letter of Marque who took their ship. Offer anyone willing to talk their freedom. They can serve aboard under any name they care to provide.'

Pearce finally got the reaction for which he was hoping. The pox-scarred face lost a degree of colour, while his whole demeanour seemed to alter until, after a long silence, which involved much lip-biting, he said, 'An offer I might accept myself, if I thought it genuine.'

'You ingrate, I'll see you damned' came from behind the door.

'You've done that already' was the shouted reply.

'It is only an offer for the truth,' Pearce added calmly.

'There are some truths best unspoken, Mr Pearce. I daresay there's a fair number of those aboard this barky already, who would be coy about their past. But I will admit to our being taken by a privateer vessel, as you have surmised.'

'Name?'

'I don't recall ever hearing it.' Which had to be a lie.

'But you were not sailing in a merchant vessel?' This got a slow nod of agreement but nothing more. 'Your ship was?'

'Smaller than *Hazard*.'

'It had a name?' Another nod admitted it to be so, but he was not willing to provide it, which could only mean this too posed some kind of threat. 'It would be interesting to know why a Letter of Marque would bother to attack another vessel, since they sail only for profit. Were you carrying anything of value?'

'Poverty was the only cargo we had' came with a hint of bitterness.

'And the fate of this unnamed ship of yours?' He just pointed downwards to indicate it had sunk, or perhaps was deliberately sent to the bottom. 'I daresay you're glad they didn't send you down with her.'

'Don't see the need to comment, given I'm sat here afore you.'

If nothing much was showing on the face, it was clear the man was troubled on what to reveal and what to keep hidden. Every reply was carefully considered, which hinted at much of the latter, this reinforced when he finally opened up a touch.

'You need to know not much more'n that, Captain Pearce, I reckon. We got into a contest an' we was bested. Put in boats, we sighted your topsails as the day came upon us and it cheered us all.'

'Enough to plan replacing your ship with mine.'

'It weren't no plan to begin with, but it was plain to Keoghan and myself you were more'n a mite lubberly.' The head jerked once more to indicate his imprisoned captain. 'That be when the notion was first aired. It were naught more than yer man voicing an idea, first to use made-up names, then not let on we had anything to speak with but the island tongue.'

'Seems quite a comprehensive conspiracy to me.'

'What I will tell you is this. Few of those who've been helping you on deck and aloft were keen on what was then proposed.'

'For which I only have your word.'

'You don't have to be mainland born to be sure of one thing. The King's Navy would never rest to find one of its ships and find it they would, lest we was prepared for wholesale murder to ensure silence.'

'Even that would not serve. Where could you go with a vessel like this and not have it remarked upon?'

'No place that I can think of.' This truth was acknowledged with a dropped head and a less-than-confident voice.

'I know of the *Bounty* story and others do too, for it was much talked of. If even the South Seas are not safe, where would you have to go to have a hope of being free of pursuit?

'Which begs the next question, what would you have done when presented with the chance to follow the specimen languishing behind yonder door. He put a bayonet to my throat, which was only a ploy to get to my pistols. Had he succeeded, he would have then sought to take control of the ship, and I'm bound to ask how far he would have gone to do so. Was he prepared to kill? I daresay he had in mind to persuade my crew to join with you.'

'This, I will grant you, was his aim. But the killing, I do not know.'

'And you? Would you have gone along with it if he had?'

'I cannot, in certainty, say one way or t'other.'

'This I find hard to credit.'

'Yet it's the truth' came without any indication of a plea he should be believed, more stated as a fact. 'Sometimes a man has to wait for the wind to know which way to sail.'

'You must have had an opinion.'

'The notion was proposed for me and I stated my doubts, but there was no holding Keoghan back once he was set on his course.'

'And the rest?'

'How much he told them I don't know. He talked to them in twos and threes, but my guess is this. It would be no more than he had to, for surprise would have been to his advantage. With a pistol at your head, he would have burnt the boats for all. From there none would see a way back, which would likely get him the support he wanted.'

A knock at the door had Michael move away and open it slightly, to show the head of Mr Cullen, a concerned look on his face. 'I require some men to help me get the marine down to the orlop deck and no one, sir, will move without your express command to do so.'

'Ask Taverner to get help on my authority.'

The interruption was welcome, because it gave Pearce time to think. One fact was obvious: If he could confine their captain, he could not do the same to his crew. They were too numerous and nor could he really contemplate returning them to their boats and casting them adrift. The proper thing to do was hand them in to some legal entity to investigate their probably nefarious actions, with the already mentioned Gibraltar the most obvious.

Yet he was on a mission already delayed. Making for the Rock, which he would have to do, before fulfilling the needs of Henry Dundas, was out of the question, and this was before any opinion Oliphant might advance. He was also desperately shorthanded, and these men had proved their superior competence.

The thought of killing two birds with one stone came to mind, this only possible because Pearce also knew one simple fact, as did anyone who served in the navy. A goodly number of those who volunteered for the service, and there were more than common gossip supposed, came aboard on the run from something and it wasn't always the law for crimes committed.

There were the irate fathers of knocked-up daughters, bad debts, youngsters running from slave-like apprenticeships. Rufus Dommet had been so engaged when Pearce first met him. This took no account of the number of crimes that could result in gaol, a rope, or transportation to the new prison settlement recently set up in Australasia. A theft of a handkerchief or a loaf of bread could see you taken thousands of miles from home, never to return.

To run for the service in wartime was a way to avoid such a fate. Once mustered on a man-o'-war, those who chose to do so were safe until the peace. The navy would never admit to their presence, even if entered under their own name, and few were fool enough to do that. For those who chose another, anonymity was guaranteed for the duration.

'You said you might be tempted by an offer I just outlined, Mr Deacon.' The courtesy of the mister was to hint at changed circumstance. 'If you were entered on the muster as Macklin, would you be willing to serve as a member of my crew?'

'What about the others?'

He asked this with a toss of his head, to indicate those outside who sat on the deck, the implication, given his determined expression, it was everyone or no one. The remark which followed could only have one person in mind.

'He might not care for their welfare but I do. Some are cousin to my wife.'

'I think it would have to apply to you all.'

'And the other course?'

'I hardly need to answer that, do I?'

His voice dropped to a whisper. 'Which still leaves Keoghan.'

It didn't have to be made plain: The man named would be impossible to include in any arrangement, which got him to the nub of the conundrum Deacon had already reached. He couldn't hand the sod over to the law on his own, for the very simple reason he'd immediately squeal on the whereabouts of his one-time crew. Any man would do to avoid a trial for piracy, of which he was certainly guilty by the actions of this night. The penalty for such a crime was the rope. Authority would have no choice but to strip them all out for trial and a similar fate.

Could he trust his own judgment, or would he be bringing to HMS *Hazard* the very danger he'd just warded off? It all depended on whether he believed what he was being told by the man sitting before him, which he was inclined to do. He recalled the moment when he'd seen them together below deck, just before he'd asked for help, the impression of a disagreement taking place, cut off by his appearance. Had they been debating this night's intention?

'I should just hang the sod,' Pearce said finally.

This became another remark which got no answer, though it did suppress the grumbling coming from the temporary cabin. This left the question of the notion being welcome with Deacon, which it might well be. There was little point in adding the two factors that rendered such an act impossible: inclination and authority, of which the former was the most important. He was not a killer by nature, added to which he had no right to convene a trial, never mind carry out an execution.

Several times he'd glanced past the man he was questioning to catch Michael O'Hagan's eye, which would have only led Pearce to the word noncommittal: His Irish friend was keeping his counsel and giving nothing away, either by gesture or expression, even if he knew the problem being wrestled with as well as anyone.

They had a crew, not only low in numbers and ability, but one yet to combine into anything like an efficient whole. He knew no details of the mission, but Michael would surely guess there could be occasions ahead where trouble was a real possibility, while reliability in action was seriously questionable. Before he decided anything, Pearce would have to consult with his lieutenants but, in the end, it would be his decision, based on his appreciation, and was that enough?

'Mr Macklin, which I shall continue to call you for now . . .' This pleased him, since it hinted at the desired solution, this slightly dented by the words which followed. 'I must, for now, keep you confined, so I will have you escorted to the cable tier.'

'That's what you get for your stupidity, Deacon!'

It was Pearce's turn to shout back. 'If you don't hold your tongue in there, I'll confine you in the heads, in the hope the stink will save me the trouble of stringing you up. Michael, call for help.'

This took a few moments, during which the fellow Rufus and Charlie were going to escort into confinement looked as he if wished to say something more, only to decide to hold back. From behind the bulkhead door came a continuous low murmur of complaint, which could be safely ignored, and this continued once Pearce and O'Hagan were alone.

'Well?'

'Sure, John Boy, you're not after asking me for a thought on the matter?'

'Please don't act the wounded spirit, Michael. I don't have time to soothe your vanity. I reckon I need to know more and I don't see my asking questions will get anything but the answers they think I want to hear. So I need you to do any enquiring on my behalf.'

The head shifted enough to take in the bulkhead door. 'Question yonder gombeen's men?'

'Precisely. But what about the man to whom you just listened?'

'There's a fair bit he's not tellin' you, but I see him as seeking to be honest as care will allow. And, for the love of Christ Risen, we could surely use the help.'

The half-hour bell, which tolled then, sounded as gloomy as ever.

CHAPTER NINE

It was inevitable Oliphant would have an opinion, and it would be one John Pearce would have to consider. But good fortune, or the unusual nature of the morning, held this at bay until Michael had carried out the task given him. He came back with a generally positive response regarding the men he now termed the "Arklows," not one of whom had been more open than their first mate.

'Not a Judas amongst them, John Boy, which oddly cheers me.'

'They must have said something, Michael.'

'I told 'em what the Deacon fellow said, an' the use of the name counted for more'n any words of mine, that and the knowledge their captain was in irons and stapled to the deck.' To a raised eyebrow, Michael smiled, his usual wide grin. 'I gilded it a bit, thinkin' it would serve.'

'It might be best if Deacon speaks with them.'

'Sure, I'd say that were sound.'

'Best fetch him then, Michael, for he can do nothing confined. But hold him back till I can take part. I need to speak to Hallowell, Worricker, and Moberly. Ask them to attend upon me at once.'

Having got Deacon from the cable tier, Michael called for Pearce to attend and he listened, as did his officers, who'd been quickly appraised of what was intended. Having insisted on English, he was pleased as Deacon explained what he'd agreed to do himself as well as what was on offer for all. This set up a degree of low murmurs as the alternatives were aired, in truth none if Pearce had the right of what they'd been about. Eventually it was settled.

Not having carried out the accustomed dawn activities, the ship had made do with lookouts, so Oliphant had been allowed to sleep longer than normal. If he was grateful for this, as well as the invitation to share breakfast with Pearce, he was equally curious as to what had replaced it and stone-faced when an explanation was provided.

'Piracy, you reckon?'

'They were privateering without the license to do so.' Noting Oliphant did not understand, he added, 'They were without a Royal Letter of Marque, which makes what such people do legal in the eyes of the law, at least at home, and it should afford them some protection if taken by the enemy.'

'Then why not get one?'

'There could be any number of reasons. Maybe Keoghan lacked the means to pay or declined to apply, reckoning it more profitable to act without it. Then again, he may have been of a stature which would see any application declined.'

'They're fussy?' came with a note of disbelief.

'Not everyone can get such a license, and there are rules by which they must abide, most tellingly the strictures against attacking neutrals. Usually those who seek them are well connected politically, or syndicates of city men who will then employ a captain and crew for a share of the profits. As a Letter of Marque, you not only pay a stiff fee to sail, you must declare to the Exchequer the value of what you have acquired from the enemy, which is then taxed, though that is much observed in the breech.'

'No sensible man pays tax willingly.'

'Without such papers, you face the rope if caught by anything navy, and it could be your own countrymen once they have you ashore. Hence the reluctance of any of these men to be open, which tells me they all knew what they were about.'

'And if such people are caught by the French?'

'They'd likely welcome the rope, given chained galley slavery would be their lot, with no hope of release even when peace came.'

'So they were sunk by whom?'

'British and I reckon a properly licensed Letter of Marque. I also suspect Keoghan was the one doing the sneaking up in the dark, hoping to profit from another's success by stealing any cargo they'd captured. It's one way of lining your pocket, except he bit off more than he could chew. I have no certainty it's the case, but it makes a kind of sense.'

'And it is your intention to take the men he led on as crew?' A nod. 'Before you tell me it's none of my business, I might as well state now, I disagree.'

'I would expect nothing less' was the jaundiced response. 'Yet I struggle to see what you can advance outside an opinion.'

'I can say this, Pearce, you have no real idea of what devilry they may have carried out. For all you know they could be murderers to a man. If you take them on, what is to stop them taking over the ship on some dark night? Leopards do not, in my experience, change their spots. I might add, my throat is at much risk of being cut as your own so recently was.'

'Which implies I've failed to think on the possibility of, what shall I call them . . .'

'Villains sounds appropriate,' Oliphant interrupted. 'I must say, I had my suspicions all was not as it should be on that first meeting with Gilligan, or whatever his true name is.'

'Which I take as rot and nothing more than hindsight. You're suspicious of everyone, even without cause.'

'You can't tell me you've not reflected on events?'

'I have and yes, I can see flaws now that did not present themselves at the time. The difference is, I lack the nature of one who, in retrospect, will claim to have seen plain what was not in the least obvious at the time.'

The words caused palpable offence, which to Pearce was pleasing, but he hurried on to stifle protest. 'But in answer to your question, the way to avoid what you fear is to mix the crew up, so no one group will have the opportunity to act as they wish. I will also ensure the officers are at all times armed, with permission to use their weapons at the first sign of dissent, never mind the kind of trouble you so fear.'

'And their captain?' came with a jerk of the head at what had been the temporary cabin. That was now gone, as was the occupant, chained up in the cable tier from which Macklin had been released. All he had was his heavy satchel, which had revealed itself bereft of the kind of coin he'd promised would be forthcoming on the shores of Ireland.

'I'm sure you have a suggestion.'

'I assume extremes are not possible, even if fully justified?'

There was no doubting what Oliphant meant by extremes. 'You would countenance such a course?'

'I find it's the best way to protect yourself against threats. It never gives anyone who might wish to harm you, even kill you, the chance to do so.'

'It's out of the question, not least because of the effect it would have on the men I hope to turn into willing members of my crew.'

'So much for your vaunted authority.'

'Which does not extend to judicial murder.'

There was little point in adding the two factors which rendered such an act impossible and already pondered upon.

'Stick him back in one of his boats and set him adrift.'

'On his own, in the middle of the ocean, in a craft he'd struggle to row single-handed. And, by the way, I have no idea of his ability as a navigator, though I suspect he is competent. I might as well use the rope you're so fond of.'

The man's eyes narrowed. 'Why do I suspect this is window dressing? I sense you've already made up your mind.'

'I have entertained some possibilities, yes. I think what suits the situation best involves a slight deviation. Unless you can provide a better alternative, it is the one I believe I'll be obliged to pursue.'

'Which is?'

'To put him ashore.'

'Nowhere near where we wish to go, I hope.'

'Credit me with some sense.'

'And following this solution?'

'As fast as we can to the borderlands.'

Pearce had failed to point out to Oliphant the notion was not without risk. To sail, as he intended, deeper into the Bay of Biscay meant there was a chance, albeit a small one, of meeting something French and armed in a situation where avoidance of a fight was impossible. To avoid this, he set course for the long, sandy, and pine-forested island of Noirmoutier.

It was an island Pearce knew from the past and one where he had been obliged to engage in a dangerous fight when on a mission to the Vendée, oddly one also at the behest of Henry Dundas. On that occasion he had sailed into the bay between the mainland and the island itself, to then face what defenders were placed there, determined men in gunboats who had to be overcome.

Not this time; his intention was to go no farther than the very western tip of the island, well away from any kind of opposition. Noirmoutier was a location which could be reached only by a causeway at low tide. It was otherwise cut off from a sparely populated mainland, strongly Catholic and monarchical in their leanings, in a region which had recently been the location of a serious revolt against Paris. Their castaway would thus face days of walking to find anyone to whom information on HMS *Hazard* being offshore was of any value.

The aim was for a speedy passage to and a quick exit from the area. In this instance the westerly wind that had been slowing progress came to their aid, obvious as soon as the helm was put down on their new course. With that and the strong tidal flow, progress was going to be rapid, which would of course be the opposite as they sought to get back out to sea.

For all the sanguine manner in which he'd massaged the concerns of a doubtful Samuel Oliphant, Pearce was well aware of the risk he was taking. This made the swearing in of Keoghan's island crewmen something to be undertaken personally, not a task to be left to his premier, as would normally be the case. Usually a ritual taking place on deck, and collectively, it was instead undertaken in the main cabin, each man brought in by Michael O'Hagan to be questioned individually.

Tempted as he was to ask about the events that had brought them aboard, such enquiries seemed best avoided: This would surely emerge in time. So the questions he posed were aimed more at their background and status. Were they married, did they have children, and what had been their occupation prior to going to sea? They were farmers and fishermen, depending on the season, it made plain neither occupation being enough to produce any surplus, the former because of poor soil. The latter, undertaken in small boats, was extremely dangerous in the exposed waters by which they lived.

If his sympathy was made plain—these the very kind of folk his late father has been so intent on stirring to political action—there was also a feeling of hypocrisy in trying to establish some form of special rapport by playing the concerned commander. To balance this, each was subjected to a stern lecture on the main clauses of the Articles of War, particularly those which referred to hanging for the guilty.

In conclusion each man was given in kind, as monies which could be set against necessities, the bounty the navy was presently paying for volunteers, a goodly portion of this going to the purser's account for things already supplied. Macklin, as he was to be called, was present throughout, to ensure no misunderstandings because of language, and there had been several, but otherwise required to remain silent and out of the men's eye line.

Michael, too, was there to help Pearce form an opinion regarding not only each fellow-Irishman questioned but the group as a whole. Last to be dealt with was the first mate himself, and with him the discussion was more complex.

'I can rate you as an able seaman but this, to me, would not do justice to your abilities.'

The look this received had about a degree of suspicion. He was, no doubt, wondering if he was being flattered, which could only have one purpose: to soften him up.

'I can rate you as a midshipman, without recourse to a higher authority, then appoint you as an acting lieutenant, neither of which qualifies for any kind of reward.'

'Which will not apply to those you've just been seeking to soft soap.'

Pearce responded with a smile. 'I think I ended with a warning of bloody retribution.'

'My lads will draw a seaman's wage, part of which they can remit home?'

'In time yes and when it is paid. There are certain papers which must be filled in and we will not be anywhere close to such an authority of some time.'

'But not me?'

'By the note of concern in your voice, I suspect it would be of value to you to do so as well?'

'It surely would.'

'Then I must enter you as a master's mate, but I would want use of those abilities already demonstrated. So let us spread the fiction of your being an acting lieutenant, which will, if Mr Hallowell agrees, give you a berth in the wardroom.'

Pearce did not add this would also seriously impede his ability to enter into quiet conversations with those he'd once led. If he was inclined to trust the man, it was not without reservations. Macklin was in the process of nodding his acceptance when a faint cry from the masthead indicated, it was to be hoped, land had been sighted, this soon confirmed with a message from the quarterdeck.

'One last duty to perform as first mate. I want you to keep those with whom you came aboard below decks until the man who commanded you is off the ship, indeed until he's out of sight. If he was to see them it would be, I reckon, necessary to gag the sod to stop him pleading for help.'

'Not many of whom would be swayed.'

'I am unwilling to risk it being even one, for their sympathy would be disguised. But such a feeling could linger and turn to rancour, which in time could affect others.'

The nod was slow in coming, which had Pearce add, 'From this point onwards, you are a member of the crew and I will expect you to act as one in every respect. This includes, as an acting lieutenant, to ensure naval discipline is maintained. I do not wish to come over as the martinet, but your fellows are not accustomed to it, while some of my quota men still struggle, so it is paramount no familiarity can be permitted.'

'I'll do my best,' Macklin replied, only to add, at an arch look from Pearce, 'sir.'

'Carry on.'

Keoghan did have to be gagged and manhandled by Michael O'Hagan to get him into a boat and keep him there, so physically did he protest. Crewed by Hazards, he was rowed ashore to a sandy beach that had no sign of habitation, to be lifted out and set down on the strand.

Michael threw him his satchel as the gag was removed by Rufus Dommet, quick to get back into the cutter.

'There's food in there and a small amount of coin, which for sure you do not deserve. For myself, I would have chucked you in the briny.'

As the cutter was rowed out to sea, it was to a litany of foul cursing aimed at everyone, promising retribution and damnation, with particular bile directed at Michael, who did not ease the man's fury by his loud laughter. Keoghan was still on the beach when the backed sails were reset and HMS *Hazard* adopted a southerly course, a diminishing dot of a stationary, squat figure in his faded red coat, who occasionally shook a fist.

'Mr Maclehose, please be so good as to tell Mr Macklin his men are no longer constrained.'

They were into the afternoon watch, with Macklin on the quarterdeck, making good speed and passing the western point of the Ile de Ré, when Pearce joined him. He ordered the helm put down to sail within sight of the near-flat southern shore, an order to make all his officers curious and, when they were ordered on to the deck, his crew as well. When he found out about the deviation, it caused Oliphant to fume, though for once he did so silently.

Ahead of them, as the spire of the La Rochelle cathedral became faintly visible, the few fishing boats still out in the deep bay, having identified the flag, were getting clear of *Hazard*'s due east course. Eventually they could see the battlements of the medieval Lantern Tower, which protected the port, at which point a flare went up soon followed by a second. This alerted the deck to the presence of a pair of cutters, guard boats patrolling offshore, they too now running for the inner anchorage, with a speedier warship closing the distance.

'Time to see if our gunnery has improved with augmentation. Mr Hallowell. Let's see if we can give those fellows in one of those guard boats a fright.'

Orders rang out to get everyone on deck at a rush. The gunner repaired to his lair to pass out the cartridge cases containing powder wads to the ship's boys, as the cannon were let loose for loading. Pearce was particularly interested in the speed and performance of the Arklows: In the absence of a true ship's name, there was nothing else to call them.

The first salvo, just after the helm was put down, did a great deal to raise the spirits of both cohorts of the crew, as it ever did. All had to be reminded of their duty, so eager were they to see the landing of the water spouts which were a result of their efforts, none really threatening the targets, if you excluded one receiving a soaking.

Sadly, reloading was a disjointed disappointment. Competent sailors the Arklows might be, but they were scarcely better than his own at reloading cannon, obliging their captain to wait before he could order a second effort that would be both wild and badly aimed.

'House your guns,' he called, which got him crabbed looks from men, inefficient as they were, enjoying themselves. 'I cannot have you wasting powder.'

'Or time,' Oliphant called.

Chapter Ten

For Walter Hodgson to be in receipt of an enquiry for his services was rare these days. Life was a lot less rewarding now than the day, many years past when, having left the army after the American War, he'd set out his stall as a professional thief-taker. This was rendered doubly so by the fact he'd been out of the nub of the game for near two years. This required him to query others, competitors in the field, to find out who, in the criminal world, might be worth chasing. Such information was not voluntarily vouchsafed.

Even so, two requests within the space of a few hours was unprecedented and also not without a degree of concern. Which one to react to first, if indeed both merited the same level of regard, which was certainly questionable? Edward Druce seeking his services had to be seen as both curious and possibly perilous; had he not seriously deceived the man, though he would satisfy his own conscience with the conviction Druce had done this to himself.

By transferring his professional skills to the needs of Emily Barclay, who'd asked him in writing to call at Harley Street, he'd acted against the interests of Druce. The prize agent had employed him and paid him handsomely not to find a particular rogue being sought by his wealthy brother-in-law. The reason for such largesse came to light only when Mrs Barclay sought his aid to get Cornelius Gherson off a charge of murder. Could he be the cause of these near-simultaneous entreaties?

Hodgson concluded he had to put Druce first, on the grounds danger, should it exist, would quickly become manifest and could be dealt with. This would allow him to approach the second enquiry with some knowledge of what was at stake, if indeed Gherson was the instigator of both. Hodgson could look after himself, not something he would say about a widow, without the man he suspected she cared for to protect her and an infant child.

His normal weapons were a billy club, manacles, and a handy pair of fists, supported by a confident manner. Rarely did he employ a pistol: In his game a live body delivered up to Newgate and justice earned much more than a corpse. He armed himself so on this occasion and had the weapon loaded, primed and well-concealed in his heavy coat, given he was about to face no common thief, but a man of means and one already known to be both secretive and dishonest. He had to be smarting from what had so recently occurred, so the possibility of Druce seeking retribution, by drawing him into a trap, had to be considered.

When he presented himself at the offices of Ommaney and Druce, it was to come into the presence of a fellow who'd wavered between determination and terror since he'd sent his clerk on the errand. This was far from new, it had been so for weeks, given the scenarios which had played out constantly in his mind. Often boosted by drink and temporary bravado, a few saw him triumph over Denby Carruthers.

But just as often he fell into despair when the nature of what he faced bore down on him, the dark night of the soul, in which he became just another victim of a man who'd stop at nothing to get his own way. These thoughts were occupying him now, which made him into a plaintive supplicant, one who saw in his visitor not just a potential fellow to be retained, but a man who could aid him in finding salvation.

'Mr Hodgson, I am so very glad you could put aside your other duties to call.'

'Not the type to refuse a request' was posited guardedly. The Druce he knew from previous dealings could be all charm one minute and icy cold the next.

'You will, of course, take of some wine?'

There was a temptation to say no, get to your business, but the quality of claret they served in these offices was of a kind he rarely tasted. On several occasions, such an offer had been far from forthcoming, the lack very obvious. The way it was being advanced now hinted any worries he had prior to arrival might be groundless. So he settled for a nod, not wishing to appear too eager.

Druce was swiftly out from behind his desk to do the honours, unusual, as any previous invitation to partake had obliged him to see to himself. To a shrewd mind, and Hodgson possessed one, this, despite the confident air, hinted at anxiety.

'I take it,' Druce remarked, back to his visitor and decanter in hand, 'you share my satisfaction justice was done in the case of Gherson.'

'I was sure you rated him guilty.'

The decanter was midair and stationary as Druce replied. His tone was tense, there being no choice but to acknowledge he must have certainly have given that impression. Quite apart from a deep desire to see a rope round the neck of a creature he found personally unpalatable, it would have solved several pressing problems at a stroke.

'I would plead I was far from alone. I would also be correct, would I not, in assuming you had a major hand in the verdict?'

'It was Mr Garrow who found the way to convince the jury there was serious doubt.'

This avoided the question of what he'd done to make a case for innocence. He'd provided an old lawyer friend with the facts of what had occurred at the Covent Garden bagnio, where the murder of Catherine Carruthers had taken place.

'Ah yes, the legal genius' was aid to avoid further comment.

Druce still had his back to Hodgson, with the wine yet to be poured. His arm was shaking to the point he'd no certainty he could hit the crystal goblet, hoping this was hidden by his body. It took a firm left hand on his right wrist to steady it enough to fill the glass. The slight tremble was harder to disguise on delivery, something Hodgson pretended not to notice.

Hodgson took a sip of the wine, before asking, in an even tone, 'Am I to take it, you have need of my services once more?'

If this elicited a nod, no words followed. From holding Hodgson's eye, the prize agent's gaze rose to stare at the elaborate plasterwork on the ceiling. He knew what he wanted but was just as aware of the care required to be exercised. He'd not missed the cagey response to his question regarding the thief-taker's previous dealing with Garrow.

The conclusion he'd reached about the way to proceed, after many torturous hours of apprehensive contemplation, was stark. Just as obvious was his own inability to bring about what seemed the only clear way out of his dilemma. The one way to secure his own safety and future well-being was to bring down his brother-in-law, a route riven with risk. The slightest hint he was acting against Denby could bring complete ruin and worse.

Set against this was the potential reward, should Denby be found guilty of conspiracy to murder, which would lead to the gallows. The thought had often had Druce nearly struggle for breath at the prospect this presented. Being childless and with Catherine dead, Denby's sole heir would be his sister, and the man possessed a fortune. This would bring into the possession of Edward Druce, as her husband, the legacy in its entirety, to dispose of as he saw fit.

Before him was a dizzying prospect, to be free of even a debt of gratitude, never mind money. To be able to not only match Francis Ommaney in funds, but to outdo him, which would change the whole nature of their unequal association. Indeed, the shoe would be on the other foot. Having finally come down on the side of action, now he had to decide how to proceed.

'I wondered, Mr Hodgson, if you felt, as I did at the conclusion of Gherson's trial, his acquittal left many questions unanswered?'

There was no engagement of the thief-taker's eye; he was still examining the ceiling, while praying his voice didn't reveal the tension gripping his breast.

'The obvious one, Mr Druce.'

Faced with a man nodding sagely and silently, Walter Hodgson was calculating what this was all about and having little trouble arriving at a possible conclusion. Druce had got himself into a tangle by doing the underhand bidding of his brother-in-law, probably innocently originally. This had turned into a morass into which he'd become trapped, having paid Hodgson for nearly two years, and handsomely, *not* to find Cornelius Gherson. Instead, he'd been charged to provide baseless sightings, which he could pass on to the man who, Hodgson eventually discovered, was actually footing the bill.

'Obvious?'

Even if he knew Druce wanted him to say it plain, Hodgson declined to oblige, waiting in silence until he had no choice but to name the conclusion. Even as he did so, it smacked of evasion.

'Do you have anyone in mind?'

'I have already provided you an opinion, Mr Druce, not a solid one I grant, but one which justifies consideration.'

Having been put away, the two drawings previously provided by Hodgson were brought back out of the drawer, to be laid on the desk once more, Druce leaning forward to give them close and silent examination.

'I seem to recall you had no luck in finding these fellows,' he said finally. 'Do you see any value in continuing to search for them?'

'Not without a clear notion of the purpose.'

'Surely the purpose would be to tar them with guilt, as the men who murdered Mrs Carruthers.' A raised eyebrow obliged Druce to add, 'It would lay to rest other areas of speculation.'

'Such as?' Hodgson asked, with a contrived air of innocence.

Druce was not about to say and once more would not hold his visitor's eye. 'If they are indeed the perpetrators, one is bound to query their motives. I cannot believe Catherine was known to them, they being the kind of creatures she'd hardly associate with.'

'Since I never met the lady, I couldn't say.'

'Refined, Hodgson, pretty, too, if lacking in a degree of seriousness, hardly surprising in one so young. It did raise eyebrows when my brother-in-law chose to marry her, the age difference being so . . .'

What this meant was left in the air as was the obvious ghost in the room. Carruthers had tried to kill Gherson for the act of seducing his wife and had failed. He'd then expended endless sums in a spurious effort to find the sod, this brokered by the man before him. He knew the object of the search was at sea, leaving him and his partner to milk the Barclay account.

It had all gone wrong with the death of Captain Barclay, his slippery clerk now without employment and back in London, looking to profit from his knowledge of the frauds. Druce had been forced to alert his bother-in-law to the fact and had probably passed on where he could be found.

Once the deed was done and Gherson incarcerated, the threat of what he might reveal and to whom did not diminish, for he had contacted Barclay's widow, so Hodgson had been employed by her to deal with him. The entry into the imbroglio of Emily Barclay opened up a whole new barrel of worms, information on the past coming to Walter Hodgson from her and Gherson.

This laid out plain the whole nature of multiple deceptions which would put Ommaney and Druce out of business and might even threaten the latter's life. Druce had no idea of the depth of Hodgson's knowledge, so there was an element of fishing going on to seek it out. In doing so, the man was revealing more than he was discovering.

What Hodgson didn't know was what was required, though he had a fair degree of suspicion as to what it might be. He had his own notion on the guilty party, but no reason to act upon it. There was no reward in hounding and finding a thief or murderer if no bounty was placed on their head. A thief-taker's task, regardless of any sense of justice, did not extend to charity: They worked to be paid for nothing less than to put food on their table. But there was a game to be played, and so the question was posed.

'The two fellows whose likenesses you're looking at. Are you suggesting, Mr Druce, I continue my search for them?'

'I see it as a way to proceed, yes.'

'I would have to widen the area. Those I have covered were close to London and, given we rate them as seafarers, it may be necessary to look to coastal parts farther afield. An expensive business travelling far and wide, as the farrago of looking for Gherson established.'

Druce was embarrassed by the reference and the word farrago and failed to hide the fact. 'Nevertheless, I think it must be undertaken.'

'We need to set my rates.'

'I'm willing to add a ten percent bonus on top of what you charged previously.'

'And will your brother-in-law be meeting the bill this time?'

This startled Druce enough to have him jerk forward in his chair. 'How do you know . . .?' He stopped himself and fought to control his voice as he added in a hissing tone, 'All you need to know, is you will be paid when you present a bill. Where the funds come from are none of your concern.'

'Of course.'

This came from a man who now knew exactly what he was being required to do, able in the realisation to present a calm demeanour. Druce, by his reaction, had nailed the real aim of the search, which was satisfying since it matched Hodgson's own deductions. Justice might be served, and he would be paid to help it along.

'I wonder if I might trouble you for another glass of this excellent claret.'

'Help yourself' was far from outgoing. 'And, after you have done so, I think our business is concluded.'

Hodgson stood and went to the decanter, quickly filling his goblet and drinking the contents.

'And Mr Hodgson' came with an insincere, friendly tone aimed at his back. 'You will oblige me in this matter by dealing with myself and myself alone, even to the point of presenting your ongoing expenses.'

The desk drawer was opened once more and a purse produced, from which Druce extracted five golden guineas, put in a pile on the desk.

'This will serve to meet any immediate expense. I wish this matter to be pursued with maximum discretion. Indeed, I think it better if, when information is forthcoming or a further payment falls due, you send me a sealed note with a place to meet. Not hard by these premises, but somewhere fairly close by where I can satisfy myself to the requirements of the situation.'

'Do you wish me to take possession of those drawings?'

'I'm sure the features are printed on your mind by now, as they are on mine.'

Druce might as well have said they're my insurance, but this fact was not imparted to the departing Walter Hodgson, a man who did indeed have those sketched images marked in his mind, as well as copies should his memory fail him.

Also being marked was a deep red weal, not the first and destined not to be the last, on the bare back of Jaleel Tolland, he strapped to a grating on the quarterdeck of HMS *Bedford*. The crew was assembled, as was the captain of the seventy-four, Sir Thomas Byard, along with his officers, the marine drummer boy rattling his sticks in front of his red-coated seniors, the regular gathering to witness punishment aboard a King's vessel. The cat, well tarred, was laid on with both force and in silence, which extended to the man on the receiving end.

Both crime and sentence had been read out before the flogging commenced, with no plea for leniency from his divisional officer. Tolland had so badly beaten a shipmate, the man was likely to be of no further use to the navy for a month or even more. What was also known, but remained unspoken, was the victim was a real hard case, a lower-deck thug who, prior to arrival of the Tolland brothers and their crew of smugglers, had lorded it over his shipmates.

To those watching, even some of the lieutenants and certainly the petty officers and crew, it was a pity the man at the grating was being punished at all. He'd removed from duty a fellow, more of a pest than any rat that ran through the bilges, in what had been a contest to see who was top dog on the lower deck. There was no doubt now who it would be, and the true test of his character was being played out before them all. Jaleel Tolland was taking it like a man, with not so much, when the cat struck, as a gasp passing his lips.

Farrier, the bosun's mate, his heavy breathing clearly showing the strain of his efforts, laid on with the last of the dozen, the cat then falling limp in his hand. A short period of silence followed, before Sir Thomas ordered Tolland cut down. As the ropes lashing him were undone, there was no collapse, no falling to the deck or the need to be assisted to make the companionway and the surgeon's attention. Tolland stood on his own two feet for a few seconds and then turned to look at Byard, fixing his captain with a steady gaze, not disdainful, but surely wanting in respect.

'I trust,' Sir Thomas said in a carrying voice, intended as a warning to all, 'you will have learned the error of your actions. Our duty requires us to fight the King's enemies, not each other.'

'Permission to go below?'

You had to note the voice fitted the man; low, deep and rasping. Then there was the face, bruised and with many a lump, for it had been a hard fight with a brawny fellow unaccustomed to losing. Not that it would have been called handsome anyway, it being the countenance of one to steer clear of. The lack of any courtesy of title was also notable, and Byard could have referred to it and considered it yet another offence. But he'd been in the navy since he was a boy and knew what from what. He recognised when an exact application of the Articles of War would not serve.

The man before him wouldn't bend, it was alien to his nature and he'd seen the type before. What mattered was how this hard case would behave in a fight with the enemy, and Byard reckoned him reliable in that regard. His kind relished a battle, be it one on one or taking on the dozen. What was needed, as with so many of his shipmates, was to apply a measure of the discretion.

'Permission to stand the men down, sir' came from Byard's premier, and this granted.

Few moved until Tolland had made the companionway and begun to descend, stiff certainly but upright, the first person to close with him his younger brother, Franklin. The face, with its livid scar, was deeply concerned, though he knew better than to commiserate: Jaleel was not one to welcome sympathy.

Instead, he accompanied him to the orlop deck and the surgeon's berth, where his back was attended to with grease as a salve, till the bells denoting the change of watch had Franklin rush off to his station, leaving Jaleel face-down in a cot. It was four hours later before they could talk, and this was done in whispers.

'We've got to get off this ship, Jaleel.'

'Which we will not do at sea, brother. Somehow we've got to get this barky into a shoreside berth from where we can skip.'

'How do you reckon to do it?' Franklin asked, for when it came to resource, he deferred to Jaleel.

'Won't happen if it don't need repair' came the hissed reply. 'So our task now is to make it unfit for staying with the fleet.'

'How, brother?'
'Let me put my mind to it. There has to be a way.'
'Carruthers?'
'Happen, Franklin. The bastard owes us.'

Chapter Eleven

Sat in the room he'd taken over in his sister's house, in which he could transact his business, Denby Carruthers was too busy with everyday paperwork to worry overmuch about the non-appearance of the ship he owned. Of the many enterprises in which he was engaged, not least as a shareholder in the East India Company, smuggling in combination with the Tolland brothers ranked as a caprice, albeit one which produced a handsome profit.

It also allowed him to use contraband goods to gift those of his associates, fellow city grandees he felt would return a useful favour, men who might help him to the office of mayor. Casks of brandy to cases of tea were seen as so much less than a bribe, more a proper gift. And for the wives, just as important in granting him the right profile, there could be a bale of silk or Calais lace.

The traffic to and from the Druce front door was steady and constant throughout the morning; messengers from Lloyds with offers to underwrite various insurance contracts, requests he invest in ventures that required careful consideration of risk, set against potential reward, as well as a knowledge of the background of those promoting the scheme.

He had interests in the Stock Exchange, buying futures on cargoes expected to be landed from around the world, as well as membership of the Baltic Exchange, engaged in ships chartering as well as cargoes of pitch pine and tar. Other correspondence related to his position as a serving alderman of the city of London.

Ships berthed when the wind and tide allowed, so no great anxiety attended the fact his junior partners were over a week late on the anticipated day of arrival. He would be informed when a messenger, usually

Franklin, showed up at the door of his own dwelling, information to be passed on by the man he'd left there to keep the place secure.

Carruthers half suspected the brothers, very much not his type, were far from diligent when it came to haste, probably too busy enjoying the fleshpots and whores of Gravelines to rush home. This obscure port was the Flanders base to the British smuggling fraternity, even in wartime. France and the traders of the Low Counties derived as much benefit from the activity as did they, while Dutch bankers were eager to handle bills of exchange, required to pay for the cargoes.

Another thing to keep an eye on, given the brothers had undertaken several successful crossings, was the list of vessels for sale. The notion had been mooted of expanding the profitable operation by buying and crewing another vessel. Thus, he had notifications delivered showing what vessels had been taken by the Excise, these being sold off at knock-down prices, to line the pocket of the person holding the required sinecure.

In addition, though of less interest, were enemy vessels captured by the navy, very rarely without expensive-to-repair damage. For once, they had put up for auction an undamaged enemy vessel of a remarkably similar tonnage to the one he already owned.

It came with both the cargo, interesting in itself, plus everything necessary to be able to immediately put to sea, including cordage and canvas. All it required were the men needed to crew it. He'd been assured this presented no difficulty, the coastal areas of Kent having no shortage of men willing to risk the trade.

With viewing taking place this very day, Carruthers decided the fresh air of a Greenwich dockside would be welcome after so much time cooped up indoors. He was obliged to handle his workload personally, including the writing of voluminous correspondence, a heavy and time-consuming burden. The need he had for a reliable clerk was pressing, the rub being in the word reliable. Bitter experience told him such fellows were thin on the ground.

Not a thought on which he wanted to dwell, given it rendered him mournful and furious in equal measure, he called to a house servant to arrange a hack for an hour hence. Then he went back to his papers.

The vessel was thought to be recognised long before Denby Carruthers came alongside, he having bought the vessel in which the Tollands sailed. If nothing else was particularly distinctive, in the broad-bottomed and dark green hull there was the figurehead, a massive-bosomed lady with an ugly face and bright red lips. Not that it was so singular as to provide a positive identity: The carvers and painters of such artefacts were not long on imagination. They sold copy after copy to whoever was building ships. A walk to the stern, surprisingly, produced no name, the board bearing it being missing.

A throng of interested potential buyers had come to the pre-auction viewing, more examining the unloaded cargo laid out in a shed than the ship itself. The same goods, perused by Carruthers, left him with the creeping suspicion he was looking, in the bales and barrels, at his own property. It matched, if not precisely, what he had indented and paid for, as well as that which the Tolland brothers had been sent to fetch home.

The auction itself being several days away from commencement, he sought out the naval officer overseeing matters, an elderly, one-legged lieutenant with a ruddy, weather-beaten face. Garbed in a plain blue coat, the fellow was greeted with contrived bonhomie, added to a genial enquiry as to his name and previous service. This established the former to be Perkins, while the leg had gone two decades past, in a fight with a Frenchman.

Flattery and commiseration had the fellow open up, with references to his obvious expertise in the matter of sailing vessels, Carruthers readily admitting his own ignorance. Was this un-named barky sound, how did he think she would sail? Finally, he enquired about the nationality, only to be told it was unknown, but most likely Dutch, given it was in good order below decks.

'Not a thing to be found in a John Crapaud ship, sir,' Perkins spat. 'When it comes to cleanliness, they are slovenly sods.'

'Dutch? I'm bound to ask where this ship was taken, Mr Perkins.'

'Off Flanders I'm told, brought into Ramsgate . . .'

'By?' came out too quickly. The man had clearly been about to say and was miffed at the interruption, which produced a hasty apology. 'Forgive me, I'm keen to know who effected the capture.'

'*Hazard* was the name mentioned' had about a tone of disapproval.

The nature of this vessel had to be enquired about, which established she was not a line of battleship or even a frigate, but a brig. Not that Perkins knew of it personally, though by the tone of the voice he was clearly less than fond of something in the name.

'And where is she now?'

'For that you'd need to enquire at the Admiralty, sir, though I reckon they'd be chary about telling a civilian her orders.'

'Perhaps the name of the man in command would serve better?'

That seriously changed both the tenor of voice and the countenance, which, ruddy already, went a deeper shade of red, while the voice, with a strong hint of Yorkshire, was a rasp.

'It do, sir, for it stinks, imparted to me by the officer Admiral Vereker sent up from Ramsgate. He was as shocked as I am myself at the name. That such a bastard should be given a ship, while honest men languish ashore, is a disgrace.'

'Would it be one known outside the service?' was a gentle enquiry. Obviously, Perkins saw himself as both honest and wronged.

'Would that it were known to all, sir. That such a man should merit a command is an abomination. *Hazard* has been given to a misshapen creature by the name of John Pearce, who should be keelhauled for his presumption of rank.'

'Why so?'

Much of what followed made no sense to Carruthers, who could not care a jot for the method by which naval officers achieved their rank. But he made a good fist of appearing interested, finally asking, 'I've not satisfied my belly since early morning, lieutenant. I trust you know of somewhere I can do so.'

'Indeed, sir, I can recommend the Admiral Benbow, which I myself use.'

'Would you care to join me? If not food, a pot of ale, perhaps.'

'I would go to a glass of rum, sir.'

'Then let it be my pleasure to provide it.'

On his way to Portsmouth, Walter Hodgson was on an errand, which had nothing to do with the search he was tasked to undertake on behalf of Edward Druce. Mind, it was to him the bill for the coach and accommodation would go, an act which would not trouble Hodgson's conscience at all. He'd said he would search the nation's seaports and none was greater in such a regard than the premier base of the King's Navy.

His interview with Emily Barclay had confirmed the cause of her problem to be Cornelius Gherson, so he was headed, on her behalf, for the location where the sod was living. His attempt to dissuade her from funding this latest request, more of a demand really, had fallen on deaf ears. This had held even when backed up by the physician, Lutyens, with whom she lodged, and he knew why.

Her late husband's clerk knew too much to be left free to babble or, even worse perhaps, pen a pamphlet telling the ever-curious public some home truths about the reasons he was on trial. He was, after all, still celebrity enough to gain a ready audience, eager to pay a penny to read his tale. Salacious enough, given the gruesome murder, to ensure increased interest, he might choose to mention his previous life and some of the things he'd witnessed. Like his life as a captain's clerk and the state of his late employer's marriage where innuendo would suffice.

With no desire to engage in idle chatter with his fellow passengers, Hodgson was afforded ample time to think. The problem to be considered was not how to satisfy Gherson's latest demand, he carried the means to do so, but to ensure such importuning of Emily Barclay ceased. He had, in his coat, the sum of fifty guineas, enough for Gherson to establish the credit he needed to undertake a position as a purser on a Royal Navy vessel, though not anything of size.

'Let him start in a transport vessel, Mr Hodgson,' Emily had insisted, with undisguised bitterness, 'and use his own nefarious ways to progress. I fully expect he will gain a flagship in record time and do so by cheating those unfortunates who look to him for necessities.'

It was known to be an occupation full of risk, pursers regularly going bankrupt, not that such a fate engendered any sympathy. No one, from captain to ship's boy, loved the breed, seeing them as rapacious scoundrels intent on extracting the last bit of copper from all and sundry. A commanding officer would be obliged to engage in dispute with the purser on the subject of beef, pork, and peas to be supplied to the crew, doubly so if it was unfit to be consumed and must be condemned.

The wardroom must seek its supplies of coal for the stove and candles by which to see from the same source, as did the cook seek wood to heat water in the galley. The crew also required their stoves to be fed, and heaven help if you lost wooden bowls, plates, or eating utensils. It would require begging for replacements. Slop clothes had to be paid for, hammocks too, for the supply of these were set against the purser's account and rarely did a parsimonious Admiralty reimburse them without argument, if such articles were damaged or lost.

But it was tobacco where they made their most tenacious antagonists: A fellow needing a smoke and short on coin would not take to weights which calculated at fourteen ounces to the pound. Even if a purser's weights came in at a proper sixteen, no one would believe it to be so. It was sad to think the fellow he was on his way to see would likely thrive on such hatred, being one to despise his fellow man, seen as something to exploit, the other obvious trait, his fear of the same people.

Rarely had Hodgson met so obvious a coward, and with this went the desire to bully if it could be inflicted without retribution. The thief-taker had met some right evil bastards in his working life, but he had to admit Gherson was a match for any of them. Two days later, he walked through the bustle of Portsmouth Point to the Spice Island Inn, where Gherson had indicated he would wait, it being easy to find.

Here lay a place Walter Hodgson had visited before, chasing felons intent on getting away to sea to avoid justice, easy in wartime. An offer to volunteer never raised questions as to why with the nation in conflict; in peace it was chancy, the service never short on volunteers.

The hawkers were at their raucous trade, selling everything a body could need in the trinket and gimcrack line while keeping an eye out for the watchmen, who would fine them if caught. Not the whores, they had nothing to worry about while plying their trade, which came in steadily, given the reputation of the promontory called the Spice Island, an attraction to even the well-heeled young buck out for risky experience. There were the usual urchins seeking to pick a pocket, not his, for he had the look of a man who knew how to deal with dippers.

The sight of Gherson might have induced pity if it was another. He looked forlorn, nursing, it turned out, a near-empty tankard, with the wear on his quality clothes taking the tarnish off the protection they afforded him. It was not a safe place to be dressed like a common tar or working man, with press-gangs as regular callers. Best to aspire to appear a gentleman and thus immune from their activities.

Increasing age was beginning to dent his looks, yet Gherson was still absurdly handsome, an angel to look at some would say, a devil at heart to those who knew him. Blond hair and smooth cheeks, added to blue eyes that could pretend innocence and full cupid lips, it was a testament to his penury that he sat unmolested by the trollops.

The look he aimed at Hodgson started as alarm, having been threat-ened with physical harm before, to then morph into hope when treated to a smile. Obviously feeling his expectations were about to be satisfied, Gherson reverted to his true, sneering type.

'Once more the messenger, Hodgson.'

'Mr Hodgson to you' was the sharp rejoinder, 'and don't forget it again.'

The changing expression on his face showed arrogance doing battle with need, a whole gamut of emotions with supplication winning out, to remind Hodgson, not that he required it, the despicable creature he was dealing with.

'I hope Mrs Barclay has sent you to satisfy my request.'

'Sounded more of a demand to me.'

'You may call it what you wish, but I need to know if it is to be met.'

The soft leather purse came out from a pocket to be laid on the table, the clunk of contact denoting the weight of the contents, which produced a look of pure avarice. A hand reached out to take it, but the purse was quickly withdrawn.

'Not so fast.'

'I demand what is mine' was a whining plea.

'It ain't yours till I say so, which is how I have been so charged to act. I give you this now and what will it be used for? Whores and drink, looking about me, the contents gone in a week, followed by another demand for more.'

'You have me mistaken.'

Hodgson's face must have shown he could not bring himself to believe this possible, which led to a gabbling attempt to convince him. The insistence being put forward was Hodgson was dealing with a changed man, chastened by what had happened to him, eager only to find a way to make his way in the world and avoid ending up in the gutter.

'You advised, outside the Old Bailey, I get to sea for my own safety. This is what I intend to do, though I can find no places for clerking. Having talked to a couple of fellows keen to retire, I have options of a purser's berth, as long as I can post a reasonable bond.'

The purse was lifted and dropped again, though to within reach of the intended recipient.

'And that's the purpose of what you hold.'

'Which I will continue to do, until we meet these options and am satisfied of your intentions.'

'We? This is unseemly. How would I identify you?'

Hodgson chuckled. 'Happen as an indulgent uncle, keen to see his favourite nephew proper set up.' About to protest, a held-up hand stopped him. 'I'm in control here, not you. You act as I say, or this purse goes back from whence it came.'

Gherson sat back, his voice low and his face oddly expressionless, but the threat issued came as no surprise. 'The consequences could be dire for the owner.'

'I don't think so. But I do know what the consequences, as you call them, could be for you. After you left me on the trial day, I went for a wet in a nearby tavern and what happened. A stranger, a fellow I've never seen in my life before, goes out of his way to engage me in conversation. Having seen me come from the court, probably in your company, he was eager to know more about you.'

'So?'

'Like asking where you might go, now you were acquitted.'

This drained a bit of colour from Gherson's cheeks, not that there was much to start with.

'Thought himself clever this cove, buying me ale and pumping for information. I spotted him following me when I went on my way, being it's in my nature to be sharp on such matters. So what was he, just a nosy bugger, maybe a Grub Street hack looking for a tale to write up and sell?' Hodgson chuckled again. 'The true tale of a man who nearly hanged would warrant a fee.'

There was little need to continue. Gherson had imagination enough to conjure up the alternatives to the notion of a hack. To let him stew, Hodgson waved to a serving girl for a second tankard and a fill, watching his man with an amused expression, as both were placed and filled from a pitcher.

'I daresay you've got to what might have been the fellow's game.' A nod. 'You might even wonder if I'm still being followed.'

Gherson was now clutching the edge of the table, drink ignored, until reassured it wasn't so. Hodgson knew how to make certain of it, not that the creature appeared convinced.

'But this I will tell you. Any demand made of Mrs Barclay again, and it is I who will be given the errand, this agreed. You must, of necessity, say where you can be found. I may choose to do as I have done now, or pass this on to someone else, who cannot be said to have your well-being at heart.'

A sneering pout. 'You're not the only one who can issue threats.'

'But I will be, once I've seen my favourite nephew placed in a position of possible profit. I will know where you can be found and will make it my business to follow you wherever you go.'

'A bluff.'

'A purser must submit accounts to the Admiralty, if he wishes to be paid for his outgoings.' Confirmation was slow in coming. 'I have acted on their behalf occasionally, pursuing tars who've committed serious crimes and then deserted to avoid retribution. I think I can say I'm well-regarded thereabouts.'

Hodgson leant forward and made enough of a sound with his tankard slamming on the table to have Gherson flinch. 'So I will know where you are, afloat or at anchor. Be assured, break the rule of silence on matters about which you should be quiet and it will not be me who will find you.'

Hodgson smiled again, broadly this time. What he'd just fabricated, an entirely imagined way to stop Gherson, worked out on the Portsmouth coach, amused him, not least because the expression on the sod's face told him he'd fallen for it hook, line, and sinker. Then he took a deep drink of his ale, before commanding, 'Sup up, nephew, and let us go to settle your future.'

The laugh, as he stood up, was so loud, it turned every head in the Spice Island Inn.

CHAPTER TWELVE

The next two days were spent disguising *Hazard*, which would allow it to sail close inshore without causing alarm. If the Dons were toying with changing sides, and the French were present in force, the last thing they would want off their borderlands was a British warship. So tarred canvas had to be rigged over the side to disguise the gunports, more framed on timber, put together by the carpenter Mr Towse, to create the impression of a shallow poop, on what was a flush-decked ship.

Pearce deplored the necessity, even if he accepted it, because he saw a very real need his crew, both sections, required to be relentlessly rehearsed in gunnery. Not the firing, for this would attract undue attention, just the hauling in and out, plus the highly choreographed act of reloading. They had to get the cannon back to where it could be deployed, added to the ability of the gun captain to oversee aim and elevation, all within the required time. Given the circumstances, this was impossible.

'God aid us if we're outed' outlined his major worry.

'Can you not fire through the canvas?' Oliphant enquired.

'The question is, can we hit anything if we did and, right now, I would say it would be unlikely.'

'It may be those you face will be no better.'

'Not a notion with which to engage in battle.'

The final touch was a Swedish pennant at the masthead. The hope was, though it would not stand close-quarter inspection, of a coastal trading vessel, perhaps on course for San Sebastian, sailing close inshore for security. Blue coats and bicorn navy hats for the officers were put away, replaced by ducks. In warm weather there was no need for coats, shirts would suffice.

What could not be disguised was the height of the masts, the main especially, also the fact of it being slightly raked, which would be beyond exceptional on a cargo ship. Pearce could only hope anyone observing HMS *Hazard* would be no expert on ship design, so would not remark it. Prior to approaching the actual border, to test the theory, he took *Hazard* into a small bay, with a tiny fishing village called St Jean de Luz, at its head.

This lay on the road south from Bordeaux, a major centre from where supplies and reinforcements must come for an army operating farther south, so the village would provide a possible staging post for a change of horses or mules. This took Pearce and his telescope to the mainmast cap, so he could see for himself if the notion was sound.

On the far side of a row of tiny ramshackle dwellings, he sighted a tall flagstaff, but it carried no tricolour. It stood in the middle of a barren patch of ground, which could have been an old encampment, but there was no sense now of a military presence. More importantly, there were men on the beach sorting their nets, and *Hazard* being offshore caused no visible alarm.

Having noted the state of the tide and marked it against the time, which could matter later on, they resumed their progress down the coast. Midshipman Campbell was now aloft, charged with the aim of observing any traffic on a not-far-inland road. He could report on the odd slow-moving cart, his vigil kept until the road trended inland and was lost from view.

The conclusion reached, in discussion with Oliphant, suggested there could be no serious military presence farther south. Thus the question was raised as to the need to go ashore on the French side of the border. On this occasion Pearce, who demurred, was obliged to bow to the opinion of his companion. He insisted Dundas would not settle for supposition; he was a man for facts.

'Or those you choose to present to him' was the barbed conclusion.

Hauling offshore, Pearce carried out a duty already left too long. In the company of Mr Williams, he had himself rowed round the ship to check the trim, necessary on a regular basis. When barrels of beef and pork, as well as water, were used up, as they were on a daily basis, a great deal of shifting was required to correct the effect on the trim of the ship. This affected the manner in which she sailed and occasioned much communication with the deck, messages passed on to those toiling and sweating to shift stores below decks.

The duty also presented an opportunity to train his quota men on the proper employment of the oars. Under the hand of Michael O'Hagan as coxswain, they worked to perfect the required rhythm, which made passage as quick and smooth as was possible on the swell of an open Atlantic. If it improved, it would not pass muster under an admiral's eye. Their very best endeavours were going to be required very shortly, given he and Oliphant would be going ashore, the first landfall designed to show the state of preparedness of the enemy forces. It, at least, came with a degree of security, for if challenged, they had their facility in French to divert any attempt at questioning their presence. Given several hours would pass before this would happen, both men took to their cots to get some sleep.

The extensive Admiralty charts provided the place to land, a bay to the north of a rocky outcrop called the Pointe St Anne, within easy walking distance of the border town of Hendaye. Observation in daylight would tell if there were soldiers present and if so, in what strength.

Pearce arose from his slumbers when the bay was sighted and went aloft with his telescope once more, to run it over a small strand of beach. This was set between rocky arms, on a shoreline backed by pine forest, with no sign of occupation, not even drawn-up fishing boats. Satisfied, *Hazard* was hauled offshore to stay out of sight until dusk.

The time had come to issue orders for what should happen in his absence, with instructions on what to do should he and Oliphant fail to return. In short, to appraise his premier of the mission on which the ship was engaged, given it would fall to him to complete it or not, as he saw fit. If Hallowell seemed eager to be informed, this was not replicated by Oliphant, who had only reluctantly agreed the man who would assume command had to know what they were about.

'I must stress, this is for your ears only, Mr Hallowell. It is not to be discussed in the wardroom or anywhere else. You will be required to deflect curiosity and be firm in doing so.'

'Which cannot be stressed enough.'

Oliphant insisted on this with a testy look, designed to drive the point home. Again, he was speaking when he should stay silent, which had Pearce shaking his head in frustration. This having no effect at all, he went on to outline the task, without naming the person who'd initiated it, which was not precaution enough.

'Be assured, we are acting on instructions from the highest in the land,' Oliphant asserted. 'Any breach of their trust will rebound extremely badly on the career of whosoever breaks it.'

'I take such words amiss, Mr Oliphant,' Hallowell responded, his tone of voice, delivered in a slow Yankee drawl, polite but firm. 'Might I remind you of the price my family has paid, so far, for our loyalty to the British crown.'

If he'd hoped to embarrass Oliphant, it failed. The Hallowell family had backed the losing side in the American Revolution, so had been forced to flee to Canada after Yorktown, leaving behind all they possessed in land and property. It made no impression on Oliphant, the man being beyond such a sentiment, which left an awkward silence.

Pearce filled it with instructions on the practicalities. The cutter would deliver him and Oliphant to the shore, the spot marked so they could be fetched off again the following night or the one after. A watch was to be kept for a flashing lantern on the treeline, which would indicate they were waiting.

'I wish you to be well offshore at dawn, the hull out of sight of land, only closing when it's time to send the cutter in for a rendezvous. Out at sea, contact with other vessels, should any appear, is to be avoided unless this proves impossible.'

Once the orders had been digested and with the premier departed, objections were not long in coming.

'You didn't say what was to happen if the ship meets an armed enemy, or we have another storm?'

'I trust Hallowell to take whatever action he sees as being appropriate.'

'Which might include running for safety.'

'That's always possible.'

'I just wondered, where does this leave us?'

'To fend for ourselves until he can get a boat in to take us off, which would be the case wherever we landed.'

Sensing there might be more argument, Pearce continued. 'If you're so certain we can't find out anything lest we go ashore, you then have to accept it's impossible to account for every eventuality, even in an enterprise less fraught with risk than this. Hallowell is a competent officer, who will, one day, command his own ship and be responsible for the decisions this entails. I have no choice but to leave him in this situation now and, be assured, I have complete faith in his ability to act sensibly.'

'I could go alone, in fact, I think I'd be more secure if I were to do so.'

'We were jointly charged with this mission and jointly we will carry it out.'

'Which sounds very like you don't trust me.'

'You may take what I say to mean what you wish.'

Silence and cold stares ensued, each keeping his thoughts to himself. For Pearce, even if he was not prepared to say so out loud, it was a lack of trust. Given the cock-and-bull story Oliphant had concocted and sold Henry Dundas when he got back from France, claiming success instead of admitting failure, he wanted to see anything of significance with his own eyes. He was certainly never going to settle for and share responsibility for a secondhand report.

Many times he'd berated himself for his failure to tell Dundas the truth, the excuses conjured up varied. He didn't like the man was an understatement. Quite apart from a personal antipathy to a bully, Pearce suspected him to be partly, if not wholly, responsible for the writ of sedition issued against his father. Given being found guilty risked a hanging, it had driven both father and son from the country in the year after the fall of the Bastille.

Both Scots and far from friends, Pearce senior and Henry Dundas had clashed as young men, their differences widening as they grew older. One became more radical and outspoken, while Dundas, ever an establishment creature, went on to cement his position as the leader of the faction of Scottish MPs. They were now supporting the government, which would risk defeat in Parliament without their votes. Besides the power this brought him, he'd become William Pitt's boon companion, not least with claret bottle.

There had, of course, been the temptation of future employment, a ship, in fact, something which he had no hope of getting from those who normally distributed such plums. To be on the beach promised half-pay penury, which would certainly make it harder to resist the entreaties of his lover that he consent to live off the legacy of her late husband. This was a thought too demeaning, given he despised the man's very name. Whichever it was, he was here now and being brought back to the present by Oliphant, who, if anything, sounded slightly cocky.

'We shouldn't need to be ashore for long, perhaps less than a full day. Would it not be better if the boat taking us ashore waited for our return?'

'I cannot see beyond the line of trees and have no idea what lies behind it, or what patrols the French might mount to ensure the security of the coastline. The idea of a boat drawn up on the beach and sailors with it, does not appeal. Besides, it would require a strong party and the men to be armed.'

'Exactly. With the numbers and weapons to hold open our route of escape should we be rumbled.'

'And who do you suggest should make up this party?'

'That is for you to decide.'

'At last,' was delivered in a deeply caustic tone, 'you acknowledge I have the responsibility.'

'Don't get on your high horse when what I suggest is logical.'

'Then I grant to you the task of picking the men for such a duty.'

'I sense a trick.'

'What you lack is any sense at all, certainly any knowledge when it comes to the scarcity of choice.'

Pearce waited for Oliphant to make the obvious deduction. But, once more, he showed, with his silence and expression, he could only factor his own needs and never included the difficulties with which they'd been landed. Had they been left with the original ship's company, Pearce might have been putting forward the very notion being suggested, but they had not.

'I invite you to look at the crew and make your choice. Will it be our quota men, none of whom are yet used to fighting with weapons, especially muskets? That's because there's been no time to properly train them, which means they would have little idea how to defend themselves, which leaves only the Arklows.'

The Oliphant countenance moved from disagreeable to piqued, with Pearce determined to drive home a point Oliphant should have arrived at on his own.

'I'm far from sure of them in the matter of desertion, or even another attempt to take over the ship, which is why I and my officers have been carrying loaded weapons these last two days. The only body who can provide even a modicum of what you suggest are Moberly and his marines. Given the circumstances in which we find ourselves, would it be wise to leave the ship without them?'

'Obviously not' was reluctantly acceded.

'So, you see, we must go ashore and act alone.'

'And if this leaves us waiting for days, which you must acknowledge is a possibility?'

'We will take ashore food enough to keep us from starvation.'

'Hardtack and cheese?'

'I've got by on less in my life.'

'I'm more content to rely on carrying the means to buy what we need.'

'As long as it's not with the flashing of gold coin.'

Of which there was a good supply, if not an abundance, provided by Henry Dundas for the purpose of bribery, but not as much as there had been originally. John Pearce had used some of the funds to buy extra gunpowder from the manufactory at Faversham. The sound, fury, and smoke of actual discharge had cheered the new men, even if it had done little for their ability.

'We must carry enough to buy our way out of trouble,' Oliphant insisted.

'Of course. Now I suggest you prepare. The sun is on the wane and we need to shortly be on our way. For myself, I must dig out civilian clothing.'

The food, which included cold beef as well as cheese and aforesaid hardtack, was placed in a dunny sack, along with flints, the lantern, and two candles. It also carried two bottles of wine, the water the ship carried now too brackish to even think of drinking. Any of that commodity to ease a thirst would have to come from the heavens or a well.

Pistols and swords were taken as a matter of course, Pearce amused to observe Oliphant's blade had a very elaborate, decorative, and gilded hilt. He also carried a tall, black hat, two items so incongruous, Pearce had to contain the temptation to mention it. For himself he had plainer head-gear, while both had satchels for more personal possessions, spare shirts and stockings, the means to shave, as well as a sum of gold sufficient to buy their way out of difficulty.

The sky, now mixed high cloud over a setting sun, provided a fabulously colourful western sunset, which predicted enough starlight to begin with, as well as a risen half-moon, by the time they made the shore. Michael O'Hagan was present to time the oars, but Pearce had ordered young Maclehose to command the boat, Oliphant whispering, to enquire if this was really necessary.

'The way you get midshipman accustomed to responsibility is to give them some.'

'He's bound to wonder what we're at.'

'So will the entire crew and they'll be concocting all sorts of theories. So for the sake of all that's holy, put it out of your concerns. Now have a care as you go down the side. I have no desire to fetch you out of the water.'

He needed help, as well as line round his waist, to ensure such a fate was avoided. The wooden battens, even in hot weather, were slippery enough to catch out the most experienced, evidenced by the amount of cursing and slippage which came from those, Michael apart, who would be rowing the cutter.

The way in to shore was fairly smooth and easy, given the tide was making and carrying them in—it would be a damn sight harder coming out. Before long, the tang of saltwater was overlaid with the smell of pine wafting out on the warmer air from the shore.

Maclehose moved to the prow, riding the swell and looking forward keenly for the first sight of a breaking wave, showing good sense when sighted. The news was whispered to the nearest oar, to be passed back to his captain, at which point both he and Oliphant took out their pistols. Should there be a shout, or any sign of a human presence, the orders had already been issued. At the sound of firing, the oars were to spin the boat and head fast for open water.

Soon they were in the breakers, white water requiring the oars to be well plied to keep the course straight. Michael O'Hagan ignored the notion of any danger to call out corrections, until the keel hit sand, a pair ordered into the water to keep the boat steady. Pearce made his way between the remainder to follow Maclehose in jumping on to sand, a hand held out to help Oliphant, with O'Hagan coming ashore as well to whisper a farewell.

'Sure, don't you be taking on the whole Jacobin army, John Boy, heathens that they are.'

'I won't. Look after the lad, Michael.'

'Don't need much of it' was imparted over his shoulder.

'You're on enemy territory, Mr Maclehose. How does that feel?'

'Exhilarating, sir.'

'I hope we shall see you tomorrow night. You know what to look out for?'

'Aye aye, sir.'

'Then be on your way.'

Pearce and Oliphant crossed the narrow strip of sloping sand to enter the trees, there being no intention to go farther till daylight. As usual, when left with time to talk about things inconsequential, the conversation was stilted, driving home how little they had in common.

Chapter Thirteen

A covered moon meant total darkness, fortunately rare. When the cloud cleared to show no more than a sliver of moon, Pearce kept himself awake by observing the night sky. As ever he felt, and he had done this as a boy, deep awe at the dense mass of the Milky Way, lying like a carpet across the heavens. An incalculable number of pinpoints of light, beset with shooting stars, leaving him feeling something more than insignificant in the face of such celestial majesty.

It was a thing many times experienced but, in recollection, if nights spent in the open loomed large, they were the exception not the rule, an occasional summer necessity when parental plans failed. Most were spent as the guest of people, from the merely curious about Adam Pearce's radical ideas, to outright supporters of his view of a corrupt society in desperate need of change. By a warm fire, he'd often listened as father and host discussed their polemical views.

Winters were no time to be on the road, so they were spent in London, where Adam would meet with his fellow radicals and those who would print his pamphlets. The main venue for such was the Grecian Coffee House, a place his father termed as the beating heart of agitation for change. John sat with him, much indulged and allowed an occasional interjection in what could be heated discussions. If there was one thing he knew only too well, it was no two radicals ever agreed on everything. Too often this extended to nothing.

If there was one unifying position, outright atheists aside, it lay within the tenets of what the religious opposition called Deism. He recalled clearly one discussion he'd been allowed to participate in, being as he was on the verge of manhood, which took place only weeks before both he and his father were arrested and ended up in the Fleet Prison.

It centred on the notion that to believe in God did not oblige a man or woman to subscribe to the Thirty-Nine Articles of the Anglican faith, even less to bow the knee to the despotism of Popery. Man could reason what was right and wrong, without instruction from any institutions, or those who claimed a divine access to the Creator. In the Grecian Coffee House, all religions were held to have become an arm of political tyranny.

This supported a world which saw bishops who only could minister to their so-called flock while living in palaces. Likewise, hypocritical divines, down to individual parish priests, ate heartily and well while their poorer parishioners wondered where their next meal was to come from, and often it never arrived. Odd, those who often objected vehemently to Adam's speeches tended the most downtrodden, wrapped in a superstition bred into them from birth. They were the ones who threw mud.

It was, as ever, circular reflections, images of faces and locations, cramped houses most often. There had been manors occasionally and on one occasion, a night spent in a proper Palladian mansion, the property of a titled and wealthy abolitionist, the horrors of the slave trade knowing few boundaries. Snatches of remembered dialogue coursed in a jumble through his mind until, eventually, it became a source of frustration. John Pearce, unlike father Adam, was a man who wanted hard solutions, not speculations based on hope.

A band of clear sky produced sufficient light to allow him to see more than just the outline of his companion, sat like him, with his back to a pine tree. Oliphant, who aboard ship seemed wedded to his cot, had nodded off, his head falling on to his chest. This annoyed Pearce, the message being he was the one to ensure they were not surprised.

Yet there was an animal quality to the man, the kind of alertness to sound shown by cats and dogs. A hand rustling of the pine needles and leafage which carpeted the forest floor caused him to jerk upright, grabbing the sword by his side, to appear fully awake.

'Was that you, Pearce?'

Tempted to play the innocent as he was, the reply was blunt. 'I observed you depending on me to keep you alive.'

'Which I will never do on terra firma. My hearing is acute and I rely on it always.'

'You see no need to stay alert then?'

'The circumstances permit it. Unless our arrival has been anticipated, there is no reason for anyone to be about. If there were, we would have been taken on the beach. As for the woods, anyone within would be blundering about in pitch darkness, making sound enough to match a charging boar, while providing ample time to react.'

'And on sand?'

'I would still hear them, indeed, I would do so if they walked on water.'

'Well, I shall trust to my eyes and would be obliged if you would do so too.'

'You may request it, Pearce, but we're not aboard ship now.'

There was no need to say more. What had been building for weeks was now a fact; they were equals and Pearce could no more order Oliphant to any act than the sod could to instruct him. The sensible thing pointed towards acknowledgment and seeking to find a way of working harmoniously, yet he could not bring himself to do it. He could reason with himself, in the silence that followed the exchange, the position taken by him was sound.

All he had to do was recall the way Oliphant had behaved when a matter went wrong on their previous combined endeavour, the need to avoid pursuit as well as conjure up a way to get back to England. He had never been open about either his intentions or his need to think for both, always putting his own survival first. He would, there could be no doubt, do likewise here and now.

It was not difficult to conjure up scenarios where he would be left in the lurch, concerns he was still chasing in the face of increasing daylight. He didn't reckon Oliphant would deliberately endanger him, on the good grounds he'd risk his own person. But would he act to save him by sacrificing himself? On what he knew of the man, the answer was a resounding no.

Breakfast was a bite of cheese and no more than a sip of wine, given it tended to induce rather than assuage thirst. Examining his companion gave Pearce some notion of how he himself looked, showing little signs of an uncomfortable night and, since both men had shaved before leaving the ship, little telltale growth of a night spent in the open.

Setting off through the trees quickly brought them to open country, the line of pines lacking depth, just enough planted to break the fierce Atlantic winds which would regularly strike such a coast. The field before them was full of wheat swaying on a light breeze and, out of habit, Pearce picked at a head of corn, crushing it between his fingers to reckon it long past the time to harvest.

'Where did you learn to deduce such a thing?'

'Wandering through summer fields, Oliphant. Now I suggest we skirt the crop, for to walk through it will leave an easy-to-see trail, one that will be visible for days.'

This they did, moving gently uphill, repeated whenever they came to another field, many without any kind of crop, yet also unploughed and again remarked upon by Pearce. The only sounds to accompany their progress was the buzzing of insects and the singing of the birds, they momentarily silent when these humans came close, with the odd startled pigeon causing alarm as it noisily exited a leafy tree.

If there was nothing in the fields the land was clearly fecund, there being, on a gently rising slope, small orchards, though the apples looked to have suffered from various diseases like scab. There were quantities of figs and plums, as well as hedges full of edible berries which Pearce, to the annoyance of Oliphant, kept stopping to pick. What was missing was humanity, people working what must be productive land, the impression hard to avoid of it being left untended.

'Where is everyone?' Pearce asked, after he'd bitten into a windfall plum, the juice of which took a swift hand to wipe away.

'Still abed, if they have any sense' came with a yawn.

'It is at this time of day, the workers are already long in the fields, which you would know if you'd spent any time in the country.'

The comment brought no response for, in passing through rows of vines, also in need of attention, they'd crested a rise to show rolling undulating scenery. Below them lay the valley of the River Bidassoa and the outline of the town of Hendaye, with the arc of a long and sandy beach on the shoreline running to the estuary.

The Spanish side rose to be equally hilly as the spot where they stood, while off to the east lay the high Pyrenees. Between them and the outline of the town, there being no sign of activity on what was still open country, certainly nothing military, Pearce posed his opinion.

'I'm bound to ask if we've seen enough.'

'We've seen nothing and no one, not even, as you pointed out, any peasants.'

'Which tells us there's no army camped near the border. Clearly the French feel no threat of a new war anytime soon.'

'I would imagine any concentration to be farther back.'

'We've seen no evidence of that either.'

'I think we require a closer look at what's in the town.'

'Not an easy place to approach without being seen.'

'Then,' Oliphant declared, 'let us not try to avoid it.'

Without waiting for agreement, he strode out along the crest, leaving Pearce no choice but to follow him, while thinking he was replicating the actions of the mad March Hare. Here the fields were unsown and dusty, much cratered, crisscrossed with the remains of trench lines and hastily thrown-up earth bastions, with evidence of destruction to both.

'Overrun by the look of it' was Oliphant's opinion.

Pearce produced a telescope to examine what lay ahead, remarking on tricolour hanging limp over what could be some kind of citadel, whatever it was surrounded by the outline of incomplete buildings, which rendered it indistinct.

'A flag which implies some sort of governance,' Oliphant decided.

Pearce looked over the far bank, to suggest the devastation to the landscape had been replicated on the southern side, evidence of hard-fought battles for control of the estuary, but again, not much sign of human activity. Moving on they came to where the first houses in the town should have stood, which would have been little more than wattle-and-daub structures framed in wood. Now they were rubble, while what wood remained was charred.

'You still see a need to carry on?' Pearce asked.

'You may remain here if you wish.'

This was accompanied by a challenging look, responded to with a shake of the head. Oliphant undid his sword belt and then delved into his satchel to produce, much to the surprise of his companion, a tricolour sash of the kind worn by Revolutionary functionaries. Slung over one shoulder and looped round his waist, it was knotted to one side and kept secure by his sword belt. The tall hat on his head seemed to complete the ensemble.

'I daresay, after your time in Paris, you will have seen one of these, Pearce.'

'What a magician you are to produce such a thing' was a less-than-sterling endorsement. 'I cannot but think you waited till now, so as to enjoy a greater degree of surprise.'

'I show a degree of foresight, only to be accused of trickery.'

The statement might have had some depth if it had not been accompanied by a smirk, soon replaced by an irritating schoolmasterly tone.

'With this we have no need to sneak around, which is a bad idea anyway. Nothing creates more suspicion than skulking about. Now let us be going on.'

The narrow, sloping streets had been cleared of rubble, but the damage proved more severe as the buildings increased in both dimensions and impairment. Progress was far from silent, their boots striking the cobbled pavé, to echo off what walls remained. The only warm-blooded creatures encountered were mangy dogs, animals who would either stare at them silently or ignore their presence as they scrabbled in the debris for something their sense of smell told them might be edible.

For human nostrils it was dust, plus the odd rotting odour of what was likely a hidden corpse. On reaching the edge of what looked to be the main square, they were faced with a large but less than whole cathedral. Certainly, if it had possessed a spire, it lacked a whole one now.

'No one about here either,' Oliphant said in a quiet voice. 'The place is deserted.'

'*Arretez.*'

As both turned to face the command, Pearce murmured, 'So much for your acute hearing.'

The unshaven pair they faced were clad in what passed for uniforms, if this could be said to include garments which approximated to rags. There was a vestige of a blue coat, much faded now, on one. The other had on a sort of smock over tattered leggings, no stockings and footwear badly scuffed enough to match his companion's worn boots. What they did have were levelled muskets, added to a look of the resolve required to use them.

'You took your time to do your duty,' Oliphant barked in French. 'Half the Spanish army could have marched through the town before you pair stirred. I've a good mind to send you to the guillotine.'

The tone was so unexpected, not least by John Pearce, it had these scruffy specimens blink, to then look these apparitions up and down with an uncertain air. Before them stood a pair of healthy and well-fed-looking creatures, dressed in good-quality clothing, which included fine if dusty footwear.

In the case of Oliphant, it was accompanied by an imperious look and a commanding tone. There was, as well, the tricolour sash he wore, a known symbol of authority, set off by a sword hilt no longer seemingly too decorative. It now appeared fitting to the impression Oliphant was setting out to create.

'Damnit, are you deaf as well as stupid?' Blue-coat mumbled something incomprehensible, which got him another blast. 'Put up those weapons. Given the look of you, they're not safe in your hands.'

All John Pearce could do was add a supportive glare as Oliphant closed with the pointing barrels, to brush both aside. The exchange which followed was a master class in bluff, as the two were mercilessly interrogated. This included references to Paris and he being a representative on mission. It also established the one in the less-than-inspiring blue coat, though there were no marks to prove it, held the rank of sergeant.

Their commander was a lieutenant, he in his quarters within the main fortification. This sat on the riverbank, to which Oliphant was directed with much finger pointing, musket muzzles now aiming at the ground. He then demanded to know if there were other pickets on duty to guard against the Spanish.

'Why, monsieur, we are at peace.'

'Then why are you two on patrol?'

'To prevent looting.'

Oliphant actually laughed. 'There's nothing left to loot.'

'For a man or woman starving, there may be something.'

'We've seen no one.'

'You may not see them, monsieur, but there are children here.'

'You're afraid of children?'

'They are growing to manhood and useful with the knife.'

'Mothers and fathers?'

'The women stay away. The menfolk were conscripted, so are either dead or still with the army.'

The head swivelled to encompass the surrounding destruction, before the sergeant spat into the dust.

'I require you to accompany me. Clochard, the telescope.'

It took Pearce a moment to realise it was he being addressed and in the same tone as this pair of unfortunates. It was as if Oliphant was talking to a servant, even to the point of being accompanied by a click of his fingers. This was no time for ruffled feathers, so a lip had to be bitten. The instrument was taken from his satchel to be passed over, snatched from his hand as the sod marched off, Pearce and the two ragamuffins trailing in his wake.

Closer to the river the defences were more substantial, not least the citadel. There was an open glacis betwixt riverbank and the fortress battlements, these sloping inwards to deflect the effect of cannon fire. Triangular protruding bastions created a star-like structure, which exposed an attacking enemy to deadly crossfire.

Even so the walls had suffered more from bombardment than the rest of the town, but being of a solid stone structure, had survived to remain intact. This was not replicated by what lay on the southern bank, an extensively damaged fortress of a more medieval design, less able to stand the effect of shot and shell.

Both presented evidence of a long and sustained artillery duel, in which the Spaniards had come off second best. An arched bridge, there to facilitate cross-border trade, was missing its central span, no doubt blown up for safety. A string of boats, which had become detached, were floating against the French bank, the remains of a pontoon structure. The planking which had formed a footbridge, which would have allowed the French army to cross, were now somewhere out in the Bay of Biscay.

Oliphant had the telescope to his eye, weaving it right and left but saying nothing, like some commanding general. He then handed it to Pearce, asking him for an appreciation, in a way that brought on a cheering thought: The man had no idea how to properly use the damn thing. Taking it and making the required adjustments, Pearce ran it over the shattered buildings of the Spanish town of Irun, but there was a difference. The fortifications on the southern bank had been roughly repaired, though he could see no evidence of their being manned.

'Your officer' came as yet another peremptory command, once Pearce had outlined what he'd seen. 'Take me to him.'

This had the telescope drop, Pearce turning to stare. He then had to compose his features in a more suitable expression, the two layabouts being present. What was Oliphant about and why was he making such a demand without prior discussion? It was clear the sergeant was struggling to know how to respond, which got him another blast.

'Don't dither, man.'

He nodded, turned to his inferior, to instruct him to return to their previous beat while he was absent. The expression this engendered, even if it was accompanied by agreement, hinted differently. Pearce guessed, once his sergeant was out of sight, he was going to find somewhere to hide. He was not going to hang about to face alone the knives of the rat-like local youths.

As they trudged along the riverbank, Oliphant dropped back to increase the distance between them and their escort, which allowed for a quiet if less-than-civil exchange.

'You need to think on your feet in such situations, Pearce, don't you know that?'

'Don't patronise me. If you're going to be thinking on your feet, recall there are four on this mission, not two.'

'Do you disagree with what I'm doing?'

'The chance to do so was never presented.'

'It must be galling to have the shoe on the other foot.'

It's difficult to continue an argument in whispers, so Pearce decided against even trying, given Oliphant was obviously paying him back for what he saw as previous slights. Anyway, there was no time. Before them lay the main entrance to the fortress, the façade showing much scarring, where both shells and musket balls had struck stone. Access was over a lowered drawbridge, which had upon it a couple of sentries, in tattered uniforms not so very different from their escort's.

'You've easily managed to overawe our friend up ahead,' Pearce whispered. 'You may find the man who commands him a different challenge.'

'One I think we can meet.'

'And if you can't?'

Pearce, who had emphasised the "you," was now wishing they'd primed and loaded their pistols before setting out from the shoreline, taking the risk they might accidentally discharge, always possible when they were not actually in the hand. Too late now, all he had was his sword. Reverting to French, Oliphant addressed the sentries in the same domineering manner, a demand one of them appraise their officer of visitors from Paris, demanding to see him.

Pearce could not help but think, if he'd addressed a British soldier in such a tone, he'd be more likely to get a boot up his arse than acquiescence. From his knowledge of the French, they were even more given to challenging authority than the sons of Britannia, but not this pair. One came close to a salute, spun round, and went through the arch of thick stone.

While he was gone Oliphant produced a good impression of impatience, huffing and puffing as he paced to and fro, this accompanied by several glares at the archway. Pearce remained stoical but apprehensive, his hand on his sword hilt, even when the messenger reappeared and invited them to follow him.

Once inside, they crossed a cobbled courtyard and were then led through a series of narrow corridors and stone staircases, to end up in a circular room, sun streaming through the narrow embrasures, lighting what were bare floorboards. There was a desk and chair, as well as a tricolour flag on a pole, but no evidence of paperwork, even if there was a quill and an inkwell.

The fellow who entered through a second door was in the process of trying to do up his less-than-clean uniform coat. Behind him, before the door was pulled shut, Pearce saw an unmade bed, carelessly scattered clothing, and what appeared to be several empty wine bottles littering the floor. In some measure the lieutenant who'd occupied it matched the disorder, appearing to be no spring chicken. He had pepper-and-salt hair and a slack jaw, with a much-lined, broken-veined, and vinous face.

Given the hand-trembling mess he was making with his buttons, it indicated a fellow not wedded to sobriety but, as he came closer the impression of someone aged diminished: If he was not young, closer examination indicated his habits had done more to add years to his appearance than time.

The first brusque questions from Oliphant established his name as Arnaud, his rank of lieutenant confirmed. He commanded no more than a much-depleted half company of men, his task to patrol the border between the coast and the inland town of Biriatou. From there to the Pass of Roncevaux, the mountains formed an impassable barrier. This established, he began a litany of complaints about his shortage of men for such a task as well as the lack of supplies from the army quartermaster, this abruptly cut off by Oliphant.

'We require a report on the state of matters in your area of command.'

'There is little to report.' This came with an inquisitive look, albeit a nervous one, to which was added, 'Which is what I have passed up to the regional command in Toulouse. Would I be permitted to enquire, monsieur, who is asking?'

Oliphant reached into his satchel and produced a folded document, which had Pearce again wondering what he was up to. This turned to a real jolt when he heard the reply.

'My credentials, Lieutenant, from the Minister of War, who wishes for an independent account regarding the border. Minister Carnot needs to reference it to those he is getting from the army command, which he does not trust.'

The surprise to Pearce was this elderly-for-his-rank French officer showed none, indeed he came close to a confirming nod. The paper was taken into one less-than-steady hand, the seals and signature examined by bleary eyes, and, unaware at least one of his visitors had his heart in his mouth, handed back.

'Can I offer you some wine, messieurs?'

Chapter Fourteen

'I still cannot believe you got away with such a farrago. It was beyond credibility from start to finish.'

'And yet, here we are, on our way back to the beach.'

'The chances of it going wrong were obvious.'

For much of the way, the chance to talk had been curtailed by a quartet of escorts provided for them by Arnaud, not that such scruffy specimens gave any sense of security. For them, the description slovenly appeared as flattery, but they did represent what they'd been told about the state of the border forces. In this sector they were no more, most of the battalions sent off several months past to fight the Austrians in Italy.

Once they'd cleared the ruins of Hendaye, Oliphant peremptorily dismissed them, which left Pearce continuing to reflect on what had just occurred. His nerves were still a touch rattled, even if they had gleaned more than could have been hoped for on coming ashore. Though Arnaud was careful not to name or condemn anyone, he as good as admitted desertion, coupled with abject leadership, had reduced what was left of the army of Roussillon to a rabble, of which the men he led stood as ample proof.

At this point Oliphant had thumped the deck so hard the inkwell jumped, though not as much as the withered lieutenant. Wine had stilled his alcoholic trembling with the first hastily downed goblet, but it returned fully as Oliphant, roundly and loudly, cursed the people sending false reports to the Minister of War. This was delivered in such a way as to make it seem as if the man was personally responsible. A poor specimen considering his rank, Arnaud became more and more loquacious, and less discreet, the more wine he consumed.

His goblet was never empty for long and, the more this so-called representative from Paris harangued him, the quicker it was despatched, till he became eager to anticipate each question put to him, all the while subjected to the same badgering and hectoring manner. He was fearful clearly of losing his posting but, at times, it seemed to John Pearce, as if he was in as much fear of his very life.

The Spanish had re-formed in his sector, moved back to hold their side of the border. As was visible, they'd repaired their defences, albeit showing no sign of aggressive intent. Once the work was complete, they had withdrawn a full league to comply with the terms of the treaty they'd signed. There was no reason to believe this did not also apply on the Catalonian flank of the mountains.

As to the blown bridge, one of the few questions Pearce managed to get in, this had been left in disrepair for reasons the lieutenant could not explain. The Spaniards had shown no sign of seeking to replace the central arch, while he would have needed the engineers to carry out the work when none existed. They too had marched off to Italy, and, besides, there were crossings farther upriver.

The lack of humanity in the countryside they'd passed through, as well as the uncultivated fields, was caused by conscription. Every able-bodied man who could be found had been drafted into the army under the 1793 *levee en masse*, this instituted by the very same Lazare Carnot Oliphant now claimed to represent. A Jacobin politician and regicide, cum-soldier of outstanding revolutionary zeal, he was famed for an intolerance of failure.

The Frenchman showed no surprise when told his visitors had come by ship, which came close to having Pearce wonder at his sanity, nor did he show any guarded reaction when told they were now going to re-join their vessel, which could only be put down to his fear.

Farewells were stiff and formal from his visitors, Arnaud near to grovelling, hinting he might deserve a good word put in for his honesty. He having accompanied them to the gate, they were now traversing the fields and hedgerows they'd passed through that morning, with Oliphant showing no willingness to acknowledge the risks he'd taken, in fact the reverse.

'Trust I know my game as well as you know yours, Pearce.'

'If the man had not been such a dolt and a drunkard, we could have ended up against a wall and shot. A lot of good your damn sash would have done you against a file of muskets.'

'The damn sash, as you call it, made what I've just accomplished possible.'

The look of disdain this produced, which should have irritated Oliphant, instead seemed to amuse him, so it was Pearce who found his bile rising. Too long a time spent in imminent expectation of summary execution failed to leave him feeling benign towards his companion, not helped by the abrupt nature of the following enquiry.

'How much do you know of what happened in the Pyrenees war?'

'Clearly not as much as you.'

'Which tells me you took no trouble to find out.'

'And you did' was a growl. 'Recall the difficulties I was obliged to deal with in the time available.'

'Of course, I did' was larded with impatience and not a jot of acknowledgment. 'London is full of French *emigres*, many of whom know me as sound in their cause. They are a good source of intelligence, admittedly not often the most up-to-date, given the time any letters take to get to London.'

'Letters?' Pearce asked, more to gain time than as a genuine query. A notion had surfaced that required examination before he could nail a way to pursue it. 'So they told you to don your sash?'

'It's a trick I've used before, one I know works. I had good reason to think its employment here would serve. Nothing in the France of the Revolution comes close to conferring such power.'

'I know a great deal of its power.'

He declined to add, it had been worn by the men who'd condemned and then guillotined his father, but it also set in train a recollection of time he returned to Paris to try to save him. Hanging around in the taverns surrounding the prison in which Pearce senior was being held, son John recalled the kind of people who filled them. There were the usual loud talkers, of course, but more who were silent, having either a shifty or a villainous appearance. Still seeking to nail the train of thought, he stopped by a fig tree.

'And no one I've ever seen wearing one has been other than a murderous scoundrel.'

'I know your opinion of me is low, but surely . . .' The pause took Oliphant's gaze to the way Pearce had stopped and was filling his satchel. 'What are you about?'

'Picking figs.'

'Why?'

'For the crew. The diet of the common seaman varies little and is inclined to render them costive. I shall give these to Mr Cullen, which will save him the need to use his probes.'

'It would serve better to stick to the subject than that which has to clear a sailor's blocked arse.'

'Picking fruit does not debar me from listening to what you gleaned from your *emigres*.'

Another man would have possibly stayed silent; not Oliphant, he was too busy with puffed pride.

'The original campaign was a disaster. The first general to command the armies on this part of the border was an old sod, an ex-Royal officer in his seventies apparently. Lost a couple of minor battles and put a gun to his head in ninety-three, no doubt driven to it by fear of what might come by staying alive. And he had good cause; his replacement was guillotined a year later for the same kind of failures.'

'Loping of the heads of unsuccessful soldiers became quite common, especially under Robespierre.'

'Precisely. But tell me, who sent him to his death?' The sash was tugged to drive home the coming point. 'The local representatives on mission wielded untrammelled power in some regions. I was told this was one of them.'

Oliphant rambled on as they moved towards the pines masking the beach, showing away to Pearce's mind at the things he'd ferreted out. Jacobin fanatics with a complete lack of any military ability, appointing and dismissing a string of commanders that, unbelievably, had included a pair of rabid revolutionary doctors, with no military experience and predictable results. Time and again the French had been routed, which resulted in even more changes of command, until finally Paris intervened to appoint a proper general.

'All very interesting' was delivered in a bored voice as they entered the strip of trees.

'The fear has not gone away and nor has the guillotine. One word from the right quarter can cost you your head. Our drunkard back there in Hendaye knows and is in terror of it.'

'The document you showed him?'

'A forgery, but a good one. I had it drawn up for me in London by another Frenchman, one adept at such things. If Arnaud had ever seen Carnot's signature and seal, which I doubt, it would have passed muster down to the very paper on which it was written. I copied it from the one you were given in the Temple.'

'Which you told me you left in Calais, with the woman you called Marie.'

'Let's say I had a change of mind, thinking it would be more use to me than her.'

'Why don't you just admit you lied?'

'You're so sure I did?'

'Going on past behaviour, I don't doubt it for a second.'

Tempted to curse the man, Pearce was well aware there was little point. It was just another example of the way Oliphant operated. The pass had been given to him, in Paris, by Régis de Cambacérès, ostensibly as an act of generosity. Instead, it had been designed as a trap and, by the time it was removed, it had both succeeded and ceased to be of use.

'What if I did? You don't come across such a windfall very day,' Oliphant added. 'Since I hoped for future employment, it made sense to keep it.'

They were on the beach now, Pearce naturally searching for any sign of HMS *Hazard*, glad there was none. 'Am I right in assuming this was planned before we left the ship?'

'Not planned, it never can be. You will recall I kept the sash hidden until we were sure there was no military force of any size in the vicinity.'

'And if there had been?'

'I would have advised an immediate return to the beach. There could only be one reason to maintain a strong presence on the border, the fear of Spanish duplicity, which would go some way to answering Dundas's confusions.'

'We best gather the means to make a fire.'

There was a long time to wait before the flints could be usefully employed, time for Pearce to cogitate on what Oliphant had told him on the way, conversation no more flowing than it had been the night before. Besides, the sod had nodded off again, annoying because it never seemed to occur to him his companion had also gone without sleep the night before and was more in need than he.

Pearce was no stranger to doing without: It was the lot of every naval officer, even more so a commander, given the vagaries of wind and weather. Yet sleep would have been hard to come by given the thoughts churning round his head. The more he recalled what had been said, as well as the way Oliphant had behaved, it pointed to certain possibilities regarding the man's past, coupled with what he'd so recently witnessed.

It was partly the manner in which Régis de Cambacérès had addressed him as Bertrand, confident in having recognised a fellow he knew well. Also, there had been no denial, not even a hint of surprise or any attempt to question the appellation, this from a man who was not only a highly placed revolutionary, but another one of the regicides who'd voted for the execution of King Louis.

Mixed with this was his reference to the French *emigres*, hoping to see out the mayhem in France by eking out a living in England. Few had got out with the means to exist in comfort and had long outlived their initial warm welcome. They were now generally seen as pests and, with the nation at war, untrustworthy to boot. Several of their number had been told to find another place of refuge, either on the Continent or the newly formed United States.

This was not the only overt threat to their peaceful well-being. Ever since the first aristocrats had fled across the Channel, a certain fate had followed. Bloodcurdling promises had come from Paris to say they were not safe, the Revolution had a long and murderous reach and would find them wherever they cowered. Oliphant knew them, he had said so and they'd given him the intelligence he'd just employed.

But this raised the question: Why would a group of people, surely suspicious of anyone not of their nationality and class, trust him? For a second time his mind was taken back to the streets and watering holes surrounding the massive stone bulk of the Conciergerie. The one-time fortress had become both a prison for the enemies of the people and home to the murderers who would condemn them. There was no trial in the accepted sense: If you came before the Tribunal, you were guilty.

But within the prison, there would be those who hoped for rescue, and surely the means to effect it existed. The warder who controlled access to the prison had been a man who could be bribed, though how far he would go and for what price, Pearce never got the chance to establish. Perhaps others had, like some of those filling the places where folk gathered in the surrounding streets.

They would not all be boastful merchants or traders satisfying their needs in food and drink. Some would be ghouls, come to see the inmates harangued, because the members of the Tribunal put on a show for their supporters. Every one of the accused was treated to a whole series of bile-filled rants regarding the past oppressions and depredations before being "justly" condemned to the guillotine. The ghouls would then follow the tumbril to the Place de la Revolution, to witness them pay the price.

Some of the people Pearce had sat alongside were very different. They were the ones who sat in sober silence or exchanged discreet, whispered conversations behind raised hands. Did they have more dubious motives for proximity to such an obscene place as the Conciergerie and the proceedings taking place within?

Had Oliphant been one of them? He certainly fitted the pattern of a conspirator, evident from the moment they'd contrived to be captured on French soil months past. It might only be retrospective in realisation, but even then, there had been an air about the man, of knowing more than he was prepared to be open about. This had, subsequently, been proven without question, as they were forced to flee Gravelines.

The use of the tricolour sash, the brio with which he had bullied, first the two men who accosted them, then their commander, could not be sudden inspiration. It was a tactic and one which looked to be well-honed. If it had been employed before, and Oliphant had admitted it was so, where and how often were obvious questions?

Hallowell would be bringing *Hazard* closer to the shore, so any fire they lit could be visible from the tops. The mixture of cloud and clear sky having lasted into a second day, too often there was the near-blinding glare of the setting sun, shining on the shore, which postponed the time when lighting their signal fire would be effective. This lengthened the time Pearce had for his cogitations, rendering them increasingly unsettling.

Never a man to be happy remaining merely curious, Pearce reckoned it was time to beard his companion, to find out some of the truths Oliphant, or was it really Bertrand, was determined to conceal. The toe of his boot hitting the sole of his companion brought him sharply awake, to ask if it was time, only to appear cross when he saw the unlit faggots. He was even more discomfited by the question posed.

'Since I've been forced to remain awake, I was brought to wonder how many people you managed to spirit out of France.'

'You would have been better employed catching up on your sleep' came the reply accompanied with a slow and annoying smile.

'I hope you're not going to deny it to be a game in which you were at one time engaged.'

'I would say the game you're playing reeks of an overexcitable imagination.'

'While I would posit what we require to do next will be many times more dangerous than that which we've just been about. I would also point out, I'm not prepared to go ashore over the border, to suddenly find a repeat of that just experienced, and I will go alone if necessary.'

'You would be foolish to do so, Pearce. And by what right do you even suggest it?'

'Self-preservation will serve and the fact you can only get off the ship with my permission. I require to know who it is I'm with and if this adds any additional risks to what is already a dangerous task.'

'And if I think you're bluffing?'

'You'd be making a mistake. "Trust I know what I'm doing," you said. How can I when things are sprung on me without warning.'

'Sometimes it's the only safe thing to do.'

'No more. If you have some kind of stratagem up your sleeve, I need to know of it before it's employed.'

'Not possible. Much of what needs to be done to stay safe is only possible on the wing.'

'So, tell me about yourself and trust to my discretion to keep it secret, or . . .'

'The question about rescuing people. Where did that come from?'

'Deduction and certain places and things I witnessed in Paris after war was declared, especially around the Conciergerie.'

Mention of the place changed both Oliphant's demeanour and the nature of the conversation: Now it was him asking questions. He listened in silence as each was answered, which included the thoughts Pearce had been ruminating on since they'd regained the beach, as well as the things he'd recalled having seen.

Oliphant wanted to know how he'd got to France and, even more, to Paris at a time when it seemed every citizen of the country was mired in suspicion, what had been his aim as well as the fatal outcome.

'You know Cambacérès is a regicide? He's also a member of the Directory.'

'I do, he was kind in the matter of my father's body and his burial, he arranged a plot in St Sulpice, instead of a mass grave.'

The look this engendered led to a query. 'You know of his inclinations?'

'He makes no attempt to disguise them, does he? Not that he pressed them on me.'

It ended with the man deep in thought and saying nothing for what felt like an age, this with daylight fading, until he said, 'Light the fire.'

By the time the boat hove to offshore, Pearce had been told much of what he wanted to know. Not everything, this was clear, but it nailed the dual identities. Oliphant was the name of his father, Bertrand of his French mother, whose father had been a tax farmer under King Louis.

Pearce required no telling, as a breed, they were among the most hated men in France, more so than any monarch, duke, or marquis.

Buying the right to tax a certain province from the King's Minister of Finance, they then set out to make a profit on their investment, which could only come from a more rapacious application of the amounts collected. Along with this came an intolerant attitude to the inability to pay, even in times of poor harvests. In danger of the guillotine, it was the need to rescue him which brought his grandson into a conspiracy to spirit him out of France, one in which he succeeded.

When this became known, the pleas to help others were hard to ignore, so what followed was several clandestine crossings to save others. This was achieved by the distribution of a great deal of money in bribes, the use of disguises, and endless skin-of-the-teeth encounters.

'Until finally I was caught,' he said, as they walked to the shoreline.

'Yet you're alive. How can that be?'

'It was not by luck' came out as larded with regret, but in the dark, Pearce could not be sure he'd got the tone right. 'And from there, I will say no more.'

Sat in the thwarts and in an enforced silence, there was time to reflect and examine Oliphant's explanation, to conclude it would be wise not to believe every word of a man who'd proved to be expert at dissimulation. The sound of the bosun's whistle welcoming him back aboard was cheering. Who would have thought he would ever take it as a sign of his coming home?

'Welcome back, sir,'

'Thank you, Mr Hallowell. You will be pleased to know we have enjoyed some success.'

Which got a look of anticipation from his premier, obviously expecting both more detail and inclusion as to what was to follow.

'For now, a southerly course would suit us best, but there's no need to crack on.'

'Aye, sir' was the response as Pearce turned to say quietly to Oliphant, 'I suggest my cabin at the next bell. We need to discuss what is to happen next.'

'Surely it's obvious?'

'To you perhaps, but not to me.'

'We are required to go on.'

'I would not question what you say. It's the how that matters.'

Hallowell more than most, given the knowledge he had, was afire to know what was being discussed as the hours went by and the bells reputedly rang. When his captain finally came back on deck, any hope he might learn was soon dashed, the orders he was given providing no clue.

'First thing in the morning, I wish the ship's disguise to be dismantled. Let us get the proper ensign at the masthead so we can return to what we are. And ask Mr Williams to lay us a course to close San Sebastian.'

'Aye aye, sir.'

'Also, I wish the guns to be loaded and ready to fire and then the run up to closed gunports.'

Chapter Fifteen

Not many men could have imposed themselves on a ship carrying a crew of over five hundred souls as quickly as Jaleel Tolland, though he did set out with certain advantages. First, he had the physical ability to establish himself as the hardest bargain aboard HMS *Bedford*, this followed by admiration for the stoic way he took the lash.

More vital was his being the head of a gang of smugglers, pressed with him into the seventy-four gunner, half of whom shared in the same watch. They naturally looked to him for leadership and would, without question, do his bidding. But most of all he was ruthless and clear sighted.

Knowing what he sought, it then only required he put in place a plan to achieve his aim, one that would need to evade too much scrutiny by the ship's officers. His main weapon was fear seconded by agitation, carried out by his less imposing but suave brother, Franklin, regarding the conditions in which the crew lived, aided by the station the fleet was covering.

They were beating to and fro off Texel, the largest of a string of islands protecting Antwerp. The capital of the Dutch, now Batavian Republic, was the base of what was now an enemy fleet. More tellingly, they were sailing the North Sea, so even in high summer, for every sunny day, there were half a dozen of grey cloud. Nor did the season obviate the likelihood of a full northeasterly or Atlantic gale, the latter very often accompanied by drenching downpours.

Monotony was the bedrock of the task, patrolling endlessly the same stretch of cold, grey water, necessary in keeping the Dutch bottled up to protect the convoys of merchantmen sailing to and from the Baltic. The supplies they carried were vital to the war effort and the nation, especially naval stores, pitch, turpentine, masts, and spars being the most obvious.

Changes of course were consistent and short-lived, as Admiral Duncan took his ships a few miles north, then reversed course to sail the same few miles south, the flags of the inshore squadron watched carefully for any sign of an impending threat. It was the task of these frigates to cover the multiple exits the Dutch could use to get their battle fleet to sea.

For this, the enemy required the wind to blow strongly from the east or northeast, which had the added advantage of forcing Duncan away from his close blockade, providing them with an opportunity for a successful engagement. The fact they'd showed no sign of doing so for months on end provided ideal conditions to stir up resentments: Any prospect of a fleet action had long been discounted by both officers and men.

Supplies from the port of Harwich being less than regular, food for the crew was the same weekly diet of hardtack, lobscouse, salted beef, pork, peas, and duff and, as the unchanging weeks went by, neither the wardroom nor the great cabin fared much better. If this was true elsewhere, indeed, everywhere in the service where fresh food could not be brought from the shore, it had ever fostered complaint. Relief did come eventually, as individual ships were detached back to the Nore to make up their stores and undergo repairs.

HMS *Bedford* had only just returned from the fleet anchorage at the mouth of the River Medway, to a duty all aboard reckoned would be a wearisome repeat of what had gone before. This provided Franklin Tolland with fertile grounds to stir up resentments, like reminding the lower deck of the long-standing and major grievance: Their pay had not changed since the time of the second King Charles.

Already established as a man about whom it was wise to tiptoe, brother Jaleel needed to take general caution to a level of dread, to create a feeling to cross him was to risk your very life. His chance to drive this home came when the prevailing westerly brought not only an Atlantic gale but, more importantly, the aforementioned heavy rain. The wind and the constant need to trim sails kept the watch on deck and regularly sent the topmen aloft, while the downpour, which lasted all day and into the hours of darkness, soaked all aboard into the kind of misery which saps awareness.

Thus the murder of the bosun's mate, Farrier, who'd so energetically laid into Jaleel Tolland with the cat-o'-nine-tails, was not difficult. Nor, in truth, was it brought about by a desire for revenge, only the need for an example which would fit his purpose. When the time came, his smugglers formed something of a screen between themselves and the quarterdeck, hardly necessary with visibility severely curtained by the conditions. This applied to most of the watch on deck, while others who suspected something might be going on were adept at averting their gaze.

Franklin held the man's attention with a stream of abuse, hard words that saw a knotted starter raised to strike, so the older Tolland could knife him from behind, rapid stabs at his exposed side which were lethal, if not yet fatal. What did for him was the cold and heaving North Sea, his still-breathing body tipped over the side by men made strong from years at sea, as well as fights to keep alive their smuggling game. Much blood was spilled, but the lashing rain soon washed this through the scuppers, to leave a deck and hammock nettings lacking any trace of the crime. Eight bells saw Tolland and his watch back below and the gang in a huddle.

'Let it be known, quiet like, once the bastard's proper missed, how he met his end and why. And hint it will be the fate of any who cross me.'

Jaleel looked around the faces crowding the mess table, to be cheered by the grins and nods of men he knew he could rely on. In no time the rumour would be all over the ship, the only people left out the officers. Questions would be asked about the disappearance of Farrier, but men vanishing at sea and in a storm, if not a commonplace, was far from exceptional.

A second's carelessness could see a topman disappear into the sea on a dark night and even immediately hove to, he was unlikely to be sighted and rescued. Likewise, anyone going aloft by the shrouds from a heaving deck could be undone by a missed footing or a less than secure handhold, more likely to apply to skylarking midshipmen than long-serving hands. Also to be considered was a deliberate act, a man so struck with the black dog, he would see death by drowning as a way out of his misery.

So when the watch on duty were questioned and none was willing to give evidence of anything untoward, the loss was accepted as a not-uncommon event. The name of Farrier was entered in HMS *Bedford*'s log as "having expired in the execution of his duties."

To stay out of his own home and away from his brother-in-law had proved close to impossible, so Edward Druce took some respite from an enforced trip to Bath, given it relieved him of the necessity to contrive endless excuses. It could also, in some measure, be named an achievement. He'd managed to secure an interview with Admiral Lord Howe, granted on the grounds of the letter the old goat had been sent, regarding the threat to his own rewards in prize money.

Missives had gone out from a discomfited Howe to the various junior admirals he commanded on the Glorious First, as well as those officers he'd criticised for a lack of zeal, to his mind what he saw as a downright disobedience of clear orders. The group holding up proceedings in the Prize Court were now informed he would appear in person should any case require adjudication. Given his present unimpeachable stature, no one would dare challenge his word, which more or less guaranteed an end to fractious dispute.

He returned to find nothing had been done by Francis Ommaney to undermine him in his absence. So, with the success of his mission under his belt, as well as being more relaxed about the security of his position, he went home in a good mood. This was soon spoiled by Denby Carruthers and not merely because of his presence. As overbearing as ever, he batted away the very gentle hint the prurient gossip, which had made him a near-permanent guest, had surely died down by now.

It was plain he had no intention yet of a return to his own city abode. Nor did he, after dinner and over a decanter of port, show the slightest interest in what his host had been up to, which, given the pride taken in the outcome, rankled mightily. Having bemoaned his lot he then surprised Edward Druce by his raising the name and abilities of Walter Hodgson, which uncomfortably reminded Druce of many things he'd been able to park in limbo.

Any reference to the man made him uncomfortable anyway, nowhere more so than in the presence of his brother-in-law. It also brought home not a shred of information seemed to have come in from the man in his absence, which was also a worry.

'You actually wish to employ him?'

'I do.'

This put Druce immediately on his guard. It was nothing to do with the fact he had engaged Hodgson on his own enquiries, which, if successful, could be hoped to yield life-altering results. The reason his brother-in-law might want Hodgson's services were not hard to fathom, so his first thought was how to avoid personal engagement. It smelled of more spilled blood, and he already had suspicions enough to keep him awake at night.

'Do you wish me to let you know where he might be found?'

This got a surprised response. 'I have no wish to deal with him directly.'

'Why not?'

'Trust me when I say it would be best to do so at a distance.'

There was little need to enquire whom he expected to act as intermediary: The hard look Druce was getting left him in no doubt. This was soon replaced by one that sought to imply Denby was a soul much put upon, his voice almost a whinge.

'The matter is delicate for a man in my position. I require someone to do on my behalf, and in short order, something which I cannot do myself.'

'He moves around a great deal' was the first excuse to come to mind, though he was given no time to expand on it.

'Of which you're hardly required to remind me, considering how much of my money he wasted in his search for . . .' There was awkward pause then, clear evidence Carruthers did not want to employ Gherson's name. It was underlined by the slight reddening of his cheeks, which made what followed very feeble. 'You know of whom I speak.'

'You intend he should pursue the same task?'

'No, no, Druce. There, the matter is closed.'

As a clear lie it could hardly be bettered, yet it was not open to challenge, unless the whole tub of worms concerning the murder of his wife were laid bare. There arose, once more, the feeling of being trapped, yet so too did all the reasons he acted as a buffer for Denby in the past. The way to avoid a repeat lay to hand in being candid, but so did the risks.

'What is it you wish Hodgson to do now?'

'I think I have had a ship, as well as its cargo, stolen from under me.'

That was a surprise. 'Are you talking of piracy?'

'Worse, it's damned close to official. A certain naval officer has contrived to convince his superiors my property was an enemy vessel and thus a prize.'

'You will forgive me, if I seem to require more information.'

'Whatever for? If the facts are plain, all that's required is proof of this larceny.'

'Where is the vessel now?'

'Greenwich.'

'Then surely the remedy is simple, Denby. You have ownership papers. All you have to do is produce them and claim, no, in fact, establish title.'

'Not so simple, Druce. It was purchased using a proxy and the rogue who took possession of her was cunning. Not a scrap of paper now exists aboard and nor does the name board still grace her stern. She has been rendered a mystery ship.'

Getting no response and with his host looking unconvinced, Carruthers was forced to add, 'The officer overseeing the auction of the cargo was good enough to let me go aboard and search the main cabin. But I did get from him a name.'

'And this officer is?'

'John Pearce, lieutenant. A rogue of long-standing, according to my informant, as well as an officer bearing a fraudulently acquired commission.'

The continuing questioning look produced the admission this information came from another naval officer, a peg-leg called Perkins, with the brother-in-law unaware Druce had posed the silent enquiry to cover for his own knowledge of the first name proposed. What was the alleged lover of Emily Barclay doing stealing ships?

'The cargo, surely there was a manifest.'

'Are you listening, Druce?' was the angry rejoinder. 'There was nothing, I told you.'

'Your proxy?'

'Also missing and surely, no doubt due to the same Pearce fellow. It's him I need to find.'

'His name is?'

'Tolland. Jaleel Tolland. I can direct your man Hodgson where to look this time. He hails from a hamlet called Beltinge on the North Kent coast, but my attempt to correspond with him has produced no result.'

'Am I allowed to ask why you used a proxy purchaser?'

'Business, Druce, which I don't expect you to fully understand.'

Therein lay a piece of condescension that would have kept Edward Druce awake regardless of other concerns, the first being he did not, for one second, believe Denby had told him the truth. The ownership documents for any purchase, if not the originals, then a notarised copy, would stay with the man who'd laid out the funds. Any notion the only proof of same would be aboard the ship was risible. Nor was he to be fobbed off with the high tone, which implied such matters were beyond his comprehension, as if, in business affairs, he was some kind of simpleton.

What followed was a night of tossing, turning, and audible groans, disturbing the gentle snores of his wife, which were a lot less troubling than the ever-recurring scenarios he'd imagined over the preceding weeks. All were speculative, the only solid fact, he would have to act as requested for, without solid and damning information from Walter Hodgson, he was still mired in uncertainty.

Certainty of his own infallibility was intrinsic to his nature, yet Jaleel Tolland was much mistaken to think he could act aboard ship as he wished, without it coming to the attention of those in positions of authority. It did not require a name, or knowledge, for an experienced naval officer to sense a shift in mood, especially aboard a ship normally reckoned content.

The ability to do so was core, as was the necessity of ensuring such feelings were made known to the captain, never such an aloof character as was fondly imagined. Sir Thomas Byard was kept informed of everything he needed to know in the daily meetings he had with his premier. A relationship not always harmonious in the service, this was one of shared purpose and general amity.

Responsible for the day-to-day running of the ship, Mr Laker had much to report which was routine. Any changes to the watch and quarter bills or berthing arrangements, an assurance, more for habit than information, the ship was clean and free from disease. Also his inferior officers and warrants were assiduous in carrying out their duties. He also brought to Byard's notice anything reported to him as requiring attention, always a long list for a ship of the line suffering the wear and tear of the constancy of being at sea. This was essential so his captain could take up any pressing matters with whoever held a particular responsibility.

The last report was defaulters, the transgressions of the lower deck, usually petty in nature and requiring no more than a loss of privileges. There were many other sanctions open to a commanding officer, from stopping grog, stapling to the deck, all the way up to the least desirable and often a last resort, a dozen of the cat.

'Am I allowed to say, Mr Laker, the list seems longer than usual?'

The premier acknowledged this to be so, aware of the way the question had been posed to imply no criticism of him personally. If Sir Thomas Byard had the right to be as rude and crusty as he wished, it was an approach he rarely employed.

'It's nothing more than impressions, sir, but the wardroom shares the view there is an increased feeling of general discontent amongst the hands.'

'And do they not have much to be discontented about?' There was no need to acknowledge this as the truth, Byard adding with a smile, 'And it's not confined to the lower decks.'

It was not the case the King's Navy was riven with dispute, but each part had their own concerns. When it came to the sailors, many officers shared their grievance over pay, while also being affronted at the static rates they, too, received. Then there was the vexed subject of the division of prize money to which all had a view they were being shortchanged. Sympathy, however, did not extend to allowing open expression, and Byard was as wedded to the maxim "no ship could be a republic" as any of his contemporaries.

'It is ever one or two malcontents who stir up matters. It shouldn't be too difficult, surely, to find their names and deal with them.'

Laker hoped there was no implicit reproof in the remark: The suggestion he had, so far, failed in his duty. If the authority to dispense discipline lay with a ship's captain, the information he required as to how to apply it came from his inferior officers, most notably the premier. Laker wanted to reply, if he'd done so, it was because the normal methods of exposure seemed to be blocked; in short, no one was even hinting at the source of disruption, a point quickly put forward.

'A little less of the blind eye might serve,' Byard suggested. 'Let the divisional officers crack down a bit and see if it lubricates tongues.'

Which again required no explanation. The Articles of War, by which the navy laid down the rules of conduct, too rigidly imposed, could work against the ship, making it less, not more, effective as a fighting vessel. Some laxity of rigid discipline was essential to maintain harmony, though it had to be measured to ensure it did not go too far. It was therefore necessary an officer had the ability to see and stop what must be curtailed, but also the wisdom not to take notice of every minor infraction.

'I will make it so, sir.'

CHAPTER SIXTEEN

The fortress dominating San Sebastian was visible well out to sea, solid, square stone walls and crenelated battlements, overlooking steep cliffs. As they closed with the shore, they could see the outer defences, which ran on all sides of the conical hill it dominated. This was the crown of a narrow promontory to the west of the wide and tidal River Urumea, sticking north like a thumb into the Bay of Biscay.

Below the fortress, the shoreline was lined with jagged rocks affording few places to land so, even to a siege novice such as John Pearce, it appeared assaults from boats would be impossible at high tide and murderous at low. He had to assume the landward defences, from where any assault would need to be launched, were even more comprehensive, not that he had in mind any kind of attack from either flank.

But, looking at what was before him, there was a very obvious moment when he wondered if the right choice had been made. This had him run over, in his mind, the lengthy discussion he'd had with Oliphant about the approach to employ. At the base of this there was one inescapable fact: Regardless of what they gleaned on the French side of the border, they were still in total ignorance of any matters of policy farther south.

The option of a repeat, of going ashore in a boat, had eventually evaporated in the face of the very obvious drawbacks. Beyond a greeting, they could not speak the language, added to which there was certainly no way the kind of tricks pulled on Arnaud would work on any Spanish counterpart. They would be two strangers and obvious because of it, seeking to gather high-level information, with no clear idea of how to go about it. Making it up on the hoof would be suicidal.

In the end, it had fallen to Pearce to make a decision, having fully explored the limited options, and his words of conclusion had been sobering. They were about to enter a Spanish port, known to possess stout defences, with no idea if they were still an ally or had flipped to become an enemy. He, as well as the men he commanded, were about to find out.

Knowing HMS *Hazard* would be sailing in under its high elevation, Pearce had decided to survey the deck from the mainmast cap, ensuring what would be seen by those on the battlements would arouse no suspicion. For the same reason, the Admiralty pennant, which might raise questions, had been taken down, replaced from the locker with that of a Vice Admiral of the White, under whose flag the previous commander had sailed.

As ordered, his loaded guns were bowsed tight against their ports, the only factor hinting at readiness being the attached flintlocks. It would require an uncommonly sharp as well as knowledgeable eye to spot such. Even less this applied to the equipment normally stored below but now laid hard by the ship's side: crows, handspikes, rammers, sponges, powder horns, and cartridge prickers.

The balls necessary to reload were already in a basket, hung just below deck level, this attached to a whip from the main yard. Missing was the linstock and tub for lit and burning slowmatch, there in case the flints failed to spark, because any trace of smoke would raise suspicions as to his purpose. More concerning, the same from the ramparts might point to an unwelcome reaction to his approach, and his four-pounder cannon, even if he could hit them, would bounce off the walls.

All he could do if he'd guessed wrong about the Dons still being allies was reply to the much larger ordnance to which he would subjected with what he had. Really, he would have to rely on the sailing qualities of HMS *Hazard*, the only thing that would get her out of range with the minimum amount of damage.

He wanted, in all respects, to be seen as what he was, a British warship making a courtesy call on an ally, which was fine if this still held. If it did not, his mission would be over: It would be plain the Dons had changed sides, so it then became a matter of survival. Every man aboard had been made aware of what was possible, so were standing by, out of sight, ready to take whatever action was required.

A search for a sign he might be sailing into danger, like evidence of the fortress cannon being manned and run out, became the focus of his concerns. Yet even from the crow's nest, so great was the elevation of the main defences, it would be impossible to see much of any activity on the higher batteries, which also applied to San Sebastian itself.

The castle and hill masked the town, which lay behind it, a string of buildings on the southern side of the navigable Urumea, as ever in this part of the world, dominated by the towering spire of a cathedral. To the south lay a curving sandy bay, some protection from the Atlantic afforded by a heavily wooded island called Santa Clara, almost central to the arc of its horns.

Most of the shipping sailing to and from San Sebastian landed or loaded their cargoes along the Urumea riverbank, but his charts indicated there was an old harbour tucked in under the walls and guns of the castle, so it was for this he aimed. Once in the river, wide as it was, manoeuvre would become impossible and he could be trapped by the fall of the tide. A relatively open bay was a much better bet.

'Anything untoward, Pearce?'

This greeting he got from Oliphant as soon as his feet touched the deck. The look it received elicited an immediate apology. 'Sorry, Captain.'

'Nothing to cause alarm but, as I've already told you, trouble would probably come by way of a forty-two-pounder cannon ball.'

'Boat putting off, sir,' called Midshipman Campbell, who'd replaced him aloft.

'Mr Hallowell, man the signal guns and stand by to reduce sail.'

Two of the small brass swivels were now mounted either side of the quarterdeck. In battle, a dozen of these were close-quarter weapons for sweeping an enemy deck, as well as this function. Using powder only, it was the task of a ship's commander to acknowledge the flag of the nation on which they were closing, in this case the red and gold of Royal Spain. In effect, it became a salute to the sovereign himself.

Twenty-one times the small charges were fired, the black smoke billowing towards the shore until the courtesy was complete, at which point it was time to hold breath and await the response. Pearce felt the air in his lungs release as the first blast erupted from the battlements, with no sign of the dreaded round shot, as the flag he was flying was properly acknowledged in a salvo of nine.

'Let's hope it's not a ruse' was imparted to no one in particular, followed by the orders to shorten sail. 'We will leave the guns as they are, Mr Hallowell, but it will be necessary to make them look harmless in case we are subject to a visit. It must be done without haste and discreetly, so nothing is seen from yonder castle.'

The boat to which Campbell had alerted them carried a pilot, who signalled *Hazard* should follow him to a berth. Having intended to anchor well out in the bay, and use Santa Clara Island as shelter, he had no choice but to obey the instructions given. This took him, slowly and under topsails, not only close to the harbour, but right under the looming cliffs. Immediately of concern were several small bastions with cannon, near to sea level, the weapons representing danger to any ship seeking to mount an inshore assault. Unmanned as far as Pearce could see, there was no sign they were a present threat.

Anchoring was carried out with reasonable efficacy, the fluke itself barely catted before Pearce was alerted to a second boat leaving the harbour entrance. An official-looking barge, it bore a large Spanish flag on a stern staff, blowing stiffly on the wind that had brought *Hazard* in from the Bay of Biscay. As all hands were on deck, the order to clear any suspicious items could be carried out without too much concern.

The launch was rowed by smartly dressed oarsmen, seen to be carrying a pair of uniformed officers, one young and in plain garb. The other took Pearce's attention because of his elaborately decorated uniform, adorned with much gold frogging. From what he knew of Spanish naval dress and headgear, learned fighting alongside them at Toulon, he was looking at someone quite senior.

He'd already established no naval presence in the Santa Clara Bay and, from what he could see of the harbour and the masts therein, nothing to give any indication of even a small warship berthed there. This did make him wonder at being called upon by someone naval, when he'd thought, if he was going to meet anyone, it would be either a civilian or an emissary from the Spanish army.

'Mr Livingston, a message to my steward to lay out some refreshments, the very best in the larder and wine store.'

The Mite scampered off to carry out the order, subject to a benign smile from his captain, pleased at last the boy was showing less timidity, reacting to an order immediately instead of with a blinking pause. The gangway was opened, with Pearce, already in his best uniform, taking up station to receive his visitor, now so close his face was hidden under a large tricorn and feather-trimmed hat.

Moberly had his marines on deck, lining them up in proper order, Pearce checking their uniforms were in good condition, their whitened webbing pristine. Finally, happy they were properly aligned, out came Moberly's sword, to be raised to his shoulder, he as stiff at attention as his men.

'Bosun.'

The pipes wailed out welcome notes as the two officers came aboard, to raise their hats to the flag. Pearce stepped forward to introduce himself in French and welcome them aboard, with an apology for having no Spanish, happy to see he'd been understood. Allowed only a brief moment to take in the face, he registered one swarthy and lined, with liquid brown eyes, underscored by dark, puffy pouches, as well as to note the expression, which was unsmiling.

'Unnecessary, monsieur, as I have no English.' The hat was lifted slightly again as his eyes began to wander over the deck. 'Commandatore Felipe de Rosado.'

'Allow me to introduce my officers.'

There was a commonplace ritual to this, as Hallowell and Worricker took a step forward. Rosado then inspected the marine guard, treating the half-dozen men lined up as if it were a full regiment. Finally, courtesies observed, he introduced the silent young fellow in the plain uniform as his nephew and aide.

'If you would care to join me in my cabin, monsieur.'

'Happily, once you have told me the purpose of your visit.' The pause was very brief before he added, in a rather brusque tone, 'We are not accustomed to the British Navy calling in to San Sebastian, unless it is for some emergency. I would say your ship seems sound in all respects, so it is not the case.'

The disarming smile Pearce produced was to cover his surprise, plus the lack of an immediate answer to a question he'd not expected to be asked. Surely such visits being, if not normal in this port, nothing to especially remark upon. And, in truth, he was stumped, so had to fall back on the most obvious reasons.

'I had hoped to make up my wood and water.'

The Spaniard took several seconds to digest this, creating an impression of unease, before saying, 'If you send in your boats, we will happily accommodate you.'

Because Rosado had moved to carry out his inspection, Pearce could see the worried face of Oliphant over his shoulder. It was obvious and had been discussed, now they'd safely anchored, if they were to find out anything, they would need to go ashore. Taking on board wood and water was not the kind of duty to require the presence of either. But he could think of no pressing reason to suggest why. It was the other face in his eye line, Michael O'Hagan's, as ever curious when overhearing words he could not understand, which led to a possible solution. It seemed a risible one to the man making it, but he had to say something.

'I also wish to beg for your indulgence, monsieur. Many of my crew are Irish and of the Roman faith. Would I be able to indulge them, while we are here, with a visit to a church of their own denomination? I fear my readings of Sunday services do little to ease their souls.'

'An unusual request from a British officer' came with a wry expression.

Oliphant's look now commanded Pearce's attention, for he'd understood every word. He was jerking his head slightly to remind the need for him to be included, while being a Papist would not serve. What Pearce came up with was a real shot in the dark: He could not just name him as a civilian passenger. The man had to have some stature.

'I'm also delighted to be carrying aboard an emissary of His Majesty King George's government. If I may introduce him.' Rosado, slightly taken by surprise, nodded as he turned to be introduced to a very stiff "passenger." 'Monsieur Samuel Oliphant.'

'A member of the government?' Rosado enquired, with an arched eyebrow.

Stuck for a reply, Pearce was glad Oliphant spoke up, and in a breezy confident tone. 'A very junior one, monsieur. I'm on route to Lisbon to discuss certain matters with the Portuguese military.'

'And these are?'

Pretending to be surprised, Oliphant gave an abrupt answer. 'You would not really expect me to answer such a question. But they are, of course, dependent on British subventions to pursue the war.'

It took several seconds for Pearce to get what was being implied; fortunately, Rosado required the same amount of time. If Spain was in receipt of British gold to help pay for her part in fighting the Revolution, so would be their Portuguese neighbour. Hard as it was to credit the man with anything, Pearce was forced to admire the swift thinking, Oliphant too having been caught on the hoof. It was driven home just how clever the invention was when Rosado, who'd had about him an air of caution since coming aboard, seemed to alter his mood.

'An allied captain and a government emissary? We should be flattered. You must both dine with me in the castle, where we can perhaps discuss the similar needs of my country. As to the crew, they are, of course, at liberty to come ashore and worship.'

'My cabin, monsieur,' came from a tight Pearce throat. 'Mr Hallowell, I trust you to entertain Commandatore Rosado's nephew.'

'Sir.'

'You have no objection to Monsieur Oliphant joining us?'

'I would be most disappointed if he did not.'

It was a half-relieved, wholly concerned John Pearce who led the way, with no notion he'd be able to take up the baton of what had just been devised. He needed Oliphant to do the talking. It proved to be a sound bit of inspiration, the fictitious junior role in government being expanded, while he listened, grateful not to have to add anything.

Rosado was more interested in Oliphant than him anyway, his seemingly innocent enquiries relating to the Portuguese expertly fielded, often by the stated need for discretion. The Spaniard was given just enough tantalising hints to keep him intrigued, without anything to establish a single hard fact about this supposed mission.

Likewise Oliphant's background in government service, his present rank probed, was seen off by obfuscation about the layers of bureaucracy in which he was enmeshed. Having drunk some decent, if not outstanding, wine, the Spaniard ran out of ways to ask the same thing several times, so indicated he desired to depart. This had all three rise from their chairs to stand, heads bent, under the deck beams.

'I will send my barge for you this afternoon.'

Without quite knowing why, Pearce replied with polite but unambiguous force. 'Surely no need, monsieur. If my Catholics are going ashore, I must go with them to ensure they find what they need. We cannot leave them to be tempted to indulge in other, less saintly, pursuits.'

A hand was waved by Pearce at his inventive co-conspirator.

'How much more so for Monsieur Oliphant, who suffers very badly from seasickness, so would welcome some solid ground beneath his feet. All you need do is give us a time to call upon you at the castle, not a place to which we will surely require to be directed.'

Rosado was left with no place to go which would not break the bounds of good manners. Not that he acceded immediately, staring at John Pearce in such a way as to make him wonder if, already hot under the collar, he was blushing.

'I will expect you at the third hour after noon when the sun has begun to diminish. Please present yourself at the main gate.'

'You're learning, Pearce,' Oliphant whispered, as Rosado and his nephew were piped over the side. 'I was caught on the hop and for the same reason as you, but it seems to have stalled him.'

'I got the impression he's suspicious.'

'I did too, which has to make you wonder why.'

'It could be dislike about cooperating with us. I saw much of the attitude at Toulon. Too many of the Dons were not happy to be fighting alongside Britannia and made no attempt to hide it. When we had to abandon the port, they were not as ruthless as they should have been when it came to destroying what was left of the French fleet. It led to a suspicion they wanted it preserved.'

'In case they came round to fighting us again?'

'That was the theory, not in this war, but at some time in the future, when France returns to normal. They see her as a natural ally against Britannia, with the Revolution as an aberration.'

'Yet he's invited us to break bread.'

'What does that tell us?'

'We're in for an interesting dinner.'

'Or a Last Supper. You'll forgive me, I've got to tell our Irishmen they're going to church.'

'There are those,' Michael O'Hagan opined, 'who might be thinkin' gratitude to be in order, John Boy.'

'From your tone, I perceive you're not one of them.'

'Sure, do I not know you too well? So best you tell me what the game is.'

'You're so certain there's a game?'

'I am and have been for a long time.'

There was no way to avoid such a stark response, also no way to explain in a partial sense. Why would he do so, when he trusted Michael implicitly and they were now at their destination? Not that there was much comfort in the telling, it being plain his friend was wounded by not being informed before.

'It was not my doing, Michael' sounded as feeble as it felt. 'Oliphant was adamant the whole situation must be confined to just we two. I could not go against him on it.'

'He would not have heard a thing from my lips.'

'I know, but he does not know you as I do and he's wedded to secrecy.'

'All the way to where he hails from and what our Charlie reckons to be a muddy past.'

'It's no good asking me about it.'

This was a deliberate ploy to avoid passing on what suspicions he'd harboured when ashore, as well as what Oliphant had done to satisfy them. These were, still, in any case, subject to speculation. No point in indulging Pelican suspicions and even less in adding to them.

'Please ask Mr Macklin to call upon me.'

'Sure, one day I might get the courtesy of a mister' came as jaundiced and parting shot, leaving Pearce to work out how to deal with what was coming, not yet fully clear what to say when Macklin entered the cabin and was invited to sit.

'I must ask you, will your men return to the ship if they're allowed ashore?' The question surprised him, of this there was no doubt, given he was physically taken aback. 'I feel I have to, at some point, find out how much trust I can place in them. Being here, in a Spanish bay, might provide an opportunity to find out. I have never enquired of your faith, but I'm sure I know theirs.'

'There's no difference.'

'Michael O'Hagan is a man who has been with me through many a trial and he, too, is a Papist. He has asked to be allowed ashore to see a priest, no doubt to confess. It occurred to me, the same may be something which your men would welcome.'

'It would be the answer to a prayer, sir.'

'But would they run?'

'There's nowhere to run to, when the only safe place is where you are.'

Prey to a sudden inspiration, Pearce carried on in a sombre tone.

'I cannot, in all conscience, allow you all ashore at the same time. But I'm minded to do so in two parties, with O'Hagan and the two watch captains, Taverner and Dommet, as escorts for both. I need hardly point out to you the risk I'm taking, which is why I will be going ashore as well.'

'I will have them swear on the Holy Cross they'll not disappoint you. If they do so, they will risk damnation.'

'Please ask O'Hagan to come back, so I can talk of what needs to be done.'

'My request, was it? Jesus, John Boy, when it comes to the double-dealing . . .'

'None of us are saints' was the Pearce interruption. 'I need to get ashore and so does Oliphant and I doubt one visit will be enough. If we do not, we have no way of knowing if the suspicions we've been sent to uncover have any basis. And if you, Charlie, and Rufus have a chance to find out anything that will help, take it.'

'Two parties?'

'Yes,' replied a rather testy John Pearce, 'which will give you an opportunity to confess twice, something I have no doubt will be required to list the number of your sins.'

This did produce a broad grin, familiar but not seen for a while. 'And here's me thinkin', John Boy, you had no care at all for my soul.'

CHAPTER SEVENTEEN

John Pearce had reason to regret being so open about the deck being under constant observation. It produced playacting from the crew, exaggerated performances of what were simple acts. This had him calling for normality, with threats to stop their grog if they didn't behave. At the same time as he showed his anger, there were elements to cheer him as a captain. A crew acting so came across as harmonious, which was promising for the future.

Having claimed his call was for wood and water, he had to send in boats and funds to take some on board when in truth he was quite well found. He reassured himself with the knowledge it never did any harm to store an excess, given no captain, or ship's cook for that matter, could ever be sure where and when they could acquire more. Derwent and the purser, Porlock, were sent along, to buy fresh provisions, bread, lemons, and greens for the crew, the same plus fish, beef, and fowl for the great cabin.

It most respects, he wished the morning to proceed with as much routine as possible. Mr Williams was indulged with the jolly boat, two men to row it with another to cast his leaded lines and tallow-coated lead weights. He began to check the depth and holding quality of the anchorage, as well as the shoal and rocky waters around the Santa Clara Island, against what was indicated in his Admiralty charts.

He would also make rough drawings of the hilly shoreline, to be perfected when time permitted, these and his observations being eventually submitted to the Navy Board. This was a common practice and a duty placed on men who held his warrant, to ensure navy charts and visual signs on the shoreline were up to date. If Rosado was watching, all he would see was common practice in any navy when at anchor, a ship's master checking the seabed and noting any changes which might endanger another ship, or new buildings on the skyline.

On deck men went about their duties, or to be more precise, when it came to his quota men, to further instruction in the multitude of tasks which had to be carried out on a daily basis. He did have one concern, which was laid to rest by Mr Low, the gunner. Having loaded his cannon out at sea, did he need to worm them to get out the balls and cartridges? Would leaving them as they were reduce their effectiveness, if and when they were required?

Such work could not be carried out discreetly, which would send a clear message to anyone observing from the ramparts they'd been unsure of a peaceful reception. Only one reason for such behaviour would make sense, even to the dimmest mind, and this had to be avoided.

'Warm, dry weather of a day, sir' was Low's response. 'And we apron the touch holes, just in case there's a dew or rainfall.'

'I need to stress, Mr Low, we must be ready to fight at the drop of a hat.'

'Which would have a simple soul like myself wondering, why that would be, your honour?'

'And wonder you must' was the Pearce response, returning, in good measure the look he was getting.

'First party is ready to go ashore, sir' was a message to kill off further curiosity.

'Thank you, Mr Maclehose. Please rouse out our passenger who, if I know him at all, will be snoozing. Mr Low, I'm sure you have duties to attend to.'

Oliphant was on deck by the time Pearce got there, to join the Pelicans and half the Arklows, all in what passed for their best attire, not much given how little they'd managed to rescue. The air of repressed excitement had their captain wonder at the power of their religion, something to which he was immune.

Michael O'Hagan had about him an air of high anticipation, which both Rufus and Charlie, indifferent themselves, took good care not to mock. It was a subject upon which Michael was solemn. Never a bully, even so, any ribaldry might not go unpunished. There was the usual fuss of getting Oliphant safely into the gently rocking cutter; he seemed determined to establish his non-sailor status by making a poor first of something he should by now be accustomed to. Michael got in a whisper to say a ducking would be the best way to oblige him to learn.

'You've no idea, Michael, how tempted I am to take up your suggestion.'

'Long as you're up for a dive in and rescue.'

'I'd let him have a few swallows of seawater first.'

The fully loaded cutter was cast off to be rowed toward the harbour mouth, with nothing in the way of haste, Pearce keenly examining what, if anything, lie ahead. He was not left to wonder for long, and the sight was far from pleasing. A file of green uniforms appeared, a dozen men lining up under the command of an officer, muskets across their chests.

'An escort?' Pearce suggested to Oliphant.

'Looks like it.'

'Makes life difficult.'

'If the truth is as we fear, they will want to keep us ignorant, so Rosado is making sure we see only what he wants us to, which is hardly the behaviour of an ally.' Responding to the look this received, he added, 'But it's not proof of anything and, if Dundas was here, he'd tell you policy can't be based on guesswork.'

'So?'

'We must be ready to take any chance that presents itself.'

Which looked to be a tall order as they made the quay. There was no smiling greeting, just a crusty young lieutenant who did not even bother to impart his name. The only information given, delivered in halting French, was to establish he was in command of the men who would escort them to the cathedral and there was to be no delay.

Not that Pearce obeyed, taking a long look around the harbour. Like the anchorage out in the bay, it contained a number of small trading vessels of the coastal type, none deep sea by their build, but nothing remotely naval. A sense of relief held until a series of shouts took his attention. Pearce turned to take note of a cutter tied up, directly under the walls of Moro Castle. Surrounded by men stripped to the waist, they were occupied with ropes and pulleys, working with some skill.

The concern surfaced when he realised what they were labouring on, lowering a cannon, a twelve-pounder by its size, from the battlements above, with others working on the tackle which allowed it to be lashed in the bows of said cutter.

'A gunboat being made ready,' he whispered. 'And I can think of only one target.'

'Do you think we were meant to see it?' Oliphant asked.

'What matter, we have now. We may well find it manned and out in the bay by the time we return.'

'Dangerous?'

'Very, if they don't want us to weigh.'

'Then you'd best ask our Papist friends to say a special prayer.'

The Spanish lieutenant, clearly annoyed, barked, and the whole party moved off, soldiers ahead and behind, to make their way through narrow streets of, at first, things common to any port: trestles of fresh seafood for sale, bakeries and butchers, warehouses, taverns, suppliers of the various chandelling goods, the thousands of objects a sailing ship required to brave the oceans. Along with this went repairers working on various craft, added to the bustle of people doing business.

Even as Pearce took in the surroundings, narrow streets, a mix of substantial stone houses and old-fashioned timber-framed dwellings, his mind was racing. He could not avoid thinking of ways, if his concerns were right, to get out of what was going to be a real predicament.

A cutter rigged as a gunboat was about the hardest opponent with which a sailing ship at anchor could do battle. Able to pick their angle of attack, out of the arc of response covered by the deck cannon, they could do great damage, while he lacked even a crew of competent gunners to fashion a response. This had been proved off La Rochelle a few days past, and by the very same size of target.

'Seem to be a lot of soldiers about.'

Oliphant's observation brought Pearce back to his immediate sur-roundings, to spot, as they walked, how right he was. Small parties of soldiers, in twos and threes, loitered in various places, certainly where alleyways and streets intersected, and they were not engaging with any-one. The passing locals, if they looked at them at all, were not inclined to smile. Many passed by with heads averted or bowed, giving Pearce the impression to catch their eye was to invite trouble.

'They're not much interested in us either,' Oliphant said, when the point was made.

'Jesus, would you look at the size of it.'

Michael's loud outburst had Pearce look up, to see before him, at the end of a narrow street, the towers of a massive place of worship. It was one that seemed far too large for the surrounding buildings, an impression diminished when they entered a sizable plaza. Pinkish-coloured stone dotted with elaborate carvings rose hundreds of feet into the air, a monument to religious belief, which must have cost a fortune to fund and several decades to construct.

Was it larger than Notre Dame? It seemed so, perhaps because it had none of the dark stone or grotesques of the Paris cathedral, carved devils and ugly gargoyles to hint at hellfire. Here it was all sculpted saints giving blessings or holding holy books or crucifixes, several framing a huge arched entrance. This, less surprisingly, was topped with a statue of St Sebastian, his writhing stone body pierced by half a dozen arrows.

Their escort split up to frame the doorway, scattering the dozens of undernourished souls, those who always gathered around places of worship in every town John Pearce had ever visited. As ever, and he thought of his father at the same moment, he tried to imagine the cost of this edifice and how poor people, like those growling at having been chased away, could be brought to see it as being to their advantage.

The voice which greeted them cut through the whispers of amazement from his crew. Heads lifted to stare in wonder at the priest, making his way down the steps leading to the massive interior. Dressed in a plain black soutane, he was yet every inch a divine. Quite young, handsome, fresh of face under ginger curls, he yet had the dry-skin countenance that seemed to go with clergymen. The sizable cross sat on his chest drew the eye, but it was what he said, in English, added to his accent, which produced the most surprise.

'The top of the day to you all. And may the Good Lord bless you.'

What in the name of all that was holy was an Irish priest doing here?

'Well, Captain, as the Archbishop said, when he was asked to provide a priest, there's not much point in a fellow confessing his sins, if the man on t'other side of the screen can't understand a word he's saying. Sure, there's no salvation to be had there either, if the sinner don't know the penance.'

Tempted to question whether salvation existed at all, Pearce held his tongue. He was, after all, a seemingly affable fellow, albeit one who produced a frown as he looked Pearce up and down.

'Do I speak right, looking at your uniform, when I conjecture you're not of the faith?'

'You do, Father Behan.' Oliphant got a look, to produce a shake of the head. 'But I bear no animosity to the Roman rite.'

'I'll pray for you anyway. Now I must get started with so many souls to tend and, from what I can gather, not one been in a church for an age. I would suggest you come inside, while I go about it, there's much of wonder to see.'

'We're off to dine at the castle, Father. The men I've put in charge have already been given their orders and will see my crew back to our boat.' With the feeling this seemed to disappoint Behan, Pearce added, 'But we may well come back tomorrow, with a second group if we get permission, so perhaps then . . .'

'I'm beginning to wonder,' Oliphant murmured, as the crew followed Behan, 'after that rogue you put ashore and what he left behind, if there are more Irishmen in the world than any other race.'

'It often seems so. If you were to talk to my friend Michael, he would tell you they have good reason to leave their homeland and seek a life elsewhere. My father said poverty in Ireland was worse than England and the landlord class close to bestial. As for priests like Behan, many have had to go abroad to train, so it might explain his presence.'

As they moved off, half the escort, plus their officer, did so too, which brought forth from Oliphant the obvious question. 'What are they protecting us against?'

'Perhaps we're about to find out.'

'The gunboat you mentioned. Does that give you the impression Rosado wants to keep us here?'

'It makes me suspect they're not keen to see us weigh, which I find hard to make sense of. I suspect we may get some hint with our dinner.'

'It might be easier, if we have to get away in an emergency, to do so by land.'

'Easier for you, Oliphant. I have a ship and the crew to think of.'

'Then I hope you have some clever ruse up your sleeve.'

'I thought that was your speciality.'

Talk was suspended while they made their way up the steep incline leading to Moro Castle. The speculation Pearce had mulled on earlier, about the defence's being deeper on the landward side, was fully borne out by what he and his companion could now see before them. The old castle was formidable enough in its four-square way, but many improvements had been made to enhance the defences.

Yet there was no evidence of any fighting, odd given it was known the French had advanced beyond San Sebastian the previous year, only to depart when peace was declared. If they'd assaulted the castle, there would be evidence of scars from the artillery that would have to be employed. Perhaps no attack had been necessary, which indicated the Spaniards had either surrendered or been bypassed and left to wither on the vine.

'I suggest it might not be a subject to raise' was Oliphant's opinion, when Pearce made the point. 'Neither one represents their army in a good light.'

Passing through this and the salutes of the numerous sentries, they came to the original entrance, beyond a deep ditch, at which point their escorts halted and retraced their steps. Over the drawbridge they were taken to the officer on duty. As they were expected, he sent a man ahead to warn Rosado, then provided them with a guide.

Pearce was well aware, as his footsteps echoed off the walls, of the similarities with the fort at Hendaye: Would they emerge unscathed from this place as they had before, and was Moro more menacing? Ten times the size, the décor was much more refined. Certain Moorish influences were obvious in both the layout of the chambers, the vaulting of the arches, as well as the mosaic decoration on the walls.

They were led to a sort of audience chamber, lit by extensive candlelight, stone giving way to glittering comfort, the walls broken up by huge tapestries of medieval battle scenes, mostly of Christian knights skewering Moors and infidels. Rosado, bewigged and wearing a dress uniform more elaborately frogged than his morning ensemble, came forward to greet them. Behind stood a group of half a dozen high-ranking army officers, all in what appeared to be their best uniforms.

Introduced to the soldiers, all of whom spoke French, they soon had wine in hand and conversation to engage in. This, like the dinner to follow, took on an unreal quality of studious politeness, with no end questions posed by the hosts, few close to none by their guests. Avoided like the plague, as Oliphant had pointed out, was the outcome of Spanish efforts against the French, it being impolite to refer to what was a clear military defeat, probably followed by a diplomatic one at Basel.

As the wine was consumed, Pearce hardly touching his, and food served, he found himself fielding enquiries posed by his neighbour Rosado, about matters at home, both political and naval. He claimed a lack of any real knowledge, which was nothing but the plain truth. The fortitude of the British government in pursuing the war could only be guessed at, while the condition and strength of the Royal Navy was, he insisted, way beyond his rank.

It then came down to specifics of his voyage; when had he weighed from home? What kind of weather had he experienced, his response exaggerating the delays caused by gales in the English Channel. These were not probed by a member of a navy that had suffered a great loss from such conditions in the reign of Queen Bess?

There were enquiries about previous service, when he joined and at what rank, Pearce reckoning it best to lie, claiming the usual route of captain's servant then midshipman. Which ships had he served in and had he participated in any meaningful engagements. Here at least he could talk, with many caveats, of the gruelling sea fight that had got him present rank, as well as his service at the taking of Toulon.

Rosado, not having been there, possessed many contemporaries who had, so was able to talk knowledgably about the events of the siege and its subsequent loss. But again, diplomacy was required by his guest. There was no mention of tardy Spanish behaviour when abandoning the place, Rosado switching to another engagement entirely.

'Is Lord Howe's action in '74 still being hailed as a victory?'

'I believe so' was the bemused answer.

'Even if he failed in his primary task?'

Pearce could only shrug as his host appeared to take some delight in diminishing the Glorious First, raising his voice to remind everyone sitting close by of where it had failed. Howe had set sail to intercept a huge convoy of desperately needed grain the French were escorting from the United States. By engaging the enemy fleet, the grain got through to Nantes and saved France from starvation.

'Had he intercepted the merchant fleet, the war would have ended two years ago.'

'With respect, sir, that is speculation,' Pearce responded, albeit tactfully, annoyed and having to cover it, by the murmur of agreement from the soldiers.

'It is nothing of the sort' was a sharp rejoinder both in tone and expression. It then seemed to occur to Rosado he might have gone too far, so he ended the topic with, 'It is, of course, easy to see certain things in hindsight.'

A glance down the table indicated Oliphant was the object of much of the same kind of questions and opinions, though Pearce, being too far away, couldn't hear what fictions were being spun to fob off those posing them. He sensed no discomfort in his deportment, indeed, he seemed to be in fine fettle and at ease with himself, able to deal with the attention of those close by, in what appeared a lively conversation.

For himself, if anything touched on the supposed mission to Portugal, the plea he was a humble naval officer, whose only task was delivery, provided cover.

'Your crew have been to the cathedral?'

'Half of them, yes.' The pursed lips seemed to anticipate what Pearce said next. 'I was hoping the rest could be taken there tomorrow.' In the face of a cold look, he could only add, half in prayer, 'I felt it would be unwise to allow all of them ashore in one group, for fear of mass desertions.'

'So you intend to remain another day?'

'If it does not inconvenience you.'

'You did not see fit to say so when I came aboard.'

'It was a conclusion I only arrived at today. I hardly felt it was necessary to request permission, monsieur, from an ally.'

Eyes locked, Pearce had deliberately engineered a moment of truth. If it was seen as a trap, it was one Rosado sidestepped with a shrug.

'I take it we have satisfied your needs?' he asked, in an abrupt change of subject. 'I saw your boats going to and fro.'

'You have been most kind.'

'What are allies for, Capitaine, if not to assist each other in times of need?'

Pearce had to avoid looking at the man then, lest his reaction show his suspicions, so he looked around the table at the rest of the guests, only to be brought back by a sharp enquiry.

'You seem to have an unusual number of boats.'

Which left a hole for Pearce to fill, as well as a mistrustful look to satisfy. 'Some were acquired on the way. We came across the crew of a wrecked vessel and took both them and their boats on board.'

'Might I ask where this happened, given you did not mention it earlier?'

'Off Brittany,' came with a dismissive wave, as if it was of no account. 'And, in truth, it did not seem relevant to the matters on which you sought enlightenment. As we were shorthanded and they were competent seamen, I have mustered them on *Hazard's* books until we reach a British port.'

'Fortuitous, if you weighed short of men.' There was a silky air to what came next. 'No doubt these additions are responsible for that of which you are short.'

Rosado was playing with him. The article which would be affected by a sudden increase in numbers of crew would be food, the effect on wood and water minimal. How to respond? What came out was partly the devil in him, but just as much a way to kill off the direction in which the conversation was going.

'I saw a cutter being rigged as a gunboat this morning, I reckoned it to be loading a twelve-pounder cannon. Quite a weapon when properly deployed.'

If he had tried to put the boot on the other foot, the Spaniard was too wily for him. He was certainly in no way thrown. Indeed, he produced a look of surprise.

'A common means of defence, is it not?'

Which was true, when you had something to defend against, and Pearce had to stop himself from asking what or who this might be. About, instead, to mention the number of armed men in the streets and enquire as to their purpose, he bit his tongue. It was not a safe subject to raise.

'I think it is time I went back to my ship. Duty calls.'

'Ah, duty, a cruel mistress.' He looked down the table to where Oliphant was sitting. 'Will your companion suffer from a similar sense of obligation?'

The sod was telling some tale or other, those listening appeared rapt, which annoyed Pearce, knowing himself to be incapable of such ease in these kinds of circumstances. Not that he could let it show, but he wanted to depart and this meant both would have to go.

'He will leave when I do.'

'Do you require a boat?'

'There will be one waiting for us.'

'Of course, how lucky to have so many.'

Pearce stood, to make it plain his desire not to respond, which obliged Rosado to do likewise. This in turn alerted Oliphant, who, after a minimal pause, carried on with his tale, which forced Pearce to wait till he was finished. Then he was on his feet, exchanging pleasant farewells.

'I will have some of the men escort you back to the harbour.'

'Hardly necessary, monsieur.'

Rosado produced another mocking smile, as if to say the proposition was absurd. 'You are our guests. What would your government say if something happened to you? And, after all, your companion has his mission to fulfil.'

Was he saying he didn't believe a word of what he'd been told? It was impossible to tell. What had been imparted to Rosado on the deck of *Hazard* would have been subjected to a whole day of consideration, to leave certain questions, which Pearce could guess at. Would a man on an official mission really delay his arrival in Lisbon by stopping off in San Sebastian, especially when the Portuguese capital was only a few days' sailing away?

'Not that he seems in a hurry to do so, of course. So, if you wish to remain with us until all your men have unburdened themselves of their sins, please do so.'

Pearce knew he was being mocked, but awareness did nothing to ease it. It was Oliphant who got the backwash of a seriously put-out companion, at least able to say they had another day in which something useful might happen.

'While, I assume, you have so far uncovered nothing.'

'Not true' was the glum response. 'I have established, to my own satisfaction, the Spaniards are useless at dissimulation. I half expected any moment to be accused of treason.'

'That bad?'

'Did I succeed in allaying suspicions? Tried my best, but I can't be sure I managed to convince anyone of our *Bona Fides*.' Seeing the worried frown, Oliphant slapped Pearce on the back. 'We're alive and, thanks to you, still in the game. I speak from experience, when I say it is unwise to ask for more.'

The boat was there as expected, under the command of the Mite, who was nervous and exceedingly glad to see his captain. So, too, were a quartet of soldiers, plus the pair who'd escorted Pearce and Oliphant from the castle, souls who dispersed back to their quarters as soon as they cast off. Once aboard, he parted from Oliphant and made his way to the stern, knowing anyone watching could see him on a deck illuminated by lanterns.

The gunboat was a worry, one he had to hope was nothing to do with *Hazard*. If it was, he then had to wonder for what purpose. The only one which made sense was a gambit to make sure when he weighed, if indeed he was allowed to do so, it was not at his own choosing. This could mean he'd sailed into a trap.

Reprising the conversation he'd had with Rosado provided no conclusive answer, bar the impression the Spaniard knew he was being fed a fiction. He did not want him here but had no way of altering matters within the constraints of an alliance. Why? The idea it was just a long and historical hatred of Britannia seemed possible, but feeble, because it would not extend to an armed response.

Pearce finally went to his cot, sure of one fact. The day had revealed nothing to provide clarity, either to his present situation or the information sought by Henry Dundas.

Chapter Eighteen

Come morning he saw the gunboat, the cannon at its prow, pointing directly at the stern lights, as if it was aimed at him personally? The men crewing it sat with their oars resting in the water, ready to react as their target swung, which it did at single anchor. As *Hazard* moved, they could do so quickly to maintain the threat, if, and Pearce was far from certain, it had been rigged for such a purpose.

Once the dawn duties had been completed and with the crew gone to breakfast, Pearce invited Hallowell and Worricker to join him for what was a meal of that rare commodity on a fighting ship: fresh provender. They sat down to eggs, smoked ham, fresh bread, and copious coffee. Missing was Oliphant, still in his cot, not that he could have added much to what followed.

It was, in effect, a council of war, in which it was established all three were fully conscious of the danger the gunboat represented. With the need for secrecy gone, Worricker had been informed of the mission on which they were engaged and the most obvious question arose. Were the Spaniards, here and now and in this anchorage, playing a double game?

If it was the case, how could they counter what they now faced and get to sea with a limit to the damage they would suffer. How effective could be their response to such an immediate threat, added to the cannon on the lower bastions of Moro Castle, which would surely likewise be on alert.

Even if they could get clear, this put *Hazard* at the mercy of the larger cannon because, eventually, they would be far enough offshore to offer a target to the long-range batteries on the higher ramparts. Darkness, and the tide would have to be favourable for a fast exit, which presented the only opportunity to act, but then the gunners would send up blue lights so as to be able to still see their target.

'Those we can do nothing about,' Pearce insisted, adding a reassurance he was far from sure was the case. 'And hitting a moving target is never easy, even from a stable platform.'

'Will we be able to get under way at all?'

'If we do not, Mr Hallowell, then . . .' The obvious conclusion was left unsaid. HMS *Hazard* would be reduced to matchstick by the land-based cannon. 'Let us try to deal with the more pressing threat, the damn twelve-pounder.'

Given the ability to quickly change position, a broadside would be a waste of powder and shot besides which a gunboat would seek to either lie off the bow or the stern. The former left the farthest forward cannon as the only weapon which could conceivably hit back, with a single ball, a very small target. Astern, there was no way to move any ordnance, unobserved, to counter it, even in darkness, the ship being lit by lanterns. Anyway, the noise of the carriage wheels rumbling across the deck would give the game away.

'Assume the sod is in place to slow us down, giving the castle gunners time to get to and load their lower-placed weapons. They are, after all, not manned and to do so will take time. If we could disrupt the first discharge from the gunboat, sir, it would afford us a chance.'

Pearce acknowledged the truth of Hallowell's point. Reloading a twelve-pounder cannon on a floating cutter was no easy task, but what damage would a single ball at pistol-shot range do, especially coming through the stern lights. It would run all the way along the deck to the manger, inflicting huge damage, killing anyone in its path, either by contact or splinters.

The brass swivels were struck below when not required, two still in place following on from firing the salute. But there were ten more that could possibly be loaded with case shot out of sight. This would be enough to do real damage to human flesh, perhaps enough to prevent the reloading of the twelve-pounder, but again, rigged, they would be obvious.

For the prow, should they move, to run out a forward cannon could be quickly achieved, but aiming it would not. The carriage would need to be manoeuvred hard round with handspikes and this would not serve. Even if the gunboat held their fire, they could easily get out of the line of aim by the simple use of oars.

'We'd best get the bulkheads down to minimise the damage.'

This got looks of real doubt from both his lieutenants, it not being necessary to point out the Dons would be close enough to hear anything unusual, prompting a look at the panelling, which cut the cabin off from the lower deck.

The wedges holding the bulkheads in place had been hammered in. It would be no easy matter to get them out without a similar tool and a lot of noise. That it would be a positive step was not questioned: none required to be told more of a crew expired from flying shards of wood than fell to gunnery.

'And we must strike the furniture below.'

Which amounted to not very much. The very table and chairs they were using, a trio more for a greater number of guests, a wine cooler, and Pearce's desk, which had the owner reflect it was like trying to maim someone with a fresh snowball. If it could be done and the bulkheads silently removed, it would mitigate mutilation, but that was all.

'And we have to take out the gunboat, which means we must use our own boats to go after it.'

Which begged the question of how to weigh, which would take time and much activity, while countering the cannon below Moro Castle shorthanded. Everything taking place on deck in daylight was visible. At night, with the moon and stars, a single sentry, and Pearce had to assume one or more, would be enough to foil their efforts and the first sail raised would show clearly what they were about.

The only thing that sounded plausible was to have the carpenter partially saw through the anchor cable, so parting it with an axe could be completed in seconds, rendering the noise irrelevant. This served to demonstrate the level of desperation with which they were having to deal. Even then Worricker pointed out there was a limit in what he could do.

Too much cut away and the cable could part under strain which, if the tide was receding and with no sails set, could take the ship on the rocky shore below the castle. Using the sweeps was equally problematic, given the time it would take to get *Hazard* moving at even a snail's pace. It was far from heartening to envisage the state of their ship if they tried and no conclusion as to how to counter it forthcoming.

It was no help when Oliphant joined them, his questions leading to a reprise of all the problems as well as the negative conclusions. The only certainty was, if any attempt was to be made, it would have to be at night and a cloudy one. Which would require the topmen to get aloft at speed, in the pitch black, to get some way on *Hazard* before she was made matchwood. It was a gloomy group who, having exhausted all possibilities and with empty plates, prepared to go back to their duties.

'You're going ashore again, sir?' asked Hallowell.

'I am,' Pearce said, before glancing at Oliphant. 'Since nothing seems to be achievable here, it might, at least, make them wonder what we're up to.'

In the silence which followed, it was unstated but accepted. Not much could likely be achieved ashore either.

On a hot windless day, Pearce's uniform coat was not the right item of wear, so he took out one made of linen, which had not seen daylight for an age and smelt strongly of camphor. The military escort was again paraded as they made their way in to the harbour, suggesting they'd only been roused out when the party were seen getting down into the boats, no doubt the latter bringing on amusement at Oliphant's cack-handedness. The Pelicans were along as well, which prompted Pearce to gently rebuke himself for not enquiring of Michael if everything had gone as he wished the day before.

Following the same route once on dry land, they noted the similar atmosphere of the day before, wondering still at the need for such a strong military presence. And why were the locals seemingly so resentful of their own troops? Coming out of the shade afforded by closely packed buildings, into the cathedral plaza, the full heat of the mid-morning sun hit them, rendering the space furnace-like.

Father Behan was waiting once more and this time, when the crew entered, so did Pearce and Oliphant, glad to be in the vaulted and cool interior. They followed the crew, out of courtesy, by taking a dip of their fingers in the font, then making a half-hearted attempt at crossing themselves.

'Now, if he's looking down,' Behan crowed, with a broad grin, 'it will make the Good Lord's day.'

Not in the least put out by the sarcasm, Pearce replied, 'I was always told he was ever doing so.'

'He'll see your sins, Captain, you may count on it. And if you ask, they will be forgiven.'

'A long list,' proposed Oliphant. 'Which will take time, even for the Almighty.'

'Physician heal thyself.'

Which got a chortle from Behan. 'I will be about my task, if you don't mind.'

Which left them to take a slow walk around the interior. Regardless of any feelings on religion, it was impossible not to admire the craftsmanship of the stonemasons who'd built this edifice. Some of it was too elaborate, much more so than cathedrals in England. But, as was the case there, when you stood beside one of the columns of stone, it induced the same admiration, the way each part fitted perfectly to the one above or below.

It was natural to wonder at the skill and commitment. Men would have begun work on this ecclesiastical edifice as apprentice masons and died here as masters before it was finished, topping the columns with equally carefully hewn stone arches. The very best at their craft would graduate to sculpting the more elaborate furbelows, which topped the shrines to individual saints, as well as images to the Virgin Mary.

Less admiration was given to the paintings on the walls, garish-coloured imaginings of the Calvary and crucifixion, plus the lamentations of those who worshipped Jesus as he made his bloody way to . . . what? This was when Pearce had to stop his train of thought: It seemed impious to question the outcome when in such a place.

'I take it you're not moved by much of this, Pearce.'

'The workmanship yes, what it represents no. I object to the huge amount of wealth and time spent on display, which should be disbursed to the poor but rarely is. I can guarantee the bishop who has this see does not want for comfort.'

'Or a mistress, if he's like the French prelates. Your priest seems a decent sort.'

'First, he's not my priest, but I agree with you. He has a sense of humour. I've met good men of the cloth and admire them, but too many of the opposite, endless critics of human frailty, who put their own well-being first, while being expert avoiders of the same strictures.'

'Can I suggest we try a diversion?' It being a question that did not require an answer, Pearce waited to hear what it was. 'I'm thinking we should take a walk.'

'And I was expecting something profound.'

'To see if we're again followed.'

'Like yesterday, you mean?'

'It may have been just to ensure we turned up as expected.'

'And if we are?'

'It limits what is possible when the time comes to get away.'

'For you, Oliphant. I've already told you I have a ship and crew to consider.'

'Indulge me.'

'Just as long as you intend to return to *Hazard*.'

'This time, yes. I won't necessarily promise on another day.'

'We won't have one.'

Oliphant found himself on the end of a cold look, but this had more to do with an unpleasant truth than what he'd just said. If he decided to try to get out of San Sebastian on his own, there was nothing Pearce could do to stop him. So his reply, while positive, was couched to avoid admitting the fact.

'I think we've seen enough of misspent riches.'

Leaving the cool interior drove home just how hot the day had become, mainly due to the lack of a wind, surely a rare event on an Atlantic coast. It was baking, but also much quieter than when they'd entered, the locals taking their siesta. This did not apply to their escorts, who were huddled in the shade provided by part of the cathedral, sat on the ground, several looking to be snoozing, the lieutenant being one.

Shaken awake, he saw two of those he was detailed to look after set off in a direction away from where he was resting. Backs to him, neither Pearce nor Oliphant saw him scrabble to his feet, but they did hear the shouts of command as well as the sound of shuffling, then steadily rhythmic boots, which had them exchange a smile.

'No other soldiers about.'

'If they've got any sense, they're indoors,' Pearce replied. 'Why be out when the townsfolk are not?'

'I suggest at the next turning, you go one way, me the other.' Sensing rather than seeing Pearce tense, Oliphant added, 'I want to see what happens. I will keep the promise I made and meet you back at the cathedral.'

'How long?'

'In this heat, not very long.'

There was no attempt at subterfuge. On reaching an alleyway to one side, Oliphant just sauntered away, leaving Pearce to carry straight on, with him edging to one side to get some shade. He was the one obliged to ignore the shout, to which he didn't react. What stopped him was the crack of a musket being discharged, that being the only saving grace. He knew, having heard it and no other sound, it surely had not been aimed at his back.

When he turned round, the fellow who'd discharged his weapon was still holding it, the smoking muzzle pointing towards the sky. Oliphant emerged from his alley, or at least his head did, to look over the same scene as John Pearce, the call he produced absurdly cheerful under the circumstances.

'I think yonder fellow has just given the game away, don't you? We're not to be allowed to wander where we please, which makes me wonder, and you as well, I suspect, what it is they don't want us to see.' He waited till Pearce closed with him before adding, 'Whatever that may be, it allows for the use of a weapon and at siesta time, which will not endear him to the slumbering townsfolk. Question is, did he panic, or was he acting under orders?'

'Why don't you ask him?'

'I think it best to assume the latter, which begs the next question. If he is, why are we and your entire crew not locked up in the dungeons of the castle? Rosado does not want us here, yet neither is he, by your conjecture, seemingly willing to aid our swift departure. And I got the sense at dinner last night the army were the same.'

'You seemed to be enjoying yourself from what I recall.'

'Playing games, Pearce, trying to draw them out, with clear knowledge they were doing the same to me. It was as if they suspected we know something, which we both know we do not.'

'I'm sure you have a theory as to what it might be.'

'No. I admit myself on this occasion, like you, to be stumped.'

The glare from the officer, when they made to pass him, was one of pure hate, while his men, seeing this, felt free to express their own frustration until he commanded silence. This was followed by an abrupt gesture to proceed back the way they'd come, Oliphant cheerfully acceding, which seemed to annoy the fellow even more.

'I think the heat is making him fractious' was delivered in a flippant tone.

'I know how he feels,' Pearce responded. 'This coat is going to come off as soon as we get inside.'

Which he did, the sweat running down his back cooling him thankful for it. It was less than a minute till Father Behan appeared. Seeing both perspiring, he offered to take them into the vestry, where there was spring water brought in from the nearby mountains by aqueduct.

'My men?'

'At mass, Captain. One of my fellows is taking it and will deliver to them the sacrament. Being in Latin, it makes no odds they don't understand.'

The vestry, poorly lit by small windows, made it even cooler than the body of the cathedral, while the water was genuinely refreshing.

'Did you hear the gunshot, Father?' Oliphant asked, as Pearce soaked a handkerchief and wiped it over his face.

'Gunshot? No.'

'Thick walls' was the response, with the explanation following. 'I'm curious, I have to say, about the number of soldiers we've seen in the streets the last two days. I get no impression their presence is welcome.'

'Sure, it's the very opposite. If it's a sin to hate, and it is, then it is one of which a lot of my flock are guilty.'

'Brought on by?' Pearce asked.

'A desire to be no longer subjects of the Spanish Crown.' This was followed by a frown. 'Which being as I'm Irish, I can well understand.'

The look accompanying those words, direct and far from as friendly as hitherto, indicated he harboured similar feelings about his homeland. Inevitably, Pearce wondered if this was why he was here. Perhaps he'd been active in seeking to rid Ireland of what many saw as a British occupation, leading to a forced departure. Oliphant had evidently deduced the same.

'So it's repression they're here for in such numbers?' he asked.

'Green uniforms in Donostia and red in Dublin.' Sensing confusion, Behan added, 'That's the Basque name for San Sebastian, which was visited upon them by a King of Leon.'

'Leon?' Pearce asked, genuinely confused. 'How long ago was that?'

'Not long enough ago to forget there was once a Kingdom of Navarre, of which Donostia was part. Have you heard of it?'

'I have. King Henry of France, the first Bourbon, fourth of the name, was from Navarre.'

'I sense you're an educated man, Captain Pearce. Not many know of it outside this part of the world.'

'My late father was keen on historical tales of assassinated monarchs.'

'Historical is it? For the Basques it might as well be yesterday. They long to be free of control from Madrid.'

Oliphant posed a fairly obvious conclusion. 'Do the Spanish actually fear a local revolt?'

'They fear a desire for independence and have good reason to do so. It's been made doubly so after what the French promised the local Basque leaders, when they'd chased the Spaniards out of the whole region last year.'

'And that was?'

'To give the Basque region of Spain its freedom. Indeed, it was promised, only to go up in smoke on Swiss soil, when the two sides made their despicable peace.'

There was a long and contemplative silence as this information was digested, broken when Pearce spoke. 'You say, Father Behan, you're sympathetic to their cause.'

'I surely am. It would set an example others could follow.'

'With little regard for the King of Spain.'

'With no regard whatever for any king, of any place on earth, but all for the one who rules in heaven.'

'Does this hold with the local clergy?'

A sad smile. 'Not the bishops, but many priests are silently supportive.'

'You speak as one of them, I think.'

'I help where I can.' This occasioned a look at the vestry door, as if there might be a listening ear behind the thick oak. 'With due discretion.'

This got Oliphant a meaningful look from Pearce, but it was not a request for permission to speak.

'Then, if you will permit, I will explain to you a problem we face.'

CHAPTER NINETEEN

The letter Pearce wrote, as the light and heat of the day began to fade, was fulsome in its thanks to Commandatore Rosado, both for his hospitality and indulgence in the matter of wood and water. It informed him HMS *Hazard*, having taken on some fresh stores, such as bread, greens, and lemons, would weigh just after high tide the following day, to continue the voyage to Lisbon.

He then referred to the solace his crew had taken from the chance to receive the sacraments. He wished his gratitude to be passed on to the archbishop of San Sebastian for the special services provided, as well as thanking Rosado himself for making the arrangements, which was an assumption.

> *As a last kindness, it has been agreed a priest should come aboard and carry out a request from part of my crew that the ship be blessed, the men also to be given a last mass, prior to our raising our anchor. It may be I am risking censure from my superiors should this become known, but I feel anything which renders my crew content should be not only allowed but encouraged.*
>
> *As a last point, I wish to add the happiness I and my country take in the present alliance. This binds out two nations against a foe who, regardless of your religious denomination, can only be described as the Devil Incarnate.*
>
> *Please accept my felicitations,*

The signature was added with a flourish, the paper sanded to dry the ink, before being handed to Oliphant.

'Do you think he'll smell a rat?'

'First we have to find out if we can sail at all. If that gunboat is still in place come morning, I'm not sure we will be.'

The call went out for Maclehose to get a boat ready in order to deliver it, with instructions to leave the letter with the duty officer on the castle gate and avoid any suggestion he deliver it to the recipient.

'Any questions, you are merely a messenger, understood?'

'Aye aye, sir.'

Hallowell was the next visitor, to be advised special alertness would be necessary overnight to watch for suspicious movement. Even more they must listen out for any sounds from the shore which came across as different to what had already been noted, especially on the lower batteries of cannon.

'I reckon it would help if the crew slept in the open air tonight, sir. Between decks it is akin to a furnace.'

The scuttle, a sail rigged to provide air down to the bowels of the ship, had failed in the lack of wind throughout the day, so Pearce could only agree with his premier. He wanted his men alert in the morning: Sweating the night out in a hammock-packed space with no air would do little to aid that.

'It will be hard to sleep tonight,' Pearce suggested to Oliphant, once Hallowell had departed. 'Even for you.'

'I never worry about that which I cannot change.'

'Easier said than done.'

Pearce had his casement windows open and went naked to his cot, knowing Maclehose had carried out his orders perfectly, but it did little to aid his slumbers. When he did manage to catch short bursts of sleep, they were plagued by visions of his ship a wreck, his crew bloody and decimated corpses, strewn across the deck. The answer to the way he felt pre-dawn, in truth a bit jaded, was to throw himself into the refreshingly cool waters of the bay.

Michael O'Hagan had never relinquished the duty this entailed, of waiting with two buckets of fresh water and several towels for his friend to come back aboard. There were no sleeping bodies on the deck now: The men, in the freshness of the morning, had gone below and were waiting to be piped up to swab the decks.

'Gunboat's still there, John Boy' the answer to a question posed before he'd dived in.

'Not a lot we can do about it. If they're determined to keep us here . . .' did not have to be finished.

'And how long would that be for, I'd be asking.'

'As long as you don't pose the question to me.'

The reply came two bells later when Pearce and Oliphant were having breakfast, a letter from Rosado wishing him a safe passage, while also referring, in exceedingly flowery terms, to the solidity and compensations of the alliance.

'I would say,' Oliphant opined, 'he's outdone us in hypocrisy.'

The Mite then entered to say the gunboat was making for the entrance to the harbour, while there was no evidence of activity on the batteries.

'Which bodes well.'

Seeing the lad still a bit nervous of him, he asked how the pigeons were faring.

'They would be better, sir, if they could fly about a bit.'

'Trouble is, Mr Livingston,' Oliphant said. 'Given the chance they'd fly right home to England, which would be fine if they were carrying a message.'

'Is there one, sir?' he asked Pearce.

'Not at the moment. Now run along, and ask Mr Hallowell to get the boats ready to go ashore for supplies. Tell him he will find Father Behan, a Catholic priest, waiting to be brought aboard. He is coming at my request.'

'You going to tell Hallowell and Worricker what we're about?'

'I will,' Pearce replied, 'when I have something rock-solid to say.'

Having been breakfasted, the crew were put to work unfurling sails, which were left to flap, telling Pearce there was a breeze, if not a very strong one. Then it was more tuition in knots and splicing, when what their captain would have preferred was something that was not possible: more running in and out of the cannon, with all the actions of loading and firing repeatedly rehearsed.

To distract himself, he took the mids in fencing practice, which came as a set of formal actions, which might serve in a duel but would be of little use in the melee of actual combat. Still, it had at its basis the need to look your opponent in the eye, for this was where his intentions would be revealed.

'Boats putting off, sir.'

The cry from the quarterdeck had Pearce at the side, eagerly looking at the folk aboard, hidden by sacks of bread, fruit, and a block of ice. He did not espy Behan until they were close, his uncertainties only partially laid to rest by the sight of him. It was all very well for the priest to say he might be able to help, but was he coming with anything on which Pearce and Oliphant could act.

'Mr Oliphant to my cabin, where I will join him presently.'

He went to welcome Behan as he came aboard with his bag, in fact to help him, given a soutane was not a garment designed for boarding ships. Quickly he admonished him to act as a stranger, with Pearce going through a dumb show of seeming explanation, which included the fact they were about to sail. He then made the gestures to indicate they should repair to his cabin.

'I am to guess,' posed an amused priest, 'it's not just the Good Lord watching over us?'

'I hope he is and you're his messenger.'

For all his outward *sang froid*, Oliphant was pacing the cabin as they entered, Behan getting a keen look and a quick demand to find if he was the bearer of good news.

'Of that, sure, you'll have to be the judge. But I don't come with empty hands.'

Derwent entered with a pitcher of lemonade, full of chunks of the ice just fetched aboard. Behan, now seated, was joined by the others at the table as soon as the servant left.

'I spoke with certain parties last night and a reply came his morning, expressing a desire to meet with you.' There was an air of the dramatic about the man, as he paused to drink some lemonade and smack his lips in appreciation, this under the keen gaze of two impatient men. 'Lord, that's very fine.'

'How, where, and when,' Pearce asked, reflecting there was often a bit of an actor *manqué*, in many a divine, especially the thunder-and-damnation variety.

'The when you must tell me. But it is suggested you stand to off the estuary of the Orioko, Oreo in Spanish, which it will be on your maps. There lies the next open beach upon which you can land south of Donostia. There's nothing but rocky shore till then, but it is well out of sight from the heights round here.'

'And whom are we to meet?' asked Oliphant.

'There will be no names, but they are strong for Basque independence.'

'Are they the same people who dealt with the French, by any chance?'

'Sharp you are, Captain Pearce.'

'Will they want anything from us?'

Oliphant got a look then and a wait for an answer. 'I would say they might be looking for aid to their cause.'

Pearce put up a hand to stop Oliphant posing the next and obvious question. Given his talent for invention, it was wise to do so. This was no time to lock themselves into any promises, and he was likely to offer the earth to get what they wanted.

'Matters to be discussed when you meet,' Behan added. 'Which you now have to tell me how this will come about.'

'We must stand offshore during the day and come ashore by night, which will require some kind of beacon to guide us, a fire perhaps. I would suggest, if it is possible, we try for two days hence.'

'Sooner Pearce, surely?'

'Sorry, not possible' was his reply to Oliphant.

'We must get well clear of the shore and well out of sight. If I were Rosado, I would send out a cutter under canvas to ensure we go where we say, which means at least a day's sailing from where we now are.'

'The same time would be required to make the arrangement,' Behan added. 'The men of whom I speak are being watched.'

About to remark on that, Oliphant stopped himself, covering his failure to speak with a sort of grunt as Pearce responded.

'Then let us go first for the day after next and set aside three nights when, if the conditions favour it, we can boat to shore. This requires the beacon to be lit every night.'

'Lit fires on the beach are not unusual in summer.'

'So you accept it should be so.'

'The location is not of my choosing. It was suggested to me. Now I must pass back to them the other proposals you've put forward.'

'Leaving us with no idea if they've been agreed.'

'If you see a fire on the beach, Captain, there is the sign they have.'

Behan took another deep gulp of lemonade, which was as good as saying take it or leave it. And in truth it was the best that could be hoped for. Even then Pearce had no idea if it would answer the question they'd been sent to root out.

'You do not object to saying mass on a British man-o'-war, Father, as well as blessing such a vessel?'

'If you'd seen some of the places I have done services, Captain Pearce, you would not ask. For many of your fellow countrymen, it is seen as a sin to be so engaged.'

'The laws against Catholics have been eased, have they not?'

'Sure, indeed they have, but it takes more than statute to change the observances of men. There are parts of Ireland where those so minded to object are the law, with no great desire in Dublin Castle to chastise them, even should it come to the death of a priest.'

This was no place and no time to get into the quagmire that was Catholic Emancipation. Bills had been passed through Parliament in the last twenty years to ease the old strictures, which went back to the days of Oliver Cromwell. They'd been fought tooth and nail by the advocates of the Protestant Ascendency, so it was no surprise matters on the ground were not as had been intended.

'I will call the men to assemble on the deck then.'

'All of them, yourself included?'

Pearce thought about it for a moment. He was inclined to agree to be present, if not to participate, so what was seen by those observing fitted with what he'd said in his letter. It was Behan who produced a reason.

'You mentioned Henry of Navarre yesterday, did you not?'

'Whom I know was a Huguenot King and a convert to your faith. One who said, in order to claim the throne of France, Paris was worth a mass.'

'Then, surely to get out from here, you would see it the same way.'

'I will observe, but not participate. Oliphant, I suggest it would look good if you did likewise.'

'If you wish.'

At first Pearce was concerned not all of the crew were prepared to join in, so the notion of an explanation, to say it was a stratagem, was an option. But on reflection it would look to observers to be what was expected, only some of the crew being of the faith. Indeed, when he made the deck, there was one very vocal objection to what was about to take place.

A waister called Harry Teach, Blackbeard to his mates, who held deeply to his Methodism, saw what was happening as blasphemy. He was by nature a troublesome individual and had, within a few days of coming aboard as one of the quota men, nearly found himself lashed to a grating and getting his dozen.

The chastisement he received, verbal rather than physical, tempered his behaviour. But he was a rare sourpuss when spotted on deck, always bearing an air of resentment, for which he saw himself as having just cause. He'd been forced into the navy and would serve till the peace, about which Pearce could do nothing, but religion was different. He could not check him; the man had the right to refuse.

'You may go below and take with you any others who object. I must say to you, though, there is a reason why this mass is happening, and it has nothing to do with sacrilege.'

There was a hiatus as Teach went to gather three others who saw their souls imperilled by being present, and they left the deck. Others, Charlie Taverner and Rufus Dommet among them, were indifferent and so were allowed to gather at the forepeak, out of the way. The rest, all the Arklows, Michael O'Hagan, and one or two others, were content to use the deck and kneel at the proper moments. Pearce took station at the stern with Oliphant, sensing a chance to draw him out regarding his past.

'I met ordained priests in Paris, even one bishop, who openly admitted they did not believe in God.'

'Younger sons of aristocrats, I would guess, forced into their vows by their families, the rule being at least one for the church, the rest for the army.'

'You obviously speak of people you know.'

'I do, but I'm not minded to name them. And don't assume me a dolt, who cannot see what you're about.'

'An innocent remark,' Pearce protested.

Oliphant laughed softly. 'Perhaps you being such a poor liar, you should seek absolution from Behan.'

The rest of the ceremony was observed in silence, the intonations in Latin floating over the space between the ship and the harbour. Pearce had to fight the desire to look up at the battlements of Moro Castle, to see if there were heads over them, watching.

It was the briefest of a rite which could go on for hours, a single priest and no altar servers to carry the bread and wine, no boys swinging incense. Concluded, Pearce thanked Behan and saw him over the side, with a quiet word of hoping to see him soon. The tide had peaked in the middle of the mass. Now it was time to find out if they really were free to go. Given his continuing concern, it was no surprise the man who bore responsibility mouthed a silent entreaty.

Hallowell's orders sent men to the capstan while others raced aloft, a third party to the bows being ready to cat and fish the anchor once the men toiling below got the ship over her anchor. Pearce wanted it to be smooth and it seemed so, the fluke plucked cleanly from the sandy seabed, to be fetched and lashed to the side of the ship.

HMS *Hazard* was moving before the sails were sheeted home and the yards braced round, the falling tide beginning to take her out of the bay. Pearce, now by the wheel, legs spread, gave orders to the helmsman to take the ship well clear of the rocks at the base of Mount Orgullo, topped by the castle.

'I think we've got company, sir,' Worricker said. 'I see a boat coming out under sail.'

'With cannon?'

'No, sir.'

'I expected no less, Mr Worricker, and it may be entirely innocent. If it is not, let us hope she only has water and food for a day. Mr Hallowell, the salute to the King's flag, if you please.'

'You're not tempted to a repeat of Falmouth?' asked Oliphant, who had been given permission to stay on deck.

'Tempted, yes. But.'

'No need to explain.'

The booms of the cannon echoed across Santa Clara Bay, as the fortress replied, Pearce again glad it was only powder.

'Rosado will think he's humbugged us.'

'He might well have succeeded' was Pearce's response. 'Mr Worricker, is that boat under sail in our wake still?'

'He is, sir.'

'Well, if he's there two days hence, I'll sink the sod.'

There was no real sense of relaxation until they were a couple of miles out to sea, well out of the range of even the largest fortress cannon. Pearce could then put down his helm and head due west on the course he would be expected to take. This showed him both a coast too rock-strewn to effect a landing, as well as the flat, marshy country that formed the Oreo estuary. He could also pick out the small arc of beach where he could land.

If he'd not been on the mission, more sail would have left his pursuer struggling to catch up. But for every mile he made, he would have to do likewise in reverse, to be in position to react if the expected beacon appeared. In fine weather, on a benign breeze, they sailed on throughout the day, the sail-rigged cutter in their wake. At night he made no attempt at shucking off his tail. His lanterns were lit so he could be kept in view, a ploy which paid dividends when dawn broke, to show *Hazard* free of the chase.

'Mr Hallowell, we will come about. Let's get up that Swedish flag once more. And tell Mr Towse we will require his carpentry skills, to once more disguise the ship. We need first of all worm the cannon, then to get canvas over the side to hide the ports. Mr Williams, I want to be off the Oreo estuary by tomorrow twilight.'

'Aye aye, sir.'

Chapter Twenty

Walter Hodgson had been surprised to see Edward Druce in his local Clerkenwell Tavern, though he was too experienced to let it show. The White Swan was not the sort of establishment frequented by the likes of a prosperous prize agent, a stranger who'd sought to conceal his presence with an oversized beaver hat, pulled low over his head.

In high summer, it was headgear with which to draw attention, not negate it. Indeed, it was the incongruity of same that had drawn the thief-taker's eye in the first place, to then prompt the question: Why choose concealment in a place where nearly everyone had something to hide and, if they were blameless, did not care?

On the northern fringe of the city of London, Clerkenwell was home to many an honest trade, while being equally supplied with the more nefarious kind. It was a place to sell things not honestly acquired, or seek a person to forge a will or lottery tickets, the White Swan being a meeting place for both sides of a goodly number of the transactions.

Hodgson frequented it for two reasons, the first it being near his rooms, added to the good quality of the food, but the second was just as important. Many a villain or fence ate and drank there and, for a man whose task it was to bring villains to heel, there could be no better source of information on the doings of the criminal class.

The notion of loyalty among thieves was nonsense, jealousy and rancour being more common. The former arose when it was reckoned another had pulled a good and profitable stroke, always the subject of boast, followed naturally by envy. The latter tended to be based on the kind of perceived slights that lasted a lifetime or a dispute over a woman. Likewise, no thief saw what they were given as fair reward for effort, so could be relied upon to provide paid-for information, which a man look-ing to earn a bounty could pursue.

The name of Gherson was bound to come to mind with the sight of Edward Druce. Hodgson had just returned from Portsmouth, where he'd been acting on behalf of Emily Barclay. The sod was now safely ensconced as a purser on a navy transport vessel, due to sail to the Mediterranean. Hodgson had good grounds to believe the rat was now out of the country, so no longer of concern, either to him or the man now seeking him out.

The temptation to out Druce with a hearty greeting had been strong but resisted. If he was a fellow for whom Hodgson had little admiration, he was also one who'd provided much employment, added to a steady stipend. Yet his coming here had flown in the face of their prior arrange-ment, which left it to him to initiate a meeting. He had not done so, for there was nothing to report.

'You will recognise my voice,' Hodgson had said as he sat down a short distance from Druce. 'But do nothing to let it show, a nod will do.'

This forthcoming, Hodgson had then slid along the wooden bench to get closer and whisper an enquiry, in which Druce was told he'd be required to account for his presence. Nothing was said until Hodgson had been served with a tankard, as well as the kind of greeting afforded a regular customer, one which enquired after his health and his prospects.

'You may speak now,' he had hissed, as the owner of the White Swan, satisfied on both counts, departed.

Druce replied with a question, 'You have nothing to say to me?'

'If I had, you would know.'

'I have another search for you to perform.'

'Is one not enough?'

'It's necessary and takes precedence.'

With something approaching disbelief, Hodgson had listened to the latest task Druce wanted him to pursue, even more so in it having little to do with his present search. A missing ship, or not missing but stolen, added to the laughable idea of the King's Navy being the villain. Not that tars were beyond larceny, and it seemed there was one, not named, in this case. To this was added to a co-owner gone missing.

'It is necessary to find this fellow and get from him the documents proving the ship to have been English and the joint property of a client.'

Hodgson had been on the point of asking for the name but had sensed it would not be forthcoming. 'And the other matter?'

'Must wait. It cannot be long till the hull is sold at auction, and we fear the cargo may have already gone. On this occasion, it will be simple. I have both a name and a place of residence for the person you need to find.'

This provided, Druce had sidled out of the White Swan with such an obvious desire to be unrecognized he drew every eye, leaving Walter Hodgson to ponder on what he'd been told. It had not made much sense to him but, as he was being paid, this mattered little. There being no need to rush, he had then ordered food and ran over in his mind a reprise of what he'd been told.

This had given him good reason to think there were truths at the back of the incident not vouchsafed, yet it had seemed a simple enough commission. Against such a sanguine view lay the history of his previous dealings with Druce, which reminded him nothing in his past actions on behalf of the prize agent had been straightforward.

Yet this one had its advantages. It would take him along the south of the Thames, lined with places dedicated to seafaring, with the only known fact the pair he was in pursuit of were of this persuasion. Thus he would be able to combine the two searches, albeit one on the way back. This long being perceived as dangerous, it required him to take with him his pistol as well as a short sword, which he reckoned might be required. Not that he was looking for a fight; their names would do.

The coach to Rochester had been swift, there being a good road and frequent travel to and from the naval and military bases around the River Medway. From there on it was less so, a slow conveyance dribbling through a string of coastal villages until it reached Whitstable, where he alighted. From there the good road went inland so, coat off and looped round his satchel, he walked the length of Herne Bay, then up the hill enclosing it to the east, which brought him to the clifftops and his destination.

Beltinge could not claim the title of village, it was more a large hamlet, though quite a prosperous one, surprising given its windswept location and lack of arable land. The shingle beach below the cliffs indicated how its people earned their crust, being lined with small, drawn-up fishing boats, as well as huts for drying nets. None of what he could see as a hull was substantial; the people here fished the Thames, not deep water.

How many times had Walter Hodgson entered a strange place to be greeted with suspicious looks? He would have no cause to wonder why here, in a place on the road to nowhere. The coastal path he'd used led on to a rutted track that ran through the settlement itself, to carry on to the east. There would be a proper road to the port of Ramsgate, but it ran inland and passed this place by.

Visitors were thus an uncommon sight, established from the looks he received from the few souls out and about. There was a clutch of buildings round a church constructed of cemented flint stone, open but empty, while a call to root out a vicar went unanswered. He suspected it to be part of a multiple benefice, which meant a preacher coming by on a horse for a single Sunday service, before passing on to the next parish, a common situation in rural England.

His method in such places was to find a tavern, in this case The Tally Ho, where he secured a place to lay his head and leave his satchel and coat, a tiny room of little comfort. This he left to go sit in the taproom, where he would order bread, apple, and cheese, sip ale, and wait. There was always at least one person of a nosy disposition in such out-of-the-way places, often many more than one, and Beltinge was no exception.

One by one a quartet of fellows drifted in, all fishermen by their garb, to order ale and sit together, seeking to appear incurious. Hodgson knew he would be eyed and examined, by folk who thought they were employing discretion, when their swift and covert glances were obvious. They would act as though his mere appearance gave a clue to his purpose, which it did not, so eventually one would be detached to enquire.

'Greetings, friend' was lacking the warmth of the words. 'Not seen you around these parts afore.'

'Which would be, friend, because I have never visited, but I have a purpose and perhaps you can aid it.' Hodgson's tankard was raised and projected, to indicate information would be rewarded. 'I'm seeking the whereabouts of a certain Mr Jaleel Tolland, a person for whom I have information which will be much to his profit. If you can tell me where to find him, I'd be more than grateful.'

The look had changed before the sentence, to one that, until it was covered up, was so suspicious it did not bode well. Having been fairly relaxed, Hodgson was suddenly anything but: He was on his guard but wondering at the need. The way this fellow had reacted was not something he'd never seen before. It was the common one which preceded a lie, not long in coming.

'Never heard the name afore.'

'So you cannot help me?'

'None around these parts so called.'

His inquisitor swung round and returned to the table from which he'd detached himself, to lean over and whisper to his trio of companions, which caused them all to look hard at him. A person less versed in the ways of wickedness might have remained unflustered, but Walter Hodgson was far from the innocent he hoped to appear. Thus his hackles were active and his mind was racing.

What had been presented as a simple assignment now appeared anything but. It smacked of the kind of task he'd spent his life pursuing, which brought home one clear fact. In his open way of enquiring about Jaleel Tolland, he could have put himself at risk and the reasons mattered little.

Would there be an immediate consequence? He had to think not, The Tally Ho being too public, so he went back to his cheese and apple, cutting into both with an air of unconcern, aware of the continued whispering at the other table, even if it was beyond his hearing. The faint buzz had about it a tone which was not one to induce comfort, so he deliberately dropped his knife, which clattered onto the bare wooden floor.

As was intended, it drew more evident attention, which lasted as he stooped to pick it up. The act of examining the blade for traces of filth showed it to be a weapon made for more than slicing food. It was long, sharp, and came to a hooked point, clearly a blade that would do serious damage to more than a crisp apple.

Still in his hand, Hodgson looked across and smiled, both to show a lack of concern and indicate an apology for being so clumsy. Wiping the blade on his sleeve, he went back to his food, all he could do to send a message he was not to be trifled with. There was no need to search his mind as to why the name had triggered such a reaction; it had and there was nothing to do about it. He could only reflect, as he had suspected in the White Swan, there were things Druce had failed to tell him.

He acted calmly until both food and ale were consumed, then stood and made for the stairs, the knife still in his hand, not hidden, to under-line the message he would defend himself. There was no point in playing the innocent by acting as if there was no threat. He knew the mood in the air too well.

Sitting on the rickety cot, he wondered who was this Jaleel Tolland? Not what he'd been told, though he may be that, too, but a man whose name was not to be bandied about in the place he was said to live. Had he been chasing a felon, he would never have been so open with the name: Over the years he'd perfected many tales to explain his presence in out-of-the-way places, but here concealment was blown.

Obvious was the need to get out of Beltinge, but when he contem-plated the long coastal path he'd walked, it was not a prospect to think on as being safe. Hodgson had no reason to be sure there would be any action to harm him, but he had to allow for the chance. Not only was there the long walk, he also had to consider the length of the day. Even in summer, he would not be afforded the time to get to Whitstable before dark.

A display was required, one to warn off anyone thinking of attacking him. So out came the pistol, to be loaded and primed, it and the short sword stuck in his belt where, without his coat, they would be obvious. Seek to assault me if you wish was the message he wanted to send, but think what might be your fate if you try.

The attitude of the owner of The Tally Ho did nothing to reassure him. From being all hail fellow well met on arrival, doubly so when he was paid in advance, he was now unwilling to meet Hodgson's eye. Nor was he very forthcoming when enquired as to where a horse might be rented, until pressed to admit there was a farm, with stables, hard by an old Roman fort at Reculver.

Walking out into the sunlight, he saw not a single soul about, which was far from reassuring. There was little choice but to stride out with an air of confidence, his boots kicking up the dust from the rutted track. The view on another day would have merited attention, the expanse of the wide Thames estuary, with many vessels making their way up- and downriver. Through a summer haze, he could faintly make out the coast of Essex.

Occasionally, coming to abrupt stop and spinning round, Hodgson could discern no evidence he was being followed, which would have been close to impossible anyway on the open, grassy leas above the cliffs. The afternoon sun, added to the screeching, swooping gulls, seemed to mock his concerns, which allowed him an ease of tension.

The farm to which he'd been directed lay at the top of a path, which wound its way down to the beach, no doubt one on which horses were employed to fetch and carry. It occurred to him here was a good spot for smuggling, only to be reminded of how many such places existed along this coast.

The farmer had a spare horse as well as a good contact in Whitstable, a farrier to whom his animal could be taken and stabled until a need arose to fetch him back. Usually, Hodgson was told, this was for a local wishing for goods to be delivered, too heavy for human carriage. The fee was a lengthy haggle, but settled eventually at what would have been too high a price for a man not in a hurry.

The nag was far from impressive, either, appearing slightly blown, but it would serve, at a push, to outrun anything on two legs. Hodgson took with him a half sack of oats and some hay, tied to the saddle, to feed the beast come morning, along with a hobble rope for overnight. Before mounting, he stuck his short sword in the hay bag in such a way it would be easy to retrieve, then eased out his pistol, which he kept to hand. With the other on the reins, and with the advantage of height to look out for trouble, he set off at a walk to retrace his route.

Nothing threatened. There was no sudden flurry of birds to indicate a hidden human. At the pace he was moving, it took as long to get back to The Tally Ho as used in coming, so it was close to twilight when he arrived outside the tavern. Dismounting after a good look round, having made a point of visibly replacing his pistol, he led the horse round to the rear, where there was a field in which it could graze.

The chance existed of it being stolen overnight and much consideration had been given to this on the journey back. Yet unless he too slept in the field, there was not much he could do to prevent it, and this was a far-from-appealing prospect. Not because it was cold, for it was mild, but he would feel much more exposed outdoors than within a room, where he could contrive to bar a door, which could only admit one person at a time.

So hobble ropes on and hay net fixed to the low branch of a tree, the horse was left to munch, the oats taken indoors where he would beg some kind of receptacle in which he could mix them come morning. The access to his room, if anything so constrained could be so called, was through the taproom, which was empty. Not even the noise of his boots on the bare floorboards brought forth the owner.

The oats were dropped and the pistol put to hand once more, aimed up the stairs as he ascended. Stopping outside the door, he listened for a half minute, which felt like an hour until, fairly certain there was no one on the other side, he lifted the latch and nudged it open with his foot.

It looked empty, but his satchel and coat, left hanging on a nail, were now on the bed, the former with the flap open. Gingerly, Hodgson moved forward, pushing the door hard to ensure no one was hiding behind. Satisfied, it was closed, he looking round for something with which to jam it, eventually employing his sword, pushed into the base up to the hilt.

Laying his pistol on the bed, he lifted his coat to ensure it was intact, not concerned, for there was nothing in the pockets. He then looked inside his satchel, to see the spare shirts and breeches were there and so was the means to shave: his razor, strop, and soap. There were a couple of pairs of stockings under which he'd placed a rolled-up tube and he felt for it now, establishing very quickly it was gone.

If such articles as were still there had been left intact, it was no ordinary theft. What was missing was the tube holding the sketches of the two men he suspected were guilty of murdering Catherine Carruthers. It took only a second to conclude there must be a connection of some kind. Why take them if you did not know the faces?

And where was he, in a hamlet overlooking a shingle strand of fishing boats, with people unwilling to identify a man he'd been categorically assured lived hereabouts. The connection dawned and this meant no waiting for the morrow. Hodgson knew he had to get out now.

Chapter Twenty-One

Sir Thomas Byard was a wily old fox and a patient one. If there was an air of disquiet aboard HMS *Bedford*, it was no tinder keg, so he could wait to let the root of the problem reveal itself. He also knew, from his long years at sea, there was a pattern to what he suspected was happening beyond his cabin walls, which would grow before it could be deflated. Thus the lengthening list of defaulters on minor charges grew day by day, which he took as a sign his plan was working.

There were few flogging offences, or at least none that breached the normal, but many instances where grog was stopped and fines imposed. One fellow caught among the goats in the manger, with no reason to be there, was condemned for a whole day to be stapled to the deck. Given the sunny weather and the denial of water, this was quite a severe punishment. All came from clapping a stopper on things usually ignored, matters to which a blind eye would normally be applied.

The one to cause most upset, and Byard knew this well, was to clamp down on gambling, in any case forbidden by the Articles of War. It had to be said, those statutes of naval discipline prohibited so much they were incapable of full implementation, lest a captain was out to invite mutiny. But sailors loved to wager and, in normal circumstances, and as long as it was not too overt, or for stakes so high it would cause bloodshed, it would be ignored.

There were only so many places such activities could be undertaken, none of them a mystery to the ship's officers. A loud set of footsteps, or a tactical pause to examine a futtock for rot, could give the players time to hide their dice and disperse. The crew were fully aware of the unofficial attitude and clever enough not to push matters. They also knew, when the blind eye was suspended, it had to have a reason.

It was a wonder neither Jaleel nor Franklin Tolland could feel the mood shifting. But then fear, which could give them power, was also enough to isolate them, denying the brothers the information their hold over the crew was not as tight as they suspected. If they were told anything at all, it was what they wanted to hear, bitter complaints about food, pay, and the cheating habits and fourteen-ounce-to-the-pound weights of the purser.

But other voices had begun to be raised, or more likely whispered, from one person to another, never a group to be trusted. Men who could not rebel against tyranny from abaft the mast were not conditioned to take it in their own area of the ship. But nor were they fools, so word, when it began to filter up to the great cabin, came through hints dropped to the warrants.

They in turn, men of long service and, purser apart, held in regard, were well able to place cryptic asides into the ears of the divisional lieutenants. Nothing solid, for they were never given names or proof of disreputable activities. But there was enough to allow a picture to be fabricated, one which pointed to whatever action was necessary to restore matters to where they should be.

This saw Sir Thomas requesting a private meeting with the commander in chief of the North Sea Fleet aboard HMS *Venerable*. With some flag officers, it would have been an uncomfortable interview but, in Adam Duncan, Byard knew he had a superior who would both listen and understand. Popularity amongst a fleet, especially on such a dull and repetitious duty, could be gained only by the wise application of attention, to both duty and the care of those undertaking it.

Duncan was such an officer, not in any way diminished by a booming Scottish voice, or his bulky height and personal physical strength. This he was fond of demonstrating, despite his sixty-plus years, much to the amusement of those he led.

'Kind of you to grant me the time, sir,' Byard murmured, as he was shown into Duncan's day cabin.

'It's no a commodity of which I'm short, Sir Thomas,' Duncan replied, rising to greet him. 'If anything, I've got too much.'

'Particularly for seeing me alone.'

There were none of the executive officers or inferiors present, no captain of the fleet or flag lieutenant. Mind, Duncan had enough bulk to make up for their absence. There was a short wait while a servant laid out wine, with the admiral subjecting his visitor to a quizzical look.

'I hope you're no going to ask fur another visit to Chatham.'

Byard smiled and shook his head, at what must have been a constant request from certain fleet captains. Always with the insistence their ships were so unseaworthy, they were in need of repair. It was often suspected the man asking was in want of a bit of comfort, plus a little conjugal time with his wife or a visit to certain places where pent-up need could be dissipated.

'No sir, in that respect *Bedford* is sound.'

'And in other respects?'

With the servant gone, it was time to speak, to lay out the fact on the level of disquiet aboard and where he suspected it emanated.

'You were gifted this gang of smugglers, you say?'

'I was, from an officer, a master and commander. I had occasion to assist him off Sheerness, when he was preparing his vessel for sea. He'd been landed with almost a whole crew of lubbers, not one of whom could be relied on to even haul usefully on a rope.'

'The whole crew? I'm bound to ask who he's upset.'

'His name, sir, was John Pearce.'

'Ah!' Duncan exclaimed. 'Then no explanation is necessary.'

'He is described as a scoundrel, sir, but I have to say, I found him to be an officer doing his best and good company.'

Duncan poured the wine and smiled. He knew his visitor liked a drink, so good company meant a fellow who could shift a couple of bottles without stagger.

'Not an opinion much shared.'

'No, sir.'

'But then I don't know the laddie. Heard of his father, of course, more than I wanted to as well. Fellow countryman, Edinburgh man.'

The manner in which the last appellation was proposed was a hint, proposed by a man from Dundee, to be born in Edinburgh implied some kind of misfortune. It was not a place to go to for an Englishman, well aware of Scots' parochial dislikes.

'I think he saw it,' Byard continued, 'as some recompense for my help. Besides, in the size of vessel he commanded, added to the nature of the crew with which he'd been landed, they might have caused him serious trouble. On a seventy-four . . .'

'They could be absorbed. Am I to suspect it's no been the case?'

For all his bluff manner and exterior, Sir Thomas Byard had never doubted the sharp nature of Duncan's intelligence, and it was on show now.

'We lost a bosun's mate a few weeks back, you may recall the night we were pounded by torrential rain. It was suspected he'd been lost overboard and entered as such. There is whispering reaching the ears of my officers suggesting otherwise.'

'Do you have a culprit?'

There was no requirement for specifics. Duncan could read between the lines as well as any man and knew Byard was hinting at foul deeds.

'I have a suggestion, but no proof.'

'Added to a lower deck who will no provide you with any?'

'I think the trouble stems from the close relationship of the smugglers as a group.'

'Was one the man captaining the ship by any chance?' Byard nodded. 'And would he be the one you think might have seen to this bosun's mate?'

'He is a hard bargain *par excellence*. He beat the man seen as such on *Bedford* in a bare-knuckle bout and came close to maiming him.'

There was a hard look then from Duncan. If gambling was not permitted by the Articles of War, it paled beside crew members engaging in bloody fistfights.

'Punished?'

'A dozen, sir, which he took without a sound, to then leave the deck on his own two feet. As I say, a real hard bargain.'

'I suspect you'll want me to disperse your problem throughout the fleet?'

'Precisely. I particularly think there are two brothers who should not be on the same muster.'

'Which makes me suspect you're not telling me everything.'

'I am happy to speculate as much as you wish, sir, but that's all it would be.'

'Do you come with a list of names?'

Byard produced a paper from his pocket and laid it on Duncan's desk. 'I'm grateful for this, sir. Had you declined, I would have had to flog the problem into submission, given any request from me to my fellow captains would likely fall on stony ground.'

This got him another hard look: Byard was not known as soft, but there were other captains Duncan commanded who reckoned him so and were freer with the cat. It was to these the men on the list would be sent.

'You will want to be compensated?'

'As long as the people provided are not just another set of troublemakers.'

'I have to leave it to every captain to decide, but they'll not gift you their best and neither would I if asked.'

The list was examined, the double entry of the name Tolland obvious in what should have been a prize addition to Byard's crew. Smugglers knew their trade, being almost without exception prime hands. No doubt this lot were, but they were also trouble.

'Your Lieutenant Pearce did not do you a favour after all, Sir Thomas. It seems he rid himself of a problem and landed you with one. This sits right with the little I know of the rascal. I should be more careful with whom you share convivial bottles.'

'I shall, sir.'

This was the only response he could give, to what was as close to an admonishment as Duncan was prepared to go. It seemed best not to empty the glass before him, but to depart, with only one more thing to say.

'I shall await your decision as to where to disperse them, sir.'

In anticipation of trouble, Byard arranged for the Tollands and their one-time crew to be confined as soon as he knew to which ships they would be sent. The list from the flagship arrived the next day, to say he must expect boats from HMS *Director*, captained by William Bligh, and the fourth-rate HMS *Adamant*, commanded by William Hotham. They would take half each on the morrow and, no doubt, trade some of their lubbers in the process.

The brothers were at their mess table, along with half their old crew. Fresh from swabbing the decks, they were waiting for the breakfast mess tubs to be fetched from the cook when the marines surrounded them. They were bearing muskets, which created a buzz that ran along the deck, for here was sight none aboard had ever seen.

'Gather up your possessions,' commanded Lieutenant Laker. 'You're shifting berths.'

Jaleel Tolland was gripping the table so hard he looked to be trying to break it. When he let go, he stood up, to look along the deck at a mass of men who would not catch his eye. It was telling the marines, even with bayonets fixed, took half a step back, only the premier standing firm.

'And if I decline to be shifted?'

'You'll do so in irons, Tolland. All of you if need be.'

Franklin, still sitting, could see the fists bunch and knew by the way his brother's feet moved to get his balance, he was about to punch the premier, which was to court a rope from the yardarm.

'Belay, Jaleel. There's no way to change what will be.'

The stiffness eased as Jaleel agreed, but he was not done, swinging his head to look in both directions and glare. 'But there are those here who've crossed me and mark it, I will find out who they be. Don't think to sleep easy in your hammocks.'

There was one voice bold enough to answer back, though careful not to show a face, enquiring if Tolland could fly or even swim. It was Laker who admonished the speaker by demanding silence.

'In irons or of your own free will?' the premier asked. 'What is it to be?'

'Let's shift as they wish us to, lads, which will get us out of the stink of this barky.'

The banging started as soon as Jaleel moved, first one wooden plate slamming down on the deck, soon followed by others until, by the time the gang were being taken below to get their few possessions, it was every man at every table and deafening.

How different it was when they came on deck. The crew on watch would not look at them, concentrating on their tasks. To do so would mark their faces in memory, which was to be avoided. But there was a group not afraid to be identified, the bosun and his mates, come to see off men who, it had been hinted, had done for one of their number.

There were two cutters alongside, one from each of the ships, each with a quartet of marines as well as those rowing. First Laker watched as the men they brought as replacements were brought aboard, and a sorry bunch they appeared. There were a couple of slack jaws and one who appeared to lack control of his limbs. Truly the other captains had descanted their least able.

'Gather them in the forepeak,' the premier ordered. 'We will swear them in when these sods are gone.'

Those departing in the first were called forward to go down the side, Jaleel, ditty bag in hand, naturally leading, with Franklin sticking close to his brother.

'No,' Laker called. 'Hold back the younger Tolland.'

This required two marines, muskets now laid aside, to pin Franklin's arms as he first protested, then began to struggle, the deep scar on his face standing out a flaring red with the effort. As Jaleel dropped his bag and went to his aid, one of the bosun's mates stepped forward to hit him hard across the cheek with a starter, the knotted-and-tarred rope leaving a deep red weal, not that the victim recoiled.

'You're to go to separate vessels. Captain's orders.'

All eyes went to the poop, where Byard stood watching the proceeding. It was beneath the dignity of his rank to get involved, as he watched the elder Tolland pushed to the gangway. It was an indication of his strength, he could stop dead and hold his position, with a couple of marines putting in real effort to get him to move.

'Never fear, brother,' he called to Franklin. 'There's not a man nor a saint who can keep us apart for long. We've been in a spot afore and slipped out of bonds and will do so again.' The voice was raised and the look was aimed at the poop. 'Even if we has to take on the whole damn navy.'

The starter was used again, again taken without a flinch, Jaleel following with cackling laughter. 'That one I'll see takes the road to hell.'

'Where I might see a known face,' was the riposte.

'Don't respond, Jaleel,' Franklin called, fearing his brother, in a temper, might admit to his crime.

'I'm as wise as I need to be. But you stay whole.'

With that he went over the side, followed by half of the men he'd led. He seemed a meek fellow as he took his place in the cutter. Being so low in the water, none of what happened on deck had been witnessed but, if any of those sharing the boat could have seen into his mind, it might have made then shudder. Jaleel Tolland had only one way to act and it would not matter which deck he was on.

It was a meek Franklin who followed into the boat from the HMS *Adamant*.

Sat in the White Swan, Walter Hodgson was reflecting on the very thoughts he'd had on his hurried departure from Beltinge, which had been chilling in the extreme. The horse had to be kept on a path barely visible, this with a sheer drop at the cliff edge only yards away. It was with some relief he'd reached the flat strand of Herne Bay and could put his mount into a canter until he reached Whitstable. There he took a room, the door of which he once more used his short sword to jam shut.

Relieved of the horse next morning, it was coaches back to London and the safety of his own locale. He put word out with the Tolland name, to see if any of his contacts could supply information. With none yet forthcoming, was it time to send a message to Druce, a man he might have strangled had he encountered him on the night of his flight.

Calmer reflection made it seem unlikely Druce knew what he was sending him in to, which would have amounted to a possibly fatal trap: He wasn't the type for something so devious. Assuming the supposed co-owner of a client's ship was called Jaleel Tolland and he was one of the villains in the stolen sketches, where did it lead? He could not honestly claim he'd found his quarry, he had suppositions that was all, while the notion of going back to Beltinge, to nail the truth one way or another, did not appeal.

The answer lay with Druce, who'd avoided naming the second partner in this so-called purchase. It took no great deductive power to posit it had to be the same man for whom he'd acted previously, whose name he'd only come by from the loose tongue of Druce's clerk. The fellow had admitted his master was no more than a go-between in the tasks Hodgson had been set, to then name the person who was really paying his fees.

At the centre of the whole tangle of the last two years, pulling strings and prepared to kill a nonentity like Cornelius Gherson, out of pique at being cuckolded, sat Denby Carruthers. Put the name of Tolland to those sketches, assume them to be partners, throw in the attempt to have Gherson convicted of a crime he did not commit, and it led in only one direction.

If he'd had suspicions regarding Carruthers before, it had been without evidence to support it and no overpressing wish to seek more. He had before him a chance to secure some, the question he had to ask himself being, what was the worth of it? Justice served was a fine thing, but it did not fill your belly.

Not sure if, in the end he would walk away, as it being none of his business, which would certainly bring no reward, he decided he could not let lie something which would constantly trouble his thoughts. He must see Druce again and get from him any facts so far not revealed. Only then could he decide what to do.

CHAPTER TWENTY-TWO

It was rarely of any use becoming frustrated when at sea. Time and tide were more likely to act with indifference than wait for no man. As John Pearce made this point to Samuel Oliphant, he knew himself to be indulging in a degree of dishonesty: He shared the man's impatience, yet took a degree of pleasure in riling him by appearing not to care.

Some of the man's exasperation came from not being able to nap throughout the day, this due to the constant rumble of gun carriages on the deck. Pearce used every spare moment to work his crew on the cannon. He stood, watch in hand, timing them, as the commands were issued, seeking the places where delays were most obvious.

He also wanted to train his midshipmen to act like divisional officers on a larger warship, each in command of a trio of four-pounder cannons, while Worricker oversaw the loading and firing of the remaining five. At this point, there was no use of the swivels, but all were brought up, rigged, and in place, the move repeated time and again to speed up the process.

It was the main-deck cannon which would be employed as *Hazard* closed with an enemy and, being light in terms of weight of shot, accuracy was paramount. Added to this, the gun crews had to be trained to use all the various kinds of projectile, because when action ensued, quick decisions would have to be made as to what to employ. In short, to go for the hull, the deck, or the masts and sails.

One part of the operation was missing, the clearing for action, there being no need. The crews were called into place, having left their guns, as they would be when not required. In between drills they were allowed time to rest and drink some small beer, needed to replace the amount of sweat caused by heavy exertion in warm weather.

'Right,' Pearce called to Hallowell, in his position on the quarterdeck. 'Let us go again.'

The bosun's whistle brought the crew racing up from below. Pearce, eyes on his watch, was also counting off the seconds with tapping fingers until the first gun crew appeared. They were followed, by the time they all got to their places, by the powder monkeys, just before those commanding each section called out the first of the many orders.

'Take heed. Silence. Cast off your guns. Seize the breechings. Remove the tampion. Handle the cartridge. Put it into the gun. Wad your cartridge. Handle the rammer. Ram home. Take off the apron. Unstop the touchhole. Handle the pricking wire. Try if the cartridge be home. Draw the rammer. Shot the gun. Wad. Ram home wad and shot. Draw the rammer. Prick the cartridge. Handle the powder horn. Prime. Bruise the priming. Secure the powder horn. Cover the vent. Handle your crows and handspikes. Point the gun to the object. Lay down your crows and handspikes. Take off the apron. Fire. Stop the touchhole. Handle the sponge staff. Sponge the gun.'

Thumbs were put to touchholes again as the barrel was sponged, even if it had not actually been fired, the search following every four rounds, to clear out any debris with a wadhook, this followed once more by the sponge. It was habit that made perfect, as Pearce marked the time, watching as the reloading drill was executed in the same set of mantra-like orders.

Compared to what he'd had originally, it was chalk and cheese and, if not yet crack frigate speed of three rounds in five minutes, it was well on the way at eight. The reloading times were subject to competition for, if it was a good idea to repeat a broadside, the time came when such rigid order could not be maintained. It then fell to individual crews to fire at will.

That, too, was coming along. He watched each individual gun captain urging his party to as high a speed as was possible, without breaking the need for rhythm. Also, those in charge of multiple weapons, the youngsters, Maclehose, Campbell, and Tennant, were acting way beyond their years and with increasing confidence, albeit looking to Worricker, who was setting the example.

The Mite, Livingston, was by the side of Hallowell, ready to act as messenger, despite it being a more dangerous position in battle than along the gun deck. For an untrained eye, it ended up looking like mayhem, but to anyone who'd been in battle, they would see it as what it had to be. Putting as much shot into an enemy and accurately was the requirement, in as short a time span as could be achieved.

'Later today, we shall have some musket practice, then put out a target for your cannon. Let us see if your aim has improved as much as your speed of loading and firing. Hands to dinner, Mr Hallowell, Tennant and Livingston to take the deck.'

This got a smile from the premier. His captain had employed a good look around the empty seas before issuing the order. It was time to give the two youngest mids a bit of responsibility.

'I don't know which is worse,' Oliphant complained, after he'd finished eating, when told of what was coming, 'the grinding of the carriage wheels on the deck or the endless banging of cannon. It gives me a headache.'

'What's worse is knowing you're in a fight and losing. This induces much more than a headache, believe me.'

'There's a good chance we will be up all night again. An opportunity to get in some sleep would be of benefit.'

'Has anyone ever told you, you're like a hibernating bear? I've never known anyone sleep so much.'

'I'm never so when I need to be alert. Like a bear, I can sleep with one eye open.'

'So can bores.'

'Very amusing.'

Oliphant taking the jibe so well indicated they were getting on better, having moved to a state where general and gentle ribbing was acceptable. Pearce was unsure if this meant he, too, was the object of a certain amount of respect, but he did know he had come to think better of his companion. The man was coolness itself in any situation requiring quick thinking.

'The firing will be of short duration. One attempt on the target each. Once it's over, we will head inshore and you can nap until it's time to take to the boat.'

'If indeed we do so.'

'I'm feeling fairly confident.'

'Often a prelude to disaster in my experience.'

There was no rushing when the cannons were fired. The gun crews were employed one by one, using their handspikes and crows on a static target, but from a moving ship, especially when it came about. This time Worricker stood aside, so aiming was as much the task of the midshipmen as the gun captains, even Livingston being given a chance to display authority. He had little problem, being liked and a sort of mascot to the crew, who would not have let him look as if he'd failed.

They were trying to hit a floating barrel, the price of which Pearce reckoned he might end up paying for if anyone succeeded. It got through the exercise intact, but he was pleased at the proximity of the landed shot. Great spouts bracketed it, not one of which had failed to drench the object.

Guns housed once more, the watch off duty were left to their own devices, the helm being put down to close with the shore. Pearce went over the calculations made by Mr Williams in the master's company, not as in any way a reproof. It was more the need to be sure they would make a landfall precisely where they had to. A mile or two off in either direction, and they might not see any lit beacon.

They were going ashore again, but in vastly different circumstances. Any reception should be free of threat, but it might not be the case. As Oliphant had pointed out, if the Spaniards knew their Basque subjects to be seeking freedom, and it could be no mystery, they would have spies watching the leaders it was expected they might meet.

It was best to be assumed danger existed and consequently it required to be guarded against. Yet what a difference the few days since Hendaye had made for, this time, Pearce was going ashore with many of the ship's company. He was now convinced he had a crew on whom he could rely. His quota men, or at least those with aptitude, were improving every day, and even the inept were less surly.

The Arklows, and he was beginning to think of both groups as Hazards, seemed more than content since San Sebastian and being allowed ashore to mass. This was evidenced by the attitudes they displayed. Quick obedience to orders and a willing attitude in carrying them out gave him more freedom with his assets.

'We will be in two boats, Mr Moberly, your entire marine contingent in one.'

'None left aboard, sir?'

'Perhaps one on the spirit room.'

Moberly was satisfied, this particular storeroom being a constant worry for a marine officer: If the crew ever got in, they would drink it dry and chaos would ensue.

'I also intend your boat should be crewed by our Irish contingent, armed and under the command of Mr Macklin. They have shown greater ability with muskets than our original crew.'

'No match for my men, sir' came across with a touch of pomposity, to which Moberly was prone.

'Obviously. You are to stand off and be ready to lay down disciplined gunfire to cover us, if we have to get off the beach in a hurry.'

Michael O'Hagan was pleased to be along, Pearce too, always feeling a bit more secure with the Irishman's muscle to hand. There was also his ability, proven often, to sniff trouble before it manifested itself, and he and Oliphant were going to be dealing with strangers. They might be Basque secessionists but this did not render them harmless. Had they not been hand in glove with the French less than twelve months past?

Pearce was on deck when the first distant smudge of the shore showed, behind him again a brilliant sight, as the sun sank below the horizon to turn the clouds in the pale blue sky into a flaring vision of orange and reds. For his purpose the weather was perfect, mixed high cloud, never so widely spread as to entirely block out starlight.

The noise of men getting ready was also present, along with the atmosphere which goes with impending action, a sort of collective tingling, mixed with jokes about prowess and nerves. Oliphant joined him as the last of the sunset turned the clouds to dark grey, his mood, unusually, far from sanguine.

'Strikes me, if these Basques cannot give us a clue to Spanish intentions, we are going to struggle to find out anything. I was with you about not just boating ashore as we did on the French side, but now we've seen how numerous the Dons are, as well as clearly suspicious, I doubt we last half an hour just barging about seeking answers.'

'I thought you never worried about things you could not change.'

'I'm not sure failing Dundas is an option for either of us, so forgive me if I make an exception.'

'Then it's best we don't.'

Maclehose called down from where he'd been placed, on the mainmast cap. 'I think I can see the estuary, sir. The light is illuminating a gap in the shore.'

Having thanked the mid, Pearce said, 'If I had a worry there it was, missing the right point of rendezvous, Williams even more so.'

'He thinks you've yet to forgive him for the gale he sailed us into off the Thames. Mentions it sometimes.'

'If he has told you so, please pass this back. It's forgotten.'

'Which will be no good to one of nature's worriers.'

'Time to man the boats. I dare not take us too far in. If it goes wrong, Hallowell has to have plenty of sea room to get away.'

'This is the bit I dread.' Oliphant groaned as he headed for the gangway.

'With good reason, but I've promised not to let you drown.'

'Not me you haven't.'

The act of filling the boats was carried out at no great pace, which allowed plenty of time to help Oliphant, Pearce armed with his pistols and sword, being the last to make his way down the man ropes and battens. The faces of those who would row him ashore were now pale blobs, all of whom had weapons by their feet, hangers and tomahawks. He felt for the first time entirely at ease in their presence, the sense of common purpose palpable.

'Bear away, Mr O'Hagan.'

The laugh from the Irishman was immediate and loud. He'd got his mister.

There was no intention to row right in to the beach, only to be close enough should a beacon be lit. So the point came where the two boats, using oars to stay steady and prows pointed east, were left silent and rocking on the swell.

'Is that a torch?' Oliphant cried, as a small flicker of flame appeared.

'Looks like it,' Pearce replied in a quiet riposte, not ready to see it as signal.

He watched it as it moved, a pinprick held aloft, entirely removed from its surroundings, like a ghost was doing the bearing, not a human hand. The second it dipped, whatever it touched flared up, probably tinder-dry driftwood.

'Haul away.' Out came his pistols, Pearce vaguely aware of Oliphant acting likewise. 'Mr Moberly, d'ye hear?'

The positive reply floated across the water as both boats began to move. It wasn't long before the first wave began to break, proof of a shelving seabed. Almost on cue, the moon appeared, low above the horizon, more a waxy yellow than white on this part of its nightly trajectory. Yet it lit up the wide water at the estuary, showing a flat expanse of silver, which diminished as it narrowed to river. Now the beacon was flaring and, as they closed, there could see, standing by it, the outlines of a group of men.

'Preparing to stand off, sir.'

'A bit closer, Mr Moberly, I think,' Pearce called back. He was as good as saying a Sea Service pattern Brown Bess musket, with its barrel shortened nine inches from the infantry pattern, was not a weapon of outstanding accuracy. 'We require your fire will be effective.'

The waves were breaking regularly now and, along with this, came the sound of crashing water, as well as phosphoresce as they hit the rocks north and south. But with a wide river mouth straight ahead, the incoming tide worked up a bore effect. This came as a low, straight, and continuously even flow, to carry them in with little effort on the oars. Other than keeping the prow pointing to where they wished to go, there was no great effort required, which meant a slight alteration for the marine boat.

'Mr Moberly, you will struggle to stand off as intended. Let the wave carry you into the centre of the estuary, where it will dissipate. It will put you well within range of yonder beacon.'

Pearce could see the ground before that article, sand reflecting the colour of the rippling flames. A soft call to Michael had him make a slight adjustment so the prow bore into the soft sand at right angles, men immediately out and up to their knees in the water, using a strong grip to keep it in place.

He stepped over the prow and dropped down onto the beach, careful with his pistols, with Oliphant likewise exercising care, this being the last moment to allow an accidental discharge. Michael O'Hagan, having issued orders to secure the boat to the beach, followed them. From the silhouetted group framed by flames, one body detached himself to come forward, the voice as cheering to John Pearce as it had to be to Oliphant.

'As your national poet says, sure, you come most carefully upon your hour.' As he'd moved to be level with them, flames lit up one side of Behan's face, which, as usual, wore a smile. 'You may put up your weapons, Captain. They will not be required.'

Behan turned and walked towards the fire, Pearce and Oliphant in his wake. The group who'd been silhouettes now became faces, albeit lacking clarity due to the flickering flames, with only one feature common. If the heat of the fire was palpable, there was no warmth on these faces. They were set and determined looking.

They spread out so their visitors could come closer, Pearce noting the priest was not wearing a soutane now, but boots and breeches, which was something to wonder at. Just how involved was he with the movement to gain independence? He rattled off a sort of speech in an unintelligible tongue, the only words recognisable the two names of the arrivals, none being provided to them.

'You may speak in French. Everyone here understands, but I'll not be using any of their names until permitted to do so.' He must have sensed this was insufficient, so Behan added, 'If you don't know them, they can't be given away.'

'Not true in reverse,' Pearce said in English.

'The people they have to worry about know yours only too well, Captain. I have explained what it is you're after and have good grounds to believe you can be satisfied.'

'Which means,' Oliphant interjected, 'you might have had the answer already, so having a clandestine meeting would be superfluous.'

There was a slightly terse tone in what had, up till now, been the same friendly voice employed since first acquaintance. 'Even if I did, I would not be at liberty to divulge it.'

'The sanctity of the confessional?' Pearce asked, as the obvious struck home.

'Sure, it is the very thing.'

Which Pearce saw immediately as a perfect way for conspirators to communicate. If it was questionable a priest should act as a conduit for such messaging, it had the virtue of security in a strongly Catholic nation. Even the famed Inquisition would pause before demanding such a sacred vow be broken.

One of the up-till-now-silent group stepped forward, his voice strong, his eyes flicking between Pearce and Oliphant, the whites picking up the firelight, which added a dramatic touch.

'I think it is time you tell us what you can do for our cause.'

'Us do for you?' Pearce asked, confused.

He was about to say it was the other way round when Oliphant cut across him, his tone confident. 'How can we, monsieur, if we have no idea what you want or need?'

Chapter Twenty-Three

'They're doing no more than ask from us the kind of conditions they were offered by the French.'

'With the slight difference,' Pearce pointed out, 'we're not a victorious army, in possession of the territory they wish so desperately to liberate.'

'They're a bit full of themselves, don't you think?'

'A tough bunch, it's true, if you believe what we were told.'

And this had been quite a list. Every defeat inflicted on the enemies of the Basques had been described and they were numerous, going all the way back to the time of Charlemagne, where they'd barred the Pyrenean passes to his retreating army. None, according to these proud representatives, had stood up to Basque military prowess: Moors, the Spanish and French monarchies, all had been driven off.

'Makes you wonder how they've ended up under the thumb of Madrid.'

'You managed to talk them into the ground, so why not the Dons.'

This got a chuckle, which indicated Oliphant had taken the dig well. He'd acted on the beach with his usual confidence, as if he had the power to alter matters. This was just as well because, as Pearce reminded him, one of the Basque contingent had named him as being a representative of the British government.

'How did they get hold of that? We didn't say anything, and I don't recall either of us telling Behan. It was a tale we made up to humbug Rosado.'

'You sure about Behan?'

'Think back.'

Pearce, nursing his coffee, looked into the near-empty cup, examining the grains as would a fortune-teller. Reprising the conversation in the cathedral vestry, nothing came to mind regarding Oliphant's invented mission to Lisbon. They'd lied to the commandatore because it was necessary. There had been no need to do likewise with Behan.

'If we did not, it means the information came from somewhere else. Do any of your recently acquired Irishmen speak French?'

'Given the level of their English, I take leave to doubt it.'

'Well, where else would it come from?'

Pearce was slightly narked at the tone, which implied not knowing was his fault. But surely none of his quota men were French speakers, which extended to his Pelicans. Hallowell and Worricker were not as far as he knew, likewise the warrants. It would have made no difference if the latter were fluent. They'd had no opportunity to pass on the information.

'Which leaves Rosado himself,' Oliphant proposed. 'He must have made the arrangements that had Behan doing the confessing.'

'To get to Behan, it would have had to come through the archbishop. He told us his instructions came from on high.'

Pearce slapped the table. 'Rosado would have told those with whom we dined.'

'I was much queried about my supposed position, so everyone present knew.'

'What about those serving, they might have overheard.'

'Possible. But take the notion it was not a servitor one step further and where does it lead? To our friends of last night having an informant in the higher ranks of the Spanish garrison and one who may have the answer we need.'

'Which means,' Pearce responded, and it was not a question.

'It comes down to how we extract it from the people Behan wants us to meet. They will know from him it's what we're after. Why meet with us if they're not going to use it to trade?'

'Which takes us back to the French offer, which we're in no position to match.'

'Perhaps. If Spain was at war with us, London might consider backing an insurrection, if the conditions were favourable.'

'But how do we get them to open up,' Pearce asked, 'without we promise it?'

Oliphant responded after a significant pause. 'Is this not possible at some future date? If we can generally thump the French at sea, to bring them to the table and make peace requires armies. If Godoy can sign away Hispaniola for the sake of gaining a treaty, what's to stop Billy Pitt, or whoever comes after him, from doing the same for their Donostia?'

'That, if I may say so, is very far-fetched.'

'What about Gibraltar? That was given to us by treaty.'

'Thank you for the lecture in history' was the ironic response. 'And Gibraltar is singular in its geography.'

'I talk only of example.' Oliphant was warming to his theme. 'Whatever they think my position is, does it exclude a guarantee from me, of Britain landing an army to help fight their cause?'

'I think you mean us. I, for one, would be uncomfortable lying.'

'Which, if you'll allow me to say so, is nonsense. And are you not lying when flying flag at the masthead of another nationality?'

'It's different.'

'Nor would you hesitate to raise a tricolour to gain an advantage over a Frenchman?' There was no point in answering such a question, the rejoinder being obvious. 'You would and employ every underhand trick in your arsenal to win.'

'There's a difference between outright lies and a ruse.'

'Should you ever meet your maker, I'd like to hear you explain the difference. Our Basque friends are doubtless playing a long game, and I refer once more, to their abrogated agreement with the French Revolution. Talk about supping with the devil. They will take aid from wherever they can find it and, no doubt, lie with ease if it suits their cause. I would do the same.'

'Which I've never doubted.'

'All I'm suggesting is we put the best gloss we can on what might be possible, in the hope of unlocking their tongues.'

Pearce was obliged to listen while Oliphant, now excited, drove home the nature of their mission. If Spain was preparing to declare war, they'd be making preparations to take maximum advantage of surprise. An attack on Gibraltar could begin as they dithered. How many innocent merchant vessels would fall to the Spanish Navy before they knew they were no longer allies?

'And what about Jervis's fleet?' was his concluding argument. 'Are you so principled you'll see them destroyed?'

'So you propose to put this forward?'

'I'm hoping we will put it forward and not just for our own sakes. And I add, if we're to succeed, Pearce, we have no choice.'

'I doubt they would just take our word.'

'But do we not have the means to indicate good faith, money given to us for the very purpose of bribery?'

'Do you think gold will do the trick?'

'It's worth a try. So, do we go back tonight with this as the plan?'

It was some time before Pearce responded. 'I'll issue the orders.'

'While I work out how to present our demands.'

'We're making demands?'

'Of course. You must always have them when negotiating. We cannot allow them to think we are mere supplicants.'

'I sense another bluff.'

'Exactly so' came with a smug air.

Oliphant did come up with a tale, which made sense to those he was addressing. In this he was aided by the absence of Father Behan, the presence of whom could have made the story harder to maintain. It seemed his pastoral duties did not allow for extended absences, but he was staunch friend to Basque aspirations and would be kept informed of progress, if any could be achieved.

Oliphant spoke next to suggest this was possible, to confirm, after a day of consideration, he felt he could act on behalf of his superiors, in laying out a basis for future cooperation. The first thing he insisted upon were names.

'His Majesty's government must have people to deal with. They cannot make arrangements with phantoms. I will require a written request for aid from some form of representative body, as well as proof it speaks on behalf of the people of the region. My companion and I will move away, so you may discuss it.'

'Why bother?' Pearce whispered as they moved. 'We can't understand a word they say.'

'It looks right. I've thought long and hard about these people, Pearce, and have them down as fanatics. Such people, in my experience, are neither honest, open to reason, or constrained by principle. If it would advance their cause, they'd probably cut our throats or hand us over to Rosado.'

'Hard to disagree.'

'I wonder if you can guess whom they remind me of.'

It took a moment of consideration before Oliphant got an answer. 'Jacobins, perhaps.'

'Exactly. I have no notion of whether their aims are justified. But I do suspect there are no ends to which they would not go to gain them. If you're still in doubt about what we're proposing to do, think on that.'

The discussion behind them went on for so long, Pearce had to call out, to remind them there was a limit to how much time they had. The boats needed to get off the beach and well out to sea long before daylight. This did little to stem the exchange, while the fire around which they gathered was on its way to being embers before a conclusion was reached.

'We will give you a resolution from our Cortes.'

'You have such a body?' Oliphant demanded, though with a degree of tact.

Even with the diplomacy, it was taken as an affront. 'We had a Cortes in the past, monsieur, when there was no Spain to suppress us. Can I remind you of those we have vanquished . . .'

'I must stress,' Oliphant interrupted, no doubt wishing to avoid another litany of Basque historical victories. 'And I mean no disrespect, when I point out to you, I have to convince those who do not know either you, or your cause. They need to be persuaded you are worth support.'

'How can you doubt it, monsieur?'

'It is not I who has to consider the possibility you could be painting a picture, which is not truly as it exists, a mirage in fact.'

The temptation to dig Oliphant in the ribs and say he was going too far was strong. You didn't have to be a fanatic to be touchy, and he was coming in high, possibly too high.

'I trust there are people in England, monsieur, who know something of our history. Mention the Chanson de Roland to anyone of refinement.'

'Can I persuade anyone with a medieval poem?'

'It speaks to the world of our birthright and achievements.'

'I will make it my business to ensure our government consults those who know of your past. But I must remind you of what it is which will sway them towards belief and assistance. Proof, if it exists, that Manuel Godoy . . .'

He had to stop then as the man to whom he was talking spat into the sand.

'. . . is contemplating siding with France in the war against our country. If it is so, we need to know when it will be declared.'

'I think, monsieur, we have the means to satisfy you.'

'And what does it take to have you reveal it?'

'We will provide you with an official request from the Basque Cortes to the British government, seeking aid to gain freedom from the Spanish Crown.'

'With named members.'

'If you guarantee to keep it secure. For this we will require armed assistance, for we will fight, if weapons are provided.'

'I will give you a letter promising to take your proposals to the highest council in the British State. I will also recommend I return to undertake further enquiries as to how matters may be progressed.'

He might have made it sound very grand, but Pearce sensed it was not enough. So he tapped Oliphant and whispered in English to once more move down the beach, there to indulge in an entirely mock dispute. There was arm waving, raised voices, even a display of huff until finally a resolution was arrived at. They returned to find the embers being fed with more wood.

'Monsieur, I was on a mission, when we stopped off in Donostia.'

'To Lisbon.'

So, Pearce thought, they know about that too. While feigning surprise, Oliphant admitted it was true.

'I had with me a gift from my government to Her Majesty Queen Maria Braganza, in the form of a substantial sum in gold coin.'

The pause was masterful, creating a perfect sense of tension, even the flames of the newly revived fire adding verisimilitude.

'We, Captain Pearce and I, are willing to pass this to you as a sign of both our goodwill and that of His Majesty King George. It is to use, as you see fit, to further your aims. I require you to confirm this will be acceptable.'

This engendered another discussion, which was more heated than the mock argument indulged in by Pearce and Oliphant, who out of politeness, moved away once more.

'Is it real or are they playing the same game as us?' Pearce suggested.

'No way to tell. And who cares as long as it reaches the right conclusion.'

'We're still going to be on this damn beach when the sun comes up.'

'We can't leave without an answer.' The sudden silence indicated this was about to be forthcoming. 'Back we go and I have crossed my fingers.'

'Provided your offer, monsieur, comes with a written commitment to seek help for the Basque people from the English government, stating your position and signed, the offer of financial help will be accepted. It will allow us to provide for you what information we are able to collect.'

Pearce wanted to say information I think you already have, provided by one of those officers at Moro Castle, who might well be a Basque himself and loyal to their cause. Not that it mattered: It could just be venality.

'If you bring the promised funds tomorrow, I hope to have for you an answer to your question. Now, I think, given it will soon be light, you should be on your way.'

'I would be reluctant to make delivery of the gold contingent upon us not knowing Spanish intentions. I think you will understand I must insist on hard fact, not guesswork. To go back to my superiors without verifiable information would severely dent any efforts I might make.'

'Be assured, monsieur, I understand what you need.'

'I will not deny they could be acting in bad faith. Gold has tempted more than one man to break a vow.'

'I don't recall any vows being made,' Pearce responded. 'A promise at best, but we are proposing to go ashore with a large sum of money.'

'Given to us for the purpose, part of which you spent on gunpowder.'

'Trust me when I say it will provide benefit.'

'So you're not prepared to trust them?'

'I have no desire to have to trust them.'

'You're beginning to sound like me.'

The response by Pearce was not designed to accept what was clearly intended as a jest. It was full of bitterness.

'I was gifted a sum of money by Dundas previously and used it as intended, yet he's still claiming I wasted most of it. If it wasn't from his secret fund, so unable to be raised in a court of law, I could be in a debtor's gaol. I'm suggesting precautions be taken and it falls to me to implement them.'

There was no long haul with boats this time. HMS *Hazard* was going as far inshore as safety would allow. This, with the slight change of an earlier high tide, put the beach within range of a pair of loaded swivels. The same tidal change would allow Moberly to take his marines farther into the estuary, while a firing tube for a blue light rocket was to be shipped in.

Michael O'Hagan was put in charge of this, taking a shaded lantern with lit tallow to provide, if he got a sign from John Pearce, the means to fire it off. He was also at liberty to do so if he suspected matters were not going as planned. The chest of gold was to stay in the cutter till Pearce signalled it should be handed over.

This should persuade the Basques, should they seek to take the money, without providing anything in exchange, they would never get off the beach alive. Even if they did, the effect of a rocket illuminating the sky would be seen for miles, which must alert their Spanish overlords to investigate.

'As long as no shot is aimed at us' was Oliphant's gloomy request.

This was said as he laboured slowly over a piece of parchment, on which he was listing promises he had no right to make and no real belief would ever be met.

'It's for threat only,' Pearce reassured him, which was only partially true. He knew, once action was set in motion, it could become impossible to control.

The nerves were jangling as they crossed from the ship to shore, a single lantern amidships, added to another on the crow's nest, to show those on land *Hazard* was present. They'd be fools not to sense the previous approach had changed and deduce why when faced with a warship.

It was all unnecessary: The beacon was as bright as ever, the same group of Basque worthies around it, with one addition. Whatever pastoral duties Behan was avoiding, he was there to oversee the exchange, behaving as his usual cheerful self. There was one comment, when greetings were complete, which hinted at a different character underneath.

'It would grieve me if we should ever meet on Irish soil, Captain Pearce. I find it easy to see a good man in you here. But there, I fear you would be just an oppressor.'

'Which I am not minded to be, Father.'

'Do you not wear a coat which says the opposite? Now, having said my piece, let my Basque companions tell you what they know.'

'They are aware it has to be worthwhile.'

'Rest assured, what you will be given is of greater value than what you fetch.'

A call to Michael got the chest brought up the beach, with Oliphant asking Behan, if he knew what it was, why he just didn't say.

'I'm sure the answer will come to you' was all he got in reply.

The document Oliphant took was much weightier than the one he handed over. The small chest was opened, to reveal a sight even more alluring in firelight than daylight, over one hundred and fifty guineas in value. Behan said something to his companions in Basque, which had their leader address Pearce in French. His referred to another peace treaty between France and Spain, this time concluded at the royal place of San Ildefonso. It was one which meant he decided on war.

'Godoy will declare on the arrival of the *Santa Leocadia*, a frigate, which is carrying silver from the Caribbean. For this he must wait.'

'When and where?' Pearce demanded.

'It is due to be landed at Vigo. When, monsieur, depends on factors of which you know more than most. But we have been informed, it's expected before the end of the month.'

'And if it doesn't land?'

'Godoy has committed Spain to fight alongside France. It will be war because it is what he wishes, but perhaps our soldiers will go without pay.'

'Then you will forgive me, messieurs, if we depart. We have no time to waste.'

Pearce was shouting orders before they even got back aboard, for the right pennant to be hoisted, all sail set, and a course laid down for Vigo. Oliphant was composing, in his head, the message he would send back, by pigeon, to Henry Dundas.

CHAPTER TWENTY-FOUR

It was a poignant moment for the Mite, when the time came to release the pigeons. Oliphant had decided and Pearce could not disagree, to despatch both on the grounds one could be brought down by a raptor, a gunshot, or even a lack of the power required for the distance. This was held to be near the capacity of such birds to home. The information they carried, minute writing on a tiny scroll, placed into a thin, featherweight and varnished wooden tube attached to one leg, was too vital to risk it not getting through. If they knew the danger to the Mediterranean Fleet, neither man had any notion of what other problems would be brought on by a Spanish desertion.

'I will ask you to release them, Mr Livingston. I fear neither Mr Oliphant nor I are competent when it comes to handling birds.'

In this Pearce was fibbing; many times in his life he'd handled birds, sometimes seeking to succour those with broken wings. Just as often he had raided nests for eggs, but he knew it was going to sadden the lad, for whom these creatures were now pets. So a touch of recompense, even flattery, was in order.

'And I also think it is time you moved to join your fellows in the midshipman's berth. It gives me great pleasure to say, you have come on a great deal. I can see the makings of a very competent seaman commanding my deck and in short order too.'

It was the lad, with his small and nimble fingers, who attached the messages Oliphant had composed, of necessity the barest minimum of information. Brought on deck in the baskets picked up at Falmouth, the boy caressed and kissed them before release, then stood watching as they headed north until there was sight of them no more.

Pearce and Oliphant had discussed the contents of what had been despatched, quickly concluding there was no room for a reference to the *Santa Leocadia*, which Pearce and HMS *Hazard* were on their way to intercept. Nor did it refer to the obvious fact, a vessel of their size would find it hard going in taking on a frigate.

'A daunting prospect,' Oliphant concluded when the odds were explained to him: heavier cannon, a much larger crew, and higher scantlings. 'Does it not occur, you're disobeying the orders given you by Dundas?'

'It's possible, if the *Santa Leocadia* can be intercepted, the Dons might reconsider. Surely this justifies the risk.'

'Not possession of the cargo?' came with a wry smile.

A secondary consideration was a justification, by the look on his face, Oliphant clearly doubted.

'Let's hope it doesn't turn out to be a false tale.'

This had been a worry, which arose not long after *Hazard* had been set on course for Cape Ortegal. The need to immediately get her under way masked any consideration of why the Basques might have concocted the story. Even if it had been examined and seen as unlikely, this did not obviate the possibility.

Yet set against the way the Dons had behaved in San Sebastian, it made sense. The mood of suspicion on their arrival, the questioning as to why, then the way they'd not been allowed to wander, meant there was something they did not want them to see or hear. This validated the quest.

'I imagine they were mighty relieved to see the back of us' was Pearce's opinion. 'They must have been worried sick we'd find out.'

'They'll be even more indisposed when they find out we have.'

The conversation now being held was the first real chance they'd had to indulge in retrospective speculation. Pearce had hardly been off the deck, to ensure they were sailing as fast as could be attained and, in the circumstances, it could never be enough. The first point of notice, Cape Ortegal, on the western shoulder of Iberia, was not far off, this being the point at which Pearce could change course to the southwest. Given progress so far had been good, he hoped to have it off his beam before the day was out.

On the desk was a chart of Vigo and its approaches, which in essence was the open Atlantic, which rendered the possibility of interception difficult. There was only so much area of sea *Hazard* could cover, which meant, to cut down on failing to sight the frigate would oblige them to stay within reasonable proximity to the destination.

Yet this could not be so far inshore as to make them visible, while farther out was not much safer. They were in waters rich with fish, as well as the boats seeking to catch them. This made sailing a box course for any length of time, even once more disguised, as risky. The fishing boats did not stay out or long and, in landing their catches they would report their presence. Vigo would be even more on tenterhooks than San Sebastian.

'And then there's the wind. We would need it to favour us to even have a chance of interception. If they have the weather gage, they can slip by us at will.'

'None of which is of much interest to me, Pearce.'

'Really?' was the response to the languid, dismissive tone, from a man slightly stung by the earlier reference to his being motivated by greed. 'I had it in mind to put you on the muster, so you could share in any spoils we might acquire.'

There was amusement to be had in watching Oliphant trying to remain indifferent. The one topic to dominate conversation in the wardroom, and Pearce guessed this to be so, would be the potential value of such a prize. It had been necessary to inform both Hallowell and Worricker of the purpose of their new course, with no requirement for discretion.

They'd hardly gone a watch before the whole ship was aware of what *Hazard* was after, which would have led to much discussion and the citing of previous fabulous captures. Fortunes had been made, which were the stuff of naval legend. It was also the stuff of dreams, to the common seaman reward enough to buy an alehouse and live off the proceeds. To a captain, a landed estate, added to a coach and four.

'In what capacity?' Oliphant asked eventually, curiosity getting the better of reserve.

'What would you suggest?'

'As close to captain as possible and take that grin off your face. Surely it doesn't surprise you I hanker after the same as anyone. The methods by which I make my way in the world do not provide for the kind of riches I might have previously expected by inheritance.'

'From your tax-farmer Grandpapa.'

'He was fond of my mother, even if she had married an Englishman and helped us live in comfort. Now she and my father are in constrained circumstances and so is he, having left his fortune behind when he fled. It would be a fitting recompense if, in filching riches of the enemy, it went some way to mitigating the loss.'

Pearce had ceased to listen. It was not actually commotion on the deck above his head, but something had changed, soon brought home by a knock on the door and the entry of Midshipman Tennant, who spoke in an excited tone.

'Mr Hallowell's compliments, sir, but a sail has been sighted dead ahead.'

Pearce was past the lad before the sentence was finished. On deck all eyes were over the bowsprit, even if there was nothing to see. Pearce headed for the shrouds and was climbing fast, even as his premier was trying to confirm the delivery of the message. He slipped past the main-mast cap and climbed on up to join the lookout in the crow's nest, asking for and being passed his telescope.

There was no more than the hint of another mast as yet and that on the rise, nor of what the sighting could be, so it required patience to wait for clarification. Once the topsails became visible, and another cresting on a wave showed them in full, Pearce knew it to be a man-o-war and, not long after, very likely a frigate. But, with the wind favouring *Hazard*, blowing the flags out to sea, belonging to whom?

'Mr Hallowell,' he shouted. 'Hoist the private signal for today, if you please.'

Which gave no guarantee, if it was responded to, he would be dealing with a friend. There was one duty which fell to a captain, or whoever took over from him if he was incapacitated, to ensure in the face of capture, the book containing the day-by-day list was thrown overboard. Sadly, there was no way to guarantee this always happened.

'And Mr Hallowell, clear for action.'

If it was a friend, no problem would ensue. If not, and it was a powerful opponent, he would have to go about and run, hoping there'd be no pursuit. He might be minded to take on the aforesaid Spanish frigate with all the risks this entailed, but there was reward possible at the conclusion of such an encounter.

If what lay ahead was French it was not here. He would not fight if it could be avoided, for the greater prize was farther ahead. All he could get from even trying to pass a larger enemy was damage, perhaps so much it would render it impossible to even engage another warship. Then there was the possibility of capture. It would not be long because he knew he, too, had been sighted. The vessel ahead, which had been on a southerly course, had come round to close.

'We may have to about and quickly' was called down to his premier, 'so make sure we're prepared.'

Really, he should be on the quarterdeck and another up here, but if there was a quick decision to be made, Pearce wanted to be the one to make it. Beneath him the flags were being run up on the halyards, a sequence of numbers and letter which were right for the month of July, these committed to memory.

The time was approaching when he would have to reverse course regardless, this while he was calculating the time until darkness, which might allow him to evade a chase. Sat here, a leg across a yard, he was swaying twenty feet, which made keeping the glass on the approaching ship difficult.

Her courses, showing now, were hauled round, swinging her slightly to the north. The clear intention, if *Hazard* was a foe, was to get plenty of sea room, which would allow for a trap by using the shore. The new course brought the flags into view, both that of a rear-admiral of the Red Squadron, plus the line of signal flags with the private signal, identifying the frigate as Royal Navy.

With her higher masts, it was obvious, whoever she was, *Hazard* had been identified first. A blast of smoke from a signal gun invited Pearce to respond, a request quickly satisfied. Back on deck and with both ships closing, it was Worricker who identified her.

'HMS *Lively*, sir. Under Captain Lord Langholm, last time I spied her in Pompey.'

Looking up at the Admiralty pennant, Pearce wondered what would come from the frigate. When a signal did rise up, it demonstrated some thought had been put into its composition. Campbell had the signal book, so it was his job to decipher it.

'Request came first, followed by, Captain, repair aboard.'

'Politely expressed. Please acknowledge, Mr Campbell. Mr Hallowell, get a boat in the water and then put the ship to rights. I'm going to smarten up. You may back sails when we're a half cable distant.'

He went below to get out of his everyday clothes and put on his best, adding an oilskin boat cloak to ward off the spray he was bound to encounter. By the time he came back on deck, the cutter was floating and manned, with Michael O'Hagan acting as coxswain. Having sent word to tell Maclehose to smarten himself up, the midshipman was waiting to accompany him.

'I take it I'm not invited?' Oliphant asked.

'If you wish for a bout of seasickness, I am always happy to include you.'

'Which I'm not. Can I ask what you're going to say to yonder fellow?'

'I'm going to invite him to join us in taking the *Santa Leocadia*.'

'Which would make him the senior officer.'

'One whose orders I can deviate from, if I so wish.'

'It would also make for a greater distribution of any reward.'

'For someone not interested in prize money no more than two hours ago, I call that a change of tune.'

'I'm merely pointing out . . .'

'Matters I've already considered.' Sensing he'd been too abrupt, Pearce smiled. 'I reckon there will be enough of such a commodity for all, while there will be none at all for failure. And who knows, whoever is in command may decline.'

Lively had backed her own sails and was now awaiting Pearce, who had actually stopped for no apparent reason to stand deep in thought. He turned back to Oliphant.

'On second thoughts, I think it best I take you along, in case he requires convincing. Mr Tennant, hot foot it to the wardroom and dig out an oilskin to fit Mr Oliphant.'

As the youngster ran off, Pearce took Oliphant's elbow to lead him to a spot a few paces away from everyone else, talking quietly. 'I would ask you to be careful how you behave. I don't know the other captain but they can be, as a breed, mightily prickly if they think civilians are poking their noses into naval matters.'

'He might be positively thorny when he hears your name.'

'True, but the notion of such a prize might perfume it.'

Midshipman Tennant came running back and the oilskin was handed over, with Williams calling for it to be taken care of, it being his.

'And,' Pearce added, as Oliphant went down ahead of him, in his usual useless fashion, 'fix your gaze on the horizon and keep it there. It might stop you turning green.'

The waters were not choppy, but there was a sea running, so every topped wave brought a spray of seawater, which lasted until they were in the lee of the frigate. Slipping off his oilskin, Pearce called out, 'Lieutenant Pearce, master and commander of HMS *Hazard*.'

He grabbed at the man ropes and hauled himself aboard to the sound of pipes. His host was waiting, with his officers, lifting his hat after Pearce had acknowledged the flag.

'George Stewart, Lord Langholm, at your service, sir.'

There was a keen look from the visitor, to see how he'd reacted to the Pearce name, but nothing untoward showed. Oliphant, with Michael O'Hagan heaving at his buttocks, appeared to unsteadily make the deck, nimbly followed by Maclehose.

As this was taking place, Pearce examined Langholm and could not help thinking he looked like a slightly older version of the Mite, and not much older at that. A head shorter than Pearce, fresh of face with blond curls, long lashes, and a turned-up nose, he looked barely out of his teens. It was hard to see him as a post captain. But then he was a lord.

'If I may introduce to you, Lord Langholm, Mr Samuel Oliphant, who's a passenger on HMS *Hazard* but also my confrere in the mission on which we're engaged.'

'I saw your pennant, sir. I have to say it made me wonder what kind of duty in these waters warrants it.' The accent was Scottish but refined, with Pearce trying and failing to place it, only registering it was not Highland or a city. 'But the deck is no place for conversation, so will you both join me in my cabin.'

'Delighted, sir.'

Just as they were about to move, one of the officers took a couple of paces forward to whisper in his ear. The head bent to listen, Langholm did not react to what he was being told. Pearce had no doubt of the content when he got a look from the fellow who'd passed on the message. In truth it was as close to a glare as was allowed by naval manners.

The amount of space afforded to a frigate captain stood in stark contrast to Pearce's own, while the quality of the furniture, and there was quite a lot of it, spoke of a man not short of a coin or two. They were invited to sit, wine was poured, and Langholm opened the conversation.

'Your mission, Mr Pearce, is it one you're at liberty to discuss if you so wish?' Sensing hesitation, Langholm added, 'I know your pennant allows you to decline to answer to a superior officer.'

'We are past the point where being reserved is the case, sir. So what I would like to do, is invite Mr Oliphant to explain to you what we've been about.'

Which surprised two people, Langholm and Oliphant. Pearce was taking what he saw as proper precautions. If the on-deck whisper had been about him, and he was close to certain it was, he did not want his name to have any bearing on what he required.

It was good to see, even unprepared, Oliphant took up the baton with aplomb, eloquently describing the aims they'd set out to resolve, without mentioning Dundas. He described Hendaye and what had been discovered of the French forces, which seemed to Pearce a good way to establish the wide remit under which they were operating.

'Following this we sailed to St Sebastian, where we were subject to the oddest reception.' Langholm must have been nearly bursting with curiosity, but nothing showed. He was stillness personified. 'The aim was to find out if the Dons are going to desert the coalition.'

'I've heard rumour it's a concern. So, are they?'

'Our information says yes. We used a pair of homing pigeons to send confirmation back to London.'

'You may not be aware, sir,' said Pearce, taking up the tale. 'The people of the Basque region are not loyal to the crown, it's very much the opposite. Their leaders have given us a written request for our government to intervene and free them from Madrid. It was they who told us the Dons are about to join with the French and fight on their side.'

'I was never sure we should extend too much trust in that quarter.'

'They're waiting for one thing before making the declaration.' A tilt of the head posed the question. 'There's a frigate on the way from the Caribbean. It's carrying the silver the Dons require to fight the war.'

'You'll forgive me, gentlemen, if I say you might have been sold a pup. I can see how tempting it is to believe in it, but . . .?'

'I think, Milord, you'd have to have been present to know one way or the other.'

'Which tells me, Mr Oliphant, you believe them.'

'We both do,' Pearce replied. 'The ship is heading for Vigo, is due to make its landfall before the last of the month, which is only days away. It's my intention to seek to intercept her and seize her cargo, which will either cause a change of mind in Madrid or hamper their operations.'

'No shortage of ambition there, Mr Pearce.'

'My request to you is we act in concert, in something of great benefit to our service and country. Naturally, while I have no requirement to obey any orders you give, I am happy to acknowledge your seniority, should it come to a fight.'

'And if I decline?'

'Then we will proceed to seek interdiction on our own.'

'With what you have on your gun deck, you could be blown out of the water.'

'Perhaps with superior gunnery, which I'm sure we possess, we will prevail.'

In the face of this blatant falsehood, Oliphant remained stoic and still, the only noticeable change in his demeanour he ceased breathing.

'If I was to agree, I can tell you it might not sit well with some, maybe most of my officers.'

'My name?' Langholm nodded. 'If you fear being unpopular, Lord Langholm, let me tell you it can become bearable.'

'I still hold on to doubts and will not say ye or nae. But let us start by you telling me how you plan to achieve this feat of arms.'

'I will happily do so, sir. But I would request we get under way for Vigo. Time does not allow for a sitting-still conference.'

This Langholm acknowledged. 'Then I suggest you send orders to your premier to take station in my wake.'

Chapter Twenty-Five

The charts were laid out on *Lively*, just as they had been on *Hazard*. This time the discussion was about the route by which a vessel sailing from the Gulf of Mexico would approach the deep bay of the Ria de Vigo. The port and town were afforded some protection from Atlantic storms by a trio of offshore islands that ran north to south, the upper pair linked by a sandbar.

Given the direction in which the bay opened, added to the location of the port on the southern bank, the easiest approach was from the southwest, skirting the channel between an island called San Martino and the mainland. After an initial study of the charts, Lord Langholm asked Pearce and Oliphant to go over their tale once more.

The latter referred this time to the formal written request, from the Basque "Cortes," he'd taken on the beach, one which he'd not seen fit to fetch along. Oliphant had to acknowledge, as a body, this probably did not actually exist, unless as a provincial assembly with constrained and local responsibilities.

'I think the real point is they see themselves as a set of politicians in a position to take and wield power should the conditions they require prevail.'

'You don't really expect us to mount an incursion to aid them, do you?'

The truth of this conclusion had to be acknowledged. 'But, this war has already thrown up opportunities. I refer of course to Toulon.'

'Not a happy example, Mr Oliphant, given how it ended. Lord Hood might maintain, had he been supplied with the troops he requested, he could have held out, but not many see this as a plausible. Those damn revolutionary armies have so far beaten everyone sent against them, so I suspect they would have done for him regardless of how many men he had. Since the abandonment of Toulon, they've chased the Austrians and Piedmontese back into central Italy.'

'All we can do, sir,' Pearce countered, 'is pass the request to those who make such decisions. It's up to them how they choose to act upon it.'

'True.' Langholm hesitated for a second after this affirmation, looking directly at John Pearce. 'It will not come as a surprise to you, once your name was whispered to me, it struck a chord with a fellow Scotsman.'

'I'd noted the accent, sir, but could not place it.'

'Galloway, Mr Pearce,' he replied with a grin. 'Rough border country.'

'Much calmer now than hitherto, I would suggest.'

'Not much' came as a hoot. 'You still have to mind your cattle if you don't wish to see them for sale in England.'

He turned to Oliphant, for whom this line of conversation meant exclusion, this made good by a short explanation of the history of the border and the Reever community of which Langholm assured them he was apart. This amounted to a description of much criminality, cattle theft, and female kidnapping. In addition there was no shortage of violence, even murder, which had been a way of life for centuries, both north and south of the line.

'I doubt your father made much headway in my part of the world, Mr Pearce. It's too lawless still for radical opinion.'

'He would not have been deterred. I sometimes thought he relished danger and opposition to the extent of seeking it out.'

'But not revolution?'

'An act which now has a depraved name, but it was not of the kind he sought. He ended up disapproving of the way things turned out in France. It might be of interest to you, they threw him in prison over there, just like our own government. And for the same reason. It seems those in power abhor anyone question their activities.'

Pearce glanced at Oliphant then to see if he wanted to say anything, but the stiff face told him not.

'He was a dangerous man, Mr Pearce. I wonder if you, too, are such.'

'Dangerous to your property, Lord Langholm, which he would have wanted either diminished or your tenants better rewarded. But he would never have wanted to cut off your head.'

'But I do have to worry if his son will decapitate my career.' Getting no reply, Langholm went on. 'You say you wish to intercept this frigate and want my help to do so. I fear, from the way you express your intention, this is to take place with all cannons blazing.'

'How else is it to be prevented from landing its cargo?'

'Like father, like son. I never heard your pa speak, but I have read some of his writings, which were served up as warnings to me by my father. There was bull at the gate quality to his opinions, as if he cared not a jot where they would lead. I think we saw this come to life in Paris.'

'With respect, sir, I'm struggling to see where this is leading.'

'If we intercept the *Santa Leocadia*, the proper procedure with an ally, and it has to be assumed this might still be the case, is to apprehend him peacefully and offer to escort him to Gibraltar. You cannot, in all conscience, just go after him with round shot, whatever you think you know.'

'And if he declines to agree.'

'Then he would require, from what you've told me and in case you're correct, to be persuaded. If this ended in fight so be it. On such a condition I think we can act in concert.'

'I have serious doubts, sir, given the cargo, any Spanish officer would agree to be escorted anywhere.'

'My opinion too. But for the sake of appearances, the offer must be made. Not to do so could result in us both facing a court.' The next point was delivered in a grim tone. 'I have to say, Mr Pearce, I would survive such a hearing, censured perhaps, but whole. You, I fear, would not. Do we have agreement?'

Pearce nodded.

'Then let us finalise our procedures, and then you may return to your ship.'

It came down to how far out to sea the two vessels could, in cooperation, cover the approaches, in a way which would not allow the *Santa Leocadia* to slip through. It was agreed Lord Langholm, in the larger, better-armed vessel, would take the southernmost position and signal *Hazard* if the quarry came in sight. Likewise, the reverse, with Pearce taking station and masking the northern channel, off the northern tip of the Isla de Monteagudo.

This was contingent on there being nothing in Vigo that could give them a fight or come out to support the incoming warship. As long as this was the case, Langholm was of the opinion fishing boats informing of their presence meant nothing. To get a message to a port with any serious naval units would take time. Knowing the Dons, it would take even longer for them to get to sea.

They were barely back aboard *Hazard*, suffering a second soaking as they crossed from *Lively*, while blessed with another glorious sunset, before Oliphant voiced what he saw as a flaw in the arrangement.

'He could sight the Spaniard and not bother with the signal.' About to accuse him of his usual rampant level of distrust, Pearce hesitated. He had to admit Oliphant was right. 'He seems to know a great deal about you and your pa, what do we know of him?'

'Not a great deal.'

It was impossible not to reflect, at this point being raised, on *Lively*'s officers. They would probably be told what their vessel was about, while knowing in whose company their captain was preparing to act. Langholm was in command, but how much did he listen to the opinion of his inferiors? Would he confer with them and be swayed to a position where the talked-of cooperation seemed unwise?

The way one of his lieutenants had eyed Pearce left him in no doubt of the presence of the normal animus. As well as this, for all his polite behaviour, and Langholm had been all gentleman, what were his true feelings? The notion a Scottish aristocrat would have warm feelings for the son of Adam Pearce was not one to rely on. It was in the midst of the gloomy assessment, Oliphant said, 'He comes across as a decent fellow, I'll grant, but I've known folk of that hue to be proper scoundrels.'

Not a comment to raise the spirits, Pearce thought long and hard before replying, while at the same time putting aside a tempting jibe. Oliphant could be talking of himself.

'I think you're forgetting one thing.'

'Do tell me.'

'Even if not to alert us, he will need to fire a signal gun in order to have the *Santa Leocadia* heave to, so he can get close enough to use a speaking trumpet. If the fellow declines he'll need to put a shot across the bows. If he does either, we will hear it.'

'Does whoever commands the Spaniard know anything of San Ildefonso, Pearce? When did he sail for the Americas, it cannot have been anything less than three months past?' The look this got was quizzical. 'Even a rank amateur can calculate sailing rates and distance.'

'So can Mr Williams.'

'I sought to occupy myself, while you were otherwise engaged.'

'In this incidence, taken as harmless. But you may well be correct.'

'From which you deduce?'

'You have a point, but not one I can do anything about. Now I am for my cot and I can hardly credit you're not already in yours.'

In making the observations, Oliphant had given Pearce much to gnaw on, but the last thing he'd said held true. If Langholm decided not to signal for him, even gunfire would not mean much. If anything of value was to be extracted for this interdiction, he would have to be in sight of the capture to share any reward. In his mind he could conjure up another vision very easily, of the *Santa Leocadia* deck swarming with the crew of *Lively* by the time he came in view.

This was a series of thought he decided not to share with Oliphant, knowing he would only deepen the worry, not assuage it. They did converse, did speculate but within limits, which had Pearce wonder if Oliphant had succumbed to superstition that made any mention of what might be coming taboo.

Two days later both vessels were at their appointed positions, sure in the knowledge they could remain in place for some time. Langholm had sent a cutter under sail to reconnoitre the Vigo roads, so they knew there was no ship berthed there of a size to cause them trouble. The only things even marginally naval looked to be the size of excise boats, and those they could easily handle.

Pearce had to cater for another problem, which was the chance his quarry would try to get by him and make the next bay up the coast. The

Ria de Pontevedra lacked the facilities of Vigo but was equally deep. Within its waters, the Spaniard could anchor, so would probably have to be cut out by a boat attack. Langholm had the lesser difficulty. To the south of him lay the border with Portugal, with no safe harbour or anchorage to which an enemy could flee.

To say there was tension aboard *Hazard* was to understate the feelings of the crew, so much so John Pearce feared the effect of disappointment. He knew now he should have kept his own counsel regarding the aim of his actions. Too much talk of rewards caused an excess of excitement, as each man aboard mentally spent his share of spoils not yet gathered, many several times over.

He relieved his own by taking time in the tops, scanning the empty seascape and, when he was not up there, avoiding any speculation of both where the *Santa Leocadia* might be and what might occur if she was sighted. He tried at all times to appear phlegmatic and indifferent, which was pure front. He was as capable of looking ahead as anyone, capable of imagining how such a windfall, should they secure it, would affect his life, and there was no one with whom he could discuss it.

At the root of this was what change it would bring to his relationship with Emily. Would he, as a wealthy suitor and acknowledged catch, still be required to hold off, long enough to satisfy a social norm for which he cared not one jot? Reflecting on how he'd come to be where he was, in command of a ship which might very shortly be in a battle, it seemed hard to believe. From being a pressed seaman, so desperate to get free he'd tried to swim to shore, he'd given himself the chance of a career in the very same service.

He couldn't pinpoint the precise moment when hatred of his lot turned to an ambition to make the best of it. It was certainly not before the death of his father, when he'd been rated as no more than a midshipman. Nor, in recollection, was it the moment when Farmer George insisted he be promoted to lieutenant, without the required examination, barking "It was his damn navy," in the face of opposition.

There was a bit of a gut wrench, as he remembered how he'd let down those who'd stood by him and fought alongside him, prior to gaining his elevation. While he dallied in London, enjoying the delights of an affair with a society beauty, his Pelicans, waiting for him in Portsmouth, had been shipped off, to join Lord Hood's fleet in the Mediterranean.

Worse was the ship in which they sailed, with an indolent captain who left everything to his sadistic premier. If he'd not been given the task of delivering secret despatches to Lord Hood, he might never have seen them again. Recalling Hood and the duties he'd been landed with did not bring pleasant memories. But once Toulon was secured, he re-encountered Emily Barclay, as well as her bastard of a husband.

Memories of the early days on Barclay's ship, HMS *Brilliant*, surfaced then, any benign recall dying in the face of the sod who'd illegally pressed him, a coward who declined the invitation to settle matters with either pistols or a sword. But all this was water under the keel. Going back to the potential rewards that might very shortly come his way raised a question. What would he do, if he was a rich man, who no longer needed to stay in the navy?

Even if he'd contemplated in his cot, a very different and pastoral life, Pearce knew whatever was to come it would have to be something active. It was one fact about himself he had come to know, perhaps stemming from his peripatetic upbringing. He was incapable of taking pleasure from inactivity and it was this, as much as anything, not excluding the need to earn a living, which had kept him in the service. Added to this, of course, was stubbornness; he was damned if he was going to let the sods who sneered at his rank get him down.

'You're not far off bloody minded' was said out loud.

The knock came a second later, the initial rush to the deck following, until Pearce realised he would merely add flames to the ongoing speculation of the crew. So when he came on deck, it was at a normal pace, with nothing in his demeanour displaying a hint of eagerness. The same did not go for his premier, who could barely repress his excitement.

'Sail, sir, off our larboard quarter.'

'Unidentified, Mr Hallowell?'

'Yes, sir.'

The reply did nothing to stem his patent eagerness, this as Oliphant appeared, the look of curiosity on his face undisguised.

'A ship, but as yet we don't know the who or the what.'

Looking at the halyards, Pearce saw the agreed signal being raised, one which would make no sense even to a fellow countryman. He and Langholm had decided against "Enemy in Sight." There was just a chance it was a signal the man commanding a Spanish warship would recognise.

'May I suggest a more measured way of behaviour? We do not want to raise hopes, do we?' If Hallowell agreed, it was not genuine. 'Now let us come about and close the distance, so we can see if it's something of interest.'

'If it is,' Oliphant said, moving away, 'I'd appreciate you send someone to tell me.'

'I'll make it my most important first action.'

The sarcasm got a crabbed, over-the-shoulder look as Hallowell enquired, 'Will you be going aloft, sir?'

He was dying to, but it would not serve. 'I think we can rely on the lookout, don't you?'

He stayed by the binnacle as the yards were hauled round, the sails taking the wind as they were sheeted home, the rudder biting and *Hazard* making her turn. Pearce was in a bit of a quandary. There had been much thought of what to do if it was the *Santa Leocadia*. Should he be prepared for a fight, or would clearing for action send a signal to the Spaniard and have him change course.

If he did, Pearce wanted him going south, to where he could just see the topsails of *Lively*. From the tops of that ship, Langholm's lookout would be able to see the *Hazard's* flags, which had Pearce yell aloft to look out for the acknowledgment. When this came, he knew Langholm, too, would be altering course, so he adjusted his to one more northerly, to cut off the possibility of the *Santa Leocadia* making for Pontevedra.

'On deck, there. Spanish-coloured pennant atop the mainmast.'

'Our quarry, I think, and on the course least expected.'

Having not discussed this with Hallowell in any detail, Pearce was obliged to explain the twin approaches to Vigo and what had been surmised.

'The question is, are we looking at mere accident or an attempt at avoidance?'

'Sir?'

'Rhetorical, Mr Hallowell,' he offered when he realised the keen look his musing engendered. 'But whatever the reason, it means it is up to us to call upon him to heave to, a task that both Lord Langholm and I expected would fall to him.'

'Does this alter the way we react, sir?'

It was odd Pearce's mind turned to the musings he'd so recently indulged in. He was faced with a choice of alternatives, with no idea of which was best. To approach the Spaniard ready to fight, and being seen to be so, because it could not be hidden. Or to wait until he refused to heave to, which would be a prelude to a rejection of a request to sail for Gibraltar. This meant he required to be forced.

It was back to the heavier weight of shot and the damage *Hazard* might sustain before *Lively* could close. The *Santa Leocadia* would be carrying a well worked-up crew, but was the standard of their gunnery as well as their rate of fire which counted? He marked the wind, which, coming off the land, favoured him, then set this against an estimate of the time Langholm would need to be close enough to effect any outcome.

Was it a sin to crave what he was contemplating? Pearce knew clearly what had been obscure in his cabin. He could never be content ashore, even with deep pockets and a contented family, when the likes of this lay before him. Action, the test of oneself against an ordinary life, was meat and drink.

'Given the relative weight of shot between us and what could very well be the *Santa Leocadia*, added to which they will not have clear sight of our deck yet, I think we must clear for action, after all.'

'Shall I send to tell Mr Oliphant, sir?'

'He'll know when his cot disappears, especially if he's in it.'

CHAPTER TWENTY-SIX

An act now rehearsed many times, this went smoothly, Pearce being sure he detected an extra degree of eagerness in the speed and application applied. There was no need to ask why, though he reckoned it was not only the prospect of what they might gain in money. The crew, as a whole, were a better entity now, the elements mixing to become nearly indistinguishable. What he saw before him was internal and good-natured competition, with no one wishing to be last.

There were still a few who would never have the ability to be a proper sailor, others who could not shrug off the way they had been recruited, but in the mass they now counted for little. Also, with the help of his observant Pelicans, those who might hamper efficiency had been moved to where they could do little harm, some put to the simple task of, at times like these, loading round shot into baskets for the guns on deck.

The likes of "Blackbeard" Teach, a bit of a pest with his constant moaning or examples of injustice, had been put working with the surgeon, Mr Cullen, a normally fetch-and-carry job in which Derwent was also employed, but not on this day. If it came to a fight, Pearce would find out if Teach had sympathy for the fellows for whom he claimed to speak, or was so crabbed nothing would satisfy him.

There was no way, even at such a distance, to obscure a deck on which such a level of activity was taking place. So it was essential to see how the commander of the oncoming vessel was going to react. If he did nothing and came right on, it could not be his quarry and might not even be Spanish. This was based on Oliphant's point of time and distance, of how long in the planning had been the idea of Godoy's duplicity?

The fact the Basques knew her name established the *Santa Leocadia* had been sent to fetch her cargo as a specific mission, with a known goal of satisfying the need for funds to pursue a war, without the previous subsidies. Thus, a British flag would be immediately seen by her as hostile.

This required Pearce to make for the mainmast cap, so he could observe the response. An assessment of the situation, given he had the weather gage, indicated he would be, in a limited sense, able to impose his will. Also, the tide was receding, meaning the oncoming vessel, at a point where the bed was shelving, was sailing into the wind as well as the run of the sea.

Both conferred a degree of advantage, yet for all the chance and blood rush of a possible battle, Pearce was not prepared to contemplate a butcher's bill just for the sake of personal exhilaration. The best outcome would be, if it was the *Santa Leocadia*, for its commander to be faced with two to one, odds with which he dare not engage.

'Vessel has changed course north,' came from Worricker, he in the crow's nest above Pearce's head. This put the last possibility into serious question, doubly so when he added, 'Rigged like a frigate, sir. And I've got *Lively*'s topsails.'

It had to be the *Santa Leocadia*. This alteration and identity were confirmed in short order, his own quandary being an apparent decision not to close Vigo. This left little doubt the Spaniard had seen *Hazard* as a potential threat. Was the change deliberate, or a ploy to see how they would behave, because Pearce had to consider he might be in a cat-and-mouse game?

'Spaniard's increasing sail,' Worricker shouted. 'Raising topgallants.'

With time in which to assess various avenues, his quarry could be seeking to guy him, to set him racing to close off the entry to Pontevedra Bay, before coming back on to his original course. This could provide a chance to alter the angle at which they would eventually face each other.

Pearce envisaged a situation in which his opponent would come back on to a course for Vigo, with everything set aloft he could carry. He would then attempt to use the time Pearce required to come round and intercept to advantage. Tactically, it was a clever move, because he would see it as forcing *Hazard* to close with him bows on, reducing the ability to employ anything like maximum firepower.

Without this, Pearce would be obliged to repeatedly put down his helm and sacrifice speed, in order to extract anything effective from his broadside. Getting back to *Hazard*'s best rate of sailing would also eat up time, enough to potentially prevent him from blocking the northern approach to Vigo. In such juxtaposed positions, the Spaniard could, as he would see it, also rake Pearce with a full barrage, not designed to kill the crew or disable his cannon, but to shred his top hamper, which would slow him even more.

How long before the topsails of *Lively* came into view? They were only just visible to Worricker, but not yet to the Spaniard? Following his recent change of course would extend the time that would elapse before he got a surprise, realised he had two enemies to contend with, not one. Pearce was hoping for this to be delayed long enough for the game, if it was such, to be played out. But he felt the need to do something to add spice, and this required he force a reaction.

'Mr Hallowell, a change of course a few points to the north. I reckon our friend yonder is seeking to game us, so let him think he has succeeded.'

The change was imperceptible, but Pearce knew it would be more obvious to a vessel fast approaching and nearly hull up. As with all things at sea, time stood still, so minutes could seem like an hour: The impression of nothing happening was one it took time to get used to, occasions when impatience was a waste of energy.

The Spaniard was holding his course and, with his increased sail, would be calculating one of several possibilities. Could he open Pontevedra Bay before it became essential to fight? Or would he follow what Pearce imagined to be his true intention, which was to humbug him. Not that the Spaniard would be overly concerned either way: The vessel before him would be seen as no real match.

Yet it took no great intellect to discern, with the cargo he was carrying, as well as the responsibility he bore, added to the known fact no outcome of a battle was ever certain, an avoidance of action was the right choice. The hourglass was well run before the next move was made, and it played into Pearce's guess.

'He's coming round on to his previous course, sir.'

271

'Thank you, Mr Worricker. I think you have done as much as you can, so I would ask you to return to your duties on deck. Mr Hallowell, we will hold our present course for a few more minutes, at which point, we will come about. Then I want everything aloft we can carry.'

It couldn't be long before the Spaniard was faced with the prospect of two against one and, by his latest alteration, he had guaranteed this would come soon. This accepted, it would be folly to assume everything would happen as was desired. You could never know if an opponent had another trick up his sleeve. Just because it was not plain to you, did not mean it didn't exist.

'Now,' Pearce said to himself, feeling confident, with the wind holding steady, he still holding the weather gage, and *Lively* closing. 'Let us see how you like being the mouse instead of the cat.'

Timing was critical, since Pearce now had very little with which to play. In truth, he was relying on the Spaniard having no idea of the speed *Hazard* could achieve at her very best. It was paramount she get across the enemy bow, crossing the T, reversing what had been tried on him.

'Let us come about, Mr Hallowell.'

And nifty it was, yet another demonstration of the abilities achieved by a now harmonious crew. *Hazard*, sprightly when well handled, was round in less than a minute, while the men who'd been manning the guns went about the sheeting home. They then rushed to the duty of getting aloft extra canvas, each addition making an impression.

Pearce observed the precise moment the Spaniard spotted his consort. He could faintly see her quarterdeck now, so marked the tiny figures as they rushed to larboard. Beyond them, faintly in the distance, was the sight of *Lively*'s battle flag. She was coming up hand over fist as expected and it looked as though it was game over.

It was at this point Pearce himself got a surprise. The *Santa Leocadia* began to come round and, if it was clearly intent on fleeing the approach of a British frigate, surely an opponent too risky to face, this did not apply to the lesser of two evils. The Spaniard was going to go for Pontevedra Bay after all, with John Pearce and his crew now right in the way.

If it was uncomfortable, it made sense. The cargo was one for which the man in command must know the Chief Minister was desperate. The

Santa Leocadia had been tasked to load it and to land it, which took precedence over any other factor, including national pride. If it could be got ashore in boats, it would be just as good as landing it on a Vigo quay.

Battle must be joined and, faced with no choice, out of two opponents, the Spaniard had naturally chosen the lesser threat. It was now John Pearce's job to either stop him or impose enough of a delay to allow Langholm to enter the action. Either way, it looked as if he, his ship and crew, were going to pay a price.

Back on the deck, in his mind reprising what he'd seen of the way the *Santa Leocadia* had so far been handled, nothing hinted at anything exceptional. But her sailing qualities were only one factor, when the cannon she mounted would be at least twenty-eight pounders. With his four-pounders, a fight at long range was therefore not an option: Pearce had to get in close.

How quickly could the Dons handle their cannon? Size of shot would be much diminished if *Hazard* could get off the faster salvoes. How nimble were her crew at sudden and forced changes of course, which might become necessary? Nothing so far observed gave a clue, all having been done without pressure.

Battle was different. Even manning ropes was far from easy when the deck was being swept by grapeshot. Standing stoic on a quarterdeck when under fire took special nerve, as did working cannon when there was as much shot coming in as going out. Quick calculation was going to be required, and Pearce knew his one advantage lay in manoeuvrability. He had to hope he was up against an opponent who could not best it.

Yet there were inherent problems. Even at pistol-shot range, *Hazard's* round shot could not hope to smash the enemy scantlings and frighten her gun crews. There would be a rate of splinters and a lucky ball might get through a gunport, but it was not something to depend upon. If he went for the sails and rigging to slow her down, while the Spaniard sought to rake his gun deck, he might see it swept of humanity, himself included.

There was no way to know what was in his opponent's mind, something he would only find out in the minutes before action was joined. This took him and a telescope to the stern, to take stock of the mouth of Pontevedra Bay, running through his mind a host of calculations. He had to assume, given it was devoid of shipping, it was not held to be a desirable anchorage, and there must be a reason.

What was Langholm's maximum rate of sailing on the present wind? How long would he take to come up on the Spaniard, which dictated the time Pearce would have to fight unaided? Were there advantages in seeking to draw him in towards the bay, especially at what would soon be low tide, fighting a larger vessel in what would be confined waters?

He drew less under his keel and perhaps, at this time of the tidal day, the stretch of water he was looking at would be doubly dangerous for the larger ship. Whoever commanded *Santa Leocadia* could be well aware the bay did not necessarily represent safety. Even if he could get past *Hazard*, he could be followed in by *Lively*, only able to boat ashore his cargo if Langholm was destroyed. Thus there was an element of desperation in the aim, the kind that might cloud judgment.

Swinging the telescope to look forward, he could see the enemy was right round now, so it was bowsprit to bowsprit, with the range rapidly closing, the time for making the right call being taken away. As a sign of this, the *Santa Leocadia* fired off its bow chasers, which sent up great plumes of water well ahead of *Hazard's* bow.

'Trying to scare us,' Pearce called as he made his way back to the quarterdeck. 'Or seeking to save us washing our decks.'

When this evoked laughter, even a few cheers, Pearce had to wonder and be thankful for their ignorance, which seemed to extend to both parts of the crew. How would they react under sustained assault? For the quota men, their only experience of being under fire occurred when Jaleel Tolland loosed off a cannon in the North Sea, the result of his aim pitiful. What of the men who looked to Macklin? How stalwart would they be?

Even if he had the most lubberly gunners in creation, the *Santa Leocadia* had more cannon. Its deck was higher, so if it came to musketry, and it might, the Spaniards would be firing down on easily observed targets. The Hazards would have to reply to men they'd be unable to get sight of, so all the advantage lay with Spain unless he could outwit the sod.

'Mr Hallowell. Please come about and head for Pontevedra Bay.' This got raised eyebrows but no objection. 'Mr Williams, to me, I need your opinion.'

There was a nervousness about the man as he approached, which did not induce confidence. He looked as though he was in expectation of a wigging. There was also a hiatus until *Hazard* was settled on her new course.

'I've had no time to study Pontevedra Bay, so it may be I will require your guidance. What do you know of it?'

'I would reckon it inadvisable, sir, to go on under such a weight of canvas.'

'Look to our rear, Mr Williams, then tell me how much time I am to be afforded if we reduce sail.'

Pearce hadn't meant to sound harsh, but the lack of grit in the man raised his hackles. Williams had been at sea most of his life. Even if he'd never participated in a battle, he surely knew the situation they were in was potentially calamitous. So he didn't modify his tone when he gave his orders, the first of which should have come from the master.

'I would suggest we need a couple of hands into the bows with casting lines. Then you must use any charts you possess to direct me in how I should proceed. The safety of HMS *Hazard* lies with you.'

The attempt to spark a sense of resolve fell on stony ground.

'Mr Williams, we have to cope with an enemy in our wake for, if we do not, he may well destroy us. I would point out, his aim is to anchor in the bay, thus he has no cause to seek capture where destruction will serve. In that case we will most certainly not enjoy any of the silver you and others have been happily spending since you found out what we're after. Do you have means to make the necessary calculations?'

'Since we were bound for Gibraltar, I sailed with a chart of this coast, sir.'

'Then kindly fetch it, so I can see where the problems lie, as well as the opportunities.'

'I have had no occasion to test its accuracy.'

'Nor will you be afforded one. We must seek to make do with what has been recorded previously.'

As he departed Pearce called for Hallowell, Worricker, and Macklin to join him, the latter to reassure the men he'd brought aboard, who would be raised in spirits to see him being included in any consultation. They came as another salvo from those bow chasers disturbed more sea, which served to show the range had decreased. What followed was imparted quietly to the trio now close around him.

'Gentlemen, I do not think I need to tell you what we face.' Grim reality was etched on their expressions, but Pearce was cheered to see no lack of steadfastness. 'I deduce, in open water, we are at a major disadvantage. So the first task is to reduce this, which cannot be accomplished without risk.'

'He's a Spaniard, sir, and we generally wallop them.'

'Well said, Mr Hallowell, but I want you to know my intentions for two reasons. I invite you to cast an opinion. Secondly, when the shot begins to fly, we are all potential victims.' Which meant, if I fall, you take over in rank order. 'Mr Williams.'

Pearce looked past his officers to where the master was standing, a chart in his hand, to then smile. 'The fellow in our wake has no idea how much trouble he's in.'

The smiles were returned, but not in the same measure. 'I'm going to take *Hazard* into the mouth of the bay at a rate of sailing only justified by emergency. I will guarantee the fellow in command of *Santa Leocadia* will not do likewise. He must know the bay or have charts, as good as or better than our own, so he will know of the dangers.'

'You anticipate he'll reduce sail, sir,' Macklin suggested.

'Just so, and well before he faces any risk. By doing so he leaves himself vulnerable. Do you agree?' If the nods were slow in coming, all did so. 'We must be doubly sharp about our duties, both on the cannon and the canvas. Our task is to stop him gaining deep water, in short to keep him from accessing a safe haven long enough to allow *Lively* to join us in the fight.'

'He seems happy to waste powder and shot, sir,' this as another salvo landed in the sea.

'Why would he not be, Mr Worricker? He thinks he's home.'

Having sent them back to their various places, he called Williams to him again, his tone gentle. 'I am the captain, Mr Williams, so the result of what follows rests with me. You are acting on my instructions, do you see it?' The nod was far from emphatic. 'Do your best, which is all I can ask of anyone aboard.'

'Aye aye, sir.'

'Now let us look at your chart so you can tell me what I need to do.'

Chapter Twenty-Seven

It was necessary to examine what Williams had dug out in his tiny cabin-cum-chart room, this carried out under lantern light, employing measuring instruments as well as a magnifying glass. Like the Ria de Vigo, Pontevedra Bay opened to the southwest, but lacked the deep water of its neighbour. The gap between it and the close inshore island of Ons was much more constrained than Pearce had realised.

The upper section of the entrance had a rocky seabed, while on the southern shore it was sandy but shallow, increasingly so the closer one got to land. In order to get into the deep inner basin, there existed only a narrow channel, which doglegged to the left and right and would require highly competent seamanship as well as much care to navigate, even at high tide. Given the present state of this, the *Santa Leocadia* should be going nowhere near it. The obvious question was, should *Hazard* be equally wary? Pearce charged Williams to mark any areas, and there were not many, where *Hazard* could work outside the channel, without either running aground on sand or ripping out her keel on those rocks.

All the while the boom of cannon could be heard through the bulwarks, as the captain of *Santa Leocadia* kept up what seemed to be a useless employment of his bow chasers, reckoned to be merely scare tactics. Had he guessed what Pearce was contemplating, or would he expect him to avoid what looked like an approaching trap?

'Let's get back on deck, Mr Williams, so I can get some visual appreciation of what the chart tells me. And bring your instruments so we can get some approximate measurements.'

The weight of responsibility on the master was very evident and, even if he wished it gone, Pearce could appreciate why. There was no way, if he felt less than trusted, this could be assuaged, certainly not in the time available. He was possibly going to be required to make decisions which normally were none of his concern.

Sure his inferior officers were doing everything required, Pearce took the chart into the bows, calling on the men there to cast their logs to hold it, this while he sought to measure what prominent feature he could see. Few stood out on the shoreline of both the mainland and the offshore island, so Williams was called upon to use his protractors to provide a rough, and it could only be that, measure of distances.

While this was being worked out, Oliphant appeared, requesting to be told what was happening, and for once Pearce decided to indulge him, given he had as much at stake as anyone and the time for the ultimate decision was nearly upon him.

'I reckon to have three basic options, one of which, I expect the Spaniard, viewing his reactions up till now, will discount.'

He explained this was to hold his course just long enough to block access to the waters between Ons and the mainland. In short, to enforce delay, if necessary sacrificing his ship to allow *Lively* to affect a capture.

'A second is to do what our opponent is expecting, namely to reverse course and promise a battle, in which the ability to manoeuvre will be the key.'

Pearce was convinced, and said so, there would no extended engagement: The Spaniard would do nothing more than seek to get to leeward of him. Yes, there would be some exchanges of gunfire, but they would be few. The man's paramount aim was to seek a place in which to get off his cargo.

The third option he could not begin to contemplate, which was to put down his helm and make for the open sea on a northwesterly course, thus declining any kind of engagement. This would give his opponent all the time he needed to affect an entry.

'Take *Hazard* out of the equation and the Spanish captain can reduce sail and make a careful approach to the bay ahead, which will allow him some hope of avoiding the dangers Mr Williams and I have already identified.'

'Since you've already discounted one, Pearce, which of the two is it to be?'

'Just hope it's the right one. Now I suggest the best place for you is below on the orlop. It's going to be too hot on the deck for a civilian and you'll only get in the way.'

'Am I allowed to wish us good luck?' Oliphant asked.

'If you feel it does not tempt providence, yes. Now, if you don't mind.'

'Of course,' he replied and was gone.

An enquiry to the lookout confirmed *Lively* was closing on the *Santa Leocadia*, but at no outstanding gain, so it would be some time before Langholm posed a real threat. She certainly would not arrive before he had to decide on his course of action.

'*Lively* signalling, sir.'

This sent Mr Campbell up the shrouds with his signal book, the message, when read and called down, producing a wry smile.

'Engage the enemy more closely.'

No "request" this time. Lord Langholm must know the amount of damage *Hazard* might suffer if he just went toe to toe with a frigate, which the message implied he should. This left Pearce with the impression his lordship was quite willing to contemplate the cost, all very well since it would not be his own. Unless he had the notion *Hazard* was running away, which reminded Pearce he was free to act as he wished.

The call went up to Campbell. 'Do not acknowledge.'

He had to do what was least expected and contrive a way to stop the *Santa Leocadia* without his own ship and crew suffering destruction. If there was an answer, it lay in the chart being held up before him. So he traced a finger over the entry channel, trying to envisage the point at which the enemy would be most vulnerable, also how he could contrive to avoid the various risks.

There was no way the Spaniard could go in under full sail, which meant he'd have to reduce and slow, adding to the time Pearce had to find a solution. The rocky seabed did not appeal, it being jagged, so even with well-cast logs and with hardly any weight, he could still damage his keel. The sandy southern section offered no such danger and had the added advantage, if he did touch bottom, the incoming tide, shortly due to turn, would float him off.

So it came down to one question: How to make the entry impossible for his opponent who, even under severe or any other kind of threat, would not cease to try because he dare not. Again Pearce saw it as being about manoeuvrability, but there was no room for such a luxury under canvas. There was, however, a way.

Odd how he'd touched at Nourmoutier on the way, which brought back memories of the action he had been forced to engage in there, for it presented a possible solution. If the Spaniard would struggle to manoeuvre in such a confined space so would *Hazard*, so he'd need to be both anchored and able to apply movement.

'Mr Hallowell,' he called. 'We need a cable up from the tier, to be snug on the capstan, one end on deck ready to employ.'

As the orders were issued, which sent men below to see to the task, and trailed by a gloomy Williams, Pearce went back to join the premier, chart in hand, then using a finger to indicate his intention.

'I wish to anchor here.'

Peering at it, Hallowell remarked on the lack of depth, which was readily acknowledged by Mr Williams. Pearce ignored his expression and added confidently, 'Once we are at anchor, I want a spring on the cable so we can change, at will and quickly, the angle at which we face our approaching friend.' He again traced the channel with his finger. 'He's going to have to get through there, and it's our task to stop him.'

Evidence of his premier's ability lay in the fact little further explanation was requested. He understood to sail through would require dexterous use of both rudder and sails, while any competent seaman would have boats in the water. These, with cables attached to bow and stern, could ease the way of the ship or afford a backup method of making marginal changes in course.

'But if he runs aground, he's done for, sir.'

'Gently runs aground, Mr Hallowell. If he hits a rock, we don't want him taking in too much water, we want the sod in one piece and seaworthy. By my reckoning, unless he has a double-sized crew, he cannot make adjustments to his sails, have boat crews in the water, and simultaneously man all his guns. Indeed, I hope he can crew so few, we will have near-equal firepower.'

'How long will we have to deal with him, sir?'

'It would be best to ask Lord Langholm. I hope he sees bringing *Lively* in too close will be unnecessary. So we need to contrive a message to advise him a boat attack would be in both our interests. If we try to board alone, I fear, with our numbers, we might fail.'

'If we're to anchor where you wish, sir, it's very close to the time to reduce sail.'

Pearce looked back to the *Santa Leocadia*, monetarily obscured by yet more water spouts from his bow chasers.

'Make it so, Mr Hallowell. And let us get out all our boats alongside and in our lee. Regardless of what will happen, we will not escape without coming under fire and the time will come when we may have to employ them.'

'Can I suggest, sir, the cutter be rigged with a sail. Once we're at anchor and our Spaniard has committed himself, it can be sent away with a message to *Lively*, detailing your intentions and requirements.'

'An excellent idea, but I doubt Lord Langholm would be pleased with the word requirements. I suggest we despatch Maclehose with something more polite, like request.'

Hallowell smiled and nodded: He knew what his captain was driving at.

'And send the Mite with him. The only place for the lad is on the quarterdeck. Call me soft if you wish, but I see him as too tender in years for such a station.'

The lack of agreement was plain on Hallowell's face, this added to no verbal acceptance. He clearly did not like the idea of favouring one midshipman over another, even if he would openly admit the quarterdeck in battle was the place of most danger.

'It is not just I who have a soft spot for him,' Pearce added. 'To the whole crew he has become something of a mascot. Put Tennant aloft with a telescope, with orders to watch for *Lively* manning her boats. Now let's be about our business.'

There were not enough hands for everything to be covered simultaneously. One end of the cable Pearce had called for, having been fed through the forward hawsehole, was brought up on deck to be dragged to the stern. In anticipation of a boat attack, weapons had to be placed in readiness. Michael O'Hagan was in charge of ensuring they would save time when the order was given to man them.

At the same time the top hamper had to be reduced to topsails, the courses wetted by the fire engine to reduce the risk of inflammation before being clewed up. In all this Pearce was somewhat redundant, the orders being carried out by his inferiors. This allowed him to observe the alarming speed with which the distance between his stern and the bows of the *Santa Leocadia* were diminishing. Soon those bow chasers could be chewing timber, not disturbing seawater.

The temptation to call for everything to happen more quickly had to be resisted, for it invited confusion. So he was left to contemplate, as Derwent arrived with his sword and pistols, he'd made a poor choice, because, just as he'd already suffered one surprise, there was always the option of another.

'Don is shortening sail, sir.'

The cry from the masthead eased his concerns, since it would slow the time before he could begin to suffer damage which, for all his sanguine attitude, he saw as inevitable. Michael O'Hagan approached to report the arms for the boats were stacked ready for use and, since Pearce was well away from everyone, he could ask as a friend, what was about to happen.

'Hands are asking me, John Boy, an' it don't look good when I say I ain't got a clue.'

The explanation was brief and basic, Pearce grinning, well aware it was Michael's own curiosity that was paramount. The message about stacked arms could have gone to Hallowell.

'If all goes well, you'll find enough of a dustup to satisfy even you.'

'Been a long time, John Boy. Sure, I'm a'feart of going soft. If it's to be boats, I will be in yours, unless you say other.'

'No chance of that, friend. I need you to hand to make sure I survive.' As a cheered Michael moved away, Pearce called out, 'Mr Williams, I hand over to you the task of anchoring us.'

This was close to the first of the two doglegs, a point at which the *Santa Leocadia* would, for a very brief period, present herself stern on and moving slowly. But for the moment it was anchoring himself that was the concern. He could clearly hear the call of the men in the bows as they cast and hauled in their logs, with *Hazard* now creeping into the arms of the bay.

As soon as Williams gave the order, the stern anchor dropped into the water, which brought on that gap between it hitting the seabed and the fluke biting, another before the cable took the strain and brought the ship to a halt. All the while Pearce was listening for the sound of his keel rubbing the sand, which would precede *Hazard* running aground. Should this happen, he could forget his spring.

It didn't come. The still-falling tide did what Pearce had anticipated, brought the bows round to face square on to the incoming sea, to rock gently on the low waves. At the same time, the cable was being dropped over the larboard side, with a boat party rushing to man the cutter. It was under the command of Macklin, whose task it was to drag the open end towards the now-rigid anchor cable and see it firmly attached.

His plan would now be obvious to the Spaniard. With the range reduced, he aimed his bow chasers at Macklin's boat, coming too damn close for comfort with his first salvo, which hit the water twenty yards from the cutter. A lesser man might have stopped his endeavours, but Macklin proved his worth, his gestures and command floating across the water.

On deck, Pearce had ordered the starboard cannon manned and, firing over the heads of the men in the cutter, one by one, they sent a salvo, one falling short and designed more to distract than damage. It took high seamanship skills to carry out the task Macklin had, but those he possessed, a hand waved to the quarterdeck to let his captain know the spring was secure.

'Come on, *sĕnor*, whoever you are, we are now ready for you.'

When talking of sea fights experienced, John Pearce being no exception, even if he rarely indulged, it was common to refer to the mayhem, to the inability to recall every detail of what had taken place. Not on this occasion: to call it action was a misnomer, given it played out at the pace of a stately gavotte. *Santa Leocadia* crept into the bay with boats in the water full of rowers, forced to stay in her wake because, for Pearce, they were an obvious target.

As soon as the range closed, the two bow chasers were set against seven four-pounder cannon, now with the wedges knocked well in, to fire high and seek to shred the rigging. The billowing black smoke, blowing away from *Hazard*, partly obscured the target, while *Lively*, trying the range without success, showed it would not be long before she, too, was able to enter the fight.

The point of danger for *Hazard* came as the Spaniard began to swing round to take the first and left dogleg, her open gunports showing the threatening muzzles of her loaded cannon, double the number of his own and three times the poundage. The broadside he feared did not come, no doubt due to a lack of men. They spoke in pairs while he required his to fire at the rapid speed he'd sought.

'Three in five, three in five.'

It was like a prayer to those who heard and, if it was closer than what had gone before, it did not hit that mark. Yet he was firing faster than the enemy, with more guns and at close range, parting hawsers and shrouds to great effect. The time was fast approaching when he needed to concentrate on the Spaniard's hull, which required the wedges to be pulled and the aim lowered.

Hazard was not immune from counterfire. She shuddered as the Spaniard's round shot repeatedly struck her hull low down, evidence his opposite number had seen the spring and knew its significance. He was trying to hole her, so *Hazard* would settle on the sand and be unable to employ it. There was a momentary thought of how this would sound to Oliphant, given it could be thudding into the hull not far from his head, but present needs soon banished that.

Committed to the course he must pursue, *Santa Leocadia*'s bow began to swing away, which exposed the boats she would need to aid her manoeuvres. Eventually it also presented her stern, the casements covered with thick wooden deadlights to mitigate the shot that, if it penetrated, would go the whole length of the deck.

'Musket fire on the boats, Mr Moberly.'

This was acknowledged as the marines on the mainmast cap let fly. The order was given to Maclehose and the Mite to get away in the cutter. Hallowell was overseeing the hauling on the spring, this slowly bringing *Hazard* round, so her broadside never ceased to threaten the Spaniard.

He was suffering, both on the frigate and in the boats, which if they were not struck by round shot found it hard to carry out the duty required by a number of near misses. Then one struck, the boat splintering just before the ball hit and mangled flesh. Taking water, it tipped over, sending the rowers into the sea, which detracted their shipmates from their primary duty in order to rescue them.

'Mr Worricker,' Pearce shouted, to the crack of case shot whistling past his head, too high to do damage and evidence of hasty aim. 'If you can take out the rudder, we will require little more.'

Having nothing with which to retaliate, Worricker could order the guns to cease firing at will, so the frenzied loading could be slowed and the aiming coordinated. His second lieutenant walked down the deck, ducking to sight each cannon once it was ready to fire. It was no broadside, but a carefully controlled cannonade with but one purpose.

Even on waves that barely lifted and dropped *Hazard*, the area of shot was both too high and too low, the latter doing the most damage to a vital part of *Santa Leocadia's* ability to steer. Chunks flew off the rudder, gratifying but not terminal. Yet her forward progress was so slow, Worricker got in another salvo just before she reached the right dogleg, and this time the effect was terminal.

It seemed as if two four-pounder balls hit the exact same spot, the pintles attaching the rudder to the hull, and what was left of the whole assembly dropping off to float in the water. The Spaniard being helpless, there was a hiatus when Pearce wondered if he would strike his flag. Yet all that was the Spaniard's boats being brought alongside, the crews hurrying to get back aboard.

The *Santa Leocadia* began to drift towards the rocky part of the bay and it seemed as if her guns had been abandoned. Yet Pearce saw the deck now as a hive of activity, with men pulling frantically on ropes, with a wooden box coming out of the hold. The boats so recently abandoned had been hauled into a position where the bulk of their ship afforded protection. He saw said box being lowered until it was out of sight and the reason dawned.

There could be only one commodity they wanted to save, their cargo of silver, and this must be prevented, but how? It would take too long to get *Hazard* free from the spring, sails in play and the distance covered.

The notion he'd had of boarding was only really viable in company with the crew of *Lively*, and he'd yet to be told she'd come close enough to intervene. It came down to numbers. To get up the frigate's tumble-home and on to the deck was hard enough when you could mount an advantage in that commodity. On its own, *Hazard* did not have it, but what it did have was an abundance of boats.

The idea that came to mind might be due to the clarity brought on by action, but it bordered on madness. Pearce knew he had to do something, having no idea of the size of the cargo of silver, how many of those boxes had to be got out and loaded into the boats, but haunted by the notion of it all being shipped ashore.

'Mr Worricker, case shot if you please and keep a couple of cannon sweeping the enemy deck. I want their efforts disrupted. Mr Hallowell, you have the deck until you feel your presence no longer required. Release the spring and cut the anchor cable. Get lines over the side so the boats can warp us close to the enemy stern.'

There was a pause then until Pearce issued the final order. 'Once all is complete, man the boats. All of them.'

Chapter Twenty-Eight

The silence felt odd, given the gunfire, followed by the amount of yelling which had just accompanied the execution of those orders. Worricker was waiting for case shot to be brought up from the hold, while Michael O'Hagan had an axe in hand and was standing by the stern hawse hole, ready to employ it. Down below the spring cable was being detached so it would work free as *Hazard* began to move. Pearce had nothing cheering from Midshipman Tennant, whom he could see had his telescope trained on HMS *Lively*, still under sail.

The level of frustration was acute, only partly relieved when the first salvo of case shot swept the Spaniard's deck, which brought an abrupt halt to the work of getting boxes out of the hold. Yet it resumed as *Hazard*'s cannon were being reloaded, evidence his opponent cared little for the fate of ship, while being willing to pay a high price in blood and crew to fulfil his mission.

Such fire would have to cease. There was no way to employ case shot when your own crew members were in the water between the muzzle and the target, this a situation fast approaching. John Pearce, standing on the quarterdeck, having wracked his brain for a plan, saw a possible solution present itself.

'Mr Worricker. Once we are in our boats, I want the larboard cannon triple-shotted.'

When Michael O'Hagan, on orders from the premier, began to swing his axe, his shipmates, having grabbed their preferred weapons along with grappling irons, poured over the side. Charlie Taverner took command of one boat, Rufus Dommet following to take charge of another. The thick cable did not part easily; it took Michael two dozen swings, by which time Pearce had got aboard Charlie's boat, ordering a move to the bows, there to take up a heavy rope end floating in the water.

This was quickly looped round the stern post, so already hauling when the anchor cable finally parted, not that movement was immediate. It took men half standing and straining on the oars to get even an inch of reaction, this only really effective when Rufus and his boat joined in. And there was O'Hagan, axe over his shoulder, shouting to his friends, 'You not be goin' without me now, will you?'

'Been tryin' to get away from you for years,' Charlie called back.

'Get another boat, Michael,' Pearce shouted. 'I suggest Mr Hallowell will not be content to remain aboard. Join him, then us on the deck yonder and do so before I have in my hand his flag.'

If *Hazard* was moving, it was at no great pace. But they were closing the gap sufficiently to make whoever was in command of the *Santa Leocadia* nervous. He'd pulled some of his men off the unloading to line his taffrail with muskets. Moberly, in the marine boat, which had once belonged to Keoghan, was alert to the danger. He had it hauled round and steadied so he could reply, the salvo fired sending heads ducking for safety.

For all Pearce thought his marine officer a bit pompous and dim, there was no denying in this situation he knew his stuff. As soon as his men had fired, he had the boat moving again as, in between the rowers, weapons were being efficiently reloaded. It was as if the lobsters were executing a drill, the previous salvo repeated as soon as they were ready.

Pearce detached Rufus's boat and ordered him to the stern, to another set of dropped-over lines, as the contest between the muskets in both boat and ship continued. Never a truly accurate weapon, it was even less so in the hands of men with little experience of its use. Thus, of the men rowing and towing, only one had so far taken a ball, Pearce immediately taking his oar as he fell from his seat.

'You'll be pissing on your hands afore this day is out, your honour.'

This comment, coming from behind, meant it was from an unknown source and was of the kind to warrant a dozen on some ships. But it brought forth laughter even from the man at whom it was aimed and he replied, albeit breathing heavily, 'As long as I'm pissing and not bleeding, I'll settle.'

'It might be him spilling his blood,' Charlie called. 'Fuckin' cheek of him.'

'Belay, Charlie, I can live with a little insult.'

A glance over his shoulder told Pearce they were getting close and doing so in relative safety. Moberly, now the range was shorter, had split his men into two groups of three, one firing while the other reloaded. This allowed him to maintain fire, which made it dangerous for those at the taffrail to raise their heads for more than a second. They were still trying to respond, but Moberly's tactic made aiming impossible.

Pearce called for raised oars, then shouted to Rufus to take up the strain. Given *Hazard* was still moving, even if it was only at a snail's pace, this rendered their task easier. The stern began to swing round, bringing Worricker's cannon on to the target. For what he hoped was coming, Pearce reckoned being any closer was dangerous, so he shouted up to his second lieutenant, 'Mr Worricker, take out those deadlights.'

The boom of the cannon was deafening, but not so much as the crack of splintering wood, some of which, had he got too close, might have damaged him and his Hazards. Yet the deadlights held, with Moberly, now alongside him, directing the pistols and muskets of his men, keeping up the rate of fire. Behind, the cannon were being reloaded by the best gun crews *Hazard* possessed.

The second triple-shotted salvo went right through the partially shattered deadlights, creating a gap big enough for two or three men to get through. The yell to close almost seemed superfluous, so eager were his men to get fighting. Moberly, now with his sword out, indicated the honour of going first should fall to his captain. In this he found willing acceptance.

'Hazards to me,' Pearce shouted as the boat bumped against the stern. One pistol to hand, he leapt for the hole, coming to a dark deck in which he could see nothing, certainly not opposition. Even so, he discharged his pistol and hauled out his sword, unaware he was screaming his head off, as were those who joined him. They had several moments when no one came to oppose them. Anyone who'd been behind those deadlights was now nothing but mangled flesh. Yet as his eyes adjusted, he saw bodies beginning to crowd a companionway.

With bayonet-ready marines on either side, two Pelicans and their boat crews at his rear, Pearce rushed forward, seeing, in what was left of any lantern light, a uniform coat, for which he aimed, sword swinging. It met metal halfway down, the clang loud enough to hear, even in the noise of what was now mayhem. The men he'd brought aboard were his responsibility, but this could not be allowed to mar his concentration, as he parried and thrust against an opponent who knew how to use a sword.

But so did John Pearce, the lessons he'd taken in Paris coming to the fore. If the eyes of his opponent, steadily holding his own, were dark brown, they appeared black in the gloom, as blade slithered off blade, both men constrained in what they could do by the press of bodies around them.

It was this that gave Pearce his opening. The Spaniard lifted his weapon high to deliver a downward, killer slash at the throat of an opponent who'd taken a regressive step. It was he who suffered, as Pearce thrust forward in classic fencer pose, front knee so far bent he was close to the deck, the point of his extended sword taking the man under his rib cage, making him fall backwards. With a quick dancing two-step, Pearce followed up, to drive home and twist the point.

Free for a few seconds, able to take stock, Pearce reckoned they were doing well, but was it well enough? Success lay in getting up the companionway, crowded with enemy sailors who could not yet get into the fight. It was only a matter of time before many of them sought another way down from the upper deck, which would increase the difficulties for the Hazards.

A voice in his ear cheered him mightily. 'Having a rest are we, John Boy?'

O'Hagan barrelled past him, axe swinging in a deadly arc, which nearly took off the arm of one before causing those around him to cower, men who could not withdraw far enough because of the press at their rear. This allowed Pearce and Michael to get a foot on the step of the now blood-soaked companionway.

Thinking they were progressing, a shout from Rufus Dommet alerted him to look along the deck. There he saw what looked like Spanish marines, advancing in a line, bayonets pushed forward and calling out, probably to their own, to get out of the way. A look around for Moberly showed him as a red coat on the deck, clearly wounded, as well as the disordered state of the other marines.

They were all fighting individual battles. He needed them and their bayonets organised enough to counter what was coming. Such a weapon, on the end of a levelled musket, was as good as a pike, able to inflict wounds at a distance, when those on the receiving end could not get close enough to retaliate. Worse, the crowd was beginning to part before them, so they would soon be stabbing those bayonets at him and his men.

Withdrawal was hampered for him, as it was for those facing a still-swinging axe, because there were Hazards newly arrived, who could not get into the fight, but were pushing forward their mates who could. Even if *Hazard* must be denuded of crew, and some of the Spaniards must have succumbed to the triple-shotted cannon fire, they were still fewer than their opponent.

If Pearce's opposite number had any sense, he would abandon his attempts to get the silver off into boats and send every man he had to fight the boarding party. Faced with this as a possibility, he had to contemplate withdrawal, which would be far from simple, and matters would get worse as soon as the bottom of the companionway was clear.

To have got so close to capture and then have to abandon the attempt would be a bitter pill, but better swallow that than lose half his crew. The first thing Pearce had to do was get temporarily out of the fight, so he could see who was where and seek to organise a tactical retreat. He hauled on O'Hagan's free arm and yelled at him to cover his back, also pointing out the line of marines now prodding the slowest of their own and with little gentility.

Not having spotted them, it was good the Irishman immediately assessed and understood the risk, moving his bulk enough to allow Pearce to disengage. If Michael was there, so would be Hallowell and it was him he sought. When he saw his blue coat, he also observed at his feet three bodies, one of them writhing, evidence the furious one-time Jonathan was a handful.

Getting him out, so he could yell in his ear, took some doing, thankfully the space created being immediately filled by a couple of the Arklows, who looked to have the same Hibernian fury as Michael, belabouring their enemies with tomahawks. In open space, Pearce yelled into Hallowell's ear.

'Is Worricker still aboard?' A gasping affirmation. 'Get back and tell him, if he hasn't already, to load the cannon again. I reckon we will struggle to hold here, but if we can get back to the boats and out of the line of fire, he can clear this lot in one blow.'

'You reckon to come back on board again?'

'I reckon to see what lies before me at the time.'

Pearce's next task was to get his mouth to a number of ears, those pressing forward, and tell them to get out of the way, but not at haste. As soon as they relieved the pressure on the backs of their shipmates, the battling away were quick to realise what must be happening and so began, inch by inch, to give ground.

Michael, even having lost his foothold on the companionway, still towered head and shoulder above the others. It was to him Pearce forced his way, because it was a situation in which he could command attention. At all costs the pulling back had to be orderly. If it ceased to be so, the chances of getting to the boats would diminish, never mind the notion of a second assault.

'Michael, back to boats but orderly. Do you understand?'

The head didn't turn, he was too busy keeping those before him at bay, but there was a ghost of a nod, which had Pearce pull back again. He wanted to find Charlie and Rufus, who, as watch captains, would also be able to control a group. Then there were the marines, spread out with no notion of anyone being in charge, using their bayonets as well as the musket butts to good effect, only not the way required, which was to form a rear guard.

The realisation he was not going to be given the time he needed dawned slowly. The press was too great and, once the mood of impending withdrawal dawned, so did the need for each man to seek his own survival. If it was going to fail, it required to be slowed as much as was possible, so there was only one place for him, at the very head of his crew and damn the consequences.

It took some doing to get through the mass, elbows employed, much cursing, too, but eventually he was at the front of the line. He pushed his way between two of his men, knowing, within a minute, it would be his sword against one or more bayonets, in a contest he did not expect to win. What he would not do was surrender.

Sword jabbing, cutting and slashing, he took out two of those who still stood between him and what he saw as his fate, only to be jostled to one side as O'Hagan joined him, his breathing heavy as he yelled, 'If we're goin,' John Boy, sure we'll do it as one.'

'Get away, Michael. That's an order.'

The shout was ignored and there was no time to repeat it, there were too many weapons seeking to do him harm. So, shoulder to shoulder, he and Michael laboured away, inflicting wounds, killing as many as possible before they reckoned to be killed themselves.

The change was so sudden and both were so committed to their task, they nearly fell forward on to the deck as the mass of men before them evaporated. They were running away and sweeping aside their own marines, who soon likewise fled. The yell from Pearce now was to rush the rapidly clearing companionway, he first and taking the steps three at a time.

By the time he made the main deck, he was just in time to see an insouciant and seemingly unbloodied captain, Lord Langholm, standing on the quarterdeck, accepting the sword of the man who'd commanded the *Santa Leocadia*. This was followed by a rousing cheer from the many dozens of men he'd brought over the side, no doubt with little opposition, it being below and engaged in repelling the Hazards.

Turning to face John Pearce, the eyes ranged over a man and uniform showing clear signs of the engagement in which he'd just been involved. Bloodstains abounded, as did various rips to cloth, while the breeches, once white, were now filthy. Langholm looked as if he was dressed for a levee.

'My, Mr Pearce, you have been in the wars. It certainly looks to be so, but I give you joy of our capture.'

Pearce wanted to say "my capture." But there was no point, as everyone not Spanish was cheering.

With so many hands available, damage to the *Santa Leocadia* was quickly seen to, so she could be warped out to deeper water, to be taken under tow by HMS *Lively* until she could be jury-rigged. The cargo which had been unloaded was safely back in her holds, one box broken to show the ingots of silver they contained. In an act of what he saw as kindness, Langholm put the crew ashore, captain included, with his sword restored. Oliphant reckoned it not a kindness at all, thinking the reception he'd get from Manuel Godoy.

There were casualties to deal with on *Hazard*, two of his quota men had been killed and several wounded, one so seriously he might not survive. Among them was Moberly, who'd been felled by a blow to the head. The atmosphere was, however, as good as John Pearce had ever known it on a ship, he being a man proud of his command and willing to damn anyone who disagreed.

'What now, Pearce?' asked Oliphant who, if he'd suffered at all from round shot hitting the hull, any damage now being repaired by Towse, it didn't show.

'Lisbon or Gibraltar for you, whichever you choose for a packet to London. For us it's a few repairs in Gib, then set course for Leghorn with all despatch, to tell Jervis of the danger he faces.'

'And the capture?'

'Gibraltar and the Prize Court, so the value can be assessed.'

'Not home?'

'You were thinking of going with her?'

'Why not? Be nice to sit above the silver and contemplate a brighter future.'

'I have some letters I would wish you to take home with you.'

'Harley Street, I suppose' came with a knowing grin.

'Can I say, I shan't miss you?'

'Perhaps it won't be forever' came the mischievous response. 'Dundas will be cock-a-hoop after this jaunt.'

'You have the ability to take the cheer out of what has, so far, been a good if tiring day.'

'Not over yet. We're having dinner on *Lively* are we not?'

'To no doubt listen to Lord Langholm, while he boasts of the ease with which he took the *Santa Leocadia* and how not one of his crew emerged with so much as a scratch.'